THE BLOOD OF OCTOBER

THE BLOOD
OF OCTOBER

David Lippincott

W.H. ALLEN · LONDON
1986

To the very, very, very rich, who were
both the victims and villains of this piece.
They have the good taste to die gracefully.

"There is a radicalism abroad in America these days that is . . . not yet a call to arms, but is definitely a call for change in society and government.

And these attacks are not coming from their usual quarters, the political extremist . . . but more significantly, from the long-suffering, basically unpolitical *middle* group in America."

—*J. F. Terhorst,*
former Press Secretary to
President Ford

Prologue

Fall, that year, was an uncertain season. A fickle jet stream had produced an Indian summer that was the longest and most oppressive in memory; old-timers had to reach back into the early thirties to unearth one as uncomfortable as that of 1981. To an already nervous and unsettled country, this peculiarity added one more degree of uneasiness: even the seasons had taken to unpredictable and sinister behavior.

Actually, weather was the least of the nation's troubles. After the recovery of the Ford years, a new administration had taken over and managed to hammer a thriving economy into a crippling disaster. Guaranteed minimum incomes, guaranteed employment, and guaranteed health plans, Americans discovered, in the end guaranteed nothing but national insolvency. Each month became a race between the rise in the inflation index and the unemployment rate.

On the surface, at least, New York's major response appeared to be a frenzy of spending. At the most expensive department stores, monthly sales figures rocketed to new heights. Van Clef, Winston's and Cartier's began to look as crowded as Korvette's at Christmas. Rolls and Mercedes were snatched off salesroom floors; Potamkin, the world's largest Cadillac dealer, had so large a list of back orders he refused to take any more. Knoedler, and similar galleries, found their walls denuded of paintings; the price of antique furniture went out of sight. The boutiques were never more crowded, the theaters more fully booked, the tables of Lutèce, "21" and Regine's more jammed—as if people were determined to spend their money while they still had it to spend, a lavish last fling, a dizzying, spinning, whirling dance of exhaustion before someone or something should call a halt. The order was not long in coming.

On May 12, 1980, New York City had defaulted on its notes; New York State followed two days later. The next

1

week, May 19, saw Detroit, Boston and Los Angeles travel the same route. For two long weeks more, Chicago held on, then, on June 3, it, too, shuddered into bankruptcy.

Given all of this, the Presidential election of 1980 was a savage and bitter episode: the country was thoroughly disgusted with both national parties and elected an Independent, Roger Welby. Unfortunately, the formulae which had made Welby seem brilliant as Governor of Maine were simply not up to the nation's crisis; Congress screamed, the unions screamed, and business screamed. At this point, a shaken Europe and a terrified bloc of OPEC nations did something far more destructive than screaming: they withdrew their extensive American holdings, compounding the already desperate situation.

In the middle of all this, President Welby's Vice President ran into a personal calamity. Old rumor advanced into new substance, and an unresolved indictment charging embezzlement of public funds during his tenure as Senator from Ohio was suddenly handed down. The Vice President, muttering and hostile, had no choice but to resign. President Welby appeared unfazed and reported he would submit a nominee to replace him by July 1, and hope swept the embattled country that a new Vice President might come equipped with new solutions to the rapidly worsening economic situation.

Then, it happened. On Tuesday, June 20, 1981, President Welby suffered a major stroke. Under ordinary circumstances, the Vice President would have functioned as Acting President, but the Constitution had made no provision for an incapacitated President who *had* no Vice President. Welby was reported to be improving and in full command of all mental processes; but he had been seen by no one outside of his immediate official family. Directives were issued, bills signed, press releases propounded, all purportedly in Welby's name, but rumors quickly began sweeping Washington: Welby was in a coma: Welby was unable to read, hear, understand, or speak; Welby was dead.

The restlessness that had been shaking the country began to surface openly. Aimless groups of unemployed, the welfare cabal and the chronically poor appeared on the streets, chanting and demonstrating—for work, for handouts, for higher food-stamp allotments. At the same time, a number of quasi-vigilante groups—the unionized middle

class and the still-employed, the hard-hats of another era—
began grouping into a counterforce. They tried to keep order, trying to force their own demands, pleading for a
return to a better day when law and order would have
prevented such near anarchy.

The aims of these two forces appeared diametrically op-
posed; about the only point they seemed to share was a
belief that anyone with any money at all was either exploit-
ive, dishonest, or had somehow stolen it from *them*.

Behind the serene facade of the White House, President
Welby was reportedly resting, still trying to decide who
should become his new Vice President. For him, for the
moneyed, for anyone who owned anything at all of value,
the fall of 1981 was rapidly shaping up as the uncertainest
season of them all.

Flying into the eye of this nervous climate on the afternoon of October 13, FAA air controllers on duty at Wilmington Airport took note of an exceptional number of
unscheduled jet aircraft—all private. This sudden flurry of
traffic, it developed, was occasioned by Ravensaugh Wetherill's eighty-third birthday, being celebrated, as it always
had been, at Usspatpenn, his estate outside Wilmington.

In view of the nation's troubled economic posture and the
reported near-rioting in the streets of some cities, there were
those who felt such a display of extravagance on the part of
the usually publicity-shy Wetherill family was unwise, perhaps even dangerous. To the advisers around Ravensaugh
Wetherill who raised this point of view, the old man gave
a simple explanation: "I've been having a party on my
birthday every year since I was four, dammit; to stop now,
at my age, would only be tempting fate." The advisers
knew better than to argue: Ravensaugh Wetherill did not
take kindly to dissenting opinions. Like many men of his
age, Ravensaugh had developed an almost childlike irritation with anything that got in the way of his small
pleasures. He had looked forward to the party, the party
was both a tradition and his due, and the party would be
held.

Thus, jets began arriving at Wilmington at about five
o'clock on the 13th, their silver wings gleaming in the last
of the fall sun. The Governors of three states (all of
whom owed their jobs in some way to the Wetherill

family) were expected; many of industry's chief executives were there; the President had sent both his regrets and his Secretary of State, resplendent in Air Force Two, to represent him. Besides a number of influential Senators and Congressmen with past debts to the family, there was a large number of people who were simply wealthy: friends whom the Wetherill family saw on a day-to-day basis, their peers, people with whom they had shared schools, experiences and pasts.

By far the largest single contingent of aircraft contained members of the Wetherill family (their personal fleet of jets was so large it was referred to in aviation circles as the Wetherill Air Force, or, more simply, as the W.A.F.). The oldest of Ravensaugh's sons, Nicholas, sixty, who looked after the family banking interests, arrived first; he was followed by Duane, the junior Senator from West Virginia. Ravensaugh Wetherill's daughter, Moira Cantrell, landed about half an hour later, her long, square face frozen into a look of dour displeasure, complaining about the trip, the pilots, and the inconvenience of having to be where she was. Her husband, Dudley Cantrell, stood beside her and listened patiently, looking alternately pained and embarrassed, but equipped with an expression that indicated he had heard all of this before.

Tracey, the youngest brother, had, as always, sent regrets, regrets that were greeted by his father, as always, with considerable relief. To most of the family, Tracey's life was a complete mystery—and one they would as soon remain unsolved. Fresh from Washington, Associate Justice of the Supreme Court Tobin Wetherill discovered his landing was sandwiched between that of the president of Northco and the chairman of U. S. Steel. Since Steel was involved in a case pending before the court, Toby almost sprinted across the tarmac when he saw who had landed in the plane following his.

Last of the Wetherills to arrive, except for a scattering of the younger "cousins," was Chase Wetherill, head of the Wetherill Foundation. Chase was Ravensaugh's favorite son, the one he trusted, the one he listened to. And when Chase had advised against the birthday party, the old man had come close to giving in; only at the last moment had he changed his mind.

Chase's expression mirrored his feelings as he helped his wife, Darcie, into the waiting limousine for the trip to Usspatpenn; his usually animated, light-hearted manner was replaced by a mask of stern displeasure. This left Darcie with no choice but to follow her husband's lead and look equally solemn herself. In the car, Chase slumped into one corner and stared out the window. As they turned into the mile-long driveway of Usspatpenn, passing through the tall brick pillars with the lion's heads on top, the mansion came suddenly into view, all its windows blazing with light. Along both sides of the drive, the topiary sculptures of nursery-rhyme figures had been floodlit, as had the entire front of the house itself. As many times as he had seen it lit up this way before, the sight still took Chase's breath away.

Darcie, in spite of twenty years of marriage to Chase, was still unaccustomed to the spectacle, and was even more stunned. "My God, Chase, but it's beautiful."

"Yes, it is beautiful. And the party is still stupid," snorted Chase. "Of all people, Graffa should know this is no time to be having a birthday party with a lot of damned money being spent in ways people can read about. The newspapers will have a field day with it."

Alongside him, Chase could feel Darcie stiffen at the implied rebuke. He was sulking and knew it. "I'm sorry, Darcie. The whole thing has me on edge."

Darcie reached over and squeezed his hand. "I know. But Graffa *is* eighty-three, Chase."

"And ought to know better."

A sigh of defeat from Darcie shook Chase out of his sulk once again. Suddenly turning to her, he threw up his hands and laughed. "Oh, the hell with it. Let's just enjoy ourselves. Didn't they have a ball at Versailles only a couple of days before the Bastille went under? Well, fair enough. I may even get drunk."

They rode the rest of the way to the house in silence. The haunting uneasiness that was nagging at Chase was not driven away, only papered over.

For most of the guests, the party was an unqualified success. Cocktails had been in the formal dining room, stripped of its usual furniture and transformed into a semi-jungle by massed banks of flowers and tropical fernery. Dinner itself was served around the edges of the indoor pool, a pool set in the center of a reproduction Greek atrium lined by polished Doric columns. Twenty-four tables of four lined each of the long, marble sides; at the deep end, where the diving board was usually anchored, a long thin table ran the width of the pool. Graffa was planted firmly in its center, with Darcie seated to his right. No explanation was offered as to where Graffa's wife was; everyone there knew. For lighting, besides some concealed indoor floodlights, the surface of the pool itself was filled with bobbing wax flowers, each holding a single fat candle. At the opposite end of the pool, a small string orchestra played melodies from thirty and forty years before, the violin tones picking up strange but not unpleasant resonances from the effect of the high ceiling and the marble walls. There was only one known casualty: a busboy who slipped and fell in. When he pulled himself out of the water, the guests applauded enthusiastically, and he bowed to them, a stiff, formal little bend at the waist. Then, as suddenly as it had begun, the party was over.

The family retreated to the library to watch Graffa open his family presents, and to listen to the rambling discourse he inevitably produced the one time a year he had them all together again. This was the real reason, Chase knew, behind Graffa's insistence on the party; as Graffa's sons' own children had grown older, they had been used as excuses for not traveling to Usspatpenn for Thanksgiving and Christmas. Turns were taken, his sons and Moira doing their duty by their father on a carefully worked-out schedule so that Graffa would have someone there for each holiday. But his birthday still gave Graffa the opportunity to corral all of them at once, and he usually made the most of the occasion.

Tonight, the discourse was short, almost hurried. Suddenly rising out of his chair, Graffa lifted his brandy snifter toward the portrait over the mantel—a copy of the painting of Hendryk Wilhelm Vederyll that hung in the lobby of the Wetherill Foundation—and said very softly: "To the family."

One by one, uncertain and perhaps even startled, the group rose slowly to its feet. Chase observed them closely; the toast was so outrageous in its melodramatic overtones only Graffa could get away with it. He could see that Nicholas—like all lawyers and bankers, comfortable with the obvious—felt perfectly at ease; Toby looked less certain, but has his jaw stuck out as if he were determined to go through with the toast regardless of what anyone thought; Duane was avoiding Chase's eyes and Chase knew that his favorite brother's sense of the irreverent was being put to a severe test; for himself, Chase decided to go along with the toast, if only to please Graffa. Then from behind him, he heard Moira say, quite clearly, "Oh, balls."

All the heads swiveled toward her, registering various degrees of disbelief. Graffa stared at Moira, his head inclined to one side, trying to focus his famously convenient bad hearing. "What? What? What did she say?" he demanded.

Moira's husband, Dudley, stepped in to save her. "She said that calls for going all the way, a toast like that calls for it, and I agree." Turning, Dudley raised his own glass, said "To the family" in a loud voice, and threw the glass with a crash into the fireplace.

"To the family," chorused the rest of the group unevenly. Following Dudley's inspired improvisation they all threw their glasses, in a scene reminiscent of a bad Boer War movie. Chase and Darcie left immediately afterward. The rest of the brothers, along with Moira and her husband, were spending the night at Usspatpenn, but Chase had come armed with an excuse for immediate return so hastily concocted he hoped no one would press him for details.

On the drive back to the Wilmington airport with Darcie, Chase suddenly found the feeling of uneasiness he'd experienced earlier in the day sweep across him again, cold and unreasonable. Had he been aware of an incident which occurred along the almost deserted highway between Usspatpenn and the airport, Chase Wetherill might have learned the reason for his unexplained concern far sooner than he did. Chase had paid little attention to a dark, shadowy shape along the edge of the road; he had felt his limousine slow as the driver cut his speed, sensing the shape was that of a wrecked car and that help might be required. But as the driver neared the shadow and could clearly see that it was an almost overturned car pulled off onto the highway's shoulder, a man with a flashlight appeared from behind it and waved the limousine on.

Quickly, the car regained its speed. Not long after Chase's limousine had passed, another car, traveling in the same direction but at some distance behind, not only slowed at the wreck, but came to a halt. Unknown to either Chase or the limousine's driver, this same car had been behind them ever since they had left Usspatpenn. The window was rolled down and the man behind the wheel stuck out his head to listen to the man with the flashlight.

"We got this pair, but there may be more ahead. Stick with them, dammit, stick with them." The man with the flashlight indicated Chase's disappearing car with a shake of his head almost as angry as his voice.

The man behind the wheel muttered, but rolled up the window against the chill night air and jammed his car into gear. With a squeal of his tires, he set off down the highway again to catch up with Chase's limousine, now little more than a pair of red dots disappearing into the horizon.

The man with the flashlight turned back to the wreck and joined another man behind it. A young blond girl in blue jeans stood beside a tall black; both of them looked as if they had not only been shaken up by the accident, but possibly knocked around since.

"They say anything yet?" demanded the man with the flashlight.

"It's all a mistake. That's what they say."

"Sure." The man with the flashlight studied the pair for a minute, then looked at his companion. "Well, anybody can make a mistake. Show 'em."

The black stiffened; the blond's eyes widened as she automatically turned her head to try to find help that wasn't there. "No," she said, her head turning again frantically. "No, please—it's all a mis—"

The words remained unfinished, abruptly cut short by a single, long burst of .45 slugs from a burp gun.

In the grand scheme of things that were to come, this execution along 912 might have seemed a small incident. To Chase, had he witnessed it, it would have seemed like the opening shots of a war.

Which, indeed, was precisely what it was.

Chapter One

*Whether in matters of criminal proceedings,
or grave illness, or famine or even war the
wealthy tend to survive while the poor
perish, because the rich have the resources
to protect themselves. The question of
equality and fairness immediately comes
to mind, but is answered by some with the
argument that this process is, in the long
run, necessary to society because it is a
societal translation of natural selection, or
survival of the fittest. In any case, the
argument is not one for we scientists, but
for the philosophers.*

> —*Dr. Regal Turgeon,*
> *Dean,*
> *the Academy of Behavorial Sciences*

Strange as it may seem, it is exceedingly difficult for the
average person to grasp the extent of wealth and power in-
vested in those labeled as the "very rich." Everyone, of
course, has heard of the Astors, the Vanderbilts, the
Rockefellers, the Mellons, the DuPonts, the Huttons and
the Fords; yet the actual amount of money they represent
is so overwhelming that it virtually becomes no more than
an abstract number. It is one thing to read, "At the top of
the 1900 group is John D. Rockefeller with his one billion
dollars; at the top in 1925 is Henry Ford with his billion;
and, in 1950 . . . H. L. Hunt is worth one or two billions
. . . the fortune of Hugh Roy Cullen . . . is reported of
late to come to a billion."[1] *Hugh Roy Cullen?* It is one

[1]*The Power Elite,* by C. Wright Mills.

thing to read of these billionaires, but it becomes another when you realize they include people whose names you have never even heard mentioned.

This fact, of course, stems from the propensity of today's wealthy to keep their actual worth hidden until death or a federal investigation forces the figures into the open. For instance, it was only the information demanded of Nelson Rockefeller during the hearings over his nomination to the Vice Presidency that revealed his personal fortune (equally matched by each of his brothers and sisters) could be fixed at $218 million.[2] Because of the Rockefeller Foundation and other devices the figure is undoubtedly a low one. Yet, the sum is still so large as to remain an abstract to most people. Again, when one of the very rich dies, the figures become public knowledge: Howard Hughes, by first reports from his Summa Corporation, could tally a mean $1.5 billion. Still, to the average person, what exactly does a billion or a billion and a half mean? (For one thing, $1 billion means that, invested at a conservative 5 percent, it earns its owner approximately $137,000 a day income.)[3]

As said before, the very rich have a penchant for keeping the extent of their wealth a private matter. No family has been more successful in this than the Wetherills. Estimates of Ravensaugh Wetherill's private holdings—not including those of his four sons and Moira, his daughter—run to about $2.5 billion.[4] The children each are estimated to have perhaps $750 million, which, when you include the Wetherill Foundation's $1.5 billion, gave the family a total economic power base of some $7.75 billion.[5] Yet, while everyone was aware that the Wetherills were very rich, no one had any idea of the proportions of their wealth until the Senate hearings on the newly passed Election Bill. Like the mysterious Hugh Roy Cullen, they managed to keep themselves well out of the public eye. It was certainly not that the Wetherill money was new. But, as with just about everything involving the Wetherill family, it was deceptive. For while no single member of the family was in his own right as rich, say, as Onassis or Getty or the Shah of Iran, taken together, the family's

[2]*The Rockefellers*, by Peter Collier & David Horowitz.
[3]*The Wetherills, an Invisible Dynasty*, by John Gallagher.
[4]*Wetherill Country: A Study in Secret Billions*, by V. L. Parsons.
[5]*Ibid.*

wealth was exceeded probably only by the Mafia's. And like the Mafia, the family was a close one. The scope of its influence was awesome, reaching into manufacturing, chemicals, metals, oils, ore, land, banking, government, the judiciary, transportation, communications and aerospace. What was unusual about this—beyond the sheer size of it—was that, with the relatively small excursions into land and banking, the family owned no part of these basic industries themselves. The Wetherills' grip on them—with the control that followed—consisted entirely in patents to processes essential to these industries' survival. On paper, this approach seemed modest; in practice, it gave the family incredible influence on the nation's economy. "The family." When a Wetherill used the word, it sounded encased in reverent quotation marks, spoken in the hushed, proprietary tones Catholics reserve for "the church," politicians for "the party," and West Pointers for "the corps."

The philosophy behind the Wetherill family's activities was new to the country, but not to the Wetherills. The original Wetherill had arrived on these shores in the early eighteen hundreds. This distinction allowed the ladies of the tribe, by stretching things a bit, to affix a minute "Cda" (Colonial Dames of America) after their names in the Social Register. That this same ancestor was a fleeing Dutch nailmaker named Hendryk Wilhelm Vederyll who earned his passage as an indentured servant was not celebrated by either the Register or New York society. The Wetherills themselves, though, delighted in the fact. With the self-assuredness that only accompanies wealth long held, they hung in the Wetherill Foundation's lobby a giant portrait of what Hendryk Wilhelm was purported to look like, his body rigidly encased in the leather apron of his trade, one hand resting confidently on a keg of hand-hewn nails.

As the new country struggled to survive, Hendryk Wilhelm discovered something: although too poor to own a house or land himself, his skill at making nails soon made him more prosperous than many of those who did. And without anyone's realizing it, he had struck upon the basic philosophy behind the present-day Wetherill fortune: possession of an elemental key to someone else's survival guarantees both profit and power while involving little risk to the possessor.

For almost sixty years, this philosophy (soon applied to the burgeoning New England textile business) had made the family no more than comfortably well-off. It was the arrival of the railroad that made them rich initially. The journal boxes that lubricated the axles of the early railroad cars were designed to a patent owned by them; so were the couplers and the machines that turned out the railroad spikes. Later, in 1871, a convenient marriage into the Du-Pont family brought the Wetherills into the chemical business early; and while the Hughes Tool Company might own the design to the actual bit that dug for oil, it was the Wetherills who owned the patent for the device that held together the rods onto which the Hughes bit was fastened.

By the time the automobile arrived, the Wetherills were ready: the spark plug, the cooling system, even the lug nuts that held the wheels in place, all were manufactured or licensed from patents they owned. And by the middle nineteen hundreds, the family's ownership of patents and elements essential to the survival of almost every basic industry in the country meant that almost nowhere in the Free World could a wheel turn, a retort bubble, or a single pound of ore be refined that didn't make the Wetherill family some infinitesimal fraction wealthier. Hendryk Wilhelm would have approved.

In general, so did the country's social arbiters. By their own choice, the Wetherills were not as formally ensconced as the Rockefellers or the Mellons or the Vanderbilts. But neither were they as permanently outcast as the Kennedys, the Fords, or the half-dozen other very wealthy clans with pretensions to permanence.

The family was a well-disciplined unit; ostentation or displays of erratic behavior were brutally dealt with. From childhood, every Wetherill was raised to believe in keeping a low profile and in service to the nation. There was no element of the guilt sometimes associated with wealth behind this stance; rather, it was arrived at as the most expedient method of keeping the family's boodle intact. Expediency in keeping things intact was a key phrase in the basic Wetherill philosophy, and the vast Wetherill Foundation was a key building block of this basic philosophy.

Eleven days after the party, Eliot Towers, personal assistant to Chase Wetherill, the Foundation's chief executive, stared out the thirty-fifth-floor window of the

Wetherill Foundation. He glanced at his watch again and fidgeted. It was two minutes after one, which made Mr. Wetherill three and a half hours late. This disturbed Towers; under normal circumstances, Mr. Wetherill's nine-thirty arrival was regulated with the precision of an Atmos clock. Towers once more searched his mind, then Mr. Wetherill's desk calendar, to discover if there could be any forgotten appointment or trip to explain the delay. Neither search was productive, and Towers went back to staring out the window. He was a very precise man, and such unexplained events made him uncomfortable.

The personal phone on Mr. Wetherill's desk—one which went through neither the Foundation's switchboard nor his secretary—rang, strident and insistent in the hush of his inner office.

"Chase?" asked a voice when Towers picked up the receiver.

"No, this is Eliot Towers. Mr. Wetherill isn't here at the moment."

"I see. Hello, Towers. This is O'Connor at Trustbank." There was a pause while O'Connor of Trustbank pondered how far one went with someone like Mr. Wetherill's personal assistant, then: "Do you know when he'll be in?"

This time the pause came from Towers, torturing the same question that O'Connor had battled a moment earlier. For Towers, the solution was easier, because he knew more about O'Connor than O'Connor knew about him; the man was in charge of various Wetherill and Foundation holdings—$4.3 billion at the end of the last accounting period—and this fact, to Towers' mind, made O'Connor more than eligible to know anything he wanted to know. "I can't tell you for certain, Mr. O'Connor. As you're aware, he's usually here by nine-thirty. All I can say is that I expect him any minute."

"I see. Well, I'll call back." The pause again, only this time longer and more profound. Finally: "On the other hand, Towers, I don't want to miss him. There's a message. Important, apparently. Could you tell him that Mr.—well, he'll know who it is—called from Washington and asked me to relay to him, that is, the message was—and I hope it makes more sense to him than it does to me—called to say that a 'Situation D' exists." Over the phone, Towers could hear Mr. O'Connor cough, probably,

Towers decided, so that he could repeat himself without appearing rude. "Situation D."

Furrowing his eyebrows, Towers leaned down and picked up a pad. "Tel Mes from O'Connor—Situation D exists." He wrote the words carefully, then reviewed the note for sense. It made none. "Do you mind if I make sure I've got that right, Mr. O'Connor?" Towers was completely sure; he wanted to be certain Mr. O'Connor was.

A polite, if nervous, laugh rattled out of the receiver. Possibly, O'Connor was wondering if he had entrusted too much to a personal assistant; more probably, he had hoped to glean some information himself from Towers' reaction. "No, I have to admit it's very confusing, Towers. Mysterious, almost." The message was repeated twice, read back twice, and agreed to be a faithful account of what "Mr.—well, he'll know who it is" had told O'Connor.

"Ask Mr. Wetherill to call me when he gets in," suggested O'Connor, a sudden briskness to his tone. "Nice to talk to you, Towers." The click was audible.

With a shrug, Towers hung up the receiver, fingering the meticulously polished brass buttons of his vest in resentment. (The vest, of bright-red flannel, was an affectation of Towers', one calculated to demonstrate that he was really a bit of a sport. Emerging, however, from the inevitable upholstery gray of his suiting, the impression was bizarre, as if someone had glued twin tailpipes onto the rear of a Mercedes 600 limousine.) Straightening up, Towers tugged the vest down to make it smooth, rearranged the papers on Mr. Wetherill's desk top, and allowed his eyes to move around the room.

Messages of the kind delivered by Mr. O'Connor, Towers felt, hinted at arrangements neither prudent for the Foundation nor fitting for the Wetherills. At the same time, though, Towers had to concede the Wetherills were a hard lot to fathom: what they apparently did for one reason frequently turned out to have been done for some other reason entirely.

The Wetherill Foundation was one example of this particular phenomenon at work. In the early thirties, Chase's late grandfather, Davenport Wetherill, had set up the Foundation in keeping with the family's tradition of service to the nation. The arrangement was also in keeping with a more recent Wetherill policy: avoidance at all costs of inheritance taxes which could nibble into the family patent holdings. (Avoiding the IRS was similarly the motive behind the Ford and Rockefeller Foundations; this method of dodging inheritance taxes also gave the families a properly benign public face.) Safe from the suddenly socialist-minded grasp of Washington, the Foundation handed out grants, subsidies and gifts to worthwhile causes with the abandon of a big-time butter-and-egg man facing a maitre d'. Some of the projects were successful, some were not; some even managed to make the Wetherills themselves richer. (One case in point: $6 million of Foundation money gave New York the land on which to build the city's extensive Art, Music and Theater Center. That the Wetherill family owned all the dilapidated riverfront land around the center was overlooked in the general outpouring of appreciation; that the value of these land holdings appreciated 500 percent when the Center was built was never even noted publicly; that the Wetherill family put up apartment houses, hotels, stores, and recreation facilities to cash in on their newly valuable land would have been considered looking a gift horse in the mouth.)

But such self-serving windfalls were unusual; in general, the Foundation genuinely hewed to the principle of service to the country. Its operations were multifaceted, forward-looking, and as open-minded as they were open-handed, seeming to reflect a sincere predisposition on the part of the family to be generous to a fault. At a personal level, the Wetherills could be equally generous: a position with any Wetherill-controlled undertaking was well paid, gifts and pensions were exceptionally generous, and the loyal and faithful were never forgotten.

Eliot Towers could testify to this personally. When his youngest son was discovered to be a victim of muscular dystrophy, the first person at the hospital was Chase Wetherill. Specialists of every conceivable kind were flown in at Chase's expense. And when the doctors made it clear that the treatment would be lifelong and enormously expensive—far beyond anything that Towers could afford—it was Chase Wetherill who quietly began picking up the bills. The only stipulation he made was that the money was not to be considered a gift (taxable to the giver), but a loan, which could later be declared in default (a tax deduction *for* the giver). As with the Foundation, Chase knew generosity can be a two-way street.

From a purely technical standpoint, of course, Chase Wetherill had no right to be controlling a family-given tax-free trust such as the Foundation: along with his three brothers and lone sister he presumably could serve in no post more active than director. To get around this, there was a functioning chief operating officer, Lloyd Carpenter, the Foundation's chairman. By exquisite legal maneuvering, however—and the appointment of Carpenter to enough Wetherill-controlled boards to keep him happy—it was actually Chase who ran the Foundation, from the buying of the first paperclip to the giving away of the last million.

Eliot Towers was extremely sensitive to the delicate balance required to keep both the family and the Foundation suspended on so precarious a highwire. This sensitivity lay behind his reaction to Mr. O'Connor's cryptic "Mysterious, almost" message from Washington; an investigative gust from a hostile Congress could someday spell disaster for them all.

"Hi, Eliot." The familiar voice of Chase Wetherill came from so close behind Towers that he jumped. "Sorry I'm so late today. Should have called you. But something came up that had to be taken care of."

Towers stared down at Chase: there was no other way to meet his eyes. Chase Wetherill was a short man, and looked at least ten years younger than his fifty years. Partly, this youthful appearance was due to his almost teen-age trimness and inevitable rich tan; partly, it sprang from a constantly changing set of highly animated facial expressions, somewhere between the boyish and the elfin. Moving his head away and up, Towers fumbled in his pocket to retrieve the O'Connor note, which he started to hand to Chase.

"O'Connor? Yes. I know about it. He reached me in the car on my way here. But I'd already been given the gist of it anyway, earlier—much earlier—this morning." Chase made one of his wonderful rubbery expressions—one of resigned pain—to show precisely how early the nub of what was in O'Connor's note had reached him from some other source. With a shrug, he slapped his attaché case on his desk top. Papers were removed and placed on the desk top; a drawer was unlocked and papers from the desk transferred into the case. As if realizing for the first time that Towers was still in the room, Chase peered at him over the top of the opened case. "I'll be out of town for a few days, Eliot." He glanced at the desk calendar. "Better cancel everything until you hear from me exactly when I'll be back." The calendar was treated to a closer look, and a sour expression allowed to attach itself to Chase's face. "Nothing there but a lot of fund-raisers anyway."

"I see. Any reservations you want me to make for you?"

"I don't think so. Hotels always seem to fit me in somehow." Although dry, Chase's smile was neither arrogant nor supercilious, but the confident smile of a man well aware that any hotel in the country would evict half of its guests finding a way to make room for him. Towers ignored the realization that his question had been deliberately left unanswered and pressed on.

"Is there any place I can reach you? People always ask."

Chase sucked at his lower lip. "No, I'll call you if I need anything. As for people asking, just say I'm away. Period."

Towers could not put his finger on any precise reason, but a sense of disquiet was growing inside him. With the Wetherills, mysteries—both business and personal—were not unusual, but this one was being guarded with unusual fervor. Even he was not to know where Chase Wetherill was going. But to ask for information not volunteered was unthinkable. With a nod, Towers folded the note and fumbled putting it in his pocket. When he looked back up, Chase already had one hand on the phone. The pose was one of dismissal.

"Well, if I can help with anything . . ."

"Of course, Eliot."

Softly, Towers pulled the door shut behind him. Mysteries such as these, he repeated to himself, were neither prudent for the Foundation nor fitting for the Wetherills.

At four-thirty that afternoon, Towers was back in Chase Wetherill's office; Chase was wearing a light raincoat and standing beside his personal wall safe (the office had two: one for the Foundation papers, one for personal Wetherill business).

"OK, Eliot, I'm about off. Take care of Judy"—Judy was Wetherill's new secretary, blond, young, and tempting—"but not *too* good care."

Towers forced a man-to-man smile. It was locker-room banter; Judy's virtue was as safe with one of them as with the other.

"And, oh yes." Chase pulled a Foundation attaché case from inside the safe and handed it to Towers. "Why don't you keep this in your safe at home." Eliot nodded; at first, the request didn't appear unusual. Because of the number of Foundation papers Towers frequently took home with him, Chase had had a safe installed in Towers' den in Roslyn, L.I. But usually the papers were those which Eliot himself selected for working on there; to be given material and asked, as it were, to act as depository for it when the Foundation's building was a far safer storage place *was* unusual and unprecedented. Chase caught the look on Towers' face.

"What's inside belongs to you anyway. Just keep it handy in case you need it."

"I don't understand."

"Well, don't worry about it. The chances are you will never have to understand. For the time being, just don't bother to open it. Even if, as I said, what's inside is yours. Just keep the case in your safe, understood?" Chase was trying very hard to appear casual, but his ever-changing set of expressions was saying the opposite. Before Towers could think of any way to press his confusion on him, Chase Wetherill had slipped out the door toward the elevator, leaving only a smile, a wave and a faint whiff of lemon verbena behind him.

For some moments, Towers stared at the attaché case in his hand. Then, he closed the office door and did something he had never done before: he disobeyed orders. Putting the case on Chase's desk, he snapped the catches open. Inside, instead of a clue to Chase's mysterious behavior, was still another mystery. The interior was filled with crisp, high-denomination Dutch guilder, bundles of them, each bundle fastened by the pale-blue paper band of Trustbank. Towers' quick appraisal of the money indicated the case must hold close to half a million dollars.

Towers' first reaction was to run after Chase, catch him at the elevator, and tell him he'd apparently given him the wrong case. But that would involve admitting that he'd disobeyed a direct command. In Wetherill eyes, any such disobedience would be considered unforgivable. The mistake, Towers concluded, would soon be discovered anyway. In the meantime, rather than take the case home, he would lock it in the Foundation's safe, where it would be far better protected than at his house. With a slight irritated slam, he pushed the safe door shut. The knot of disquiet was rising inside Towers again; in all these years, he had never known Chase to keep currency of any kind in the office, or, for that matter, anywhere else. As with royalty, Wetherills considered cash a commodity to be dealt in by others. The knot grew. For what did Chase mean—the contents of the case belonged to him? Towers only wished it did.

On his way out the door, Towers began slipping into his fall topcoat before remembering that, although already October 24, it was still hot outside.

These days, you couldn't count on anything.

The Brannigan put the shift into drive, but kept his foot on the brake. Glancing left to make sure nothing was coming, he pulled slowly out of the used-car lot and eased himself into the stream of cars. Traffic at this hour would make the return trip from Long Island City to the Wetherills' town house lengthy and hectic.

"Brannigan," Chase Wetherill had said that morning, "I want you to buy a car. Used, but low mileage. Dark. Nothing flashy." Chase had paused to do some mathematics. "I wish it could be a four-door sedan, but I guess it'll have to be a station wagon. And not a Buick or a Chrysler wagon, dammit, a Chevy or a Ford."

"Are you sure now, Mr. With'rill," the Brannigan had answered in his rich Irish brogue, "you wouldn't be happier with a motorsickle and sidecar?"

Chase had laughed. The Brannigan was one of the few people who could kid Chase to his face and make him smile at the jibe; Chase relished the whimsical Irish humor and brashness of the man—along with the paradox of his color—and had quickly moved him out of the stables and into the house, then out of Ireland to the States, as sort of combination aide-valet-chauffeur and court jester. The Brannigan knew his last role was pivotal to his success, so both the brogue and the whimsy grew richer the longer he stayed in this country. No one had ever accused the Brannigan of being dumb.

A small truck cut in front of him, the driver leaning on his horn and shaking his fist at him fiercely. The Brannigan treated him to his widest smile. "And a bowlful of shamrocks up your ass, too, bucko." But he pulled the car farther to the right to give the truck plenty of room. Nothing must happen to this car; it was special, very special.

"I want you to register the car in your name," Chase had told him, reaching into his pocket. "In your name and use some phony address. I'll explain why later, but the name part's very important." A roll of bills was handed to him. "Here. This should cover it."

The Brannigan had stared at the wad and whistled softly, tilting his head as if an idea had just occurred to him that required weighing. "There's this bang-tail I keep hearin' about, Mr. Wetherill—"

"*Move*, Brannigan. And be back by three," he added, suddenly looking genuinely stern. "With the registration in *your* name, remember."

The Brannigan sighed. "Done, guv'nor." One of the prime requisites of a court jester is knowing when to stop. Whistling cheerfully—and before Chase was even quite aware of it—the Brannigan was out of the room and on his way. To buy a car—and in his own name.

Alwynn Aloysius Brannigan was born May 12, 1944, in the grim little town of Ballyshannon, County Sligo. His father (name unknown) was a deserter from the United States Quartermaster Corps Battalion billeted in Northern Ireland; he had slipped across the border into Erin just long enough for a series of passionate dalliances with the young maidens of the Western Counties. As it turned out, one of these was with a certain Meaghan Brannigan of Donnegal, after which he vanished—although whether back into Northern Ireland, to England, or to an obscure death at the hands of some infuriated Irish father remained uncertain. The result of the intimacy was more concrete: a boy child. In itself, the event of a fatherless son would have caused small comment; with so many Yanks crammed into England and Ulster, such things happened fairly regularly in Erin. But the soldier with whom Meaghan had bedded was himself unusual: Brannigan's father had been, as the locals like to put it, "as black as an Englishman's heart." And during the game of genetic roulette which followed, the chamberful of genes and chromosomes delivered a baby of the same ebony shade as his father. Many Irish girls with illegitimate children raised them as their own; Brannigan's color made this awkward. Almost as soon as she was weaned, Meaghan Brannigan's progeny was shipped to a Catholic orphanage.

The child, with its strange and unaccustomed complexion, was not looked upon too kindly at the county orphanages; Brannigan could still remember his mournful progression through them, from Sligo to Gungala to Dungarvan to Kilrush to Galway (which sounds a good deal prettier in the famous song about its bay than it looked to Brannigan from the window of a run-down orphanage). But the constant moving from place to place in the end turned out to Brannigan's advantage: the meeting and adapting to constantly changing new faces, the ceaseless coping with the ill-disguised hostility of the Catholic sisters, and the perennial awareness of being different from the other children (who, while blunt, were far kinder to him than the nuns) simultaneously sharpened Brannigan's wits, his instinct for self-preservation and his sense of humor. Very young he learned that it hurts less if you laugh at the world before the world can laugh at you.

Once released from the endless chain of orphanages to the world outside, Brannigan was fully aware of the effect he had on strangers the second he opened his mouth. The rich, rolling accents of Erin pouring from an ebony-black face was a combination guaranteed to rattle anyone. And while others might have played this paradoxical mixture down, the Brannigan—a name attached to him by the other orphans at Dungarvan because he was such a hell raiser—played up the difference for all it was worth. He had used it profitably when he first met Chase Wetherill at the stables in Tullamore; he had used it effectively a few minutes earlier at the used-car lot in Long Island City. "Jack, the Smiling Irishman"—whom Brannigan correctly suspected had never been closer to the old sod than the Shamrock Bar on Eighth Avenue—had been stunned when he heard Brannigan speak; and even though his customer was paying cash for an expensive Chevy station wagon, had been unable to contain himself. Leaning over, he had had to ask, "Say, are you putting me on, fella, or what?"

Brannigan had given him nothing more than a sly, fellow-countryman's wink, then: "Sligo. You know how it goes, bucko. Black Irish."

The joke was not original with Brannigan, but the expression of bewilderment on Jack, the Smiling Irishman's face had made the disinterment of such old material worthwhile. And without giving the salesman time to recover, Brannigan had driven off with a broad smile. He had never owned a car before, and the feeling was a good one.

Brannigan's brow clouded. Chase's mysterious reasons for buying the car, and for some of the other arrangements he had told him to make, were becoming more worrisome.

"Pull off somewhere," Chase had directed him, "and dirty the car up a little. You know, splash a bit of mud on the body and perhaps put a few dents in the fenders. Maybe kick in the license plates a little, too. I don't want the car to look too new—those dealers always polish them up like crazy."

Dirt on a clean car? Dents in new chrome? Beat-up license plates? Chase was acting strangely, and the fact made Brannigan uncomfortable. Acutely uncomfortable.

Something was up. Something he wasn't being told.

Chapter Two

Asked to elaborate, Burns [Arthur A. Burns, chairman of the Federal Reserve Board] attributed the collapse of czarist Russia before the Bolsheviks in 1917 and the rise of Nazi Germany after the first World War "in large part" to the ravages of inflation. "Uncontrolled inflation," Burns warned, leaves a nation "wide open" to attack by demagogues who "exploit the sense of misery and frustration" of the people.

—Financial Page, N.Y. Daily
News, *Wednesday, July 31, 1974*

Darcie Wetherill stood in her dressing room staring at Chase with disbelief. As he had demanded, she began, with visible reluctance, taking off the knitted suit she'd just finished putting on.

"I said something simple, Darcie."

"What's simpler than Chanel?"

"I meant something that *looked* simple, not classic. You know what . .." Chase stopped; Darcie was teasing him and he'd bitten. "Dammit," he half-growled. "Look, you know what I mean. Something like—well, maybe a sweater and skirt."

Darcie threw up her hands and stepped out of the suit's skirt; with a muffled snort of resignation she began rummaging through the shelves marked "Swtrs." "If I'm lucky, maybe I can find one with moth holes."

Chase forced a laugh. None of this, he knew, was easy for Darcie, and he owed that laughter to her. When nervous or upset, she occasionally took refuge behind the little-girl giddiness she had just displayed. He could re-

23

member the first time he had met Darcie—at an inordinately formal dinner dance in New York. At the last minute, the seating arrangements had been switched around and, peering at the place cards, she found she was to be seated next to Chase Wetherill, an awesome experience for someone her age. Momentarily rattled, she had said nothing for a second or two when he first sat down. Then, turning her eyes on him—the widest, most innocent, honest eyes Chase had ever encountered—she proceeded to awe the awesome Wetherill sitting beside her. "Are you really as rich as they say?"

Chase was stunned. The subject of their wealth was something no one ever mentioned to any Wetherill; it would have been considered both rude and ugly. Yet, the simple directness with which Darcie had put the question cut through the party's underlying hypocrisy without seeming either rude or ugly. Chase sighed, appearing deep in some calculation. Finally: "Yes, I suppose I am." He paused for a second and smiled. "And *then* some."

"How wonderful!" Darcie had laughed, almost clapping her hands in glee. "I was afraid you were going to say something condescending like, 'Well, I get by' or 'You know how people exaggerate.' How wonderful! And what fun that you're able to enjoy it! Most rich people I know either pretend they're poor or that they're embarrassed by having money or that they don't like being rich." She paused, then let the heart of her basic philosophy be seen. "I hate—absolutely can't stand—hypocrites."

To a man always afraid he may be liked more for his wealth than for himself, the appeal of her directness was overwhelming.

No great beauty, Darcie Wetherill was as trim and compact as her husband, but exuded a soft, feminine charm and an almost regal elegance that made her seem far prettier than she was. At forty-eight, her face still had a strong aquiline handsomeness to it, with forceful, perpetually widened eyes that restlessly searched the faces around her for any hint of the hypocrisy she so loathed. Darcie was the perfect wife for Chase, a constant series of surprises springing from the two sides of her personality: impulsive and childlike, witty and direct, determined and challenging, honest to a fault.

The combination of determination and challenging nature had, about ten years earlier, produced an explosion between them which neither of them ever mentioned, though neither of them had ever forgotten it. Unknown to anyone but Chase, Darcie had quietly become an ardent feminist. To Chase, this presented no problem: in his own mind he had gone through his usual tortuous process of seeing both sides of the question in depth and emerged favoring the concept totally; in fact, he found it difficult imagining anyone taking any other position. His only area of disagreement was where feminism—like so many other activist movements—produced its own kind of prejudice. Where the disagreement began was Darcie's impulsive announcement one day that she was about to embark on a series of speaking tours in behalf of the sagging Equal Rights Amendment.

Chase was appalled. For the family, the ramifications were huge. But even with that, the argument was civilized enough until Chase, trying to make a point, struck the raw nerve of her ego. "Don't you see, Darcie, what they're trying to do? They're using you, dammit, they're using you to get the Wetherill name."

Darcie flared. "What do you mean, 'to get the Wetherill name'? Didn't it ever occur to you that I might just have something worth listening to all on my own?"

"Would they have asked you if you weren't a Wetherill?"

"I don't know and I don't give a damn. They asked *me* to speak, not a name."

"You're kidding yourself, Darcie. What they want is the name. And when they use the name, it brushes off on all of us—on me and the Foundation, on Duane in the Senate, and could make Toby have to disqualify himself every time Equal Rights or anything close to it comes up before the Supreme Court. So it's not just a question of what *you* want to do—the whole family is involved."

Darcie exploded. Chase could never remember seeing her so angry. "The family. I'm fed up to here with the damned family. The family, the family! Do you have to wait until the family tells you what to think?"

Taken back, Chase tried to slow her down. "Darcie, you're not letting—"

"Well, I'm not like you, Chase. I'm not a Wetherill. I only married one. I don't take my orders from the family. Screw them."

"Christ, Darcie, but you make it tough. You won't listen. But it's because of the family that I'm going to have to tell you not to—"

The choice of the word "tell" was unfortunate; later, Chase wasn't even sure it had been what he meant to say. But Darcie didn't wait to find out. Standing up, she headed for the door of the library, pausing only long enough to spin and call back to him: "No, Chase. Because of the *family* I'm going to have to tell *you* something. Goodbye." Then she stormed out of the house and disappeared.

At first, Chase didn't know where she had gone, but his underground soon reported that she had moved into the Colony Club. The role reversal was so complete—irate wife storms out of house and moves into her club—that Chase couldn't help be amused, even though finding anything funny in the situation immediately made him feel guilty. Neither was the subject even mentioned when, five days later, she returned.

"I'm glad to be back," she had said, kissing him on the forehead.

"I missed you," he had answered. And the book was closed on the matter.

She never made the speeches, although she contributed heavily—and anonymously—to the movement, some secret part of her hating him for not having the directness to say what he personally thought, family or not, and some other part of her hating herself even more for not having defied the family. The damned family.

Now, this many years later, she wondered why a recollection of her short-lived defiance should surface. Certainly Chase had said nothing to evoke the memory of the matter. She turned and stared at him, trying to find an answer. Then she saw the tiny lines of concern building around Chase's eyes. She stopped the unbuttoning of a folded gray sweater and looked at him with a confident smile. "Don't worry, Chase. I'll be all right."

"I know. I just hope everybody else will be." He continued watching her, and when she turned around to him to reach for something, he kissed her lightly on the back of the neck.

"You tickle." Even though he couldn't see Darcie's face, Chase knew his gesture had been appreciated. She turned around with a sweeping gesture, dressed now in a simple sweater and skirt, a monochrome of light and dark grays.

She was still more chic-looking than Chase really wanted, but he lacked heart to push her any further. "Kids ready? We've got to get moving."

"As they'll ever be. Emlyn's suspicious. Dina's complaining. But the twins can't wait: they think it's some kind of great adventure. In other words, about the reaction you'd expect from that bunch."

"About the reaction you'd expect from that bunch." Chase repeated the words to himself; it was a fair summary. The four Wetherill children were as varied a lot as you could find in any one family anywhere.

For some years, Dina, the eldest, had appeared headed toward the social whirl, a private world of subscription dances and chinless young men in which any Wetherill was considered desirable prey. Sometime during the last year, though—almost precisely, it seemed, when she turned seventeen—Dina had abruptly shaken herself loose from the butterfly existence and gone to the other extreme. The laughter and endless telephoning of the year before had disappeared, replaced by an intense, almost moody introspection. No one was sure what sort of people and causes she might be involved with, for they saw little of her, and she discouraged any discussion of what she was doing or whom she was seeing. Some of the possibilities unnerved Chase. There had been no need to tell Dina to dress simply today; her present wardrobe appeared to consist entirely of various shades of faded blue denim.

With her brother, Emlyn—at sixteen, a year younger—no such dramatic change had taken place, only an intensification. From the time he was practically little more than a child, he had been completely absorbed with advanced physics and theoretical mathematics, subjects which mystified his mother and father and left Emlyn intense and withdrawn. To his teachers, he was a serious student with a brilliant future; to Chase, Emlyn was a disembodied brain attached to a gangling frame, immune to all efforts at being trimmed, combed or shaved. He would have felt a lot better if the boy had laughed once in a while; sometimes Chase wondered if Emlyn had ever been a child at all.

But 't was the thirteen-year-old twins that were both Chase's chief delight and worry. Identical to an eerie degree, the twins would appear every day dressed in the same clothes (even without knowing what the other would be wearing), and could finish each other's sentences. They led lives so closely bound they seemed in perpetual conspiracy against the world. This very closeness was what worried Chase. His own younger brother, Tracey, had been one of such a pair of twins, and he hadn't worked out at all well (the other twin, at seventeen, in one of his few separations from Tracey, had been found dead under circumstances so mysterious Chase himself had only discovered what had happened to him two years ago; the subject had always been out of bounds, even within the family). Sometimes, thinking of his own Jeremy and Raven (for Ravensaugh, Graffa's name), the dark suspicious brooding about Tracey and his dead twin would haunt Chase and cause him to shudder. But Jeremy and Raven were so exuberant, so full of fun, so rambunctious, the cloud of doubt would quickly melt away. From downstairs, he could hear them now, shouting at each other, a sort of taunting chant directed probably at either Dina or Emlyn. With a smile, Chase looked at Darcie.

"Perhaps if you get Nettie to pump some food into them, they'd simmer down."

"No, they'll just go on raising hell on full stomachs instead of empty ones. But I suppose it's worth a try." She picked up the house phone and gave instructions to Nettie downstairs in the kitchen.

Chase checked his watch. "Brannigan should be here with the car pretty soon, so maybe you'd better hurry things along. He's all set to go; we have to be too."

Darcie seemed stunned. "We're taking the *Brannigan* with us?"

"It may turn out to be more a case of Brannigan taking us with *him*."

Darcie pretended to busy herself with little details of packing, although her muttered "The Irish . . ." did not escape Chase's ears. She was neither particularly fond nor approving of the Brannigan, but had never made an issue of the man. For one thing, she knew she was in the minority; the kids adored him, and so apparently did her husband. But the Brannigan's coming along was something she hadn't counted on, one more irritation in an already painful and disturbing situation.

Chase decided the matter shouldn't be allowed to pass unmentioned, a small festering sore. "He's needed, Darcie.

In these circumstances, he can turn out to be a tremendous help."

She stopped her busywork and stared at him. "I'm not arguing with you, Chase. It's just that Brannigan's Irish whimsy begins to grate on my nerves pretty quickly. A whole trip with him . . ." She snapped her bag shut. "You did say only one suitcase each, right?" The question simultaneously gave Darcie a chance to change the subject, yet by underscoring how little they were allowed to bring with them, made the addition of Brannigan more pointed.

In frustration, Chase shook his head. "I think I'll grab a bite myself. Want anything?"

"For this whole mess to go away. It's so damned extraordinary, so hard to believe. If it could just turn out to be a dream. But I suppose that's like waiting up for the Tooth Fairy."

Chase's only acknowledgment of her statement was a small, sad nod. Then he checked his watch again. "I'll see you downstairs."

After he left, Darcie looked around the room for a moment. For fifteen years, this particular room had been so much a part of her life it was hard to imagine existing without it. Every piece of furniture, every picture, every *objet*, had been personally selected by her. Deserting the room was like running out on an old and very dear friend.

Darcie sighed. Although Chase had long ago explained the ideas that lay behind the "Situation D" call this morning, she had never fully believed them; yet the urgency with which Chase was acting, the suddenly dogmatic attitude he was displaying, forced her to accept that he considered them valid. It was not his usual manner. (She had no way of knowing the hours and days that Chase had devoted to arguing with himself what he would do if a "Situation D" call really ever *should* come.)

Giving the room a final, loving glance, she turned and left, sad, disquieted, uncertain. Part of her life was in that room. How much of it, she was only to discover in the crucible of the coming weeks.

The Brannigan turned off Park Avenue at 64th Street and headed down the two short blocks toward the Wetherill house. The activity on the streets for this time of the year was, as always, bustling. Farther uptown, though,

Brannigan had experienced an uneasy feeling, as if the people on the streets were waiting for the other shoe to drop. He could not put his finger on it. Up in Harlem, it was not unusual to see knots of people leaning against buildings, talking, laughing, killing time. The only difference he noted was that, because of this year's high unemployment rate, more people were available to lean against the buildings than usual. As he drove farther downtown, though, he experienced a curious sensation that some element was missing. When he turned the signal indicator to show he was making a left, checking to see there was no cop to catch him going through the yellow light, it finally struck him: nowhere, during the entire trip back into town, had he set eyes upon a single policeman. For a moment, Brannigan tortured the idea, then dismissed it. The drizzle of cold, light rain had increased, and more cops than usual were probably inside their patrol cars, "cooping" to keep themselves dry. A honk behind him forced him across Park before he was ready to go, at the same time pushing the sense of foreboding from his mind.

Spinning the wheel hard—the Chevy's power steering was not all that Jack, the Smiling Irishman, had promised—Brannigan drove slowly through the narrow arch and into the garage forming the front of the house next to the Wetherills' and closed the heavy doors behind him. From the outside, the Wetherills' house, a narrow, four-story affair with Georgian overtones, looked reasonably modest —if any town house in the East Sixties can be said to fit such a description. It was only when you got inside the house itself that you realized how large the structure really was. The buildings on either side of the house proper, owned by the Wetherills but rented out commercially, had their rear windows bricked up; this allowed the Wetherill house to spread out behind them in the shape of a fat T. What from the front, then, looked unpretentious enough to suit the Wetherill passion for a low profile, was, for the city, huge, probably about thirty-five rooms.

Inside the garage, Brannigan went into the house through an interior door and started upstairs to report to Chase. On the way, he crossed the entrance hall: Jeremy and Raven, each with a half-eaten sandwich in hand, were playing some elaborate game involving who could race around the oval-shaped hall the fastest and get back "home" at the base of the circular staircase. A small row

of bags was neatly lined up to one side of the stairs. Tray
of milk clutched in her hands, Nettie was trying to restore
order, but the twins, perhaps sensing that today was a day
in which all the rules went by the boards, paid little attention to her threats.

In the usual roughshod manner that made all the children worship him, Brannigan took charge. Moving swiftly
across the black-and-white-squared marble floor of the
hall, he grabbed one twin under each arm and began
swinging them around so fast their legs were almost paral-
lel to the floor. "All right, now!" he roared over their
screams of delight. "Pipe down, you young louts, or I'll
bash your bloody little heads together, I will."

More yelps of delighted pain and pretended fright. Brannigan appeared a slight man, but he was as powerful as an
ox. On occasion, he was also about as restrained. The
screams and the laughter and Brannigan's roaring all came
to an abrupt halt as Raven's flying feet kicked a bowl off
one of the bombé chests flanking the living-room doors.
The crash that followed was loud and final, followed by a
gasp from Darcie Wetherill, who had chosen precisely that
moment to make her descent down the stairs. (The bowl
was Tsu-Min, circa 1720.)

"Oh, my now," gasped Brannigan, staring awe-stricken
at the shattered remains on the floor. "Pretty thing it was,
too." His eyes rose to meet Mrs. Wetherill's.

Darcie smiled weakly. This was neither the time nor the
circumstances to lecture Brannigan. Besides, given everything else that was happening, the loss of a bowl, valuable
or not, was academic.

"I'm sorry, Missus. It was my fault, you understan', not
the lad's."

"Nothing to worry about, nothing to worry about at all.
It's insured," Darcie lied, this time managing a more con-
vincing smile. The twins sighed in relief. "But do as the
Brannigan says: pipe down, you two. We've got a lot to
get done."

"Indeed we do," agreed Brannigan, suddenly stern.
Moving quickly forward, he handed them each a bag to
carry. "Here. Start loading all of these into the back of the
station wagon. It's in the garage. March, now!"

Subdued by the Brannigan's unusual seriousness, the
twins, after an exchange of glances, slowly picked up the
bags and began lugging them out of the hall.

For a second, Darcie's and Brannigan's eyes met and locked. They were both aware that it was only this pressing situation that was forcing this new togetherness. The unspoken truce had to be observed. As with most truces, the reasons behind it were more pragmatic than philosophical.

Brannigan turned on his widest grin. "Are you sure, Mrs. Wetherill, there's nothing I can fetch down for you?"

Darcie bit her lip. "I don't think I'll ever be sure of anything again." She looked upstairs for a second, then came down the rest of the way. "Thank you anyway, but there's nothing you can do. Nothing anybody can do."

The car was crowded to the point of discomfort. Seven people plus minimal personal luggage is a lot for even a station wagon to handle. And the luggage, since it included a heavy footlocker which Chase and Brannigan had put aboard at the last minute, took up far more room than anyone had expected. (The footlocker, however, was an important item. Since what might happen to U.S. currency was uncertain, it held the most reliable kind of hard currency: gold and silver coin.) Looking around from the front seat, Chase could only wonder how he had ever imagined they could travel in his first choice, a four-door sedan.

Since the bags could not be distributed, the riders had been instead, creating a curious seating arrangement. Brannigan, of course, was driving; instead of his usual black alpaca coat, today he was resplendent in a sports jacket to make him look less like a servant and more like a civilian. On the far right-hand side of the front seat sat Chase, looking strange and unkempt to his family since he was without his usual necktie. (The twins, of course, had hooted at the sight, and then were thundered into silence by their father.)

Squeezed between Brannigan and Chase was Darcie, tense and uncomfortable. The reality of what they were doing had not really reached her until she had climbed into the car. Directly behind the three of them—on the short two-seater—were Emlyn and Dina, staring straight ahead like strangers on a bus. The rear seat held the luggage, the footlocker, a mysterious long package wrapped in a blanket, and—the twins, who were already wrestling, falling onto the floor, and giggling, lost in their private world.

As the car pulled out of the garage onto the street, the early dark of late October surrounded them. The streets had the enchanted air of fall to them, people moving behind the brightly lit windows of the houses in the Sixties, their movements purposeful yet indistinct behind the rippled glass or sheer curtains that townhouses of the area used to ensure privacy. Along the sidewalks, people hurried purposefully, struggled to find taxis, or headed for subway stops and newspaper kiosks, packages clutched to themselves. Between Lex and Third, stopped momentarily by the honking traffic, Chase watched as the door of a small bar swung open to reveal its brightly lit interior; for a moment the door stayed open and inside you could see a fanfaronatic crush of patrons standing around, drinking, laughing, and talking, frantically celebrating something. A blare of the jukebox music reached the car just before the door swung closed again.

The very ordinariness of that scene—in contrast to the overloaded station wagon crammed with its premature refugees—made Chase feel unreal; he struggled to convince himself once again that their flight was necessary. The suddenness of O'Connor's phone call had left Chase shaken and unsure. Although he was careful to let no indication of his misgivings show, he knew Darcie was even less convinced.

"Are you *sure* we have to go?" she had asked, pausing at the door into the garage after bussing Nettie on the cheek.

"The only thing I'm not sure of is whether we shouldn't have left the moment we got that call this morning. And we'll find that out soon enough."

Brannigan honked his horn at the cars ahead of him, trying to make them react to the traffic light. Slowly, almost reluctantly, the cars began to move spasmodically forward. At the entrance to the East River Drive, they swung south and went across the 58th Street Bridge; Chase's plan was to stay off the Triboro and the major parkways. Threading their way now through the erratic, dingy streets of Long Island City, they turned again, and still using secondary routes, headed toward Long Island itself.

The traffic was lighter, but they were not sure of the

way. Chase struggled with a folded road map, trying to find street names along the way that matched those set in tiny type on the detailed map insert. Progress was slow. The neighborhood they were passing through was row after row of undistinguished two-family houses, mostly in need of paint, and punctuated regularly by small stores, shops and bars. The streets themselves were narrow but empty, lined with cars parked bumper to bumper, looking stark and grim in the long shadows cast by the overhead street lights. Twice, glancing behind him, Chase thought they were being followed: a small gray two-door Ford seemed to keep reappearing in the rear-view mirror. But after keeping track for a while, Chase decided it was his imagination and smiled inwardly: he would make a very nervous criminal.

After they had turned left onto a narrower street, euphemistically named Avalon Drive, and driven two or three blocks farther, the street abruptly changed. The housing was the same, respectable if depressing, but the sidewalks, even the outer edge of the streets themselves, were full of people. They were mostly blacks, with a scattering of young whites, their long hair held in place by rubber bands and pieces of cloth. They all looked strangely out of place in this bastion of middle-class bleakness.

"Where the hell did *they* come from all of a sudden?" Chase asked of no one in particular.

Brannigan laughed. "It's the long hair that does it, you know: sucks the brains right out through their skulls, it does."

A snort came from Dina, a giggle from the twins. While they were stopped, again waiting for one of the frequent traffic lights to change, the crowd began moving off the sidewalks and spilled into the streets, youths climbing over the bumpers of the parked cars to get on the roadway. When Brannigan honked, the side of the car was slapped hard several times.

Chase turned around to Emlyn and Dina. "Better lock the doors. Probably unnecessary, but you never know." *He* didn't know, certainly, and that caused the disquiet growing inside him to mushroom.

Ahead of them, a yellow El Dorado coupe that Chase had seen pull out of a factory gate earlier was blowing its horn in loud and imperial trumpetings, trying to clear for itself a path through the crowd. Several of the youths slapped the El Dorado's hood; others had taken the blast from the horn as a challenge and planted themselves directly in front of the car. The window on the left side of the Cadillac rolled smoothly down and the driver leaned out, swearing loudly at the crowd and telling them to get the hell out of his way.

A taunting shout rose from the crowd as the young blacks yelled back. Quickly, they surrounded the car, hammering on its hood and sides, swearing back at the driver, shaking their fists, chanting something Chase couldn't make out, although it sounded like "jobsjobsjobs." One young girl threw something through the window of the car; the driver shook his head and wiped his face, then pressed the button to roll the window back up. A cheer rose from the mob; the pounding on the sides increased, and another girl darted forward and wrote something obscene on the windshield with her lipstick. The crowd cheered again; several of the stronger youths began rocking the car from side to side.

Over the futile blasts of the Cadillac's horn and the chanting of the mob and the raucous confusion of individual shouts and curses, Chase heard a new sound: it was a voice that had the echoing, tinny quality of having come from a loudspeaker. "No, gaddamyouall, you got the wrong car," the voice bellowed. "It's the one behind. The one behind. They're in the station wagon. You got the wrong car . . ."

Chase went hollow. From the beginning, it had struck him as more than chance that just while he and his family were passing through the area the crowd had chosen that moment to erupt. Twisting himself in his seat, Chase could see a short, frail-looking black with a wispy goatee standing on the roof of a parked car, shouting his commands through a bull horn, waving his arms, manipulating the crowd like a conductor, moving them inexorably toward Chase's car. On the roof of another car, Chase had just enough time to see a CBS television crew, sweeping the scene with their portable camera.

"Get going, Brannigan. Jesus, get going!" Chase was startled at how long it had taken him to react and give his order, but the true meaning of what was happening had taken that long to sink in. As a result, he hadn't even noticed that Brannigan was already doing everything that he could think of to get the station wagon and themselves out of the crowd, now swarming over the car in mushrooming numbers. From Brannigan, all Chase got was a glancing dart from reproachful eyes, a sort of "What the hell do you think I'm *trying* to do, Mr. W'thril?" look. The car, Chase realized, was lurching up and down from Brannigan's struggles, a violent alternate braking and acceleration, attempting to force the Chevy through the crowd pressing in from its rear.

Fists pounded on the windows; an angry sea of faces contorted themselves, screaming at the occupants; the entire hood was covered with men, some flat on their stomachs, some kneeling, beating on the windshield in rhythm of the loudspeaker's relentless chant of "jobsjobsjobs." As Chase looked, he could find the angry, same distorted mouths at all of the car's windows, snarling, shouting, a school of black piranha, their jaws grinding in frustration against the glass of the tank that separates them from their prey. No one inside the car had spoken since the mob had been diverted from the El Dorado to them; at first, the twins had pointed out individuals, a little in excitement, a little in sheer fright; but even they had fallen silent. Chase and his family began swaying back and forth as the mob started the car rocking from one side to another. Finally, Darcie screamed, "Oh, Chase. *Why?*"

Chase merely shook his head and raised one hand; he was frantically trying to decide whether he should break out the shotgun to scare the crowd. Outside of a lot of shouting, the throng so far had done nothing to endanger them physically, and the gun might be what would provoke them into greater violence; on the other hand, it was clear that the violence was directed and controlled by the man with the goatee. From behind him, he was startled to hear the twins suddenly speak for the first time since the incident had begun.

"Dad! Dad! Behind us! There's a man . . ."

". . . waving a gasoline can and pointing at the car." Jeremy, as he so often did, had completed Raven's sentence for him.

Chase spun around in his seat; Brannigan halted his futile efforts to back his way through the crowd. They could see the man with the goatee, still on the car roof, waving a bright-red five-gallon can back and forth in rhythm to the chant of "jobsjobsjobs." His other hand, the one holding the bull horn, pointed toward them. Putting the bull horn to his mouth, the man broke into the crowd's chant with some words neither Chase nor Brannigan could understand, and then started a new one: "Burn 'em, burn 'em, burn 'em!" The mob roared, then picked up the new words and cadence. Chase felt his skin prickle and the sweat began to break out all over his body.

With a sudden shout and a great heaving motion of his free arm, the man with the goatee sailed the gas can into the crowd, hurling it as far as he could. What looked like a thousand hands wrestled for possession of it, moving it relentlessly toward the station wagon. Scrambling to the rear of the station wagon, Chase yanked the blanket off the shotgun and began stuffing shells into his pocket.

"Mr. Wetherill . . ." Brannigan's voice had a strange sound to it, halfway between confusion and hope. "Listen."

Chase blinked, then frowned, trying to fathom the meaning of a distant rumbling, a sound which grew clearer and closer even as he listened. The mob had heard it too and stopped, frozen into position as if by a photographer's flash bulb.

Through the unreal silence, broken only by an occasional mutter or shout of confusion from the outer edge of the mob, the new sound grew increasingly loud. Brannigan, with one hand on the shift lever, appeared about to start jockeying the station wagon again, but Chase shook his head and stopped him. At first he hadn't been sure of what he was hearing inside the sealed car, but as the sound grew louder, Chase recognized the heavy frequent blasts from several different air horns, and an unmuffled racing of heavy-duty motors of some sort. The mob turned to look for the man with the bull horn. He had disappeared.

Bewildered, the throng stood motionless for a second. A new and closer blast of the air horns—raucous and ear-splitting, the kind that fire engines use in an emergency—galvanized them into action. As abruptly as they had appeared, the whole writhing mob began to vanish, disappearing down side streets, diving over fences, racing into alleyways. Chase sighed in relief. The police—granted, a little late, but nevertheless, in time—had arrived. And from the sound of it, complete with a riot squad and heavy equipment.

The interior of the station wagon suddenly filled with
voices. Chase, cutting through the babble, speaking loudly
and confidently. "Relax, everybody. It's over. Everybody
all right?"

Brannigan bubbled: "The pol-is is generally not my favorite people. But in this case I'm willing to make an exception." Emlyn laughed in his nervous, adolescent way
and said, "Whew!" Dina remained silent. The twins leaned
forward, squirming with excitement. "The way they were
moving that gas can toward us. Do you think . . ?"
asked Raven. From beside him came a whispered aside
from Jeremy. "Of course, that's what they were going to
do. Fry us. But Dad was getting the shotgun and—"

Chase decided to restore order. "OK, now, I said everybody *relax*. The police will have plenty of questions to
ask." His own statement sent a sudden chill through
Chase; this was no time to be getting mixed up with offi-
cialdom of any kind. "Brannigan," he began.

He never finished the sentence. Another blast from the
air horn, this time from almost on top of them, ended any
talk in the Chevy. The street suddenly seemed filled with
burly-looking, grim-faced men. Some wore coveralls, some
were in plain work clothes, a couple sported hard hats.
Most of them were middle-aged; all were white. Each man
had a red-and-white arm band tied around his right arm,
and all of them carried clubs of some sort, while several
were equipped with what appeared to be riot guns. Chase
stared. There wasn't a policeman among them.

The snorting, coughing sound of a heavy diesel engine
stopped as the cab of a trailer truck pulled up beside
them. The door on the passenger side opened and a tall,
lean man, with yellow-brown dark glasses, dressed like the
rest except that his arm band was pure red instead of the
red-and-white, climbed slowly down from the cab and
stepped onto the road. From inside the cab, Chase could
hear the jumble of indistinct distant voices coming over
the truck's Citizens Band radio. The other men made way
for him as he advanced toward the station wagon with the
deliberate, possessive, slightly bored air of a traffic cop
about to give a ticket. Chase couldn't yet pinpoint it, but
there was something unconvincing about that particular
man in those particular clothes, as if he were dressed up
for a part. As Chase rolled down the window, the man
stuck his head partway into the car and, with the same de-

liberateness, examined the occupants. Ignoring Brannigan at the wheel, he addressed himself to Chase.

"Where are you people going?"

"The airport." Chase was uncertain whether to add "officer" or not, but decided at least something pleasant should be offered. "And thanks for showing up when you did. That was close."

The man ignored the offering and studied Chase. "The *airport*?"

"Yes, you see I have to—"

"The airport's closed. Nothing going in or out of Kennedy now."

He nodded vaguely in the direction of the side streets and alleys the throng had disappeared into. "Them people did it."

Above their heads, a jet taking off from Kennedy almost drowned the man out. Chase hesitated for a fraction of a second, then gambled. "Well, there's still a few going out, I guess, and my kids have never been to a big airport before and I promised them, you see. We're from Watertown, way upstate, and—"

"That so?" A trace of ugliness had crept into the man's voice and he stuck a thick, short cigar in his mouth. It didn't look right; his performance seemed strained, and Chase struggled again to figure what it was that made the truck driver's demeanor so unconvincing. The man continued to stare at him. Chase had hoped if he could get inside the airport grounds, he could make it to Butler Aviation—the private aircraft area—where one of the family planes was waiting. Tracking down and alerting his crew had been one of the things he'd devoted the morning to. Even now, although the roads into the airport might be overrun and blocked by more gangs of "them people," the field itself was obviously still open and operating. But to get there was going to take this man's active cooperation.

Yet Chase had a number of questions he wanted to ask him. Who were he and his men with arm bands? Why had they rescued his family and himself? How had they happened to show up at precisely the critical moment? As with the mob earlier, Chase suspected the answers were probably buried deep somewhere inside "Situation D." But before Chase could begin to question him, the man appeared to have read his mind. "Nothing personal, but the best thing—the only thing, in fact—is for you and your family to head back home."

The make-believe quality which had been bothering Chase snapped into sharp focus; a lapse in the man's truck-driver accent had not gone unnoticed by Chase. Even heavily masked, his pronunciation of the word "personal" was the giveaway; he pronounced the "per" in "person" like the French pronounce *"peu"* in *"petit peu,"* a clear indication that the "truck driver" was pure, old-school, upper-class New York—and probably Harvard to boot. He was as much a truck driver as Chase was from Watertown, N.Y.

"You wouldn't want me to disappoint the kids, would you?" Chase clung to the lie, smiling at the workman hopefully.

Chase felt himself being studied even more intently. Suddenly, the man burst out in a laugh, slapping the sides of the station wagon. Then, the newly lit cigar was spat out and the face turned dead serious. "Look, Mr. Wetherill. Nice try, but, face it: we didn't just turn up here by accident. We've had a man tailing you for three days— that man right back there. We thought you might try something like this."

Stunned the man knew who he was, Chase turned around to see pulled over to one side of the road the small gray sedan he'd thought he'd noticed on the ride out. The driver, now wearing a red-and-white arm band, leaned against the car's front fender, grinning.

"What the hell are you doing having me followed? Who are you?" A sinking sensation told him he already knew the answers.

"You was pretty glad to see us a little while back. And we're only here to help you Mr. Wetherill. The fact is, we's so concerned that nothing happens to you, please consider yourself under our protection. To make sure you get home safely, we'll even put a man in your car to ride back with you, courtesy of the Citizens Action Committee." There was a pause, then, more softly but with underlined menace: "Also, in case you decide to—well, leave the city in some other way." The man's affected language was disintegrating, but the threat implied in his words remained intact.

The Citizens Action Committee. So this is how they are going to come out into the open, thought Chase. All happening—although much faster than indicated—as secret documents outlining "Situation D" had predicted. He stared at the man with the red arm band. "You're not putting anybody in this car, dammit. The police . . . I'll stop at the first policeman I see. . . ."

The man, stuffing a new cigar in his mouth and trying to light it, choked. Chase couldn't tell whether it was because of the high wind or because the man wasn't used to his props yet. With a sigh, the truck driver gave up the attempt, removed the cigar, and stared at Chase. "*What* police?"

Chase foundered, remembering the absence of a single patrolman the entire ride out.

"Schuler!" commanded the truck driver. "On the double. Ride back in the car and see that Mr. Wetherill and his family get home all right. Then go into the house with them and stay there until I send someone along to relieve you. We'll take care of your car."

Without a word, Schuler began to climb into the car. Beneath the light work clothes, Chase could make out the unmistakable bulge of a gun and holster at the man's waist.

Chase Wetherill now realized that his first instinct to leave for the airport the moment he'd gotten the call that morning had been the right one.

They rode back toward the city in painful silence. Schuler, a short, compactly built man, was seated beside Emlyn. For reasons obscure to Chase, the man had insisted on sitting on the short middle seat of the wagon; when Schuler wouldn't give up his demand, Chase gave in.

"Sit in the back with the twins," Chase had ordered Dina. Schuler, unlike the man with the truck driver, seemed authentic, and Chase felt safer with his daughter separated from him. Grumbling as always, Dina climbed into the back seat, jamming herself in with the luggage and the squirming twins. Schuler sat down beside Emlyn, saying nothing. And when Chase turned on the Chevy's radio, Schuler at first leaned forward as if to object, but then something occurred to him and he settled back down in his seat. Spinning the dial, Chase was baffled; all regular programming seemed to be continuing uninterrupted, and even CBS, with its steady diet of nothing but news, made only the most passing of references to the disturbances.

The jamming of some of the roads out to Kennedy, for instance, was passed off as "spotty demonstrations by the jobless continues in the Metropolitan Area . . ."

The sensation was eerie: he and his family almost set on fire by one unidentified mob, which had appeared out of nowhere, seemingly intent on pouring gasoline over his car; then rescued by another, equally unidentified mob whose leader announced they had been following him for three days and had now planted an agent in Chase's car "for his protection." A television crew on a car top ready to film his immolation, yet all radio stations pretending nothing unusual was happening. Eerie, impossible—and frightening. With a grunt of disgust, Chase flicked off the car radio.

The silence was oppressive. Darcie caught his eye with a question, but Chase shook his head. Twice, Brannigan raised his eyebrows at Chase, to which Chase made a flat, passing gesture with his hands, an unspoken "There's nothing we can do."

Brannigan either didn't get the signal or chose to ignore it. Without warning, he suddenly broke into loud singing of "The Cruiskeen Lawn," an old drinking song, in Gaelic. (Because it is the national tongue, all children in Ireland are taught the rudiments of Gaelic; yet only those brought up in orphanages or state schools ever really seem to learn it.)

As they paused for a light, Brannigan turned around to Schuler behind him. "Just trying to cheer up the young-'uns in the back, y'understand. That fracas with them heathens back there shook them up a mite, as well it would anyone."

Schuler shrugged.

Nor did he pay any particular attention when Brannigan began turning his head to direct it at the twins, talking casually in Gaelic, laughing a lot, as if jollying them along. Brannigan, so fluent in the language, had been teaching it to the twins; there had been no particular reason for this, except that the twins were natural mimics and delighted in doing anything Brannigan suggested. Now the twins chattered back. The message finally reached Chase. In this peculiar, guttural language, Brannigan and the twins could do something no one else in the car could: hold a conversation in private.

This time the twins joined him in singing:

"Gra-ma-chree ma cruiskeen
Slainte geal mavourneen
Gra-ma-chree a coolin bawn bawn bawn
Gra-ma-chree a coolin bawn."

On the last repetition of *"bawn,"* Chase, who had deliberately been keeping his eyes straight ahead, heard a thudding crunch. When he spun around, Schuler was slumping to the floor. Behind him stood Raven with a tire iron; Jeremy was bent over the edge of the seat with a heavy wrench, both from the car's tool kit.

"Good lads!" exclaimed Brannigan. The Chevy began slowing down as Brannigan searched for a place free of parked cars where he could pull over.

Darcie had looked around at the same time as Chase: for a second she was too stunned to speak. Her poise returned to her as she gave an automatic command. "Sit down, sit down," she ordered the twins. Then, watching as Emlyn lowered the unconscious and bleeding Schuler to the floor, the full impact of what had happened hit her, and her hand went automatically to her mouth. "Oh, my God, Chase. What are we getting into?"

Chase shook his head and pointed out a spot for Brannigan. The empty space was in front of a small warehouse, now darkened for the night, and far enough from any street lights to be safe from the eyes of passing traffic.

With a small lurch, Brannigan pulled the car over to the curb. Turning around, he spoke to Emlyn, who looked baffled and a little stunned from having to cope with the motionless Schuler.

"Open your door, Emlyn," said Brannigan very slowly and steadily, "and push the dear man out into the gutter." Emlyn looked blank for a moment, and didn't obey until his father nodded in approval.

Jeremy watched, his eyes so widened that they seemed to fill his entire face.

"Is he . . . is he . . . all right?"

"Will he die?" asked Raven, staring at Schuler.

Brannigan laughed. "Oh, a little cosh on the head never hurt a man, Jeremy. His noggin may be a little on the sore side, y'understand, but it takes a lot to knock the divil out of a brute like him."

After Emlyn had closed the door, Brannigan swung the

car back out into the light traffic. In the brief time that Chase had had to study Schuler before Emlyn shoved him out the door, the open and ugly wound at the base of their rider's skull had been shocking and definitive.

"Sit back down, kids," Chase said cheerfully. "The man will be fine." Reaching into the glove compartment, he withdrew the road map. Part of the morning's efforts had been devoted to alternate plans in case escape by air proved unfeasible; the immediate challenge in reaching any of the stand-by destinations was to find a route that allowed them to keep to secondary roads. And, in the new circumstances, with Schuler soon being missed and their own escape realized, the station wagon would have to be exchanged for a car no one yet knew about. Chase considered. Buying another car was now too risky. *Steal* one?

He smiled grimly. The notion of a Wetherill reduced to car theft somehow amused him.

Chapter Three

Harry Schultz plans to sell his plush town house and move to the Netherlands because, he writes in The International Harry Schultz Newsletter, *the Dutch understand "horse sense." And James Dines, another market letter writer, is contemplating moving to Switzerland. "Paper money—and its buying power— will continue to fall lik₂ the bones of prehistoric animals into the La Brea tar pits," declares Schultz.*

—Newsweek, *July 29, 1974*

The first warning of the difficulties that Chase and the nation were about to have was dimly sensed some time before by his secretary. She had come into his office looking strangely rattled, and told him that his father was on the phone.

In her job at the Foundation, she had long ago ceased to be impressed by the people Chase regularly got calls from, whether corporation presidents, Governors, Congressmen, or even, on occasion, the White House. But in her entire eight years with Chase, speaking directly to Ravensaugh Wetherill was something that had never happened to her or to anyone else she knew. In fact, it didn't happen all that often to Chase, either.

Old Mr. Wetherill—Graffa—considered the phone his enemy; except in emergencies, he never used it himself, and he had, in his younger years, discouraged his guests and staff from resorting to it by having all the phones in his mansion coin-operated. This single eccentricity had, over the years, given rise to a wealth of penny-pinching

45

folklore concerning him: Ravensaugh Wetherill was so cheap he had pay phones in his house; he carried his lunch to work in a brown paper bag; he never left Usspatpenn because the driveway was so long he considered the gasoline for the trip too expensive.

Actually, Ravensaugh Wetherill was a delightful old gentleman, and not only relished these stories about himself but promoted them. His principal reason for not leaving the grounds was Chase's mother, who had plunged into premature senility some twenty-five years earlier.

Over the phone that day, Graffa told Chase he had to see him immediately, and Chase, without any real argument, had agreed to fly down the next day. When he tried, however, to get some inkling from him as to the reason for this sudden command performance, his father kept saying, "What? What? Speak louder, Chase; I can't hear you." As Chase had suspected for years, some of Graffa's dislike of the telephone was more convenient than actual.

Settling into the back of the car that Graffa had sent to the Wilmington airport for him, Chase relaxed and half-dozed in his seat. Wilmington is pleasant in the early spring, and Chase enjoyed the half-hour ride to Usspatpenn (a corruption of the small block letters engraved on so many of the devices that kept the Wetherills rich: U.S. Pat. Pen.), and didn't really become fully awake until the car drove through the gate of the waterfront estate.

It was enormous. To make it appear less ostentatious, Usspatpenn was hidden behind a mile-long Georgian brick wall; unfortunately, this only made the estate seem larger, as if a country club, a small college, or a flourishing Catholic retreat must surely lie between the wall and the water beyond. Chase shook his head and stared down the mile-long driveway, immaculately lined with Lombardy poplars. Behind them, he could see the topiary sculptures—evergreen bushes of various kinds trimmed and pruned over the years to resemble characters from Mother Goose. Once, these had been the delight of Virginia Wetherill, Chase's mother. Her condition had long ago caused her to lose interest in them, and now, when she confronted these living statues on one of her rare excursions out of the house, she stared at them as if they were strangers trespassing upon her property.

Driving past them, they evoked memories of his childhood. Chase could remember how the green figures seemed almost alive each time a light breeze from the water stirred their branches, delighting him and his brothers with their endless procession of nursery rhymes. The Old Lady Who Lived in a Shoe was still in place, marshaling her brood (carved out of yews) around her; an andromeda Humpty Dumpty still threatened to fall off an arborvitae wall; a diminutive pyracanthean Jack was, as always, preparing to do battle with a privet Giant, who rocked in the wind.

Today the living sculptures seemed out of place and unreal. Staring out his window, Chase studied them intently, as if the green figures could somehow recapture both his youth and an era when this kind of opulent landscape gardening didn't seem so out of joint with the times.

As the car slowed and pulled up to the front entrance of the main house, he saw Granger, Graffa's major domo, waiting at the door for him.

"Hi, Granger," called Chase, bouncing from the car.

"Mr. Chase," answered Granger, with just the slightest hint of a bow. "It's good to see you, sir. Your father's been looking forward to it all day."

Chase bounded up the stone stairs to pump Granger's hand; the gesture, it was obvious, made Granger uncomfortable. "How is he?" Chase noticed that Granger seemed to be barring the door.

"Very well, Mr. Chase, all things considered. He keeps us on our toes."

"Where is he? Downstairs? In the library? Out on the terrace?"

"Upstairs, sir. In the third-floor sitting room. He uses it a lot these days."

"Fine. I'll go see him right now."

Granger remained blocking the door. "If I might mention it, sir. Would you please be sure to use the elevator? Your mother . . ."

"Don't worry, Granger," Chase said with a broad smile, as the man stepped aside, pushing the door open for him to enter.

Inside the cold dimness of the main entrance hall, Chase saw Mort Evers, in his usual coveralls and engineer's cap, carrying a sheaf of papers on a clipboard and about to disappear through a door into the service area. Evers paused, hesitated, and tugged at the peak of his cap. "Afternoon, Mr. Chase." The twang was of Maine origin, although Chase had always been suspicious of how authentic it was.

"Hi, Mort. Things well?"

"Bad spring, bad spring, Mr. Chase." He readjusted the clipboard and smiled, displaying his gold tooth. "Too wet, but I reckon we'll survive."

Chase nodded and watched Evers disappear. Today, Evers had seemed unusually cordial; ordinarily he was totally uncommunicative. Evers was in charge of the grounds for all the Wetherill estates, shuttling men and machines up and down the coast as needed for major jobs. Although Graffa swore by the man, Chase rarely used him; his own properties were, to the extent he could afford to bypass a centralized operation like Mort Evers', handled by grounds-keepers from outside Mort's team. This procedure hadn't increased Evers' fondness for Chase any.

A maid appeared out of nowhere. "Granger asked if you were staying for supper, Mr. Wetherill." Chase nodded and made his way to the elevator, pressing the button with dread.

The door slid open. Inside, on a small campstool planted directly in front of the rows of buttons, sat Virginia Wetherill. "Up! Anyone else for up?" his mother called from her campstool. For the first time she looked at Chase, registering no recognition of any kind. "Nobody else." She sighed sadly and pressed the button again. "Slow day."

The short trip was agonizing. His mother had been like this for years, but neither the best experts on senility nor the top psychiatrists had been able to explain her belief she was running an elevator in a department store. This she did all day long, from the time she got up until she went to bed, apparently quite happy, with various members of the household staff taking turns discussing the weather with her, the only subject his mother believed appropriate for an elevator operator to discuss with the store's customers.

Chase longed to lean over and kiss her, to hug her, to remind her who he was, but had been told by his father never on any occasion to do so. The doctors, Graffa said, had explained that the thin, fragile string connecting her to whatever shred of reality she still possessed depended solely on her belief that she ran a store elevator. Graffa rode the elevator himself quite frequently, and Chase suspected that his move from his beloved library on the ground floor to the third-floor sitting room had only been an excuse to give his wife one more passenger.

"Third floor," she said matter-of-factly, looking at Chase without expression.

"Thank you. It was a very pleasant trip," he said, and stepped out of the elevator.

"Down, please!" called the maid Chase had just seen on the ground floor. "Down." The girl was panting, and Chase correctly assumed she had run up all three flights so that his mother would have a passenger for the return trip.

Shaking off a small shudder, Chase headed directly toward the third-floor sitting room. He saw his father look up from his book and headed off his attempt to rise by rushing across the room, embracing the man, but subtly forcing him back in the chair as he did. "Hello, Graffa. It's great to see you."

"Chase!" said his father, holding him back to study him. "My, but you look well." Graffa was sitting in a club chair not too far from a small fire that burned in the fireplace; behind the large chair was a standing lamp with a bulb of special intensity to make reading easier for him. He looked small and thin and fragile, but the eyes were as sharp as ever, and Chase knew the brain behind them was a long way from retirement to mental shuffleboard. "Sit down, sit down."

Pulling over a small ottoman, Chase settled down in front of him. "I *am* well, Graffa. But how about yourself?"

"Capital, capital." Graffa then laughed. "If it's still safe to use a word like that in a semi-socialist society."

"Good. Great. How about Mother?"

"You saw her." Graffa studied his fingertips for a second, then looked back at Chase with an anxious expression. "You *did* come up in the elevator?"

"Yes."

"Good, good. She loves passengers, you know." Graffa pursed his lips and shook his head. "It's all very sad." A drink was suggested and accepted, with Graffa pleading— not too convincingly—for Chase not to make his too strong.

"Weak, weak, weak," he sighed. "At my age, digestion becomes flaccid, you know. Rich foods, good wines, strong liquor—all things you still want, still think about, still dream about. Can't handle them any more, though. Frankly, I resent the loss of my digestion more than the theft of my prostate." Graffa laughed. So did Chase. The tension was broken.

Across the room at the bar, Chase mixed their drinks, whistling softly. Graffa's was no more "weak, weak, weak" than his father really wanted it to be.

"Now then, Chase," said Graffa, pulling on the scotch and soda and pretending to make an unpleasant face. He settled himself down into the club chair and got down to business. "As I'm sure you have guessed, I didn't ask you to come all the way down here to discuss either the state of my intestines or my glands. There's something I want you to undertake for me."

Chase nodded; he had no idea what it would be, but he also suspected, whatever it was, he would do it.

Graffa studied Chase's face closely. "You may not like it, you may not agree with it—in fact, you may actively oppose it—but it's for the family. And as you know, I have always depended on you in these things."

Again, Chase nodded. The buildup was unusual; ordinarily his outspoken father went straight to the point of things. "Of course." Chase paused, waiting.

Graffa bit one corner of his lip and appeared to search for precisely the right words. "I'm not sure how to put this to you, Chase. For one thing, it's conceivable what's in here"—he tapped the paper-covered book in his lap—"is a false alarm. Although I doubt that. But I've had some people, some very talented people, looking a few years ahead for me. Economists, social engineers, geopoliticans, sociologists. Those types. I thought they might develop some information that would be of use in developing new patents. What they worked with, beyond their usual tools, was some quite extraordinary"—Graffa looked away, almost as if embarrassed—"intelligence that fell into my hands. When they began, their mission was to explore the future course of business environment, how it would alter people's lives, the implications for our patent holdings, the extent to which it would affect the country's political structures."

Watching Graffa, Chase could see his father struggling with himself and strained to lighten the mood for him. He gave a low whistle, then: "Economists, geopoliticans . . .

you're treading pretty liberal territory there, Graffa. Next thing I know you'll be telling me you're a Democrat."

With a wave of his hand, Graffa dismissed Chase's weak attempt at humor; his expression remained grim. "As I said, that was the mission I gave them. They expanded on it. Got their hands on some 'eyes-only' documents that are totally shattering. Put them together with other intelligence available to them. And what they arrived at—the conclusions they came up with—are terrifying. Untenable. Monstrous." He stared at Chase. "For the first time in my life, Chase, I'm afraid. Plain afraid."

Chase didn't know how to respond. Most men of his father's years, you could write such a statement off as paranoia. But not with Graffa. Once again, Chase found himself floundering, and forced a booming laugh out of himself to conceal his confusion. "Well, Graffa, you know economists."

For the first time Graffa looked angry. "Dammit, Chase. Stop trying to humor me. It isn't just economics, it isn't just business. What they uncovered affects the whole spectrum of life in this country, its future, its freedom. Listen, Chase." Graffa's voice sank to a hoarse whisper, the report waving at him in reproach, his narrowed troubled eyes boring into his son. "Listen. Read. It's all here. Facts, documents, projected dates, inevitable conclusions." Graffa flipped some pages in the book, searching for something. With a small grunt, he pulled a yellow Telex from an envelope at the back of the book and, leaning forward from the eerie semi-dark of his wing chair, handed it to Chase. Chase took it, scanning it quickly, then rereading it. He had always found government documents difficult to grasp; this one was harder to understand than usual:

LA CALIF 12 AUG 80 XXXX QBR SYNPAC FOR THE EYES ONLY XXXX FOR THE EYES ONLY XXXX SEC'Y DEFENSE DC XXXX CONFIRM RECEIPT XXXX TLX CODE JJ3463 XXXX

TEAM 206 ACHIEVED PENETRATION TI (TEAMSTERS INTNL) AS OF 3 AUG XXX 206 REPORTS IT BELIEVES LAPD COMPLETLY ORGANIZED XXX FURTHER REPORTS LEVELS FROM PATRLMN TO SGT CONSIDER SELVES MORE ANSWERABLE TO TI THAN LAPD OFFICERS XXX OTHER SOURCES INDICATE SAME HOLDS FOR ATLANTA BOSTON CHICAGO DE-

TROIT HOUSTON SAN FRANCISCO ST LOUIS NEW
YORK XXX LAST NAMED BELIEVED BY TI LESS RE-
LIABLE DUE HEAVY MINORITY CONCENTRATION
XXX206 ALSO CONFIRMS PERSISTENT RUMORS NA-
TIONWIDE EFFORT UNKNOWN VARIETY SCHEDULED
LATE NOV THIS YEAR XXX OTHER TI SOURCES CON-
FIRM XXX TEAM 206 DIRECTED INCREASE EFFORTS
TO FIX NATURE SCOPE & EXACT DATE OF SAME.

206 REQUESTED AUTHORITY USE EXTREME MEA-
SURES ACHIEVE OBJECTIVE XXX AUTHORITY
GRANTED EIGHT/EIGHT/EIGHTY ONE XXXX TLX
CODED JJ 4363 XXX END XXX END XXX SIGNED
COLBERT SYNPAC XXXXXXX

Chase raised his head from the Telex toward Graffa. To
Chase, Graffa appeared to have almost disappeared into
the shape of the club chair, a dim shadow edged by the
sudden harsh light from his special reading lamp, only his
eyes piercing the darkness to stare at him. Chase glanced
back at the Telex, unwilling to accept its implications as
quickly as Graffa would have him. "Well, the Teamsters'
organizing of police is common knowledge. This merely
confirms that it's gone farther than anyone thought,
doesn't it?"

Graffa wheezed in exasperation. "All the way, dammit,
all the way." His fragile fingers tapped the report on his
lap meaningfully. "I don't know whether you're being
dense on purpose, Chase, or what. But that part there—
'nationwide effort of unknown variety'—'scheduled for late
November'—the reference to 'last named—New York—
believed less reliable because of heavy minority concentration'—can't you put those things together and see what
this report sees?"

Chase ignored the question and began going in another
direction. "God, Graffa, this Telex went to Defense. They
must have followed it up."

"They followed it up all right. Look at that signature
again."

"So? Colbert. He quit."

"He didn't quit. Those 'extreme measures' mentioned
there. Somebody got killed; the union got upset. Senate investigation into why Defense *had* agents in the Teamsters.
You know how Senators handle anyone doing anything to
a union. Colbert didn't quit; he was forced out. Sup-

posedly died in a private plane accident two months later.
Very convenient. Particularly since he didn't die in an accident or anything else. Back at the same old stand at
SYNPAC, only everybody thinks he's dead. Gives him
plenty of room to move around in."

Chase forced a laugh, but it had a hollow ring. "I think
the people who put your report together, who got you
these documents—God knows how—are chasing shadows.
Airplane accidents that didn't happen. Maybe it did,
maybe not. Now, this Telex"—Chase waved the paper in
the air—"about something supposed to happen in November 1980. Obviously, it didn't."

"Obviously." Graffa's voice was edged with sarcasm, a
tone he rarely used with Chase, although he was famous
for using it witheringly on other people. "That's only one
piece of evidence, Chase. The Teamsters' original timeta-
ble was thrown off by the Senate incident. What was
scheduled to happen in November 1980 is now set, according to recent papers we've come by, for 1981."

"These papers you keep coming by . . ."

Graffa laughed. "There are people moving around everywhere, you know that. Banks. Banks are the primary
channel that moves them in and out. We've got banks, the
Rockefellers have got banks, the Mellons have got banks,
all God's chillun got banks. And what the Rockefellers, the
DuPonts, the Morgans, the Mellons and the Harrimans
know, *we* know. It doesn't work the other way around, of
course. Because our bank is bigger than anybody else's, so
we only give them what we want them to have. Not only
banks, but the military-industrial complex. Our patents are
a powerful lever there. We have more; we know more."

"All right, so the Teamsters, and I suppose some other
unions as well, are planning something for November.
What?"

Graffa tapped the report. "This points out that things
have changed. The unions today are the real middle class.
Very unlike Marx and the laborers against the shopkeeper
bourgeoisie and the ruling classes." Graffa leaned forward
from his chair into the light, retrieving the Telex from
Chase as if he were afraid his son might disappear into the
gathering darkness with it. "And that Telex—there's a lot
more documents like it included here—gives you a picture
of that newly organized element of the middle class. The

militant, subversive labor union, yet one that is highly open to manipulation."

Chase studied his fingertips, trying to figure out where Graffa was heading. "It's not a pretty picture, certainly. But I don't quite understand what all the panic's about."

Graffa snorted. "You're not that dumb, Chase. You're playing dense to irritate me. Imagine, for instance, if someone was able to unionize the Army in the same way—the Dutch Army already has been, you know."

"All right, the police thing—I think the Army will be damned hardnosed about letting themselves be organized by any union—the police thing could put a lot of power in the wrong hands. But if anyone ever tried to use it—well, the Wagner Act never envisioned a police strike being used for political ends." Chase thought for a moment, brightening as he shaped a possible scenario. "In fact, it might even get *rid* of the damned Wagner Act, once and for all. As for what you're worried about, the government would take care of a police union in one big hurry, if it got out of hand."

"If the government wanted to, it would."

"That's pretty cryptic."

"So is this." Graffa reached into the folder and produced another document, this time a heavily annotated Xerox of an FBI "For the Eyes Only" report. One section of it had been underscored in red ink:

. . . same sources indicate funding and direction for unionization of local police units provided by Citizens Action Committee (CAC) (see Report, Task Force "W", 774b323, 5 Apr 79).

Penetration by Bureau into CAC top level ineffective as of this date, but same sources in earlier verbal report were able to identify the following:

Christian Randlehurst, Palm Springs, Calif., personal aide in Reagan 1976 campaign effort.

James Gattleby, New Orleans, La., former District Attorney.

Whittley Brown, Montgomery, Ala., Dirctr, Alabama Political Intelligence Unit, set up by Governor Wallace, July 1971.

Gen. Luis d'Esteverra, Miami, Fla., C/S and CIA liaison for Bay of Pigs incident.

Richard Albemanner, Key West, Fla., industrialist (Albemanner supplied covert funds for Nixon Defense Fund— see Task Force "W" Rep., 558f209).

Maj. Gen. Abram Cord, La Jeune, La., Dirctr of Training, US Marine Corps.

All above-named identified from photographic surveillance. Bureau trying to effect recognition of other persons observed in frequent company of same.

. . . same sources further suggest Task Force "W" may itself have been penetrated by CAC. All files to be destroyed, effective this date.

Chase sighed. As with the Telex, any government document, especially one with the overtones of secrecy, appeared to specialize in being obtuse. The names mentioned in the FBI report were impressive, although dated. Most important of all, either he was missing something or the report made no sense. Still holding the report in his hands, he looked up at Graffa. "I don't get it. These names—well, they're all from the far-right fringe, disgruntled conservatives of one sort or another. Why the hell would they be behind a union, for Christ's sake?"

With impatience, Graffa reached forward and took the FBI document out of Chase's hands. "Because a police union gives them a private army. To use against anything they want."

"The government? Oh, come on, Graffa."

"No, they don't need an army to use against the government. President Welby's stroke did that *for* them. But against *this*, yes." Graffa burrowed back inside his report, pulling out a Xerox like a magician producing a rabbit. It was once again a Telex from the supposedly dead Colbert:

NYC 15 MAY 81XXXX QBR SYNPAC XXX FOR THE EYES ONLY XXXX REPEAT FOR THE EYES ONLY XXXX SEC'Y DEFENCE DC XXXX CONFIRM RECEIPT XXX TLX CODE JJ 5758b XXX:

ANSWER QUERY YOUR TELEX 13 MAY XXX PLA
(PEOPLES LIBERATION ARMY) LOOSE AMALGAMA-
TION ELEMENTS OF SLA, BLA, PANTHERS, CASTRO
ACTIVISTS, AND VETERANS OF ANGOLESE & RHO-
DESIAN OVERTHROWS XXX SOME PLA DIRECTION
PROVIDED BY TWO (THIRD WORLD ORGANIZA-
TIONS STRATEGIC ARM) XXX STRIKE FORCE
DRAWN FROM CLUB (CUBAN LIBERATION & UNITY
BRIGADE) AND ARBUC (ANGOLAN & RHODESIAN
UNITY CORPS) XXXXX

PLA IS WELL SUPPLIED, AMPLY FUNDED & DEDI-
CATED XXXX REPORTS PLACE ARMS & WEAPONS
DEPOTS IN MAJOR CITIES AND OUTLYING AREAS
XXX INFORMANTS REPORT SAME APPROX DATE
FOR DISSIDENT ACTION ON PART OF PLA AS
INDICATED IN PLANS OF OPPOSING PROCESS OF
POLICE UNION CONTROLLED BY CAC XXXX

IF THESE DATES HOLD, CLEAR INDICATION OF
CONSPIRACY AT HIGHER LEVEL UNIDENTIFIED
AT THIS TIME XXX RECOMMEND FULL ARMY
ALERT FOR DATE FIXED AS APPROXIMATELY
FALL 1981 XXXX SITUATION BECOMING CRITICAL
BY THAT DATE XXXX DESTROY AFTER READING
XXXX REPEAT DESTROY AFTER READING XXX
TLX CODE JJ 5758b XXX END XXX SIGNED COL-
BERT SYNPAC XXXXXXXX

Tilting the Telex sideways, Chase tried to read something scrawled diagonally in the margin. The handwriting
was poor, the initials undecipherable, but the intent inescapable: "notify Colbert recmdtn approved, but disregard.
Do *not* repeat do *not* notify Army of content or date
noted in this msg." The Telex was less dramatic than either
the first one from Colbert or the document from the FBI.
Yet to Chase, the handwritten scrawl on the margin of the
second Telex made it the most frightening of all. The conspiracy Colbert had noted in passing was real. Floundering,
Chase fumbled for palliative words. "Frightening, sure.
But mostly hearsay. No hard facts. Bureaucratic hysteria."

"No hard facts?" Graffa brandished his report. "I don't
know how much harder you can get them."

"That FBI report, those Telexes—they must have gone
to other people besides Defense. The Army—"

"You saw the notation on that second Telex. Those reports didn't go anywhere."

"The FBI was involved; they made out their own report. The CID, the CIA—"

"Both the FBI and the CIA had their wings clipped by Frank Church and the Senate. If either agency *had* found anything out, nobody'd ever hear about it."

"Congress itself, then."

Graffa gave a bitter laugh. "Say anything bad about the Teamsters Police Union and you're anti-union. Say anything bad about the PLA and you're a racist. You know Congress. But the report, these documents, make it pretty clear what's in the cards. Clandestine groups—the PLA and the CAC—on a collision course. Committed to violence. Heavily armed, well financed, with backing in high places we don't even know about. Everybody else caught in the middle. And a government that can't—or won't—do anything."

"Somebody *must* be." Chase felt irritated and confused; too much had been thrown at him too quickly to be absorbed.

"A handful. The same people who tried in the thirties. They're putting money behind the CAC—the Rockefellers, DuPonts, Mellons, Morgans, Fords, Getty, big business. They're no happier with the CAC than you and I, but it's better than the alternative—the PLA." Graffa looked away, almost with embarrassment. "I've given a little myself."

Chase flared, wondering how much Graffa's definition of "a little" really was. "Christ, Graffa. That makes me sick."

"The whole thing makes me sick," Graffa answered coolly. "But it exists, it's there, and all the wishing in the world won't make it go away. We have to face the facts, not the wish, because when you have two extreme points of view like the CAC's and the PLA's lined up against each other, there's no point in debate. Both the PLA and the CAC are counting on inaction—lots of talk, but no action. And any idiot can see the trouble with that." He brandished the report at Chase. "What you'll find in here shows that it's precisely that inaction that the PLA and the CAC are depending on. The traditional passivity of the uncommitted middle class—the real middle class, not the new one—to make moving them in their direction easier.

A middle class that's fed up, torn in half, dragged under on the one hand by welfare people who won't lift a finger to support themselves, and pushed around on the other by a mammoth, but corrupt, inept, centralized government. Fed up—battered by inflation, squeezed dry by taxes. Fed up, demanding change, but with no idea of what they want things changed *to*. A middle class so tired it's wide open to manipulation. Extremists at both ends—the CAC and the PLA—using this fact to try to swing the middle class their way, scaring them to death with what the opposite extremists will do if they take control."

Chase shifted uncomfortably. Inside himself, he knew, he was struggling to find reasons not to believe what Graffa was saying. The words were so unbelievable they could be dismissed easily, yet gnawing at Chase was a dreadful fear that in that route lay folly. Not believing was the easy way. What was difficult was to assess the facts objectively, to reach a rational conclusion built on a pyramid of implications, half-facts, and reports that might or might not be valid. "A great deal of the stuff you've said, Graffa, someone else could argue and turn out to produce the opposite of what you're expecting. Nobody can be sure of what will happen with that—"

Graffa held up his hand to silence him and dove back into the folder of notes for a moment, then emerged to stare at Chase. "It would take a fool not to see what will happen. The closest analogy is the Weimar Republic, where the Communists and Fascists both tried to win over the middle class, manipulate them, to gain control of Germany. That's what makes the analogy so shattering. The gist of what's in here—of what has already been documented and verified—is terrifying. The details of what the report states is not just what is possible, but what is probable. That is what seems nearly beyond comprehension." Settling back, his eyes glistening in his own private darkness, Graffa began reading more excerpts from the report. "Listen, Chase, listen. It's all here."

Chase listened. As his father had said, it was all there. Dates, documents, facts, item after item spelling out the basic machinery of two vast conspiracies (one being plotted by the PLA, one by the CAC), projections, a consensus on future events, and recommended contingencies covering plans to follow, depending on whether the PLA or the CAC was the victor. There was even an occasional

demurrer, as if whoever had written Graffa's report found
the conclusions so distasteful he had to pause every now
and then to try to poke holes in his own logic. Graffa's
hand waved in the air for emphasis—he was reading excerpts, not the whole report—his small, bright eyes continually bobbing above the paper-covered folder to make sure
Chase was still following him. Even though the report was
written in the dry, precise language of clinical objectivity,
Chase found himself agreeing with Graffa's original comment: it was terrifying.

Still, even as he listened, Chase was already putting up
obstacles to accepting the findings at face value. Many of
the conclusions were too sweeping, he told himself; any
number of the generalizations were open to argument, and
even the root facts themselves were open to challenge. But
the details of the conspiracy kept adding up, one by one.
He kept reassuring himself the report was only terrifying
if the documentation was beyond challenge. The facts
might not be wholly accurate, the "intelligence" tainted,
the logic suspect. Suddenly aware that Graffa had stopped,
Chase looked up.

His father put down the report and stared at him. "Do
you see what I mean, Chase? It takes a little time to hit
you fully—certainly it did with me, anyway—but do you
understand the implications? I've only read you portions
of it, of course, but do you grasp what it's trying to say?

"I don't know."

"Don't know! For God's sake, Chase, that's no answer."
Graffa reached for his drink, slumped back into his chair,
and glowered at him, shaking his head. He brandished the
folder at him. "I can't vouch for this thing one hundred
percent myself. It's too complicated for an old man like
me. But I *do* know enough to have a point of view."

"Well, Graffa, you've thrown an awful lot at me all at
once. If the input is correct, the conclusions are inescapable. But there's a lot I can't evaluate: the quality of the
background research in the report . . . the caliber of the
people who put it together . . . the reliability of the
documents . . ."

"Oh, grow up, Chase." With a disgusted snort, his father
slapped the report shut and glowered at him. "If you
worry too much and too long about the right and wrong
of something, you eventually wind up doing nothing. It's a

paralysis of the will, as old as Hamlet. For God's sake, boy, make up your mind and *act*."

Once again, Chase flared at Graffa, something highly unusual for him to do. "Act. *Act?* What the hell am I supposed to do? Buy a gun, dig a hole, crawl in a cave, or what?" He listened to his own words in shock. Graffa seemed unperturbed, looking at Chase more with pity than anger. Chase sat blinking at him, knowing the old man was right. "I'm sorry." It wasn't much of an apology, but it would have to do. He was having trouble believing what was in Graffa's report because he didn't want to believe what was in the report. And perhaps the report wasn't proved enough to require any action—yet. Not Hamlet, precisely, but close enough. Chase sighed heavily. "What is it you want me to do, Graffa? You said something about the family."

"Situations A and B, as described in the report, are bearable. Unpleasant but bearable. Situations C and D— well, they're almost unacceptable. I don't know which it would be worse to have win—an oligarchy of the left or a junta of the right—but either one would create an untenable position for us. I never thought I would find myself saying this, but the only possible solution, should either C or D develop, is to get the family and the holdings out of the country. I would start by transferring the patent rights to dummy corporations in Switzerland immediately. Your brothers and sister should be warned; I have no idea whether they'll accept the idea of leaving or not. But at least they should be given the chance. Set up some sort of system for later that will alert them in case of a C or D. Then, if that happens, get out yourself, too."

Staring at Graffa in disbelief, Chase heard a tight, nervous laugh come out of his own mouth, an almost adolescent mannerism, a device struggling to overcome an inability to accept what he had just heard his father say. "Run away. Jesus. I thought I was kidding when I said you were suggesting go hide in a cave or something. I can't run away—it's impossible. Transfer the patents . . . Switzerland . . . run . . . the whole idea is unthinkable. My God . . ."

Graffa appeared to remain unfazed. His pale-blue eyes fixed themselves on a spot somewhere above Chase's head. "Unthinkable? So's the idea of a lifeboat. Until the ship starts to sink. Then, by God, the lifeboats had better be well stocked and in good shape." The spot above Chase's head was abandoned and the eyes lowered to lock themselves with Chase's. "I'm not saying pick up and go tomorrow. But start making the plans. Laying the groundwork. Just in case. It isn't in the Wetherill makeup to leave something that important to last-minute improvisation."

"Neither's running."

Graffa snorted. "If we have to, we should run like we held a patent on it."

Chase was still stunned. He had too long been trained in the Wetherill concept of duty to be anything else. "Run . . . run." Chase kept repeating the word with different inflections, as if he might find one that would somehow make the word acceptable. He couldn't. "But Graffa. We owe the country more than that, don't we? Christ, we can run because we can afford to; most people can't. We owe those people a little return on all they've given us—not just the money, but the help and the work and the respect. We owe them something more than hightailing it to Switzerland when the going gets tough. I ought to say, *if* the going gets tough—that report of yours could be dead wrong." For a moment, Chase sank in thought, his lips compressed, his eyes wandering around this comfortable, familiar room. "We've been brought up—you, all of us— that our duty is service to the country. God knows, you yourself have beaten it into our heads since we were kids. And whether we find it convenient now or not, it's fixed in us—for good. You just can't expect us—you can't expect yourself, for that matter—to suddenly throw it away and pretend it never existed."

Graffa's eyes, suddenly back in the light, narrowed; a small smile appeared at the corners of his mouth as he listened to his own words—said over so many years—being thrown back at him. Then, the eyes narrowed further and the smile vanished. "Never get into a fight that you know you can't win, Chase. Under ordinary circumstances, I would agree with you. Stay and fight. But the circumstances aren't ordinary: we can't win. In this case, our real service to the nation is to survive. If any of this really does happen, doing that within the country would become impossible. Whatever takes over won't last forever. The family can always return and pick up the pieces, help reestablish the old values, and help put the country back together again. *That,* Chase, is our duty."

Numbly, Chase nodded. A part of him kept insisting that Graffa's explanation was wrong, that it was only aging hysteria. But, as always, Graffa had an almost hypnotic influence on him. Quickly, Chase ran through what would have to be done. The prospect of trying to explain the report and Graffa's instructions to his four brothers and Moira was unpleasant, perhaps futile. But Graffa was probably right: contingency plans had to be prepared, even if none of the report's predictions ever came true. He nodded again. "I'd also like to read the report myself, so—well—oh, hell, you can give me a copy to take home."

"No, I can't. There is only one copy and I keep it here. So you can either read it here or not at all." Leaning forward slightly, bringing his face back into the light again, Graffa handed the report to him.

Still dazed, Chase took the copy and said he would go to the library to read it through. The room was eerily silent, and from the hall Chase could hear the door of the elevator sliding open, followed by his mother's voice cheerfully calling out, "Down, please. Anyone for down?"

This insane footnote added the proper touch of surrealism to a day already unreal.

Chase had done as Graffa had asked and warned his brothers and sister—with varying degrees of success. As he had started out on the tour for Graffa, Chase had tried to predict what each one's reactions to the report would be, and his siblings had not let him down. Nicholas, an affable panda of a man, had listened gravely, but quickly shrugged the report off. Almost imperceptibly, he changed the conversation to the possibilities of winning the Bermuda race with his twelve-meter, then segued smoothly into the predicted yield of some municipal bonds Chase had never even heard of.

Toby, oldest, most gentle-spoken, and probably the most intelligent of the brothers, who had first been a brilliant lawyer, then a distinguished federal judge, and had finally, during a period of conservative backlash, been rewarded with the ultimate appointment—a seat on the United States Supreme Court—heard Chase through meticulously, hands folded across his stomach and removed only long enough to take an occasional note on a long yellow legal pad.

Then he announced his decision: "Poor Graffa. Age gets to us all, I guess." There was no possibility of an appeal.

Moira, the lone sister, and her husband, Dudley Cantrell—successful enough in his own right but because of Moira's vast wealth pegged forever as a man who married money—jointly laughed themselves silly each time Chase went into a new facet of Graffa's report. "At least," suggested Moira, "that PLA crowd—or whatever they call themselves—might put some life back in the Everglades Club." More laughter. Chase suspected that underneath all their banter, both Moira and Dudley were a good deal more affected than they let on.

With Duane, the family's junior Senator from West Virginia who had rebelled against the position Wetherill money had bought him and suddenly turned liberal Democrat, the response was tight-lipped. He was Chase's favorite brother and one with whom there were no feelings unshared; but in this case, Duane elected to keep his own council. Duane's only comment had been consistent with his politics: "What I'd like to know is how private persons can get their hands on government agency documents."

There had been only one brother Chase had been unwilling to try to predict a reaction for: Tracey, the youngest brother. Tracey's reactions to things were as mercurial as his life style, but that day, when Chase had used that same phrase about Tracey, trying to assess for Graffa how each brother would react, his father had stunned him.

"If what you're trying to say is that Tracey is a pansy, why don't you come right out and say it?" The word itself had startled Chase—it was oddly antique—but also because he had never imagined Graffa knew anything about Tracey's private life. (Even the press shied away from mentioning him; because of the family's clout, rumors about Tracey were quietly buried.)

Graffa had snorted. "Don't look so surprised. I know all about it. Tracey keeps a houseful of boys so young they ought to be out shooting marbles instead of whatever it is they do with him. How do you think his twin Rodney was killed? In the men's room of Grand Central. Gentleman at the next urinal took exception to one of Rodney's suggestions and bopped him. Young Rodney hit his head on the tile floor and died. We didn't know anything about it until the man's trial, when his defense lawyer produced all sorts of witnesses to prove that both Rodney and Tracey spent most of their free time in fairy parlors. Case dropped right then and there."

Tracey's actual reaction to Chase's call had been one of panic. He wanted to leave the country, not tomorrow, not the next day, but that day. To hell with his home, his belongings, his properties. The money could be sent after him. He would become Chase's agent in Switzerland, starting tomorrow. He would . . . It had taken all of Chase's persuasive powers to cool Tracey down, to assure him that he was talking not of something bound to happen, but of something that *might* happen. Not today or tomorrow, but, if it happened at all, maybe not for years. And even then, any departure would have to be taken with the greatest care and the most exquisite deliberateness. Yes, Chase would keep him informed. No, there was no point in hiring a bodyguard. To himself, Chase smiled.

Now, as he and his family drove up the coast in flight, the smile was no longer appropriate. Because if Tracey's reaction had been spectacular, it had been no more spectacular than the report prepared for Graffa had been correct. It was now crystal-clear to Chase that, point by point, item by item, the report's predictions and projections had been almost eerily on target. But Chase was jarred out of his train of thought by a sudden sounding of horns. The light had changed. He dropped the station wagon into "drive" and darted through the intersection.

On a desolate stretch of tidal-basin land near St. Inigoas, Delaware, an unusual flurry of automobile traffic was taking place. Virtually all the cars were limousines, looking out of place in this flat stretch of sand and scrub. At a point perhaps a mile from their destination, each car's progress was halted by a set of heavy iron gates across the road. The cars arrived at this point, one at a time, obeying the instructions of a concealed traffic-light system two miles farther back on the sandy road; in this way, no two cars could arrive at the gate at the same time and cause a line-up of cars outside the entrance. Once at the gates, an armed guard would exchange some papers with the limousine's passenger. After the guard had had the latest arrival double-checked over the phone, the gates would open and the car would drive on in. Perhaps five minutes later, the traffic signal up the road would once

again change and the next car would make its way to
the gates, where the same process would be repeated.

About a mile inside, the limousine would reach its destination and pull to a halt. For a moment, the car would
stand motionless in a thicket of bushes from around which
the scrub growth had been cleared, leaving a large exposed
area. The car's driver did not seem surprised at this barren
and bleak end to the journey: rather, he seemed used to it,
as if he had been here frequently before. He would merely
hold the door open, allow his passenger to emerge, and
then quickly drive off down another sandy road to the left
of the clearing.

Although each of these unlikely men had arrived sep-
arately, their actions were identical: they would speak into
a microphone standing upright beside the bushes, a door in
the ground would open to reveal a brightly lit interior set
below ground level, and the man would enter, his feet
echoing hollowly on a flight of cement stairs as he descended. Then the door would close and the area would be
plunged back into darkness.

Down in the brightness below ground level, the Executive Council Meeting of the Citizens Action Committee
was being called to order. To the politically well-informed
outsider, it might have come as something of a surprise to
learn that so powerful an organization met in such bleak
surroundings, or that all of its meetings were held in an at-
mosphere of such secrecy. To even more Americans, it
would have been a shock to learn that such a body even
existed.

But almost any outsider would have been startled to discover that the first item on the meeting's agenda was, as
always, a prayer—for the preservation of the United
States.

It was a macabre footnote to an already sinister performance.

Chapter Four

*West Palm Beach, Fla. (UPI)—Some
buyers are contracting for as much as a
year's supply of dehydrated and freeze-
dried food items, sellers said. Many of the
buyers take elaborate precautions to keep
their identities secret, fearing that if their
names were known, their food hoards
would be raided by hunger rioters during
what the buyers believe is a coming period
of severe social unrest in the U.S. Jim
McCarthy, a former deputy sheriff . . .
said: "They certainly don't want their
neighbors to know there's $1,000 worth of
dehydrated food in their garage."*

*—United Press International
Wire Story, Dec. 17, 1974*

Once out of New York, they headed directly for the old
U.S. Route 1 and began following it up the coast. Inside
the car, no one appeared to be saying anything. For Emlyn and Dina to be quiet was not unusual; for the twins to
stay silent for any length of time was. With a sinking
feeling, Chase began to suspect that they were uncon-
vinced by Brannigan's and his assurances that the man
they had hit would be all right.

"Jeremy," whispered Raven, after a long, long silence.
"Do you think . . ."

". . . we killed that man?" finished Jeremy for him. "I
don't know, but . . ."

". . . I think we . . ."

". . . Did."

66

"So do I." Jeremy pondered a moment, "In a way, it was self-defense."

"Besides . . ."

". . . Brannigan told us to."

"Do you think . . ."

". . . we'll go to jail? I don't know."

Jeremy shook his head, his eyes staring at Raven, "All that blood. We must have killed him."

"Let's not . . ."

". . . think about it any more."

"Right."

For a moment, they looked at each other searchingly; the look was the only security they trusted completely. In their mirror-image world, Raven always asked the questions and Jeremy always answered them. But Jeremy needed the questions as much as Raven needed the answers, so their interdependence was total. For another mile or so they continued silent. Then, from Raven, excitedly: "Let's play . . ."

". . . license plates!"

In front, Chase was relieved to hear them giggling and exuberant again. He was not as cheerful. Questions as to where they were going, how they were going to get there, and what would happen when they did troubled him. Originally, he had planned to keep all factors leading to decisions to himself, letting only Darcie know later in private. She had guessed this and disagreed.

"I think," said Darcie, just after they passed through Harrison, "you'd better tell everybody where we're going, how we are going to get there, and what to expect."

Chase gave her a grateful glance and turned himself sideways in his seat so that he could talk to everyone equally well. "Fair enough. The first thing we have to do is get ourselves another car. People know this one is ours now. So, somewhere along the way, we have to get a new one before they find us." He turned around and addressed the twins directly. "That man you knocked unconscious was one of them. The worst he's got is a sore head, but he's undoubtedly told his friends what happened and they're probably out looking for us already."

Raven leaned forward over the back of the seat, holding Emyln and Dina. "We think . . ."

". . . we killed him."

Chase could feel Darcie's hand grip his arm. Struggling,

he managed to sound matter-of-fact. "I doubt it. Believe me, kids, it's very unlikely."

"Yerra, and didn't I say you didn't?" asked Brannigan. "All you did was make a small dent in King Kong back there."

Chase hastened to follow the twins' laughter with one of his best rubbery expressions, causing them to break up again. Deftly, he used the laughter to change the subject. "We can't buy a new car, so we'll have to 'borrow' one."

Raven could not let this pass. "You don't mean borrow, Dad . . ."

". . . you mean steal."

"All right, steal. But we're in trouble, and it's like— well, like a man dying of thirst on the desert who finds a full canteen of water somebody's left behind and takes it—to save himself."

"Wisha, and the Brannigan's building up a powerful thirst himself." Brannigan made an outrageous noise with his lips that so tickled the twins that their concern over the man began to vanish.

"Now," continued Chase, "I think we'll stop in the next town and get something to eat. While we're doing that, Brannigan will drive around and find us a car." Chase paused, then leaned over Darcie toward Brannigan. "You *can* hot-wire one, I hope: people don't leave the keys in them much any more."

Brannigan made a face indicating he wasn't sure. "At home, you see, a man can leave the keys, because not all that many people know how to drive. Hot-wire the ignition . . . I think I know how, but blessed if I'm sure."

"I can." Emlyn's statement startled Chase; he'd almost forgotten the boy's touch with anything electric. Advanced mathematics and theoretical physics took on a new light.

"All right, Emlyn. Good. Very good. You go with Brannigan. A station wagon again. But nothing distinctive. Dina, you and your mother and Raven will eat in one place; Jeremy, you and I will find another."

An immediate howl of protest rose from the twins. Darcie turned around to shush them, but it was Chase who did the explaining. "Twins are too remarkable a sight; somebody'd be bound to notice if they saw you together. From now on, kids, I'm afraid in public, we're going to have to keep you separated." The protest from the rear

seat continued, even though the twins could see the logic
in what their father said.

Darcie added a note of adult logic. "It's the same reason
your father and I are going to separate places. Two
people, together, always seem more familiar."

Emlyn unexpectedly spoke up once again. As always,
his voice was calm, his speech measured. "Putting aside
for the moment the question of *why* we're going anywhere, Dad, if we could know *where* we were heading, we
might have some ideas."

For the first time in a long time, Dina spoke. She already knew the answer: eavesdropping, she'd heard it discussed between her mother and father months earlier. But
she had her own reasons for wanting to be sure. "Emlyn's
right. We *all* ought to know."

"All right, then. Perhaps you should. We have to go
someplace safe, someplace where we won't be found by
those other people—like the ones out near the airport.
Your mother and I discussed this some time ago. The place
in Mount Desert is too well known. Besides, we may
have to stay wherever we go for some time, and Maine's
pretty cold to handle in the winter. The place in Hobe
Sound is also too associated with us, not to mention a long
way away. That leaves us your mother's house on the
Cape." Chase looked at Darcie for a second, then turned
back to the children. "We've practically never been there,
and the place is thought of in connection with your
mother's family, not the Wetherills. It's not too far, and
this time of the year the area's pretty empty. I don't think
anybody even knows we have it."

"Except Mort Evers," noted Darcie. "His men did some
clean-up work on the trees after that big blow last year."

Chase's stomach did a flip-flop: he had not known Evers
was aware of the place. "At any rate, that's where we're
headed."

"Mr. Wetherill . . ." Brannigan was pointing where
Chase could see a small group of people milling about on
the edge of the road, mostly blacks and a few young
whites.

Chase looked around him. The area they were passing
through was a small industrial town. "Let's get off Route
1. This place must have a main drag somewhere. What the
hell town is it, anyway?"

"Port Chester was the last sign I saw. But I don't think

I'd go into the town itself, y'know. Want to chance the thruway until we get around it? Wisha, but I seed a thruway sign about two blocks back."

Chase thought for a second, then nodded.

Brannigan made a U-turn and headed back down the street, although the other cars were already beginning to back up behind them. Part of the crowd began to press on them, not because of their car in particular, but acting on signals from a man equipped, like the last one, with a bull horn. By the time the station wagon had neared the ramp to the thruway, the other stopped cars and the surging people had blocked the street except for one small empty place in the middle.

"Go for it, Brannigan, go!"

With a lurch and blast of his horn, Brannigan raced toward the rapidly filling opening. "Put your bloody heads down," commanded Brannigan to the car in general. The man with the bull horn could be heard yelling over the strident blasts of the Chevy's horn. The crowds surged to fill the street in their path. Chase thought he heard shots fired, but he wasn't sure. All he knew for certain was that the speed of the car was now too great for anyone to stop it. There was a slapping sound, a series of small thuds, and Brannigan, missing the on-ramp because of the clip at which they were traveling, fought with the wheel, bounced the car across part of the on-ramp access divider, and finally wrestled the station wagon up the road onto the thruway.

"Good going, Brannigan, good going." Chase's voice broke with emotion.

Brannigan's face lit up with a momentary glow of pleasure. "Sure, a regular Juan O'Fangio I am." Then, very softly, he whispered, "I'm afraid, though, we clipped a couple of them. That last thud . . ."

Just then, the twins set up a racket from the back of the station wagon.

"Dad, Dad. there's a little hole . . ."

". . . in the rear window."

Chase was almost snappish. "Just be thankful it's only one."

Brannigan turned around to stare at the bullet hole, then returned to his driving. "Only a little way until we're past this infernal town, and then it's back to U.S. 1 and dump this outrageous jalopy."

Traffic on the turnpike appeared normal—perhaps a little heavier than usual but moving without piling up—and it did not take long before they bypassed Port Chester. Chase marveled there was so little indication of trouble on the thruway; an unusual number of heavily loaded cars seemed the only possible sign that others too were in flight. A few miles past the town, they turned off, heading eastward again until they hit the Old Post Road, U.S. Route 1. The first eating place Brannigan picked, Chase vetoed. "We don't want any place with a parking lot. Find a greasy-spoon type."

Suddenly, Brannigan pulled into a parking spot in front of a shabby-looking diner on the main street. "It looks greasy enough, but I can't vouch for the cutlery. They may use their fingers."

"OK. Darcie, take Dina and Jeremy to this one. Emlyn—no, Emlyn goes with Brannigan. Raven and I will be at the next one down the street; it looks about as bad."

Darcie looked at the ramshackle building in front of her. "Except yours probably has a bar." She smiled, squeezed Chase's hand and began collecting Dina and Jeremy.

A grumbling Raven had already been sent up the street to wait for his father; Chase got out and watched Emlyn climb in beside Brannigan. "As soon as you get the new one, we'll dump this," he told the two. "Be careful, and for God's sake, don't get caught."

Emlyn leaned out of the car window on the street side and looked directly at his father. "Are we being chased, Dad? Those people back in New York—do they think we did something wrong to them?"

Chase wondered if that was what they did think.

"*Did* we do something?" persisted Emlyn.

"No, we didn't do anything." Chase paused for a second, then added with a sigh, "Not on purpose, anyway. But, yes, son, someone is after us."

Brannigan, sensing the difficulty Chase was having, told Emlyn to close his window, then started up the street toward Raven. From behind him, he could hear Dina whistling softly as she sauntered toward her mother.

"What the world needs now is love, sweet love," was the tune.

When Eliot Towers, Chase Wetherill's personal assistant, reached the lower-level boarding gates of the Long Island trains, he found the same signs he had seen posted outside the commuter gates on the upper level: "Train Service Temporarily Suspended." Added beneath in bad, magic-marker writing, "Until Further Notice. Check Conductor." Towers had gone down on the escalator hoping the Long Island trains would be exempt from whatever was causing all the confusion on the upper level. They weren't. And as a veteran commuter to Roslyn, he was not surprised to find no conductor to check with; this was standard procedure when anything at Amtrak fell apart.

Back on the upper level, he realized the place was completely jammed. He had seen it was crowded as he paused on his way to the escalator, but had not been aware of how packed until he actually entered the vast waiting room. It was difficult to make even modest headway through the dense, undulating mass of people shoving and pushing against each other, scanning the electronic train board for news that didn't appear. Eliot Towers rarely drank, but he began making his way across the room to the Iron Horse Bar. It looked marginally less crowded inside, and if he was lucky he might even find a place to sit down. As he fought his way across the waiting room, Towers was surprised at the heat generated by the milling crowd. He found unpleasant the odor of stale sweat, overheated bodies, and children too long in their clothes.

Inside, Towers saw the reason the bar looked empty from the waiting room: almost all the customers were crowded at the far end staring up at a television set suspended high in one corner of the room, a leftover, he decided, from the World Series a few weeks earlier. Those looking at the set were silent, but the handful still at the bar occasionally tried to talk to each other. A florid-faced man on the fringe of the crowd under the set turned around and silenced them with a bellowed "Quiet!" As if to defy the man, the sound from the set suddenly became louder: you could hear angry shouts, the honking of horns, a distant crackling of small-arms fire, and the chant "jobsjobsjobs."

Towers could hear an announcer's voice, struggling to stay calm, saying that some of the material was explicitly violent, and that viewers might want to consider whether it was suitable for viewing by children.

The first tape was from Long Island City and showed a mob beating on the windows of a station wagon and the arrival of the CAC and their trucks. This was followed by footage from Los Angeles, showing crowds blocking traffic and overturning cars on Wilshire Boulevard, their rioting and chanted "jobsjobsjobs" seeming somehow unreal among the palm trees and Kodachrome sky of the coast.

The final tape came from Detroit, where the announcer explained that an executive had come out through the gates of the Chrysler plant to reason with the crowd gathered outside his factory. A nervous factory guard had fired a warning shot over the mob's heads; then he and the other guards fled inside the building as the angry crowd surged toward them. The executive was left to fend for himself. Over the chant of "jobsjobsjobs" the mob dragged the executive about twenty yards and tied his hands to the back of a flatbed truck that was parked near the gates. Someone climbed into the cab of the heavy truck and began blowing the horn. The crowd scattered, parting in front of it. The truck slowly drove down the street, yanking the man on the end of the rope behind it. But as the truck went faster, he fell down and was dragged along.

Then the truck slowed to turn around in an open space. The man managed to struggle to his knees, but the truck started back down the street toward the gates, yanking him down again. This time it drove past the mob at full speed, blowing its air horn in triumph; the man's body bounced along on the road behind it, turning and twisting from the rope, rising high into the air each time the truck hit a bump. The mob of blacks roared its approval.

The people in the bar gasped. Towers could only find strength to thank God that the man was, by now, almost certainly dead. The twisting and turning was only a hideous mock struggling, the motion of a lifeless body being dragged along the pavement at high speed.

The fear that had been growing in Eliot Towers became unbearable. Pushing his way through the people who had by now crowded in behind him, he went to the almost empty bar and ordered a double scotch on the rocks. The bartender, his eyes riveted on the screen, spilled as much on the wood surface of the bar as he did into Towers' glass.

It was not until Towers heard a familiar voice, calm and commanding, that he turned back to the television set. On screen was one of the network's anchor men. His voice and his face were familiar to Towers, but he rarely watched television and could not place the man. After the frenzied, frightened-sounding voices of the announcers covering the on-the-spot commentaries in L.A. and Detroit and New York, the man seemed a mountain of calm, something familiar and reassuring, and Towers tried to listen.

But the crowd seemed less interested in the anchor man than they had in the action shots and started talking loudly. Towers could only make out an occasional sentence. The anchor man made no attempt to characterize the disturbances as localized. In fact, the gist of what he said was that these scenes were typical of a phenomenon that had suddenly appeared out of nowhere that day and that the same sort of mob violence was surfacing erratically, but in many different parts of the country. The question of why the National Guard had not been activated to put the action down was raised, but the anchor man explained that President Welby had federalized all National Guard units and the states could no longer issue orders to them. The absence of the police remained unexplained; they had completely disappeared from the streets of all major cities and were to be found only in a few remote towns with two- and three-man forces. (So far, no one had mentioned that these were the precise forces which the Teamsters had thought uneconomical to try to organize.) The Governors of the states involved were pleading for action before the situation got completely out of hand, but Washington so far had remained officially silent. Only President Welby's Press Secretary, Edward Rombert, had even mentioned the subject, lapsing into glittering generalities such as "not overreacting to a frightening, but not basically dangerous, situation," "a pressing need for a calm overview in face of what could be blown out of all proportion by the media," and that "in time, when there is no danger of escalating the emotions inherent in all such disturbances, the President will issue an appropriate statement."

When he again turned away from the set, Towers looked at the bartender, who shook his head slowly, as if saying he couldn't explain this confusion either. Towers slapped a couple of bills on the bar and hurried out.

The caseful of Dutch guilder in the Foundation's safe made sudden new sense. There had been no mix-up of attaché cases earlier; Chase had meant for him to have it, to take it home and keep it. Somehow, Chase had known what would happen today, and the call from O'Connor about "Situation D" appeared to be part of the answer. Towers took a taxi and went directly to the Foundation building, giving the driver ten dollars to wait for him. He removed the case from the safe. On the way out the door, Eliot Towers for the second time today broke another Wetherill rule and opened Chase's desk, withdrew something and put it in his pocket. The night watchman gave Towers a curious glance as he swept back out the doors and then sat back down by the door.

Inside the taxi again, Towers thought for a second, then asked: "How much to Roslyn?" The driver turned around with a surprised look.

"You kiddin', buddy? With all this crap going on? Nothing doing."

"How *much*?" Towers hand flipping through his wallet and the insistence of the message were part of the elaborately executed ballet taxi drivers and their passengers were performing all across town tonight.

"One hundred fifty. I know a way around the trouble spots. None of them goof-off rioters. Lousy bums. But it's cash in advance or no dice. I been to Pelham with one deadbeat already."

"Seventy-five now, seventy-five when we get there." Towers wasn't just bargaining; seventy-five was all he had in his wallet.

"Shit. No dice, buddy. Like I said, I been stiff-armed once already."

"I only have seventy-five with me. The rest is at the house."

"Sure. That's what the other guy said. But it's all up front or no ball game. Sorry."

With a sigh, Towers pretended to open the door. Then he withdrew what he had taken from Chase's desk. It was a small snub-nosed .38.

The driver took him to Roslyn.

"And it is your contention that Gallagher *versus* Nevada provides the state's only precedent against the

plaintiff's class action?" asked Associate Justice Tobin
Wetherill, glowering impressively down from the bench.

"Yes, your honor," answered the attorney for the class
action. He was nervous, and wasn't entirely sure whether
the question indicated that Justice Wetherill was leaning
toward or away from his brief.

"Of course," continued Toby, "this court is never too
interested in the precedents of other courts, as I'm sure
you realize. On the other hand, if we are to engage in the
game of precedent-playing, I'm not entirely sure that the
one cited by the Senate of Nevada wouldn't militate as
much *against* as *for* the case. For instance, in Section III
thereof . . ."

Toby's law clerk smiled faintly. The Justice had scared
the young attorney (among those allowed to appear before
the Supreme Court, anyone under forty was considered
young), yet was now subtly letting him know his class action had merit. This meant that Justice Wetherill, who
could be extraordinarily caustic when he wanted to, liked
this lawyer, making his first appearance before the high
tribunal. Wetherill had spotted him as a comer, put him
through the wringer a little, and was now gently guiding
him out of the woods. In spite of his pose of impartiality,
the Justice had a way of encouraging the exceptional and
the talented, picking them out as they appeared before the
Court, and sometimes almost helping them make their case
for them.

Davin Brit, Justice Wetherill's law clerk, watched, the
note for the Justice held tentatively between his fingers,
admiring the by-play before the bench. Certainly Justice
Wetherill looked every inch the Supreme Court Justice.
Taller than Chase—in fact, almost as tall as Tracey—he
was heavier, but in no sense corpulent. His face was lean,
topped by a mound of silver-white hair of such brilliance
that Brit sometimes wondered if the Justice might not use
an occasional cosmetic rinse; his voice was deep, and,
when angered, had a tendency to boom, although generally it was used in such a soft, modulated tone that the
voice only hinted at the power it could produce. Watching
the performance intently, Brit again felt the note between
his fingers and pondered what action to take. The Court
was quite precise in its own unspoken rules on such matters.

These rules explained why Chase had had such a difficult time with the law clerk earlier in the day. Four times Chase had tried to reach his brother Toby—more formally known as Tobin Wetherill, Associate Justice of the United States Supreme Court—and each time had run into a stone wall in the shape of Davin Brit. Although Chase wasn't even sure the Court was in session (it was: today was set for the hearing of oral arguments of several cases, of which Gallagher *versus* Nevada was only one), the law clerk seemed unwilling or unable to even try to get a message to him. Brit was well aware of the Court's inner disciplines, and that no Justice was to be disturbed during the hearing of oral arguments for anything less than a personal crisis of the first magnitude—something, say, such as a death or sudden illness in the family, matters which even the Court had to admit could strike the mere mortals who composed it.

In spite of considerable prodding from Brit, Chase had refused to produce such a personal crisis: it was something, he had told Brit, of the most extreme urgency but something that only he could explain to his brother. During the luncheon recess, Brit had flashed Chase's first three messages at Toby as he made his way down the corridor; the Justice had glanced at them but not really read them, and brushed Brit aside with an impatient gesture.

Therefore, in the final of the fourth calls, Chase had gone as far as saying that he must speak to his brother immediately, that it was a matter of "life and death." This was the content of the message Brit now held in his hand, struggling with himself as he tried to decide upon a course of action. He could slip up behind Justice Wetherill and hand him the note, but could easily receive even more violent treatment than he had during the luncheon recess. If, on the other hand, Brit didn't take this risk—and something *had* happened that the Justice should know about—Brit could just as easily be rebuked for leaving Justice Wetherill unnotified.

With a weary collapse of his frame, for Brit already knew that he would lose whichever course he followed, he slipped up behind Justice Wetherill and handed him the message from Chase. Justice Wetherill held the slip of paper in his hands for some moments before opening it; he waited until Justice Simms began berating the lawyer in front of him in the colorful, brutal style which had made him famous. Almost casually, Wetherill slowly opened the note, read it, and then closed it—folding the paper into a neat square before slipping it into his pocket. On his face, as he turned to give an answer to Brit, was a look of extreme annoyance, possibly even a touch of anger. He shook his head vigorously at Brit and returned to watching Justice Simms perform. The unwritten rules had been breached for nothing, and Brit knew Justice Wetherill wanted him to be sure he realized the fact.

Silently, Brit left the podium and walked back to his office, sulking a little. Justice Wetherill had one of the finest legal minds in the country; to serve him was both a privilege and a sure road to any career in law he might want to follow. But working for the bastard was frequently not only unpleasant, but painful.

Brannigan and Emlyn pulled up outside the bar-grill where Chase had been eating for about twenty minutes; Emlyn was driving a new Ford station wagon, while Brannigan still drove the Chevy. As soon as Chase saw them through the window he hurried out.

"No trouble?"

"Yerra, not a bit. Hot-wired easily, it did. Emlyn here has a fine future ahead of him."

"Good, good." Chase clapped Emlyn on the shoulder. Then he turned to Brannigan. "What about license plates? Whoever you stole that from will report it, and that makes tracking us easy."

Brannigan gave Chase a sly look. "Already done. We pinched the front plate off one car, and the back plate off another. Emlyn's idea."

Chase looked confused. "But then the plates aren't the same."

"We know that, Dad. But a policeman only gets to look at one plate at a time. So the two plates being different won't matter. If we'd lifted both plates from the same car, it wouldn't take long for someone to put two and two together."

Brannigan beamed at Emlyn like a proud teacher. "See, Mr. Wetherill, a man loses one plate and he figures it fell off, but he loses both, and he *knows*. So the police start looking for a car with those plates. I tell you, the boy holds genuine promise."

"Sometimes you frighten me, Emlyn," nodded Chase. "Now, let's collect everyone and get moving. We'll drive a little out of town and transfer the luggage, then drive the Chevy off something steep. No point in making it easier for anyone."

Five minutes later, with Chase at the wheel of the new Ford, they set off to find a place to dispose of the Chevy.

In the end, getting rid of the car turned out to be surprisingly easy. Driving along a back road, not too far past Port Chester, they came to a small bridge overlooking a dam; the water appeared deep and the grassy slope leading to the artificial lake would make putting the car underwater simple. The luggage was transferred by the twins; the heavy footlocker was carried from one car to the other by Chase and Brannigan.

Chase was about to go back for one final load from the Chevy when he saw Raven and Jeremy unwrapping the 12-gauge shotgun he had bundled in a blanket and jammed behind the seat of the rear compartment.

"Put that down!" roared Chase. The shotgun was loaded, and although locked on "safety," leaving the weapon where the twins could find it had been stupid. "Give it to me." Chase snatched the shotgun away, furious with himself.

Darcie looked at the twins, whose mouths were open in hurt and surprise; they had never seen their father really angry, nor were they used to being yelled at.

"Never, never, never . . ." Chase's words trailed away as the anger drained out of him. "I'm sorry. But that thing's so damned dangerous."

"Are you going to kill somebody?" Raven's voice was filled with wonder.

Chase forced a laugh. "Of course not."

"We did." Jeremy let the words hang there, terrible in their simplicity.

"Oh, don't be ridiculous." But the look on the twins' faces proved they didn't consider themselves ridiculous at all. Chase's heart went out to them. They were torturing themselves with that, in spite of what he kept telling them, was the truth, and what they knew was the truth, and all the reassurances he could offer would never make them believe otherwise. The strain was showing on their faces. Chase kicked himself that he hadn't left when his instinct told him to and thus avoided this toll on Darcie and the children. It was his fault and no one else's.

Brannigan took the gun from Chase, rewrapped it in the

blanket, and stashed it in the back of the Ford wagon. Chase had wanted to put it somewhere else, out of the twins' way, but didn't want to place any emphasis on the gun's importance now. Brannigan had the Chevy's license plates tucked under one arm. With Emlyn, he jammed the accelerator down, then jumped out of the car as he slipped the automatic shift into drive. There was no way Chase could see Brannigan wince as the car roared down the bank into the water, nor would he have understood the expression of pain on his face if he had. With that car, already tilted sideways as the water poured in through its open windows, went Brannigan's very special feeling about the first car he had ever owned. His back turned, Brannigan clutched the license plates tighter to himself and walked slowly from the sight. Behind him, he could hear the bubbling as air was forced out of the Chevy.

"Look! Look! Its' capsizing like . . ."

". . . the *Poseidon*."

Brannigan shook his head and tucked the license plates away under the floor mat of the Ford. The twins' ebullient laughter floated up from the slope below, and Brannigan could hear Emlyn saying something in an excited tone as the Chevy finally disappeared completely. But Brannigan never even turned around.

Tracey Wetherill had received his "Situation D" call from Chase that morning about six o'clock. Even Tracey, who was an early riser, had been caught still asleep by the early-morning call; to any of the rest of the people in Tracey's apartment, it would have seemed the middle of the night.

The call was short, barely giving Tracey time to light his first cigarette of the day. But although short, by the time Chase hung up, the call had jarred Tracey fully awake. The memory of Chase's message from Graffa to him a year earlier was still very clear, and the reality of what Chase was saying now on the phone called for action.

No one else, including the staff, would be up for some time, so Tracey threw on a dressing gown, made himself some coffee, and wandered around the apartment, trying to figure out what to do—or, rather, how to do it.

As New York apartments went, Tracey's offered ample room for wandering. Perched on the top of a forty-five-story apartment house overlooking the East River, the triplex penthouse had been specially designed and built for Tracey as an integral part of the building. Tracey himself lived only on the lower floor; the upper two were mostly taken up by a large two-story Thermopane enclosure, a sort of luxurious greenhouse in the sky, where Tracey could indulge his passion for organic gardening on a grand scale. What Tracey grew here was a long way from simple house plants: everything from azaleas and rhododendrons to chrysanthemums was forced into bloom on command; a small patch of Gentlemen's White (with the aid of fluorescent lighting to make up what the sun lacked) produced small harvests of tender corn throughout January and February; even in the coldest parts of winter, the setup boasted crops of lemons, apples, and cherries plucked from the miniature fruit trees. In fact, the whole apartment put such a load on the building's structure that Tracey had had to buy the floor below his own triplex to support it: that entire floor was given over to I-beams and special reinforcing devices so the weight of the earth wouldn't collapse his elaborate garden in the sky.

Tracey blinked at the bright, fluorescent lighting, put down his coffee cup after checking the humidistat, and decided his two-story glass garden needed more moisture. After a minor adjustment of the dials, he carried the coffee cup with him and sat down in one of the Sidney Greenstreet rattan chairs to work out a plan. For a moment, he thought he heard someone else moving around the apartment, but dismissed it; nobody but the plants and himself ever got up before noon. (Besides Tracey, four boys were currently in residence. Thorley—who had once been Tracey's lover, but had been progressively downgraded to companion, then butler—now lived in the servants' quarters in the unoccupied floor below the triplex. On this same floor were Tracey's elaborate sauna and private gymnasium, fitted in among the crisscrossing reinforcing beams.

The few times Chase had been there—and Chase still made an effort to see Tracey, more than could be said of the rest of the family—he had been struck, as always, by the fact that the boys all bore so strong a resemblance to Tracey. (It never occurred to Chase that this meant they also bore a strong resemblance to Rodney, Tracey's deceased twin.)

Rodney was at the heart of Tracey's problem. Unlike Rodney, Tracey was a homosexual more by default than instinct. In appearance, there was nothing in the way Tracey acted or thought that would have led you to suspect him; Rodney had been a walking advertisement. Tracey led the carefully guarded life of a middle-aged homosexual, and it was only from what he chose to tell about himself that Chase and others knew anything about him at all.

Unlike Chase, he was tall, perhaps a half-inch over six feet, and even trimmer. At forty-six, he had the lithe build of an athlete, a tennis player or a skier, even though he was none of them; the trimness and compactness of movement was the product of an hour's agonizing exercise executed daily in his small gym. When he was younger, Tracey had been subject to frequent and easy arousal by girls his own age, but nothing had ever come of it. If it hadn't been for Rodney, something might have.

And Rodney's death, instead of releasing him, had only seemed to imprison him more closely.

Since Rodney's death, much of his time had been spent in a pointless search for the mirror image of his dead twin; through the long nights in bleak bars, the futile cruising of endless streets, the unsatisfying plunges in and out of random beds, Rodney's face had haunted him, a dim, beckoning recollection of someone he could feel safe with, someone he could understand and be understood by, someone he could love without fear of hurt. Yet, Rodney had hurt him constantly. So, at the same time, the recollection of Rodney carried with it the aura of someone he had resented and hated and never forgiven for robbing him of his individuality. More than once, Tracey had wanted to explain all this to Chase. "I know you don't approve of how I live, Chase, but . . ." he would begin, and then stop in embarrassment. Not for himself, but embarrassment for Chase.

Sitting in the chair, staring at the empty coffee cup, Tracey wondered if Chase would have understood. He doubted it; he barely understood his imprisonment by Rodney himself. Chase's early-morning call today had shaken him, yet he sat there and wondered if Chase would remember his visit to this apartment the day he showed up to brief him on Graffa's report. Tracey knew he had panicked at what Chase had told him, but a lot of things had contributed to his high state of nerves. In those days, Tracey was keeping a young boy named Dirk, a boy so dimpled and curly-haired he looked like a parody of Shirley Temple. And Dirk had chosen that occasion to act his worst. For a long time, sitting curled up on Tracey's white couch, Dirk had said nothing, just twisted and untwisted a gold chain supporting the coin that hung from his neck, around his fingers, At times he twisted the chain so tightly the flesh of his finger turned dark.

And when Dirk finally did speak, Tracey could have wished he hadn't. With some embarrassment, Chase had tried to explain that he had a "private family matter" to discuss with Tracey, a statement which Dirk apparently took as an insult. For when Tracey agreed and asked Dirk if they could be alone for a few minutes, Dirk abruptly uncurled himself from the couch and stalked off, pausing at the door only long enough for a single hissed observation: "I'm leaving for good, Tracey. I'm not one of your goddam fruit trees; you don't own me. Tonight you can fuck a ripe pear."

To avoid the embarrassed silence, Chase had plunged into the serious matter of Graffa's mission. Tracey had been deeply embarrassed, listening with one ear to Chase while reassuring himself that Dirk would be back.

In retrospect, of course, both Chase and he had been right—Chase about the report's predictions, he about Dirk. Now action had to be taken; his decision was made. Pushing the button on the phone that connected him with the servants' quarters and Thorley, Tracey woke him and told him to make preparations for a party tonight. A gala. He was less sanguine than Chase about their chances of getting to the airport; those things had a way of suddenly going out of control. A party had allowed Fulgencio Battista to escape from Communist Cuba; it might just work here for *him*.

By ten that evening, the "gala" at Tracey Wetherill's triplex was swinging into high gear. Many of the guests had been reluctant to come, citing the street disturbances in the city, but Tracey had talked them into it—the party, he had told them, would get their minds off their troubles.

The party would also get Tracey out of the apartment house without being seen, his only real reason for giving it. Earlier, while Chase was still in his office at the Foundation, Tracey had called him back and explained he was not going to try to make the plane Chase had waiting at Kennedy for them. Instead, he told Chase, he was going underground into a sort of "safe house" he kept in the Village. When asked why, Tracey reported that Thorley, his butler, had noticed some curious-looking men hanging around the apartment-house door all day. "Not only that, Chase, but the doorman told Thorley these men had been asking questions about whether I was home or away—you know the kind of thing. Well, I don't know who they are and I don't want to find out. I guess the same sort of people already have the airport covered. As I told you this morning, I can slip out of this place without being seen pretty easily, but I won't be able to get away from a bunch of whatever-they-ares that bottle me up on some road to Kennedy. I think you're crazy to try to make the airport yourself this late. It's safer to hide."

Chase hadn't argued, although at the time he thought Tracey was overreacting. They had wished each other luck, and promised to keep in touch, working out a code so they could make contact without using the phone.

Tracey glanced around the party. Thorley and some waiters from the caterer were busy passing drinks and hors d'oeuvres; the combo in the corner of the greenhouse was doing its best with "Lili Marlene" while one of the guests struggled through his imitation of Marlene Dietrich. The group was largely male, with a scattering of borderline-case women; all of them looked out of place surrounded by a thriving corn crop and an orchard of miniature fruit trees. Even though there hadn't been much time to prepare, Tracey had told his guests it was a "Come-as-you-will-be-at-the-End-of-the-World" party, and they had complied with full costumes, some quite elaborate.

The costumes were an important part of Tracey's escape plan. His bags were already in a rented station wagon, parked around the corner. At the most opportune moment he could find, Tracey and three of his guests (already prepared and ready) would slip out. The guests, in full costumes, would go down the front elevator and cause a commotion at the front door of the apartment building, while Tracey, dressed as a ragmuffin, wearing a hippie wig, and made up to look much younger than he was, would go down the service elevator. While the mysterious men waiting outside were busy trying to figure if Tracey was one of the three costumed men in the front, Tracey would slip out the back door, climb into the station wagon, and disappear. At the party, the only people who would know of his departure were the three accomplices (who thought Tracey was coming right back) and Thorley (who knew he wasn't).

Tracey signaled the three and nodded to Thorley. Four and a half minutes later, he was heading down the East River Drive in the wagon, trying to remember where to turn off to get to the Village. For just a moment before he turned onto the drive, he had looked back and up and seen the brilliant lights of his greenhouse blazing against the sky and it had made him feel like crying. Being alone always made him feel like that.

Chapter Five

It was the best of times; it was the worst of times, it was the age of wisdom, it was the age of foolishness ... it was the season of light, it was the season of darkness, it was the spring of hope, it was the winter of despair ...

—*Charles Dickens,*
A Tale of Two Cities

At nine a.m., only three hours after Chase had received his own early-morning telephone call, a curious scene had taken place at Usspatpenn. A series of conferences had been held between Graffa and Granger, Miss Dark (Mrs. Wetherill's nurse), and Dr. Chatteris, the young physician who devoted himself full-time to looking after the ageing Wetherills. The substance of this hastily held meeting came as no surprise to any of those people; only the timing was news to them.

Granger plunged back into the staff quarters, called the members together, and after his own talk to them, assembled the entire group in the large entrance hall. Dr. Chatteris leaned on the railing of the upper level, his hands hanging loosely over the edge of it, his legs crossed, to keep himself separate from the maids, cooks, chefs, housemen and gardeners. Graffa appeared at the head of the stairs and began a slow descent, stopping at about halfway down: Mrs. Wetherill stayed at the top of the stairs, staring blankly ahead of her, clinging to Miss Dark, not understanding why she hadn't been allowed to go to her elevator.

"This," announced Graffa, his voice clear and steady, "is a sad day for all of us. On the strong advice of Dr. Chatteris, my wife and I will be leaving for Hobe Sound in a few hours, and the move will be a permanent one. I regret that circumstances caused this decision to be made on such short notice, but arrangements have been made to soften any financial discomfort you might otherwise encounter."

To the stunned employees, Graffa then proceeded to explain that all would receive envelopes from Mrs. Gaster with one year's pay, that those with more than five years' service would receive small annuities, and that those with longer service would receive proportionately more. Any of them near retirement age would receive the same benefits they would have had they attained the stipulated age. With a sad shaking of his head, Graffa added that he was sorry that they could not continue to use their quarters here until they relocated, but noted that the house was being put on the market immediately and he would have to request that they leave by the end of the week (it now being already Wednesday, this announcement was the one statement that was met by a ripple of displeasure).

In closing, he noted the respect and admiration in which he held all of them, praised them for their many kindnesses and considerations, and again repeated his regrets that the move had to be made so precipitously. "With the thanks, then, of Mrs. Wetherill and myself, and with appreciation for your long service and personal devotion, we extend to you our sincerest wishes for your speedy relocation or pleasant retirement, whichever happens to be the case. God bless and thank you all."

The staff applauded politely, although not enthusiastically, and Granger and Miss Dark quickly left the room: that they would be going with the Wetherills was no secret, nor was the obvious corollary that they thus did not have to concern themselves with such details as new jobs, new homes and uncertain futures.

"Wave to them," hissed Graffa at his wife as he climbed slowly back up the stairs. She looked at him without comprehension, and Miss Dark moved Mrs. Wetherill's arm up and down in an approximation of a farewell salute. Looking back, Graffa waved again cheerfully, then turned his head and hid behind his handkerchief, as if overcome.

Some of the older members of the staff, many of them with years of service at Usspatpenn, were genuinely moved. There was only one flaw in what Graffa had said: virtually not one word of it was true. Granger, Miss Dark and Dr. Chatteris knew this; Chase had been told of the plan months before when he had questioned what Graffa was going to do if circumstances forced the family to leave the country. Chase expected him to come with them, of course.

Graffa had laughed and quickly made it clear he had no intention of going anywhere. "Certain fine old wines travel badly," he had explained. "And your mother and I fit that category." Then with a gesture, he had kicked back the Aubusson in the library and shown Chase the elaborate alternative he had had constructed years before, back in the days of the atomic fall-out panic. It was a two-story affair, a lavish underground duplex apartment, even boasting a tiny two-story elevator so that Graffa's wife would not become disoriented. In the storerooms was enough freeze-dried and dehydrated food to last for five years; a supply of electricity was guaranteed by molybdenum storage cells and by the same sort of solar batteries that power weather satellites; fresh air came from ventilating shafts whose entrances were carefully concealed all over the grounds of Usspatpenn, below and close to low shrubbery, beside great trees, even inside some of the topiary sculpture. All of this was maintained, trimmed and clipped personally by Mort Evers, the only man even at Usspatpenn who was aware of the underground setup. When Chase had protested that in this sort of thing the fewer people who knew the better, Graffa had turned testy. "Mort's a very valuable man. You may not like him, Chase, but I trust him completely."

The underground hideaway had impressed Chase—it would have anyone—but its very perfection worried him. Undetectable, unknown, impenetrable, the place reminded Chase of the Maginot Line—and with all the same weaknesses. But Graffa's instincts were probably right: trying to move his wife out of the country would have been the same as a death sentence.

Now, a year later, Graffa's long-ago preparations were being speeded into operation. While the entire staff was lined up outside the housekeeper's door for the checks, Graffa, Mrs. Wetherill, Dr. Chatteris and Miss Dark climbed into the back of the car driven by Granger (the chauffeur had been among those let go, so Granger had told him he would take the Wetherills to the airport himself). Thus no one was around when the car, after pulling away from the house, stopped along the driveway, beside the green statue of the Old Lady Who Lived in a Shoe. Carefully, Mrs. Wetherill and Miss Dark alighted and Granger walked behind the shrubbery with them, pulled on a complex of underground levers, and admitted them into one of the tunnels. He then got back in the car and drove until he got to Jack the Giant Killer, where Graffa stepped out of the car with Dr. Chatteris and entered the underground tunnel hidden in the shrubbery around the Giant's feet.

To complete the fiction, Granger pulled the shades in the rear of the car and drove past the guard at the gate. Later, with the shades pulled up to show how empty the car was, he would return, parking the car ostentatiously outside the house. He was to appear for an hour every day to organize the staff's departure before entering the shelter for good himself.

Only one thing had been overlooked in the preparations. And this oversight, springing from a quixotic misjudgment on Graffa's part, was to prove the most expensive mistake Ravensaugh Wetherill had ever made.

The farther Chase and his family got up the Connecticut coast, the more obvious it became that other people besides them were on the move. More cars, loaded with families and all their portable possessions, were showing up on the turnpike than earlier, but as yet these individual fleeings had not turned into the avalanche of cars Chase had expected. The news, then, was not yet general information. Earlier, when he had tried to listen to the radio in the Chevy, all Chase had gotten was regular programming. Now, in the Ford, the radio worked erratically, but what news there was about the disturbances was played down, referred to as "isolated incidents" or "unexplained demonstrations." The other people on the road, fleeing like Chase, must themselves have been operating on private information. It was Brannigan who pointed out the absence of the state police. Chase shuddered.

At about Norwalk, Dina suddenly leaned forward and tapped her father on the shoulder, pointing ahead to a gas station. "Can we stop there, please? I mean, it's urgent. Ladies' room."

Brannigan automatically began slowing down. Chase appeared irritated, and Darcie turned around in the seat to face Dina. "But, darling, we practically just left the diner . . ."

"Cramps."

Her answer left no one with anything to say. The twins giggled because they didn't understand the code, but could sense it was something neither to be argued with nor discussed. Stopping a few feet short of the Esso Station itself—so as not to run over the heavy rubber lines that would signal a customer—Brannigan pointed to a small sign half-hidden behind a brick baffle that protected the restroom doors. "Over there, Dina."

"Do you need anything, Dina?" her mother asked, the slight edge of annoyance in her voice ill-concealed.

Dina stepped out of the car, letting her small knapsack-like purse dangle from one hand. "Everything's in here. Sorry to hold everybody up."

"Damn." Chase buried himself in his roadmap after he watched Dina disappear into the door behind the brick baffle. Darcie looked at him.

"It's not her fault, Chase."

"None of this is anyone's fault, but here we are."

Behind him, the twins became restless. They tried to continue their game of license plates from the side of the road, but the cars went by too fast. The quiet in the car had been oppressive, and left alone in silence, their minds returned too quickly to the "dear man" with the bleeding head Emlyn had dumped in the gutter.

Brannigan began to whistle some obscure tune, but after a long imploring look from Darcie, he abandoned it with an apologetic smile; he could see the tenseness building in her.

Dina seemed to be taking endless time, but Chase said nothing. Too much had been said already, and he was determined not to be the first one to comment again on how much time they were wasting.

He didn't have to.

"Golly," said Raven, "but it's . . ."

". . . taking forever." The twins probably would have said more, but a look from Brannigan silenced them.

Chase and Darcie exchanged glances. Although the first to rise to her defense, Darcie didn't trust Dina completely, and the length of time she had been inside the station could no longer by explained by the most succinct code words. On top of this, the day's events had left Darcie scenting trouble at every turn. "Maybe I'd better go check. She'll be furious, but—"

"Go check." Chase's tone was stern and worried at the same time.

Less than a minute later, Darcie came running out of the ladies' room, banging her shoulder on the building's corner as she raced back toward the car. "Chase! Chase!"

Both Brannigan and Chase bounded out of the car; Emlyn's door opened only seconds later and he too jumped to the pavement. Chase, halfway to Darcie, turned around to him. "Stay with the twins, Emlyn. And all of you, get back in the car."

Chase grabbed Darcie. She was holding onto her left shoulder where it had hit the brick wall, but pointed toward the Ladies' Room with her right hand. "The mirror. On the mirror. Oh my God, Chase."

With a yank, Chase pulled the metal door wide open so violently it made a hollow, clanking sound as it crashed into the brick. At first, looking at the mirror, Chase thought the writing was in blood. But stepping closer, he could see it was scrawled in lipstick. "When you gotta go, you gotta go. So I went. Luv, Dina."

Standing just behind him, he heard Brannigan whistle. Chase felt a conflicting series of emotions sweep over him: hurt, anger, worry, doubt. Had Dina really left of her own accord, or was this more of the day's seemingly calculated peculiar and frightening events? Chase came out of the restroom and pushed past Darcie, with only a reassuring squeeze of the arm to let her know he realized he should be stopping to commiserate with her. In a half-trot, he went around the baffle and into the gas station itself. Inside, he faced a beefy, sleepy-looking proprietor leaning against his popcorn machine, listening without apparent interest to a crackling Citizens Band receiver. "Did you see a young girl come in here?"

"Nobody."

"She was in the ladies' room."

"Ladies' room's outside. So is gents'. Nobody been in here."

A bulging chaw of tobacco was shifted from one side of the man's mouth to the other. Staring at him, Chase slapped a ten-dollar bill on his counter, and added a description.

"She was sixteen, blond, dressed in Levi's."

"Oh, that girl." The man spat in a ringing coffee can on the floor. "Went around back, she did, and got into a Volkswagen bus."

"A Volkswagen bus?"

"Young guy at the wheel." His eyes studied Chase appraisingly. "She wanted for something?"

On the edge of explaining more, Chase felt a sudden cold spasm of fear seize him. The Citizens Band radio was now reciting a list of cars whose occupants were on a CAC list as "urgently wanted: apprehend if possible. Report immediately to CAC HQ." Among the cars listed was the license plate of the Chevy station wagon, along with a happily inaccurate description of himself and his family. The twins and Brannigan, however, made identifying the family frighteningly easy. Another spasm of fear swept over Chase: he had seen the service-station operator jotting down the numbers of the wanted license plates. It was time to withdraw quickly, and without giving the man any reason to become suspicious. Chase laughed casually. "No, no. She's not wanted for anything. Just went on ahead without telling us, I guess. You know kids. Thanks a lot."

No expression registered on the station operator's face. Chase left, forcing himself to move as matter-of-factly as he could manage.

Darcie seized Chase as soon as he came out of the door, but he led her back toward the car, pushing Brannigan ahead of her with a nod. "Let's get out of here. He doesn't know anything."

They drove for several blocks before Chase told Brannigan to pull over to the side. Quickly he decided to edit out any reference to the man listening to a CAC radio band. "I don't know what we should do," he told Darcie. "Dina left from the back of the station. In a Volks bus, with a young boy at the wheel. We have to assume that it was of her own free will. I think that character in there would have said something if it wasn't."

"How could anyone know she would be here? She didn't have time to phone from inside, and, anyway, wouldn't the man have mentioned it?"

"I don't know how anybody knew. And the only phone is right in the office. So you're right—she couldn't have called from there."

"She used the phone at the diner." It was Jeremy speaking, hesitantly.

Chase spun around and stared at him. "She *what?*"

"Used the phone at the diner. When Mom was in the ladies' room. But I wasn't supposed to tell. It was a promise."

"Oh, Chase, this is becoming a nightmare." Darcie shook her head and was close to tears.

"It's been one since that call at six-thirty this morning. But there's absolutely nothing we can do now to find Dina. I'm sorry."

Carefully, Chase reviewed his logic. Apparently of her own free will, Dina had climbed into a Volkswagen van driven by a young man, name unknown. Finding her by themselves would be impossible, since both VWs and young men were hardly in short supply. On the other hand, the man at the Esso station could have been lying. Since he could have been allied with the CAC, in some way, it was at least possible that he might already have turned Dina over to them. For a moment, Chase wrestled with this new terrifying possibility. It didn't make sense, he decided finally, because if they had known who she was, they would have known who *he* was, and by now, he and his whole family would have been, in the words of the Citizens Band receiver, "apprehended." Yet going to the police would be unwise. He didn't know which side they were on, if any, and besides, he was driving a stolen car. The only possible solution, then, was to continue their slow progress up the coast to safety, in the hope that Dina would eventually show up on her own; she knew their destination. Anything else would endanger the whole carful of them. The greatest good for the greatest number. All very logical. But it fell pitifully short of what seemed to be now absolutely necessary. And that was to do something bold.

Brannigan's voice startled him. "Did you know, Mr. Wetherill, you was grinding your teeth? I had a great-uncle did that. Ground 'em down so far that for the last forty years of life he couldn't eat anything but mashed potatoes."

The twins giggled and Emlyn snorted. Chase stared at Brannigan. "No, I didn't know."

It had been that kind of day.

The pair of binoculars swept an uncertain path through the tropical shrubbery, trying to focus on some figures on the dock too distant to make out clearly. Each time the man tried to adjust the glasses better, a car would rush by on A1A and interrupt his concentration. He swore at the inefficiency of the binoculars, at the cars, and at his mission, finally handing the inexpensive leatherette-covered set of Mitshubi X100's to his companion.

"There's something going down at the dock, but with these damned things, I can't make out what."

The man beside him took the glasses and tried. "She's there. *He's* there, and they're talking and waving their arms at some other people."

The first man picked up a walkie-talkie. "Something's doing down at the dock. Keep an eye out."

Ignoring the crackle from the receiver, the two went back to the binoculars, taking turns, trying to compromise between getting a better picture and not moving so close that they would become visible. Both of the men wore work clothes that made them uncomfortable; the material was too heavy and they were sweating profusely in the steamy Florida undergrowth. Worse, they could see no early chance to change: their mission was part of the operation to "protect but not interfere with" the Wetherills. The house these men had under surveillance was Dudley and Moira Cantrell's, outside of Palm Beach. What concerned them was one of the Cantrells' boats, moored offshore, a gleaming sixty-five-foot power cruiser, *Whim III*, built for speed.

At the other end of the walkie-talkie were three more men, even less appropriately dressed than those on shore: they wore ill-fitting, heavy-weight suits and white shirts and had even started their hastily ordered boat trip wearing neckties. One of the three, who had a deathly pale complexion, was forced to wear his faded fedora to avoid a painful burn.

Their boat was as incongruous in these waters as the men themselves—an old paint-heavy motor launch, built sometime before World War II, and no match for the *Whim III* if she ever really got going. If Moira and Dudley Cantrell should board their cruiser and head out to sea, the men's mission was to cut the Cantrells off before she got up speed. They were to board the cruiser with their shotguns, and place Moira and Dudley under protective custody.

"Can *you* see what's going on?" the offshore walkie-talkie in the fedora asked. We don't dare use the binocs on them from this close; I saw their captain pointing us out to someone already. Bert's trying to eyeball them from the cabin, but"—the voice took on a disgusted sound—"I think the bastard's sea-sick."

The man on shore clicked his talker switch to indicate he'd heard, and tried the glasses again. They didn't help. With a shrug, he lowered the binoculars from his eyes and spoke into the walkie-talkie. "They're just as hard to make out from here. But sure as hell *something's* going on."

Indeed something was. Moira was having an argument with Captain Struthers, a man who had served her for twelve years, first on the *Whim II* and now on the *Whim III*. Dudley fidgeted and the two crewmen looked off into space trying to pretend that they weren't there. After Chase's early "Situation D" call that morning, Moira had, as Dudley had told her to, carefully stayed close to the radio, nervously twisting the dials, but had heard nothing. The nerves relaxed a little; Moira began to feel better.

But as the day wore on and friends from Palm Beach began to call, reporting little incidents, the new self-confidence evaporated. Even Dudley started to feel anxious. And then when they heard on the radio spotty reports about the growing street demonstrations in New York and elsewhere, Dudley reached a decision.

"We'll climb onto the *Whim,* just in case, and head for"—although Dudley knew exactly what he was going to suggest, he tried to make the destination appear spontaneous—"and head for Sail. The whole thing will probably blow over. Chase and his gloomy predictions sound pretty close to hysteria, but there's no point taking chances. Yes, Sail. We'll loll around there for a week or so."

Moira had never liked Sailfish Island. Once it had been an island the yachtsmen cruising down the Caribbean had used for a layover port. No longer. Thirty miles off the coast, almost exactly opposite the line separating Georgia from Florida, it had also been a deep-sea fisherman's paradise. Then, twenty years ago, the Wetherill family had bought the island: homes, stores, marinas, the town, its small hotel, land, farms—and the natives who inhabited all of them. Although technically still a part of Georgia, its six square miles were in actuality a private family preserve, one which some of the Wetherills used more than others, but a place to which any of them could retreat without fear of intrusion by the public.

Moira Cantrell was one of the Wetherills who used the island as little as possible. Sail was all right, she supposed, if you liked deep-sea fishing the way Dudley did, but the island had always scared Moira a little. The islanders were so poor, so hungry-looking, always begging things from the Wetherill boats when they put in there. Tentatively, she put forth a mild objection: "Are you sure it's safe? The islanders . . ."

Dudley looked at her with contempt. "Sail," he said firmly.

Sailfish Island was what all the arm-waving on the dock was about. Captain Struthers was telling Moira the facts as he saw them, and they allowed no room for Sail. Telling her and trying not to get fired was not easily navigated.

"Sailfish Island, ma'am, worries me. Really worries me. I've been picking up odd chatter on the ship-to-ship from freighters going past Sail, and there's trouble of some sort there. I don't know how bad, but trouble." Captain Struthers was unable to express the degree of fear the scattered reports had produced in him; eloquence was a rarity in men who spent their lives on the sea.

"Nassau, then. Or the Out Islands," persisted Moira.

"Worse, Mrs. Cantrell." Struthers stared her directly in the eye, thought for a second, and struggled to reduce the fears generated by the ship-to-ship chatter to some sort of logical, sensible position. "Bermuda, probably all right. Or Central America—we've got enough fuel. But the Bahamas or the Out Islands—well, some of what I picked up about Sail could probably be true of them, too. And the Bahamas got native governments, which could make it even worse. You're just asking for trouble."

"No, *you're* asking for trouble." Moira studied him for a moment. Unable to think of an ultimate insult, she instead gave an explanation that sounded almost apologetic. "Mr. Cantrell has some important business decisions to make, and he needs complete seclusion to reach them. On Sail, nobody can bother him." She continued to stare at Struthers, wondering if he believed her. She doubted it. Dudley had made his decision—he always made them for Moira and himself—and she had never questioned them once. For a woman with all her money, this sort of subservience was unusual; then, so was their whole relationship.

But Struthers' arguments about Sailfish Island were reinforcing her own reservations about the place.

Struthers studied his shoes. He didn't believe her, and he knew Mrs. Cantrell knew he didn't. But this was one of those situations where no matter what you said, you were wrong, so saying nothing was the only possible safe course. "Captain," Moira suggested, "we could certainly at least take a look at Sail. You said a lot of boats were going past it. We can find out what the up-to-the minute situation is from one of them—the radio telephone—or from the head caretaker. And, if it's bad, turn around and try Bermuda. Bermuda—Crown Colony—nothing can happen there."

"No, we're going to Sail. Period." Moira was so startled by Dudley's words that she spun around, twisting her heel and almost falling. For a second, Dudley's and Moira's eyes locked in combat: he had never contradicted her in front of people before. She crumpled.

"Yes, Mr. Cantrell is right. We're going to Sailfish Island. I forgot that his business . . . Yes, Sail."

Captain Struthers stared at the ground, pondering. He had a choice: he could ignore his gut feeling and take them to Sailfish Island, or he could quit. The payments on an Elgin fishing boat he was planning to buy as a charter boat when he retired made the decision inescapable. "If you order me to."

Her head moved up and down to indicate the order should be considered given. The two crewmen handed Moira into the launch and Dudley climbed in behind her. At the *Whim III*, the steward helped her out along with Dudley. Then for the first time since her argument with Struthers, they were alone.

Moira was furious. "You reversed me in front of people. You saw I was trying to change things because of what the Captain said, and you contradicted me. The crew will think I'm an ass."

"They already do."

"Dudley, you're never to contradict me again in public."

The slap caught her off guard and almost knocked her over. "Shut the hell up."

"Dudley—"

"Oh, go below and give yourself a douche. Maybe it'll make you easier to live with."

With one hand still pressed to the side of her face,

Moira meekly went into the salon. When she saw the steward, though, she straightened up and swept regally past.

In the curious pattern of their lives, both she and
Dudley immediately felt better—although Dudley was a
little nervous that the fulcrum of the argument had to center around Sailfish Island. Orginally, he had tossed it out,
without really caring too much one way or the other; now
going there had become a matter of principle. He would
prove to the whole bunch of them that Sail was a safe
place to go if it killed him.

"Everybody hang on," shouted Struthers suddenly from
the flying bridge. "There's a boat out there I don't like the
looks of. We're going to take off at full throttle."

The boat had been bothering Struthers for some time. It
was unusual for a launch like that to hang offshore for so
long. He had seen the outrigger fishing lines they had extended over their stern, but he had also seen they were
never tended. And a man deep-sea fishing in a sinister
black fedora? While not understanding who they were or
what they wanted, he suspected they were up to something
and that that something involved the *Whim*. For that reason; he had had Jenkins lie flat on the deck and weigh the
anchor on the port side, away from the side of the *Whim*
the launch could see. The action did not go unnoticed,
however.

"There's a guy on the deck pulling up the anchor. Can
you see him?" asked the man with the on-shore walkie-
talkie.

"No, but I do see something going on up at the bow.
Looks like they're going to take off. But I don't get all the
secrecy. Do they know why we're here?" The man on the
launch had pushed back his fedora and was now using his
binoculars openly, without any pretext of being uninterest-
ed.

"Stop 'em. If they start to move, cut across their bow
and stop 'em," commanded the on-shore walkie-talkie.

His hand on the twin throttles, Struthers ignored most
of his start-up procedures. Only the bilge pump was run to
make sure no dangerous fumes had built up. "Now!"
shouted Struthers and jammed both throttles forward. The
Whim III quivered for a second, then leaped forward with
a roar of its powerful diesels. Standing beside Struthers,
crewman White grabbed at a stanchion to keep from being
yanked off his feet. From below came a clattering of china

and glassware as the steward struggled with loose items flying around the main salon. Below, Struthers could hear Moira scream and begin shouting for her husband. Dudley started to shout something back, something Struthers couldn't understand, but his words ended in midsentence; Dudley had fallen to all fours in the open cockpit of the stern.

"Jesus," crewman White complained, holding on with one hand, examining the other where it had banged into a cleat. Struthers only had time to glance at him. He put the *Whim* in a wide arc and headed straight for the beam of the launch. He could see the scrambling on her; her engines had been started at the same time as his and he could guess the man at the wheel was going to try to cut him off. Setting his teeth, he kept the *Whim* headed dead at the launch. At the last second, he eased off to starboard and shot past the launch's stern, a great white cloud of foam shooting out from either side of her hull as the *Whim* planed across the gentle swells of the Atlantic.

From beside him, he heard a groan. At first Struthers thought it was White complaining about his banged hand. Too busy to look, he heard a dull explosion from astern; it reminded him of the starting gun for the America's Cup, where last summer the *Whim* had served as Committee Boat. A strange thump from beside him finally forced Struther's head to turn: White had collapsed to the deck, lying in a pool of his own blood. Spinning around, Struthers could see that the man with the fedora, leaning against the cabin of the launch, was firing a high-powered rifle at them. Putting the *Whim* into a sudden, violent zig-zag, Struthers bellowed for Jenkins to come up on the double. Then he looked down again at the fallen man, studying the fast-growing pattern of blood, and noticing for the first time a ragged hole near the base of White's skull.

Sailfish Island was three miles long, two miles wide, and surrounded by roughly one hundred square miles of reef waters—deep enough to allow the smaller Wetherill boats entrance, but too shallow for their larger deep-draft yachts or freighters. Similarily, the single airstrip was large enough to handle only the lighter jets of the W. A. F. Potential visitors from fishing boats or offshore cruisers were discouraged by notations on the charts of the area, as well as by signs lining either side of the single narrow channel into Sail's harbor. For those who tried to fish the waters too close to shore anyway, there was a patrol boat equipped with a loudspeaker and a crew of fierce-looking islanders. When the Wetherills had first bought Sail, some of the bolder yachtsmen still tried to use what had formerly been the marina to fuel up. The Wetherills' superintendent had to put to sea in the patrol boat and somewhat vigorously suggested this was no longer an acceptable idea. Gradually the message sank in, and the Wetherills gained the privacy they had prized for so long.

Once, many years ago, the island had been a British colony, a part of the British West Indies, but it had been ceded to Georgia after the War of 1812. Georgia didn't cede it to anyone until approached by the Wetherills' land agent; even at that, Sailfish Island would probably still be in public hands if the Governor of Georgia hadn't been badly in need of campaign contributions.

The island retained many of the overtones of a sleepy British colony. What streets there were were unpaved. There were virtually no automobiles except those belonging to the Wetherills and the jeeps used by the Wetherills' staff. Its one hotel, the Compleat Angler, run by a somewhat unraveled pair of spinsters, had been closed the day after the Wetherills bought it. At last count, Sailfish Island had a total population of nine hundred and sixty persons. Nine hundred of these were native, while the rest were mainly leftover American whites from the old days who couldn't face returning to the mainland and reality. There were also about twenty whites imported from the Georgia mainland, including the superintendent and the security men. These lived in a compound completely apart from the other island residents: the Wetherills rightly considered this hard duty, and for every two months actually working on the island, a man was given three months' vacation on the mainland.

Among its assets, the island could boast tuna and sail fishing, two fire jeeps and one constable (also native). If there was little employment on the island (most of the natives and stay-behind whites were on welfare), there had been twice as much as before the Wetherills bought it; with a typical Wetherill sense of service to the nation, Wetherill money attempted to launch cottage industries, improve the farms and rebuild the small school. They also put up a minimal but serviceable hospital, imported a doctor (it

was not the Wetherills' fault that the only M.D. who
would take a job there had a long record of addiction to
his own pills), and, at the same time, gave the islanders
electricity, television, sewage disposal and a deep-seated
burning resentment of the family.

For all that the Wetherills had done to improve their
bleak existence, the islanders were grindingly poor: they
ignored repeated offers to substantially improve their own
farms, rarely attended school, refused to work in the cottage industries, and ignored the doctor completely. Apparently it was more satisfying to remain at starvation
level and blame the Wetherills for their plight. The small
number who did work for the family, either in their homes
or on the docks or in their gardens, were considered
"Uncle Toms."

The sullen, overwhelming preponderance of native population was the reason Captain Struthers felt this was no
time for the *Whim III* to be calling on Sail. As with the
B.W.I. (and the Virgin Islands), Struthers had suspected
agitators had been there working among the natives, struggling to set them against the whites. And with the Wetherills, he knew their job would be an easy one. Ordinarily,
he would have considered the islanders on Sail too sleepy
to be dangerous, but he hadn't been to the island in two
years and a good deal might have changed. There was the
twenty-man security force, of course, but given present
conditions, no one could be sure if they were even still
there. To Struthers, then, Sailfish Island was a gamble, an
uncertain sanctuary, a place to be avoided—if not out of
fear, out of prudence.

The wounding of White had forced him to change his
plans. They could not go back, and while going forward
was dangerous, at least Sail had a doctor. Although he had
examined him carefully himself, Struthers could not tell
how badly White was injured. The boy remained mostly
unconscious, but his heartbeat and pulse seemed strong
enough. With the help of Mrs. Cantrell, who insisted he be
moved out of the cramped crew quarters and put into one
of the forward staterooms, there was hope for him. It was
Moira who bathed his wound and bandaged his head and
who undressed him and got him into a pair of Dudley's
pajamas. She also sat in a small chair beside the bed, holding his hand and gently reassuring him during the rare
moments of consciousness.

Because of headwinds and the injured crewman, the *Whim III* didn't arrive off Sail until almost four a.m. Lying offshore, Struthers scanned the the dock area for some signs of activity, trying to figure out if it was safe to bring the boat in and tie up. The usual lights visible on the dock were not to be seen, nor were there any to be seen on the island itself. Nobody in the security shack answered his repeated radio calls. In themselves, these facts were hard to appraise, but they worried Struthers enough so that he decided not to try docking until morning, and the *Whim III* hove to about a mile out to sea from the docking area. To move any closer, they would have to wait. Instructing the steward and Jenkins to post alternating two-hour watches, Struthers stretched himself out on the long sofalike seat behind the wheel on the flying bridge. What guns they had aboard had already been issued; Struthers himself took the only pistol. For a long time he lay on the seat, tossing, trying to figure out where they could go after they had had White's wounds looked after—assuming even that could be accomplished. Finally, almost without realizing it, he fell into a restless sleep, a sleep made more fitful by a series of noises from the stern that didn't quite make sense.

They made sense to Dudley Cantrell. Moira had been right: today was the first time he had ever challenged her in public. Behind the scenes, it had always been Dudley who made the decisions, and this private game had delighted him. But the strain of the day's events had caused the game to pall, with the result that Dudley had changed the rules abruptly. To him, Chase's early-morning call and Captain Struthers' mutterings about intercepted ship-to-shore calls had been abstract observations. What was clear to Dudley was that someone, for reasons unknown, was after them, and Sail seemed a safer place than most to hide from them. On top of this, Dudley somehow felt responsible for White's being wounded, perhaps doomed to die from his injuries. And, for what it was worth, Sail Island could boast a doctor.

Slipping back to the stern, he motioned Jenkins over to him. "The skiff," he whispered. "Help me lower the skiff into the water." Jenkins looked at him blankly; he had no orders on this. All Struthers had told him was to keep a sharp watch on shore and to be sure no one boarded the *Whim*: no mention had been made that the owner might want to debark from her. Holding the rifle Struthers had issued him loosely, he shook his head in confusion.

"I don't know, Mr. Cantrell. Maybe I'd better wake up the captain."

"Don't be stupid. I told him what I was going to do earlier. Let him get some sleep."

"Well, I don't know. . . ." Jenkins was torn. Mr. Cantrell was the owner. Certainly, the captain had not mentioned that he would be climbing into the skiff during the night, but on the other hand, he hadn't mentioned that he wouldn't be either.

Dudley pulled the clincher. "I'm going to get the doctor off the island while everybody's asleep. For poor White. The captain would be helping me, only we were afraid Mrs. Cantrell would hear us and get upset."

To Jenkins, the mention of White was the clincher. White was an old and dear friend of his and he could guess how badly he needed Sail's doctor. Moreover, the deception of Mrs. Cantrell sounded like something the captain and Mr. Cantrell might easily have worked out. Quickly, he helped Dudley lower the skiff from its davits on the stern into the smooth water, waving as Mr. Cantrell rowed swiftly toward the shore.

The feeling that he was finally doing something immediately made Dudley feel better. Soon, he would come back with the doctor—if indeed there was any reason they shouldn't all be ashore. About a half mile from the *Whim,* Dudley started the outboard and made straight for the docks. As he grew closer, he could sense something wrong with the picture, but it was too dark for him to see what.

As he approached the pilings, Dudley turned off the outboard and glided in on the momentum. But it was only when he was almost on top of the docks that he saw the hulks—the burned out remnants of the whole fleet of boats the Wetherills kept there. Supply boats, patrol boats, the mail boat, launches, all of them. Those that hadn't already capsized or sunk were still smoldering, a thick gray smoke billowing from them every time a breeze stirred the air. Dudley stared. Struthers had been right; Sail was no place for them, for anyone, to be. He turned around to start the outboard, but it was too late. All he heard was a faint whoosh as three men jumped off the dock on top of him. Something hard hit him on the head. What little light there was in the sky over Sail went out.

The sun rises early on open water, and although it was late October, its first pale rays were visible on the horizon by five-thirty. Everybody aboard the *Whim* was already up. Moira had discovered Dudley was not in their stateroom two hours earlier and called Struthers. From the crewman Jenkins, they learned where Dudley was, and in spite of his deep misgivings, Struthers quietly and slowly moved the *Whim* toward Sail, changing from his safe position a mile from shore to a somewhat less secure one, perhaps a quarter of mile from the burned-out hulks in the dock area.

"We have to go get him. My God, we have to go get him!" Moira was almost hysterical, and it startled Struthers.

"We can't ma'am. Not until it's fully light. We have to wait till we can see what's going on." There had been light enough for him to see the superintendent's house and his staff's quarters had been burned to the ground; their fate was obvious.

Some sort of recorded trumpet call over the loudspeaker riveted their eyes on the shore. A small crowd of islanders was gathered at the end of the docks, not far from the base of the fishing dock's twin flagpoles. To one side stood the game-fishing rack, a shiny chromium bar that ran horizontally to the ground and was suspended some eight feet above it by a heavy stand; three large hooks—from which the biggest fish could be hung—extended vertically from this bar, which was topped with a scale giving the weight of each marlin, swordfish or sailfish bagged. Struthers remembered it well. Countless Wetherills and their guests had posed standing in front of it, their trophy hung from one of the hooks, leaning against the giant fish proprietarily, waiting to be recorded for posterity by the island's obliging photographer. Today the catch appeared to be large. A huge marlin—perhaps five hundred pounds—hung from the hook on the left end, its pale-white underside glistening in the early light; from the hook on the other end was suspended a swordfish so large the tip of its spearlike nose scrapped the ground. With a broad smile, a garishly dressed islander—he was wearing a white suit and a plaid tie, the costume topped by a broad-brimmed straw hat several sizes too large for him—bowed toward the *Whim*. On the dock, a loudspeaker broke into an ancient recording of "God Bless America," performed, from the sound of it, by Ivor Norvello and his Champagne Boys. As the islander struck a possessive pose beside the marlin, leaning against the white fish with one hand, the native photographer rushed forward and took his picture, while the small gathering of natives applauded with hoots and catcalls.

The tall islander nodded to someone they couldn't see, and three additional natives emerged from behind the low stonework around the flagpoles. Between them they carried a trussed-up and struggling Dudley.

"My God." Moira wasn't sure what they were planning to do, but her instincts told her that Dudley was already as good as dead.

Dudley, dressed only in his shorts, was carried quickly toward the center hook. Around his neck was a knotted loop of thin but strong fishing line; another loop of the same line was fastened on the end of perhaps six inches of wire leader. With a great deal of pushing and heaving, the three islanders lifted Dudley up and fastened this other loop to the center hook of the game-fishing stand, made sure the loop over the hook was secure, and then turned and walked away. It was a simple but murderously effective setup, designed to leave Dudley to be slowly garrotted by his own weight.

The process did not take long. For the first few moments, he kicked and thrashed, but the movements only tightened the line around his throat to the point that, even through their binoculars, they could see a thin ring of blood appear around his neck where the line cut into his flesh. In only a few minutes, his body began going alternately stiff and flaccid, while the kicking of his feet grew less visible. Slowly, his head sagged backward, his mouth open and gasping for air like a wounded fish come to the surface of the water. His hands, tied behind his back, provided a suggestion of dorsal fin, a suggestion heightened by the convulsive heaving of his pale, sagging stomach. The feet, also tied together, would first straighten and stretch themselves to a point, then flatten again, the heels pressed together like a ballet dancer's, giving the eerie impression they formed the skeleton spine of a fish's tail. As they watched, the convulsions grew further and further apart, the body turning and twisting on its hook less frequently, until only the mouth, opening and closing, still appeared to move.

At first, Moira had been too stunned to make a sound. Her hand had grabbed the gunwale for support, but she had remained mute. Then, as the full realization of what she was watching hit her, both hands rose to either side of her narrow face and she began to scream. The sound was unearthly. It tore at the slowly brightening sky in wave after wave, a sound without any discernible pitch or timbre, only modulations in tone, a sound somewhere between a shriek of terror and a wail of visceral anguish.

Struthers watched as Moira began crumpling to the deck; she was caught by the steward, who, almost tenderly, led her below to her stateroom. Turning his head, Struthers heard an uncertain cheer rise from the crowd, which he supposed came in reaction to the light of the flashbulb as the islander was photographed posing beside his trophy. Almost immediately, the throng began dispersing, as if glad to get away from the scene. At first, Struthers thought perhaps they were frightened by what they had done and were leaving before someone showed up to hold them accountable; but watching their ambling disappearance into the tropical growth farther back from the docking area, he saw there must be some other reason. Looking through the binoculars, Struthers could see the uniformed bodies crumpled in front of the security staff's burned-out houses. The islanders had no reason to fear reprisals from that quarter. No, Struthers decided, the islanders had done what they had set out to do, and now felt both a little awed and stunned at their own actions.

Dudley's execution was repayment for years of smug indifference, first at the hands of the yachtsmen-tourists, then of the Wetherills; it was the release of a long-smoldering hatred for these arrogant Americans who tied up at the docks every winter: it was the reaction against all the years the islanders had had to smile obsequiously and beg scraps of food, had been condescended to, made little of and patronized by the Wetherills.

As Moira was led below, Struthers nodded to Jenkins to weigh anchor. Crewman White would not find any help on Sail, and Struthers found himself wondering what had happened to the doctor and the other resident whites on the island. The fate of the superintendent and his staff was clear, but there had been no sign of the others. Probably dead, he decided, but he doubted if as cruelly dispatched as Dudley; that was a refinement reserved for the Wetherills. Without even referring to his charts, Struthers gunned the diesels and headed due south. They would detour around Cuba and make for Yucatan; if they ran short on fuel, they could always put into Mexico. When Jenkins appeared on the flying bridge, Struthers told him to go back to monitoring the ship-to-ship international wavelengths. His first instinct was that the pursuit of the Wetherills had more behind it than a simple vendetta against a very wealthy family. The radiomen of the coastwise and inbound foreign freighters were always in conversation with one another, and he might learn something of the bigger pattern he suspected was shaping up.

"It's pretty grubby."

Chase Wetherill had made the statement in apology, looking at Darcie as she tried not to express her feeling about the run-down motel he had pulled up in front of. "It looks clean, anyway. That's something for it," Darcie said brightly.

Chase had never ceased to be amazed at Darcie's cheerfulness when confronted with problems, but today's situation was the worst thing either of them ever had had to face. He kept wondering how deep her reservoir of calm really ran. Dina, for instance, had been barely mentioned, although they were both sick with worry over what might have happened to her, and were aware that they were totally helpless to find out anything about her. Some unspoken understanding had been reached between them that the subject of Dina would simply be avoided until they were in a position to do something. Chase squeezed Darcie's hand and again surveyed the motel. They were in Hanson, Massachusetts, a small industrial town just short of the Cape.

There were several good hotels and some excellent motels nearby, but Chase had steered away from them. Driving farther he had spotted this motel from the road and decided it was so run down his family would attract little notice. Even at that, they were splitting up into two groups, separating the twins, to make possible recognition more difficult. Darcie's only complaint had been that since they were so close to the Cape, they should go right on to her house in East Dennis. Chase had vetoed this for several reasons. He wanted to watch television and find out how bad things had gotten before going any farther;

he wanted to work out a route to their refuge of last resort if Darcie's house should prove unsafe; he wanted Brannigan, minus the Irish accent, to drop in at some scuzzy little bars he had seen to find out what people were saying.

"All right then," Chase said firmly to the occupants in the rear of the car. "Mother will drive into this one and take a room for herself and Jeremy. When she's safely set, we'll take the car and Raven, Emlyn and I will drive into that one down the street and register there. Brannigan, I'm afraid you'll have to—"

". . . spend the night at the local fleabag," finished Brannigan for him. "Wisha, I see the need, mind you, but if I begin to scratch tomorrow, you'll all be knowing why." The twins immediately began to howl at the thought of being separated.

"Why can't we be in the same hotel?"

"I've already explained that."

"Your mother and I don't like being separated either, but it's necessary."

"We've always—"

Chase shook his head vigorously. "I don't want to hear any more about it. We're all doing things we don't like."

Before Darcie and Jeremy, the latter still protesting, drove in and registered at the first motel, Chase and she had a moment together, alone on the sidewalk. Darcie reached out her hands, each hand gripping one of his forearms tightly. "Chase, we just can't go on pretending Dina doesn't exist. We've got to do something. I just don't know what, but something. Can't we call the police?"

"I haven't seen a policeman all day. I don't know what they're doing—or for whom."

"Well, what about some of her friends? One of them must know about this boy and the Volks bus—who he is, what he does, where he lives."

"We don't know many of her new friends. And we don't know which side they're on anyway."

Darcie exploded. "Their side, our side. We don't know this. We can't do that. My God, Chase. Are you going to shilly-shally about our own daughter?"

The words stung. Chase shook his head, trying to avoid an area in which he knew his answer was probably wrong. "If she doesn't show up in a couple of days, I'll go looking for her myself. She knows where we're heading. There's nothing else I can do now." Even with his head turned slightly away, he could feel Darcie's stare of disbelief. He tried another tack. "In the meantime, I'll call some people. Dick Mellon and Carter Morgan, maybe. One of them will know what's going on now—really going on—and we can find out if it's safe to bring in the police. It's not much, but it's all I can do." Not only wasn't it much, but calling people outside the family was a terrible gamble. Phones could be tapped, calls traced. That was why he had stayed away from any telephone calls to his brothers; he could get not only himself, but them, into deeper trouble. Chase shook his head again and sighed.

He looked so thoroughly miserable Darcie took pity on him, moving her hands down from his forearms to his fingers. "I'm sorry for what I said, Chase. I'm just so damned upset. Goodnight. And remember, I love you."

"Don't worry about Dina. Don't worry about anything. It's going to be all right."

Chase was back in the car with Emlyn and Raven— Brannigan had been dispatched to find his own lodgings, as well as to bring Chase a bottle of scotch—before he realized he hadn't told Darcie he loved her. For Christ's sake, he thought, events had him so worried he couldn't even say goodnight without clouding the issue with second thoughts.

Chase's telephone calls to Dick Mellon and Carter Morgan—made from a roadside telephone booth a good two miles from Hanson itself—were disturbing. The phone at the Mellon place in Seweickley rang a long time before anyone answered. In fact, it rang so long that Chase was just about to hang up, his free hand ready to collect the dozens of quarters the operator had demanded for the first three minutes. Abruptly, the phone was picked up and Chase heard the coins crash into the box below. "Mr. Mellon, please," he began. It suddenly struck him that Beedle, the Mellons' longtime, old-world butler, had not answered the phone with his usual chilly, "Mellon residence." Instead, the receiver, although taken off the hook, remained silent. Chase felt a small shudder go through him. "Is Mr. Mellon there?" he asked, his voice tentative and uncertain.

"Who's calling?" The voice didn't belong to Beedle, nor did it belong to anyone whom either Beedle or Dick Mellon himself would allow to answer his phone. It had a rough, abrasive quality to it, and an accent, although unidentifiable, that would have been more at home in a steel foundry than domestic service.

"I'm trying to reach Dick Mellon," Chase insisted. "Can you tell me if he's there?"

"Who wants him? He's here all right, buddy, but—"

Chase hung up. The damned thing was happening in Pittsburgh, too, then. Or at least in the Mellon part of Pittsburgh. For all he knew, Dick was dead; he tried to remember from his OSS days how long it took to trace a call, and concluded he was safe on that point: no one could trace a call to Hanson on the basis of so short a conversation.

More coins were deposited as Chase dialed Carter Morgan's number on Long Island. To his surprise, Carter answered the phone himself. Once he had identified Chase, his voice was maddeningly casual. "Oh, hi. I thought you might call. Hold on just a sec, Chase; there's a call coming in on the other line, too."

The line went dead as Carter pushed the "Hold" button, a silence followed by some static on the line, and a series of clicks. Carter's voice came back on the wire, cheerful but apologetic. "Sorry. No one's answering downstairs today." In the sudden pause, Chase began to say something, but was interrupted again by Carter. "Just lighting a cigarette, Chase. There. No, it's out, damn it. Hold on." Another pause. "Okay. Sorry again. Where the hell are you, Chase. You sound a million miles away."

Chase ignored the question. "I was calling to find out what the hell's going on. The riots, the disturbances, whatever you want to call them. How big a problem. How widespread. I almost got myself killed on the way here."

The voice on the other end of the phone remained calm. "Oh, them. Nothing to worry about, Chase. That bunch of wildmen—PLA, or whatever they call themselves—stirred up a few incidents, and a lot of noise, but nothing much more. All under control here, now." The pause again, then incredulously: "You almost got killed. On you way where?"

"Well, it didn't seem just a lot of noise, Carter, to me or to Darcie."

"It's all over, Chase. Forget it. Anyway, some people from the CAC were there to bail you out, so there wasn't anything to be worried about to begin with."

Because Carter Morgan was such an old friend of

Chase's and of the family's, Chase only had just begun to notice some very obvious facts. The delays and the stallings could be merely time-buying excuses to keep him on the phone so the call could be traced, which would account for the clicks and the strange static on the line too. But most significant of all was that Carter knew he had been rescued by the CAC. Carter was one of them, or allied with them. "You prick" was the best Chase could come up with as he angrily slammed down the receiver.

Checking his watch, Chase could see that the call still had been untraceable. Small comfort. Staring at the graffiti on the phone booth's wall, he sadly pondered why someone like Carter would become involved with the CAC. And, again, why should the CAC be so interested in tracking him down that they would use Carter Morgan to help? Was it the Wetherill family's wealth and position that made them targets? No, that would explain the PLA's interest in them, but not the CAC's; they had people like Carter Morgan working with or for them. Chase grimaced. He couldn't shake the notion that he and his family were somehow prizes—trophies—wanted dead or alive: dead by the PLA, alive by the CAC. Fugitives, pursued by two opposing sets of bounty hunters.

Reluctantly, he decided that no one except the family could any longer be trusted. Making a sour face, Chase checked the small notebook he always carried, stuck in the fistful of coins the operator demanded, and dialed the most reliable of the "cousins," Derek Wetherill, in Cambridge.

There was no need to keep track of the time on this call; it was painfully short. Derek's voice—desperate-sounding, almost a scream of panic—answered, apparently expecting the ring to be a return call from someone else. He gave Chase no chance to even identify himself. "Police? Police? Isn't this the police?" There was a sudden brief pause; Chase began to answer but got no chance. Desperately from Derek: "For Christ's sake, whoever you are, get off the line. I'm waiting for—Police? Police? What— Jesus Christ . . ."

The phone made a funny, hollow sound as it was dropped or torn from Derek's hand. Over the line, Chase could hear the breaking of glass and splintering of wood, followed by a scream, although whether this came from Derek or not Chase had no way of knowing. At one point, he thought he heard gunfire, but wasn't sure. And rising above all of these separate sounds, a growing, swelling, throbbing mutter of angry voices. Abruptly the phone went dead.

Chase left the old-fashioned wooden phone booth and climbed into his car. Sitting there, he thought, What in God's name is going on? Are they after all the Wetherills, even the "cousins"? Violently, he hit the steering wheel with his hand and put the Ford into gear.

Alan Peletier whistled as he drove the Volkswagen bus along the Connecticut Turnpike. The back of the bus was partioned from the front by a flexible folding door, and behind it, Dina Wetherill was changing out of her denims into a dress. This fact alone would have startled her parents, particularly her father, who for the last two years had pled with Dina to get into something more feminine. That the Levi's bothered him may have been one of the reasons Dina wore nothing else. On the other hand, Alan had only to mention his preference once, and Dina accepted it. Since then, whenever Dina climbed into the bus, the first thing she did was change into the softest, prettiest and most feminine clothes money could buy. But only for Alan.

"There," said Dina, climbing into the seat beside Alan. She was dressed in a simple, almost gossamer Halston, and as Alan looked at her, he couldn't help but smile. He didn't deserve someone as stunning as Dina.

"Where are we going?" she asked, watching him check the exit numbers as they drove up the turnpike.

"I thought we would stop off at the Red Coach, have dinner and then go back to my studio. I have a new LP— Eugene Ormandy and Beethoven."

"Wonderful." Her answer was not without silent sarcasm; she loathed Beethoven. What Dina really wanted to do was reach over, unzip the fly of his immaculately pressed gray flannels, and bury her head in his lap. But she knew Alan clung to his image of her as a delicate and untarnished flower, as much as he clung to the image of himself as an eighteenth-century gentleman. If he knew the sort of things she had been into before he entered her life . . . Biting her lip, she restrained herself and stared out the car window. A small frown appeared on Dina's brow as a car passed them, the people inside leaning out of the windows and chanting something familiar to her, their fists beating the air. "There hasn't been any trouble up here yet?" she asked. "New York was—well, New York was frightening."

"It won't affect anything up here. Just the city. The usual ghetto crap."

"Mom and Dad are trying to leave the country. Dad seems to think it's going to spread all over. And that it isn't just the blacks, it's—well, I didn't understand what he thought."

"They're worriers. And I doubt if even things in New York are really all that bad: you just ran into a trouble spot." Alan was lying and knew it. He had heard the rumors all day long, but it would be over tomorrow—it had to over tomorrow. If he told himself that enough times, it would be true.

He turned the car off at Exit 13 and headed for the Red Coach Inn; to their surprise, its signs were out and it appeared closed, though there were many cars in the parking lot. "I've never known it to be closed," Alan said in wonder, the uneasy feeling creeping over him again. He dismissed it. For Dina's benefit, he produced a look of bewildered whimsy. "Is today some kind of holiday or something?"

"You don't think—?"

"Of course not. Maybe they didn't pay their electric bill. Or the IRS. Or something. We'll go back to my place. I've got some spaghetti."

Dina smiled, but the smile lacked conviction. She sensed something wrong, and was glad when they pulled out of the parking lot.

There was indeed something wrong at the Red Coach Inn. Milling about inside were about fifty young blacks and the usual handful of whites—all members of what was known at the PLA. Less than an hour before Alan and Dina drove up, they had calmly murdered the manager and locked the entire staff in the freezer.

Darien, only a few miles from the Red Coach, had been marked for destruction, and the Red Coach was the staging area for the operation. The town had been picked not so much by design as for convenience. With Stamford on one side and Bridgeport on the other, there was a ready pool of blacks for the PLA to draw on. Further, many of them worked in Darien or in the other commuter commu-

nities very like it, doing the floors, the laundry, the gardening and occasionally—but only very occasionally—the
head of the house. From working there, the PLA agitators
knew these people would be filled with a resentment and
smoldering hatred of their white employers, whose men
daily departed to work in the city, while their ladies lolled
by their pools or kept themselves busy with endless bridge
tournaments. A little built-in anger always made the agitators' job easier. And Darien's life style, as seen from a
kneeling position on the kitchen floor, was enough to irritate anyone. The bill was about to be collected.

Alan's apartment was an unusual place, with old-fashioned twelve-foot ceilings, and at each end of the living
room, an elegant marble fireplace. In keeping with his
identification with the late eighteenth century, the walls of
the room were covered in claret-red damask; the draperies
were of a heavy watered silk of the same color and
flanked by muted, exquisitely executed oil portraits that
gleamed from inside their heavy gilt frames. The apartment was fully electrified, but Alan preferred candles.
There were masses of them: chandeliers, candelabram,
épergnes, sconces—all crammed with flickering tapers
banked as thick as fall flowers.

By now, as he always did in the complicated game they
played, he had put on a loose silk fencing shirt with wide,
flowing sleeves, tightly gathered at the wrists and trimmed
in the same ruffled lace that decorated its front. His
trousers were of tight-fitting puce twill; instead of a fly,
two rows of white pearl buttons ran down the front of the
pants, a sort of Dr. Denton arrangement, only backward.
When he bent down to give Dina her glass of port, she
stared at the trousers, unable to take her eyes away from
the bulge he produced in them. By arrangement, she
docilely sat sipping her port, listening to chamber music,
and generally maintaining what Alan saw as the restrained
formal attitude of an eighteenth-century lady, highborn
and distant. That is, until Alan finally seized her and
dragged her into his bedroom.

There, the rules of the game changed. Dina could un-
leash herself, tearing, biting, scratching, wrapping herself
around him, while he allowed himself to be undressed.
Then, as if unreasonably provoked, he would fall upon
her, as savage in passion as he had been polite before.
Tonight, though, Dina was having a difficult time working

herself into this fantasy, unable to shake her wave of
uneasiness. Alan was a little distracted himself; the worries
kept intruding upon his fantasies, as persistent and undis-
missible as the PLA's chant of "jobs, jobs, jobs." Tearing
himself free of them, Alan entered her so suddenly that
she cried out, and they both lost their doubts and fears
and awareness of the world around them.

Staring at the gray images on the small television set,
Chase Wetherill sat on the edge of his bed in the Cape
View Motel and watched the late-night news with a feeling
of defeat. The uprisings had been covered, but not given
any real sense of urgency; the earlier footage which had
so terrified Eliot Towers in the Iron Horse Bar was by
now replaced by much milder, more conventional "local
disturbance" films. For whatever their reasons, the networks and the stations were playing the story down.

Small indications, however, of just how extensive the
trouble actually was kept creeping into the commentaries
in spite of this. A Southern Senator appalled by something
the PLA had done; a Northern Liberal demanding an immediate investigation of how a neo-fascist organization
like the Citizens Action Committee could have grown up
wthout anyone in the government knowing of it; two different Governors trying to find out why both the National
Guard and the police seemed to have fallen off the face of
the globe. Harry Reasoner described the situation as "delicate," John Chancellor labeled if "baffling," Walter Cronkite's wording was that President Welby's promised
statement tomorrow would come "tragically late."

Tragically late. Chase rolled the words around in his
head, knowing they described him as accurately as they
did the President. Yet, he had done everything he could.
All of his brothers and Moira had been notified about
"Situation D," with the exception of his older brother
Toby. (Justice Tobin Wetherill had continued to remain
unavailable, in spite of Chase's four separate attempts.)
No one could ask more of him. The reaction from each
family member had been different, but only the one from
Duane had scared Chase. He hadn't been able to reach
Duane until just before they left, but his reaction had been
far from reassuring, especially coming from a U.S. Sena-
tor.

"I know, I know, I know," Duane had said. "The reports beginning to come in down here are incredible. All hell's going to break loose on the floor. The Pentagon won't answer its phones. The President can't be reached. There's talk of impeachment. Hell, I can't go. My duty's here." There had been the sound of a lot of other voices in the room Duane was speaking from, and Chase realized he was getting off the phone hurriedly.

Chase felt closest of all to Duane, and sitting alone in this bleak Hanson motel room while his family slept, he suddenly wished Duane were here. Stirring his drink moodily, he wondered how Duane was doing and where he was. (At that moment, Duane was fighting his way through Washington traffic, heading for Georgetown and a meeting with some of the other Senators in preparation for a full session of the Senate, later that night.)

Tragically late. The words he'd heard on television a few minutes ago haunted Chase. There was nothing of the "tragically late" in the way Duane was conducting himself. Unlike Chase, there hadn't been a second's hesitation on whether the right thing was to flee or to stay and fight. "Hell, my duty's here," Duane had said—and meant it. To Chase, who was still torturing himself on this point, Duane's crystal-clear vision of what his duty was, what his obligations were, what he had to do for the country, only made Chase's lack of conviction more pointed. Graffa's rationale, "The family's duty to the nation is to survive and that's all there is to it," seemed suddenly hollow.

The warm scotch he was holding abruptly tasted foul. (The Cape View Motel's ice machine did not work.) Holding his glass forlornly, Chase sighed and walked over to turn off the television set. In the other bed, Raven and Emlyn lay side by side; Raven was sleeping fitfully and kept calling out Jeremy's name, his arms flailing at Emlyn, who would mutter in his sleep and shove him away.

For a moment, Chase stared at the silent television screen, thinking about the heavily doctored news broadcast. It seemed that the violence had been made to appear far less than Chase himself knew it was: the widespread nature of it had been glossed over. Like a hurricane or a tornado, its path seemed capricious and random, but his calls to Pittsburgh, to Boston, to Washington, plus his experience on the way to Kennedy, told a different story than the networks. More and more, Chase was coming to the conclusion that Darcie's house on the Cape could only be a temporary hiding place, if usable at all. This left him with his refuge of last resort, a falling-down farmhouse outside Salisbury, Connecticut. He winced. Chase had seen the place only twice, but he remembered its shortcomings all too well. Feeling a little foolish, he had reluctantly bought and provisioned it just after being shown Graffa's setup, halfheartedly planning to fix the place up later. Salisbury is in the northwest corner of the state, where Connecticut abuts both Massachusetts and New York. After a lot of looking around, Chase had picked the spot because of the beauty of the Berkshire foothills, and because it was still an area of undeveloped countryside, where people in the neat little colonial town nearby minded their own business and were relatively unconcerned with what was happening outside their immediate surroundings.

The one big problem was the house. He had never gone ahead and finished the repairs to the house as he had planned. The roof leaked, the heating system was wood-burning, there were broken windows, and the whole place was overgrown with weeds. But it was, he decided, even in these extraordinary circumstances, safe. A year's supply of canned and dehydrated food was stored there, so while the fare might be boring, at least no one would starve. The thought of asking Darcie to cope with the discomfort and primitiveness of the place (it had no inside plumbing; the contractor commissioned to install it had simply never shown up) appalled him. Turning on the electricity would involve too many outside people; they would have to do without that as well. Chase cursed for not having followed through on the house more aggressively.

As he sat swearing at himself, two problems simultaneously solved themselves in Chase's mind. He had felt that once Darcie got moved into her beloved home in East Dennis, it would be cruel to ask her to leave it for the shambles of the house in Salisbury. But what if they never *went* to Darcie's house in Dennis? Stored in its garage, he knew, was a portable generator on a trailer he could hitch behind the station wagon. If he went out to Dennis tonight, hitched up the generator and its trailer, he could keep Darcie from ever setting foot in the place at the same time as he provided the Salisbury house with a supply of electricity independent of the electric company.

It made sense. And it would spare Darcie yet another wrench.

Writing a note and sticking it in the mirror over the dresser, Chase climbed into the station wagon and headed for East Dennis. He had thought of bringing Brannigan along, but had no idea of how to get hold of him or even too clear a picture of where he was holed up for the night.

Traffic was nonexistent and the sky was clear, with a brilliant scattering of stars thrown across the crisp October heavens. When he finally reached the house, perhaps three-quarters of an hour later, he put out his headlights and drove into the driveway blind. The place was surrounded by a peaceful silence, broken only by the sound of gentle waves washing the shore. Out in the small gray-shingled shed to one side of the house, he found the generator; it would be easy to attach its trailer to the Ford. On his way back to the car, something—an instinct, a feeling, a small flash of light moving behind one of the windows—stopped him. He stood stock still and waited. The flicker of light appeared again, then vanished.

Chase tried the door; it was locked. Silently he pulled the house key from his pocket and slipped it into the lock, turned it, and softly opened the door. He could hear nothing. Quietly, Chase went back, reached into the rear of the Ford, and reentered the house, carrying the shotgun, still wrapped in its blanket, under his arm. There was no sound of movement, nothing to indicate anyone's presence. Cautiously he searched the kitchen, the dining room, and the living room; no one was there. It was only when he opened the door to the library, a spacious room overlooking Nantucket Sound, that he finally discovered the source of the light. Directly opposite the door was a large bay window with a handsome Early American desk facing outward from it. As he moved into the room, someone behind the desk turned on a flashlight so that the beam hit Chase directly in the eyes.

"Well, now, Mr. Chase. I figured you might just turn up here. Yessir, I did."

The Maine twang fell upon Chase's ears as unpleasantly as ever. But with it, a great feeling of relief swept across Chase: this was no prowler, just Mort Evers, probably going from one of the Wetherill places to another, making sure that all the empty ones were locked up and made fast against the uprisings.

"Oh, Mort, it's you," Chase said with a small laugh of relief. "I wasn't sure, but I thought someone was inside, and with all that's going on, I didn't know who I might find."

"Yep, just old Mort."

The light continued to shine in Chase's eyes, which made him blink hard. Abruptly, his sudden feeling of relief disappeared, replaced by a hard sinking shock. Visible in the pale circle of light the flashlight spilled onto the desk itself were a couple of objects that took Chase's breath away: the dim, barely recognizable stripes of a red-and-white armband, and, beside it, the ice blue of a forty-five.

"I don't think that you should have killed that man out by the airport, Mr. Chase," began Evers, his fingers inching their way across the desk top toward the revolver.

The twin blasts from Chase's 12-gauge shotgun blew most of Evers' head away and sent it splattering through the leaded casement windows of the window beyond into the waters of Nantucket Bay.

Chapter Six

*For the first time since my marriage, I'm
watching every penny I spend. For
Christmas, I bought only practical gifts.
We made all our own Christmas tree
decorations this year and we had smoked
salmon instead of caviar.*

—*Countess Isabelle D'Ornano,
"W," January 1, 1975*

The headlights of the car cut through the early dawn
fog with a bleak and resentful glare. In spite of the light
traffic all the way, Chase Wetherill and his family didn't
arrive at Salisbury until almost seven in the morning. And
even this required driving far faster than Chase cared to.

But after his encounter with Mort Evers at Dennis,
Chase decided he could not afford the luxury of waiting
until morning to leave. At this point, he had no idea how
far the CAC's arm might reach, and no way of knowing
how many of their men had known that Evers was laying
for him at Darcie's house. Thus, he could only guess at
how long it might be before Evers' body was discovered
and the alarm sounded. Waiting until morning and driving
across Massachusetts in broad daylight struck him as too
dangerous.

Chase awoke an exhausted Emlyn and a resentful
Raven from their sleep, hurried them into their clothes,
shoved them grumbling into the car, and drove to the
other motel where Darcie and Jeremy were.

As quietly as he could manage, Chase found her room
and rapped softly. There was no answer. Further gentle
knocking still produced no response. Finally, Emlyn asked
his father for a credit card, slipped it into the crack between the door and the frame, and pressed it once or

twice. After a rapid up-and-down sliding motion, the card struck something that slid back on the locked bolt, and the door swung open.

Emlyn looked at Chase, his face a mixture of pride and guilt. "Old housebreaker's trick. It always works unless the lock is a deadbolt job." Emlyn's study of his father's baffled expression apparently was less than reassuring. "I read about it somewhere," he explained.

"I don't give a damn if you took lessons from Willie Sutton. It worked."

Without making a sound, the three of them slipped into Darcie's room. "Put your hand over Jeremy's mouth, Raven, and I'll take care of your mother. We don't want anyone to panic and start yelling."

Darcie sat bolt upright, eyes staring with terror, unable, in the blackness, to see who had clamped a hand over her mouth; Chase's urgent whispering in her ear took a moment or two to sink in. Jeremy thrashed violently the second Raven's hand first touched him, but with the mystic communion the twins had always shared, knew whose hand it was even before Raven had a chance to speak.

Quietly, Chase explained the situation, although omitting any reference to the shooting of Mort Evers.

"What about Brannigan?" asked Emlyn. "We don't even know where he's staying."

That had bothered Chase ever since he had decided they would have to take off earlier than they planned. He realized that scouring the flophouses of a sleeping town for Brannigan could only draw attention to them. The conclusion was inescapable: prudent logic demanded they desert Brannigan. Brannigan knew where the house in Salisbury was, and he could make his way there on his own. But Darcie solved the nagging of Chase's conscience. "Don't worry, Emlyn. Brannigan told me where he would be— just before he took off. He was afraid something might happen and I'd need him. He's at someplace called 'The Bogs.' "

A little driving up and down the streets of Hanson's poorer neighborhood revealed Brannigan's lodging: a non-descript, unevenly shingled old house with a flickering neon sign hanging in a flyspecked front window, "The Bogs—Transients and Permanent Guests Welcome," the sign proclaimed in a sickly purple flicker.

Chase looked at the building with a dour expression.

"We don't know how to get in, or even what room Brannigan's got once we do. As for getting him out without waking anybody . . . well, I don't know. The whole town could hear us."

"There's one window open in front," noted Raven.

"And the Brannigan always liked to sleep in a cold room," added Jeremy. "He said it reminded him of home."

"The Red Zoomer!" they both suddenly hissed in unison.

Raven ran back to the car, and came back a moment later with a bright red Frisbee. With a lot of whispered advice and encouragement from Jeremy, Raven took careful aim and sailed the Frisbee cleanly through the open bottom half of the window. A small crash was followed by a grunt and the cautious appearance of Brannigan's head in the window. Frantic pantomime indicated to Brannigan that he had to leave, unheard and unseen. For a second he stared at the group on the lawn. Then, after a single nod of his head, he simultaneously waved his hand and disappeared from the window.

Five minutes later all five of them were in the car and headed for Salisbury.

The pale light of an October sun, chill and mist-laden, did little to improve the grim appearance of the house in Salisbury. In front the grass was tall and overgrown, and the long private road little more than rutted gravel. The building itself, an old Federal-style manor house built in the eighteen hundreds, looked bleak and forlorn; there was a noticeable sag in the middle of the roof and the windows were black and forbidding.

"Well, this is it. Home. For a while, anyway." The false note of enthusiasm in Chase's voice made Darcie unable to resist a sideways glance of despair. For the sake of the children, she stifled her usual directness. The twins did not.

"It looks like it . . ."

". . . might fall down."

Emlyn had said nothing. He sat still for a moment, studying the place, but quickly disappeared around the side of the house to explore.

Even Brannigan's perennial optimism had a muted note to it. "Lot of good life left in that house. Built back when people cared. I been all through it, y'understand, when I was laying in the stores. Very solid, it is."

"Does the plumbing work?" Darcie, as usual, asked the one question no one wanted her to.

"Strictly speaking, there isn't any." Chase laid the facts out for her. "There's an outhouse, of course. In back, not too far. And after a while, well, maybe we can figure out something for inside. If the generator works, we'll have a semblance of electricity. First, we have to rig some way for running water and heat."

Darcie took this string of small shocks with apparent calm, although her lips were pressed tightly together when she finally spoke. "Well, we'd better start moving things inside. The footlocker first, I think. The bed linen's in it. I mean, there *are* beds?"

Her question had just enough hint of dry humor that Chase smiled. "I can't vouch for them, but, yes, there are beds." Leaning over, Chase took both of Darcie's forearms in his hand and squeezed them in appreciation.

"Five beds to make," said Darcie with exaggerated resignation. Then it struck her that she had forgotten that one of the family wasn't with them. Her face turned grave. "I mean four beds." She turned toward Chase with a suddenly stricken look. "Oh, Chase, dammit, what are we going to do about Dina?"

"She'll turn up. Don't worry. It may take a little time, but she'll turn up." Chase spoke firmly, wishing he felt as confident as he sounded.

From around the other side of the house, Emlyn arrived, flushed and excited. "Dad, there's an old greenhouse out behind. Some of the glass is gone, but that's easy to fix. With fluorescent lighting and hydroponics we could grow stuff all year. Also, there's a stream and an old grist mill, and maybe—"

"Frisbeeeeee!" screamed the twins for no reason, and dashed off in the direction Emlyn had come from, tossing the bright-red plastic disc back and forth between them.

Darcie sighed. "I wonder if Maggie Rudkin started this way." A suddenly plaintive expression crossed her face as she turned toward her husband. "Oh, God, Chase, but I hope all this is really necessary."

Chase, who knew it was not only necessary but critical to their survival, kissed her lightly and led her up the uneven front steps and through the sagging doorway of their new home. As they entered, they could hear the scurry of terrified mice heading for their dark hiding places inside the walls.

Darcie thought she knew exactly how they felt.

The *Whim III* pulled into Hamilton's unreal, pastel-hued harbor at about noontime, some twenty-four hours after leaving Sail Island. Nothing there had changed since Moira had last visited Bermuda: the neat pale-pink houses with their blinding white roofs, built of crushed coral shell and looking like shallow unfinished pyramids, still ringed the harbor like colorful toys; the water and the sky were the rich, fantasy blue of old Kodachromes. The small yachts scurried back and forth across the bay, manned by young men and women, their blond hair in sharp relief to immorally bronzed skins. Everything was the same, yet everything was different.

Moira felt a sudden catch at her heart, remembering the last time they had been here, with Dudley insisting on running up the pennants and calling orders to the crew and laughing like a schoolboy. Today, only one flag fluttered from the spar of the small, raked mast on the flying bridge—the required yellow quarantine flag to notify Her Majesty's Officers of the Port that a foreign vessel was coming into its waters. Moira was wearing a light dress and her head was wrapped in a colorful scarf to keep her hair in place; her only concession to grief was a pair of dark glasses dredged up from somewhere below by the steward to hide the swollen eyes.

"There it is, Cap'n, over there, by Wharf Two," she heard seaman Jenkins call to Struthers. A gleaming white ambulance with a huge red cross waited for them at dockside. Seaman White was still alive. Struthers had radiophoned ahead that he had a badly injured man aboard. The authorities in Bermuda had said they would expedite clearance for the sailor, although there seemed to be some hesitation concerning the rest of the party aboard; American ships fell into a doubtful category, at the moment. Unless she could get off the islands, Moira figured so did her future.

Climbing to the narrow deck closest to the slip, Moira watched them carry White in a wire-basket stretcher up and onto the pier. She had wanted to say something reassuring to him, but could see that his eyes were closed again; instead she settled for brushing a lock of hair away from his face.

From the dock, Moira heard a familiar, unnerving flapping sound, the flap of a halyard on a flagpole striking the wood in the brisk breeze. Looking up, she could see the Union Jack flapping brightly in the sun, and her eyes squinted for a moment to study it. Her face twisted into a mask of pain: this place, the semi-tropical sun, the blinding blueness of the water, all had too many terrifying recollections of Sail.

Moving toward Struthers and an officer in a British Navy uniform standing on the foredeck, she ignored the salute the officer gave her and addressed Struthers directly. "I'm going ashore, Captain. There are some things I need. I'll be back shortly." She paused, then: "And you'd better get some sleep. You must be exhausted."

Both Struthers and the British officer hesitated, as if each of them were about to say something but was waiting for the other to start speaking first. She used their confusion to barge past them and strode down the gangway, this time acknowledging with a curt nod the British officer's uncertain but automatic salute.

Firmly, she strode across Paget Place, where an ebony black policeman in a gleaming white uniform directed traffic beneath a striped umbrella, and reached the sidewalk on the opposite corner. She looked farther down the street, past Trimingham's, thought she saw the building she wanted, and walked toward it. For Moira Cantrell had no intention of returning to the *Whim* shortly. Or, for that matter, ever. Earlier that morning, she had opened the wall safe in their cabin to check the supply of cash always kept on board. Looking inside, she was reassured to see stacks of American bills and foreign currency as well as the letter of credit she maintained at Trustbank. Carefully, she stuffed the letter of credit and as much cash as she could carry into an ample white-and-gold beach bag; the rest of the cash she hid in one of the lockers. Just before she left Bermuda, she would call the ship and tell Struthers where it was and instruct him to pay off the crew and himself. The *Whim* itself would be her parting present to Struthers. For herself, she never wanted to see or hear of it again. Or of Sail. Or of Bermuda.

Inside the British Airways office, she marched up to the counter and asked the attendant, a nice-looking young

man in a pale-blue uniform, when the earliest flight could
be arranged for Switzerland. She supposed she would have
to go via London, Moira noted, but that really didn't matter; her most urgent request was to leave Bermuda as soon
as possible.

The attendant appeared rattled. To Moira he looked
very young. Pulling something from beneath the counter,
he hid behind an unfolded flight schedule. "We have a
midafternoon flight to London today"—he turned the
schedule slightly to make reading a footnote easier—"and
from there, we have a direct flight to Geneva. You did say
Geneva, didn't you?" Moira hadn't, but let the point pass
with a nod. The attendant plunged back into the flight
schedule. "To Geneva one and a half hours later," he finished breathlessly.

"Fine. First class, if you have a seat. This time of year
you certainly should have plenty."

A form was produced and the young man began writing, then paused and straightened up. "Your passport is
U.S.?"

It was Moira's turn to appear rattled. Her passport.
How could she have been so stupid? Obviously, she
couldn't fly to London without one. The attendant was
staring at her with an embarrassed expression; his question
had been so simple.

"I don't have it with me. It's on its way here."

"On its way?"

"From the States. When I left, I hadn't really expected
to be going on through to London from here. It should arrive . . ." Moira quickly estimated how long it would take
to buy a forgery here in Bermuda. She wasn't used to such
trafficking, but there were crooks almost everywhere, and
no reason the pastel-pink landscape of the island should
exempt Bermuda. "It should arrive the day after tomorrow."

The attendant turned the form Moira had begun filling
out so that he could read her name. "Well, Mrs. Cantrell,
you see—that is—company policy, you understand—but
the fact is, I can't even make your reservation until I have
proof of citizenship. The passport. This afternoon, obviously—I mean, it's silly, but—this afternoon will be impossible."

Moira had known where he was heading long before the
attendant had begun to fumble his way through the ex-

planation. Part of her longed to beat her fists on the counter and lecture this ineffective employee of a subsidized airline for trampling on something as sacrosanct as her right to go anywhere she chose, anytime she choose. But she knew she had to be sensible. What had happened on Sail Island had happened, at least partially, because of events on the mainland. And if this was true, how long would it be before the infection spread to Bermuda? No, escaping from these terrible islands to Switzerland was too desperately critical a step to jeopardize by putting the young man in his place.

"I see," said Moira calmly. "Well, the passport will be here roughly the day after tomorrow; I'll come back." She delivered her most gracious smile, turned on her heel, and walked back out into the blinding sunshine.

Moira had no clear plan how to go about finding the criminal element in Bermuda. Struthers could probably have accomplished it easily for her, but Moira was determined not to return to the boat and was already planning which hotel to have herself taken to. And a forged passport wasn't something you asked about at a hotel desk.

The idea hit her. A pawnshop. Even Bermuda must have pawnshops, and a pawnshop was the next thing to stolen goods, which were first cousins of thieves, extortionists and forgers. Automatically, she patted the beach bag, which beside cash, held a good deal of her summer jewelry.

Somewhere in that collection of diamonds, emeralds and platinum lay the key to her getting to Europe, and the more she thought about it, the more convinced she was that getting to Europe was the key to her survival.

In a small wooden structure, weatherbeaten, perched unevenly above the water on sagging stilts, and not far from the docks of Hamilton, Moira Wetherill Cantrell finally found a hock shop. The place was dirty and smelled of a sweet, cloying odor Moira could not identify. From ceiling to floor, the walls and cases were lined with unreclaimed items, each one carrying a small tag with its price. The items were almost all personal: guitars, fishing equipment, record players, radios, tennis rackets, snorkling equipment, an outboard motor, cameras, television sets, costume jewelry, a bust of Queen Elizabeth (carved out of coral and commemorating her 1975 visit), dinner trays, breakfast trays, tea trays, hors d'oeuvre trays, trays to carry trays—all of them a pathetic reflection of the private misery of others. Moira peered closely, trying to see if any real jewelry was displayed. Perhaps such items were kept in back.

A polite cough caused her to turn and face the store's owner. He was not Jewish, as she had expected from her literary knowledge of pawnbrokers, but a tall elegant mulatto. "May I be of help, ma'am?" His voice was deep and rich.

Moira felt her confidence crumbling. The man was too polite and too elegant even to despise, something which would have made the situation much easier for her. "Well, I don't know. That is—I've never met a man in your profession before."

The pawnbroker's face never changed expression. "Of course, ma'am. The process is really quite simple. I wish I could say it was entirely painless, but only people with a difficulty of some variety come here. As with a doctor, I am not necessary until something goes wrong. Then I am very necessary indeed." His laugh was gentle and friendly, presumptuous perhaps, but in no way unkind. Moira relaxed. Then, she remembered that the islanders on Sail Island used to smile, too, and shuddered.

With a look of determined impatience, Moira faced the man: "You see, because of the situation at home . . ."

"You are not the first American lady in here today, ma'am, if that's of any comfort to you."

Moira felt irritated that this man was lumping her with tourists, gamblers and drifters, out of funds and peddling a watch to buy a meal. "I have some items of jewelry here," she announced quickly. "I was wondering if you could tell me how much you would buy—pawn, I should say—them for."

The pawnbroker took up position behind a small glass counter equipped with a strong light and various jeweler's tools. "Certainly."

Down on the counter went the Patek-Philippe watch, its face surrounded by almost ten carats of oblong diamonds and topped by a large square-cut emerald. The pawnbroker watched in awe as Moira reached into her purse and added the Schlumberger canary diamond ear clips, the Clafin diamond and sapphire pin, the Oriental ruby pendant on its chain of alternating diamonds and emeralds, and went back into her bag to start piling platinum and jeweled bracelets, arm bands, gold chains, and random brooches on top.

"Ma'am," he said in a near whisper. "Enough, ma'am. Too much, ma'am. This is a small concern." Nervously his fingers brushed across the mound of jewels. As if in automatic response, he put the jeweler's loupe to his eye and gave cursory inspection to the smallest piece of the diamond work he could find.

Inside Moira, something wrenched as she saw her possessions piled there, a pathetic monument to the world's lack of social order.

With a small sigh, the jeweler removed the loupe, surveyed the pile again, and looked at Moira. "Ma'am, exactly how much money is it that you need?"

For a second, Moira stared at the man with a blank expression. The idea of "needing" money was so foreign to her that putting a value on the need had simply not occurred to her. "Well . . ." Blinking a little, she surveyed the heap of Harry Winston.

"Ma'am," said the pawnbroker quickly. "Please understand, you have offered me such valuable items I can't possibly handle anything but one of the smallest pieces. Therefore I need to know the minimum figure your requirements demand, and, perhaps then, we can reach some accommodation for you."

"Well," she repeated. "I could probably scrape by with a thousand—until my money comes from Switzerland."

"A thousand," said the pawnbroker sadly. "I am not sure I have even that much money to my name."

"Seven-fifty." Moira spoke the words quickly—with an evident note of pride. She was getting the drift of the game now; it was like an auction in reverse.

With one finger the man poked around in the pile, finally spotting and withdrawing the most modest item he could find: a heavy gold wristband set with a large single tourmaline. Moira watched as the pawnbroker examined the piece. "I realize, ma'am, this is worth far more than that," he said, "but it is the best I can do."

"Sold." The pawnbroker had looked at her with a small expression of bewilderment. Moira wasn't sure the word was right, but it did end the transaction.

Neatly, the pawnbroker tied a small tag to it, accepting without question the patently spurious name Moira gave him. He was just beginning to wrap the wristband in green felt when Moira stopped him. "Actually," she began, "there is something else you can do for me. Something that would mean you could forget 'keeping' the wristband for me completely. It would become"—Moira groped for a delicate word, but could only come up with the obvious—"well, it would become a gift. And I might even add this." Moira fished through the pile and withdrew the Claffin diamond and sapphire pin: "For good measure."

The over-large head of the mulatto pawnbroker raised itself slowly, his eyes locked with Moira's, suddenly expressionless and unmoving. "This thing you wish me to do for you. This favor. I am to presume, ma'am, it is illegal?"

Moira nodded, feeling a sudden prickling in her skin. "I suppose. That is—you see—I need, well, I want an American passport. Mine got lost somehow and I don't want to go through all the red tape and—"

The pawnbroker sighed, holding up his hands with the fingertips raised delicately to stop her. "You have a picture of yourself, ma'am, of the right size."

"No. But I can get one taken."

"Please, ma'am. I will arrange that." He looked at her suddenly. "No extra charge. I would just prefer it that way, ma'am."

"Very well." She managed a smile, although the smile had one meaning to her and another to the pawnbroker.

"Please, if you would be so kind, ma'am, as to be here at five this afternoon. The process will take about two days."

"Fine. And thank you."

The man bowed slightly, his smile small and wistful. "I trust the lady will come upon better times."

With a sweeping gesture, Moira shoved the rest of the pile over the edge of the counter back into her bag. The solid clunk the jewelry made was embarrassing, and Moira tried to cover the sound with a small laugh. "Thank you very much," she repeated. She wanted to say more, to tell him how he had, in some strange way, given her back her dignity. But the door behind her opened and a sun-tanned young man, dressed in ragged cut-off shorts and dragging a worn-looking surf-casting rod behind him, barged in and slammed it on the counter with a defensive stare. The rod's end almost poked Moira in the face and she had to duck.

"How much, Uncle?" demanded the youth in the remnants of a British accent.

"Be careful how you wave that thing around," shouted the pawnbroker at him. "Can't you see a lady is trying to get past?" He shoved the pole away from Moira, smiled, and bowed to her again.

Moira left. Unlike those of the natives of Sail, the pawnbroker's smile seemed genuine.

Two days later, convinced that it would be spotted, Moira Wetherill Cantrell hesitantly presented her forged passport to the emigration officer at the Bermuda airport. He barely glanced at it. And after a few questions to determine that she planned no protracted stay in the U.K., the British officer stamped the passport perfunctorily and waved Moira through into the debarkation area. An attendant from British Airways quickly took her in charge and escorted her to the First Class Lounge, which appeared deserted except for a man and his wife about Moira's age.

Gratefully, Moira slumped into one of the lounge's overstuffed chairs, her bag of jewelry resting in her lap. It had been a nervous few moments. Moira was not used to having to deal with bogus documents. While the passport had looked right enough to her—stamped with the raised seal of the United States across the somewhat dowdy-looking picture of her—she had had no idea what might be wrong with it in the eyes of the emigration man. The pawnbroker had nothing to lose if the document was an extremely poor forgery; he could simply deny Moira's story that he had provided it and that would be the end of that. But the passport had worked and Moira felt reassured enough to order herself a scotch and water.

Across from her, a couple sat in their chairs, only occasionally even bothering to look at her; they appeared deep in conversation. The husband was prematurely paunchy, with an unusually red face and the air of a Rotary Club activist about him. His wife was a long string of a woman, sharp-faced with harlequin glasses that pegged her as a woman trying to appear sophisticated but not making it. Glancing up from a copy of the *Bermudian*, the man smiled at Moira and appeared on the edge of attempting a conversation. Moira contrived to become intensely interested in the contents of her beach bag. The people opposite her seemed about as innocent as it was possible to be, but so many things had happened in her life lately that she was automatically suspicious of anyone and everyone.

The first call for the flight was announced at 2:12 p.m., and Moira rose to her feet and began advancing toward the check-in counter. Dr. and Mrs. Clemson—Moira had heard one of the airline attendants call them that—stood up as well, moving toward the same desk at an angle, still talking to each other in soft tones. Moira, her bogus passport in one hand, the beach bag full of diamonds in the other, quickened her pace; she was determined to get on board first. Dr. Clemson appeared to sense her urgency, and nodded for her to go ahead of him. Ida Clemson found herself with her husband's arm suddenly holding her back: she looked up and tried to see what was slowing them down. As she did, her left heel appeared to catch on a loose edge of the boarding carpet, and she fell into Moira while struggling to maintain her balance. In the process, Ida's flailing arm knocked the passport, the ticket and the other papers out of Moira's hand. Apologizing profusely, the woman steadied herself by holding onto Moira's wrist, while her husband Dr. Clemson was scrambling to retrieve the scattered papers and passport, handing them back to Moira and laughing at his wife's clumsiness.

"Ida, if I've told you once about those damned skyscraper heels of yours, I've told you a thousand times. It's not as if you were short or something."

But Ida Clemson was too busy with her apology to Moira to even listen. "I'm so sorry. That rug. I don't know why they haven't fixed a thing like that. Someone could get hurt and sue."

"It's all right," Moira assured her. "Perfectly all right. I know how those heels can be." But something was happening to Moira she didn't understand at all. The lounge, the apologetic woman standing on one foot and clutching her arm, the officers at the entrance gate, seemed suddenly to grow very, very far away. A strange roaring filled her ears, and the room began to slant beneath her feet. She tried to scream, but while her mouth could open and her tongue move, no sound was produced. Through a moving blur, Ida's face smiled at her.

Instead of Moira, it was Ida who screamed, yelling for her husband to catch Moira quickly. Moira never saw the crowd that gathered around her, never heard the hastily summoned "Dr." Clemson talk about a presumed "cardiovascular accident," never felt herself being carried to a waiting car so that she could be sped to a hospital it was not planned that she would ever reach.

Chapter Seven

According to popular myth, both American blacks and
Irishmen are supposed to be born with naturally splendid
voices. Since Brannigan was an equal mixture of the two,
his voice should have been magnificent. It wasn't. He had
no difficulty in carrying a tune, but his voice had a strange
sound to it—guttural and piercing at the same time, as if
the late Senator Everett Dirkson's vocal cords had been
grafted onto those of a boy soprano's. In fact, the most
that could be said of Brannigan's voice was that it was
filled with enthusiasm and could, when he felt happy, be
loud—very loud. Today, Brannigan felt happy.

"Oh, the strangers came and tried to teach us their ways,
But their ways are no better than ours are,
And you might as well go chasing after moonbeams,
—or try light a penny candle from a star."

Driving down U.S. 8 on the way home from a shopping
expedition in Millerton, he sang as he pushed the Ford
along the brilliantly sunny, smooth surface of the highway.

134

Since he was alone, all eight verses of "Galway Bay" had been completed without anyone pleading for him to stop. They had been in Salisbury almost ten days, but the sky was still a clear October blue, the trees were in their most garish stage of red and yellows, and Brannigan felt at peace with the world. As he was later to reflect, his state of mind may have been tempting fate.

He felt so at peace that he barely noticed the sudden confusion of cars ahead of him, and came close to bar- reling into something before he realized what was causing the backup. A little ahead, he could make out that a road- block of sorts had been thrown across the highway; it was manned by men wearing the bright red-and-white arm bands he remembered all too well from Long Island City. Fear seized Brannigan. Each car was being searched and the drivers were being examined, their drivers licenses in- spected, their license tags checked. Even if he weren't a fugitive, Brannigan could never survive this checking process. He was driving a stolen car, whose front and back license plates did not jibe; the car registration was made out to some unknown woman in Port Chester; and he was black, which would automatically subject him to particu- larly hard scrutiny. On top of this, he suspected his own name, neatly typed on his driver's license, must be on some sort of list. By now, the CAC would surely know his name, what he looked like, his background, and whom he worked for.

Slowing the car so abruptly he could hear a small scream as the tire treads gripped the road's surface, Bran- nigan checked the rear mirror to see what was behind him: more cars like his, all suddenly putting on the brakes and reluctantly forcing themselves into a ragged line to go through the inspection point ahead. If he were to make a U-turn on the highway and begin heading in the opposite direction, he would immediately be labeled as someone who didn't dare show his face at the roadblock and pursuit would follow swiftly; staying in line would force him to go through the checkpoint and therefore be equally disas- trous.

A little ahead and to the left, Brannigan could see a small dirt road leading up the side of one of the surround- ing hills before it disappeared into the shallow valley be- tween them. With luck, this road would bring him out where he could get back to Salisbury without running the

CAC road barrier. Brannigan took the only chance he figured he had. Blowing his horn and waving his arm out the window to show he wanted to turn off to the left, Brannigan tried to make the cars ahead give him enough room to pull out of line. Everyone turned to stare at the car reckless enough to blow its horn in defiance of the roadblock: at the checkpoint; the men with the arm bands themselves looked up and studied him. Slowly, the cars ahead edged themselves over the the far right of the road, and Brannigan, swearing, yelling, and wearing an expression of high indignation, drove past them directly toward the checkpoint, then slowly began to turn up the dirt road, as if that had been his destination all along.

At the checkpoint, Brannigan could make out a good deal of confused activity. Men behind the barrier were running around and pointing, but as yet, there apparently was no decision made to chase him. For a moment, Brannigan thought he had gotten away with his ruse, and started to slow the car to avoid further bouncing on the rutted road surface.

"Halt!" commanded a sudden voice. "Stop that damned car. Halt, or I shoot." In the dead center of the narrow road loomed a man, his rifle held at the ready, his legs spread slightly apart. That he happened to be there at all, Brannigan could see, was by accident, not design. For at the base of a tree near the road stood the remains of a picnic—a thermos bottle, a lunch box, and the inevitable crumpled paper. The man, wearing a CAC arm band, had been taking his luncheon break when Brannigan turned up his road, and attracted by the noises from below, he had seen him coming and taken up his position.

Brannigan made the only choice he could. Pressing his foot hard on the accelerator, he gunned the station wagon. The wheels spun for a second in the dirt, then caught, and the car surged forward, straight at the man with the rifle. The sentry was either surprised, inexperienced, or both. Trying to get out of the way, he fell over backward as the car roared past him. Although shaken, he recovered quickly. The first shot was into the air; the next two were straight at Brannigan's receding rear window, and Brannigan could hear the glass shatter, the whine of bullets and the thunk of other shots plunging into the car. Driving as fast as the miserable state of he road allowed, Brannigan could only see a little of what was now going on at the

roadblock. Two jeeps, their red lights flashing, were barreling around the roadblock, but were slowed by the traffic
jam their own roadblock had caused. Then Brannigan lost
sight of the checkpoint entirely as the narrow road took a
sudden turn to the right around one of the hills.

He was on a small plain, a sudden flat surface between
the hills, and began looking around for someplace to hide
himself and the car. He could not hope to outrun those
jeeps on this kind of road in a station wagon. On the rise
of a small hill to the left, he saw a farmer on his tractor.
The man had stopped, and was looking from roadblock to
Brannigan and back. Just below the slope was a barn, its
wide doors open. Brannigan stopped his station wagon
twenty feet from the farmer. For a second, their eyes
locked. The man shrugged slightly but showed no other
expression. Then Brannigan quickly drove into the barn
and pulled the doors shut behind him. From outside, he
could hear the tractor begin moving again and pressed his
eye to a wide crack in the weathered boards to look out.
The farmer's tractor was turning the ground over for the
winter: the man appeared absorbed in his work and
largely indifferent to what might be going on around him.
A few minutes later, the two jeeps, full of men with rifles,
ground to a halt on the dirt road, and Brannigan could see
the farmer being questioned about him.

His heart pounded and he felt the adrenalin race
through his body, wondering if the farmer might not simply raise his finger and point toward the barn. A sudden
noise from above him made Brannigan nearly climb out of
his skin. His eyes, growing used to the darkness, could see
a barn owl, its enigmatic eyes saucerlike, perched on a
beam and staring down at him. It gave a low cry, ruffled
its feathers again, looking through rather than at Brannigan, in its ceaseless search for rats or mice. The owl
gave its cry again.

Outside, the CAC men were all shouting at the same
time, waving their arms. The farmer raised his arms a couple of times in a gesture of "I don't know," and then finally, as if giving evidence against his will, raised one arm
and pointed down the dirt road. The motors roared and
the jeeps tore off, the men in back struggling against the
bad jouncing the road was giving them.

Brannigan waited, his heart still pounding. From behind
him, there was a sudden whoosh of air and the small

strangled squeak of a mouse as the owl pounced on it, returning to its beam with the creature in its beak. Brannigan could see the mouse struggle, then disappear whole inside the owl. About five minutes later, he heard the roar of the jeeps returning and watched them roar past him down the road toward the roadblock.

Pushing open the doors, Brannigan backed out the station wagon. The farmer was still on his tractor, the blades of the harrow turning over rows of earth as it made its way across the field. Brannigan began driving down the road away from the checkpoint, but stopped the car and leaned out his window to speak to the man, who continued his harrowing. He was still close enough to the road, however, to hear Brannigan shouting at him. With impatience, the farmer throttled back the tractor to hear him.

"Thanks. I don't know what else to say. But sweet mother of Jesus, thanks."

For a second, their eyes again locked. Then the farmer, still expressionless, shrugged noncommitally and returned to his harrowing.

Brannigan drove slowly down the road until he reached Connecticut 186, which would take him around the checkpoint, back to Salisbury. There was a lot to do. New license plates would have to be stolen. Ideally, a new car, too. But it would probably be safer to paint this one; perhaps Emlyn could figure a way to do that. And Chase would have to be told. Brannigan squirmed. Chase had warned him to stay off the main routes, and Brannigan hadn't. Beyond that, Brannigan knew Chase was worried sick about Dina, was worried about their safety at the farm, was concerned about his brothers, his father and the whole family. With a sigh, Brannigan decided to tell him about the road blocks casually, to work it into some other conversation, eliminating his own close call from the story. That way, Chase would get the information without having too much new to worry about.

Slowly, Chase climbed back up the ladder with some shingles tied to his back, followed by Brannigan. Although the day was a chilly one, both men were sweating. On Brannigan's black skin the perspiration glistened; on Chase, it was lost in a two-day growth of whiskers, and the beaded sweat caused him to look even grubbier than he felt. For most of the day, Chase and Brannigan had been shingling the leakiest parts of the roof. Only about a third of the job was finished, but Chase's whole body ached from the effects of muscles long unused being pressed into service. Although his body ached, he found himself tremendously proud of the slow, steady progress of new shingles across the roof.

Brannigan's reaction was more of a practical sort. "Yerra, no wonder we Irish love thatched roofs. They're easier on a man's back." Two days had passed since his confrontation with the CAC roadblock and he had yet to tell Chase of it; one excuse after another had so far spared Brannigan the inevitable.

Chase surveyed the shrinking supply of shingles. "We'd better pick up some more of those, Brannigan. This roof is bigger than I thought."

Brannigan, who so far had done all of the shopping in nearby towns like Sharon, Amenia and Lakeville, appeared to hesitate, as if he wanted to brush the suggestion aside with some irreverent comment, but couldn't. He hammered for a second, then stopped and sighed, his face wearing an unaccustomed look of solemnity. "Picking things up around here is getting a mite troublesome, Mr. Wetherill." Raising the hammer, he turned back to his work, then stopped once more, staring at the shingle he had just nailed down. "Roadblocks, don't you see."

"Roadblocks?"

"Connecticut 7 and U.S. 8. More checkpoints than roadblocks really, but just as effective. I've found a way around them by using the back roads, but I don't know how long it will be before they think of that themselves."

Chase was staggered. Why such a concentration of roadblocks in a quiet area like Sharon? His immediate reaction was to believe any such flurry of activity must somehow be aimed at his capture, but his sense of logic quickly overcame his growing paranoia. If the CAC even suspected he was in the neighborhood, they would be using far more direct methods to track him down than roadblocks. The only other explanation he could come up with—that a network of such roadblocks existed nationwide—was less easily dismissed. In the end, though, Chase realized that any such undertaking would require so vast a number of people it was improbable at this juncture. He was, then, left with no answer. (Chase could not know that nearby Great Barrington housed the CAC headquarters for the entire Berkshire foothills area, or that the roadblocks springing up around Sharon were in the nature of a test to discover if such a system would ever be feasible countrywide.) Baffled, Chase was seized by a new fear.

"Are they in the towns, too?"

"Not so's you could notice. No one with arm bands, anyway. But they may have someone planted, you know, in each town, keeping his eyes open. Not identified, y'understand, just acting himself. A postman. A shopkeeper. It could be the local doctor or, saints preserve us, the village priest. That's why I try to spread buying things between so many towns now. A black in these parts is as rare as an honest landlord, and a black who is spending a lot of money to boot would be sure to draw attention."

"Well, we'll just have to let Emlyn do some of the shopping, then. Or Darcie. My beard isn't up to hiding behind yet."

Brannigan nodded and they went back to their shingling, Chase pounding in each nail as if it were a personal enemy. The idea that peaceful New England villages like Salisbury and Sharon—particularly Sharon, with its picture-postcard Congregational Church and its chaste rows of white colonial houses—might now be infested with CAC agents and local informers presented an incongruous picture, but one, Chase supposed, that was safer to accept than ignore.

A noise from below made him look down. Emlyn was struggling with some cable, and Chase slid down the ladder, shook himself, and walked over to him. "How are you doing?" Chase paused, then forced an inquisitive smile. "Not that I know *what* you're doing."

"In a couple of days, I'll have us tied into the main cables down on the road. The electric company will never know unless someone goes up that particular pole to repair something. But I'm going to cut a groove into the pole and putty it over, so there's not too much chance of their noticing even then. Once we're on the main circuit, we'll have more juice than we know what to do with."

For a moment Chase stood staring at Emlyn. The image of his son as a lonely child who had immersed himself in mathematics and physics to escape from his peers disappeared as he studied him. Who, Chase wondered, had been escaping from whom? "Goddamn, Emlyn. You're something, really something. I only wish it hadn't taken—oh, hell, you know what I'm getting at, Emlyn." Chase shoved his hands in his pockets.

Emlyn blushed. "I know. And thanks." Without a word, Emlyn went back to fussing with the ends of the cable, his frail shoulders and bespectacled face bent too close to his work, making him look like an elderly Swiss watchmaker.

Tousling Emlyn's hair as he passed him, Chase climbed the uneven front steps into the house. The place was bedlam. Raven and Jeremy were stacking wood for the kitchen stove and the fireplace; the process involved one of them standing at the door and lobbing a log across to the other. The percentage of logs dropped to logs caught was high, but the resulting crash, for some private reason, would leave them both helpless with laughter.

Chase winced as a particularly heavy log slipped from Raven's hands and hit the floor with a thunderous crash. The twins whooped. "Hey!" called Chase, but his voice was lost in their laughter. "Stop it, dammit!" he bellowed: the twins turned toward him as if seeing him for the first time. Shaking his head, Chase continued across the room, "Okay, okay. Just try and keep it down a little, will you? The whole house shakes every time you guys miss one."

Almost the second he stepped through the door into the kitchen, the laughter and the crashing began again. To his surprise, Darcie seemed unperturbed. She was staring intently at the instructions on the back of a package of some dehydrated mix, experimenting with various recipes from the emergency supplies against the day when the stores in town might, as Chase had warned, run out of food to sell. Dipping one finger tentatively into a mixing bowl, she raised it to her mouth to taste the result. Her expression reminded Chase of a little girl who had just been force-fed Pepto-Bismol. With an exaggerated movement of her lips, she wrinkled her nose and turned her startling-wide, childlike eyes toward Chase. "After a couple of days on this stuff, we'd be willing to eat the bark off trees. Like Ewell Gibbons."

Chase struggled with himself and forced a small smile.

"Correction," announced Darcie, taking another taste. "We'd be willing to eat Ewell Gibbons."

Abruptly, Chase changed the subject. "In a couple of days, Emlyn says we'll have all the electricity we can use.

That means we can pick up a shortwave set and find out what's happening. What's really happening, I mean."

No reaction came from Darcie; she was back studying the directions on another package. Chase stifled his irritation. "That Emlyn—well, he's quite a kid."

The light look abruptly disappeared from Darcie's face and she set the bowl down beside the food mix. "So is Dina."

Walking around to her, Chase tried to put his arms protectively around her, but she moved away. "Look, Darcie, I feel just as worried about Dina as you do. But for the moment there's simply nothing we can do. We have to wait and see what happens, review our options and then decide what the best way is—"

Staring straight at Chase, Darcie yanked off the apron. "You've been saying that since she disappeared, and if you don't start doing something about finding Dina pretty fast, I'll do it myself." With one hand to her face, Darcie crumpled the apron into a wad, threw it on the floor, and ran from the room.

Bending down, Chase carefully picked the apron up and folded it into a neat square, gently pressing the fabric on its edges with his hand. Almost tenderly, he put it on one corner of the kitchen table. His new growth of beard itched, and Chase rubbed it. Darcie had struck his most sensitive point. She knew he had no options to review, no plan to follow, that he was helpless to act. And was taking the fact that there was no reasonable course of action out on him. She was, Chase felt, being unfair. In light of what was happening, he was doing the only thing anybody could: nothing. But the frustration of it was monumental.

The anger in him suddenly boiled over. Chase made a fist and slapped it hard against the kitchen wall in frustration. From the other room, the sound of the twins and their deafening wood-stacking irritated him even further, and he found himself hitting the wall a second time. That, he told himself, was stupid. If he was going to hit something, it might as well be a nail into the shingle on the roof. Swearing at himself, he strode out of the room and outside, climbing quickly up the ladder, to join Brannigan in his work.

On the hill behind the farm, a pair of eyes, glued to an inexpensive pair of binoculars, watched Chase walk out of the house, up the ladder, and onto the roof. He was a pale, bespectacled man about fifty-five or sixty, who looked out of place here in the outdoors. Lying flat on his stomach, he had been watching the house below for well over an hour. With a thin smile, he could see that neither of the men on the roof knew much about using nails and hammers, much less shingles, and therefore were probably from a city somewhere. With the built-in snobbery of all rural people, this fact alone was enough to make the observer suspicious. The binoculars focused on the man who had just stormed out of the house and joined the black man on the roof. Through the binoculars Chase's face came sharply into focus, and the observer noted the scraggly growth of whiskers. The black man had been in his store to make small purchases; the white with the scruffy growth, never. Perhaps he was waiting for the beard to grow before he dared show himself. Unquestionably, there was something familiar about his face. Small things, granted, but when added together, perhaps more than passing reasons for suspicion and further investigation. In any case, the activity at this old farm should be reported to his superiors; his bosses would know what to do with the information and might even praise him for his speed in following orders to "report any suspicious newcomers to the immediate area." Carefully, the binoculars were put back into their carrying case and the observer crawled back a few feet, then stood up. His knees creaked, and an expression of pain crossed his face.

His chiefs at the regional CAC headquarters might know what to do about the newcomers, but the man could wish they knew what to do about aging bones and atrophied muscles pressed into their service.

Chapter Eight

Whenever the Vice President and a majority
of the principal officers of the Executive
Departments . . . transmit . . . their
written declaration that the President is
unable to discharge the powers and duties
of his office . . .

> —*Section 4, Article XXV,*
> *Amendments to the Constitution*
> *of the United States*

When the twenty-fifth Amendment to the Constitution became effective, on February 10, 1967, its framers considered they had done a more than thorough job of protecting the country from any possible future state of leaderlessness. Briefly, the amendment provided for the succession of the Vice President to the Presidency in case of death or removal—the word "removal" was the important new addition—and for the appointing of a Vice President by the President, should that office become vacant. At the same time, it provided that the President, should he find himself unable to continue functioning, should notify the Congress and allow the Vice President to act as "'Acting President" until he recovered. Most significantly, remembering the situation of Woodrow Wilson, when the country was for all intents governed by Mrs. Wilson after Wilson became sick, the present amendment allowed the Vice President and a majority of the executive and Cabinet officers to declare the President incapable of functioning, with the Vice President becoming Acting President until the situation was resolved, either by recovery or death.

At the time, no one gave much thought to what might happen if there was no Vice President and an ailing

144

President refused to step down. There was, for instance, no provision for the Speaker of the House to become Acting President. Not much thought was given to this oversight because February 10, 1967, was pre-Watergate. No Vice President had yet been compelled to resign under fire; no President had yet been forced from office.

The framers of the Twenty-fifth Amendment would have considered themselves less thorough if they could have envisioned the summer of 1981. Two months earlier, Samuel DeClerque, a Republican, had been indicted for embezzlement of state funds while Governor of Ohio; the incident would have been of small import except that De-Clerque was Vice President of the United States at the time. Under considerable pressure, he resigned.

President Welby had already begun searching for a new Vice President, pointing out to Congress that the uncertainties of the economy would demand fast action on his final nomination, since to leave the country without a guaranteed succession in the face of domestic crisis was unthinkable. His nominee's name never reached the Congress. On June 20, 1981, President Welby suffered a stroke, and with the perversity common to many stroke victims, flatly refused to resign.

The framers of the amendment would have shuddered. As with most of recent history, the Congress was Democrat, while the Administration was not, and there was considerable support for the President's position among the Republicans in Congress, who now viewed the Presidency as their last stronghold of power. Worse, from the framers' viewpoint, the Supreme Court itself had in recent years become increasingly politicized, and supported Welby's refusal by a five-to-four vote (Associate Justice Tobin Wetherill, vacationing in Europe, was flown back and cast the deciding vote).

The country was in a leaderless stalemate. Welby was never seen in public, but declared himself, through his press secretary, Edward Rombert, to be in a rapidly improving state. His mind, Rombert also added, had never been sharper. Use was returning to his left hand, and the droop on the left side of his face was barely visible any longer. Since no one either heard or saw the President except the men directly around him—all the attempts of the Congressional leadership were rebuffed—there was considerable leeway for rumor.

Too late the few framers of the Twenty-fifth Amendment still alive realized their work had not been thorough in the least, but actually quite shoddy. In the light of these events, few of them would have tried to defend their work; all of them would have been appalled if they had been privy to a telephone call made in Washington on the late afternoon of November 5, 1981.

You could see the man's back, but that was about all. He sat silhouetted against the fading light of late afternoon, swivel chair raked backward, feet propped up on some sort of table behind his desk, watching the peaceful rose colors in which the last sunlight bathed the marble facade of the Capitol Building. The phone was held loosely in his right hand; into this, the man's voice—breathy, deep, almost an actor's voice—spoke with a booming authority.

"Traynor?" it asked. "Tristram Shandy here. Scramble."

A pause followed while a button on the receiver was pressed at each end of the line, and the electronic device—not the classic "scrambler" of World War II vintage, but a computerized voice encoder that made interception or tapping virtually impossible—was brought into action.

"Set? Good. These instructions are urgent and I want no argument about any of them; there isn't time. First of all, to get around the Court decision, Congress is planning a special session after the White House news conference this evening. Talk of impeachment, of course. We can't allow that."

The voice paused. Apparently, in spite of its direction that there was to be no argument, some sort of negative reaction was coming from the other end of the wire. The voice's owner passed his hand over his hair, smoothing it down, in a small show of annoyance. "I'm aware of all that. Now, if you'll just listen . . . Very well, then. Contact our friends in the 'opposition'—Higgins is the top contact—and have him advance his operation in this city. To tonight. And I want it escalated to full scale—the works. The Weimar Torch thing we discussed as an option some weeks ago. Understood?"

Apparently the person at the other end was having considerable difficulty accepting this order. The man using the code name Tristram Shandy, listened for some time, his head nodding up and down mechanically, giving an occasional grunt to indicate that he understood what was being said but didn't necessarily agree. "I'm aware it's difficult. Impress on Higgins that I'm aware of just how difficult it is. But tell him to get it done. Then, have him go to New York—and, well, you know how to handle that matter."

The voice paused again, listening but not agreeing. "Yes, I know. But that's the way those things go. Now, then. At the same time, the full stops should be let out across the country. Tip off the networks. Change from interest to concern. That will require some very fast footwork on everybody's part, but we have no choice. Also, Operation Pull-Plug should be advanced so it is coordinated with all of this. Understood?"

This time there was apparently an outpouring of protests from the other end. The hand was used to smooth down the hair again, this time a little more vigorously, as if patience was growing thin. "I realize all of that. But those instructions are imperative. And immediate. I suggest you get moving right now. We'll be talking"—there was a pause while the voice's owner appeared to consider some facet of what he was saying—"but don't you call me, I'll call you." The pause that followed was filled with an irritating little laugh, an attempt at some humor made by someone not used to the art. "I sound like an agent."

The voice itself seemed to realize the humor wasn't very funny and placed the receiver back on the phone, giving an angry little grunt of impatience. As he turned in his chair to do this, the man's face became visible for the first time. Down the street, Congress would have been infuriated to discover who had held this end of the conversation. Most of the country—if they had recognized the speaker —would have been similarily outraged. The lone member of Congress who had argued in 1967 that the Twenty-fifth Amendment was not comprehensive enough, that there were loopholes in it big enough to drive a truck through, would finally have been justified in his solitary stance.

But all the fury, the outrage, the justification, would have counted for nothing. The truck had already been driven through the loophole.

"Why do they always have their special programs in the middle of the good programs?"

"Always," echoed Raven.

The twins were condemning President Welby's news conference, before it even began. Like all children, they hated change, particularly when the change would affect some favorite program of theirs.

"Shhhh!" commanded Darcie. "It's going to be a very important announcement. You should watch it." She had ordered dinner forward by an hour so that the whole family could see the conference on the tiny portable set Brannigan had bought in Amenia.

"How can you have a Presidential news conference without a President?"

"Some conference," agreed Jeremy.

"His press secretary handles the questions for him and reads the statements the President wants people to hear."

"Nuts. We'll play Scrabble."

"Or anything."

Darcie gave them a stern look as they marched out of the room, but was unable to suppress a smile once they could no longer see her. Much like herself, the twins increasingly had an ability to put their fingers on the heart of an absurdity. And what could have been more absurd, more Alice in Wonderland, than a Presidential news conference without a President?

Chase actually expected little more from the speech than the twins. Sitting in the living room, glued to the miniature screen, he and Darcie sat as close as they could get without completely cutting off Emlyn's line of sight. Brannigan stood, some distance back, more listening than watching.

To the Wetherills, as to anyone who at least expected something encouraging from the press conference, the program came as both a shock and a bitter disappointment.

Press Secretary Rombert stood beneath a mammoth photographic portrait of President Welby, facing the camera and assembled newsmen with a friendly, if apologetic, smile. He would, he had announced, first read some statements from the President, then as usual take questions from the floor.

The statements were neither very encouraging nor very informative. Yes, Rombert stated, of course the President was aware of the disturbances and sporadic clashes in the cities. But the President felt sure that the American people would regain their calm shortly, as he was completely convinced the economy was about to experience a dramatic upswing. Keeping Americans from panicking, Rombert said, was one of the President's major concerns. For instance, the President had federalized the National Guard to prevent individual governors from overreacting and using troops against citizens who were merely exercising their right to protest. To answer a question before it was asked, Rombert quoted the President as saying he did not feel any sort of conspiracy lay behind the uprisings, rather just some Americans "letting off steam" after a long hot summer. To help ease any remaining tension, Rombert added, the President was appointing a Congressional committee to explore the problems lying behind the sudden show of feelings. In conclusion, Rombert noted, the President hoped that all Americans would rally behind him in gaining control of a situation that was built largely on exaggeration.

Chase Wetherill looked at Darcie and shook his head. It was a mishmash of platitudes so out of scale with what they knew was going on it might have been delivered by a man on another planet. The gatherings of newsmen seemed to feel the same way. The "play-it-down" approach they had been following since the onset of the trouble was replaced by a concerted barrage of questions, pointed, penetrating and accusative. It was as if someone had changed the media's signals in midgame, and Rombert was clearly unprepared for what was thrown at him.

No, Rombert said, the President's health was improving steadily. No, he could not explain the rash of rumors that the President was disintegrating. The fact was that his mind was sharper than ever and superbly capable of coping with the situation. No, it was ridiculous, perhaps even irresponsible, to suggest that he had given any thought to stepping down.

Was the President—was Rombert—aware that there was a special session of Congress being called, that committee meetings had begun this evening, and that one of the items being taken up was the matter of impeachment? Yes, both he and the President were, but considered it of no consequence.

To the question of why the National Guard, since it had been federalized, hadn't been used to put down the disturbances in some cities where there was widespread disorder, Rombert said the President did not feel it appropriate to have one American taking up arms against another. The riots—Rombert fell into using this word by error and tried to change it to "restlessness," but laughter from the newsmen made it impossible—the riots would die down without the use of force. No, he didn't know why the police were absent and had no explanation of why they didn't even try to keep order. That, as Rombert pointed out, was something for the newsmen to ask local authorities, not the Administration. No, he had already answered that, the President's health was improving, not deteriorating. And he had also answered the question about impeachment. All Americans, Rombert repeated, should listen to what the President's prepared text had to say about remaining calm and—

"Shit," Chase said suddenly, and leaned over to switch off the set. It was not an expression he used often, and Emlyn looked up in surprise. Brushing past him, Chase slipped into his topcoat and walked out the front door; he thought some fresh air might clear his head.

Like most Americans, Chase found himself bewildered by events rushing past him, although most Americans had not found themselves as deep in the middle as Chase and the entire Wetherill family did: in the very first few hours of the uprisings, the PLA had tried to kill them, and they had to be "rescued" by the CAC, only to discover that being rescued by the CAC was the same as being imprisoned. Their escape from them had led to the twins' accidental killing of one CAC man and Chase's shooting of Mort Evers. As a result, they were now being vigorously pursued by both sides.

Chase found the accumulation of facts hard to believe: Dick Mellon in the same boat as they, Carter Morgan apparently working with the CAC, Dina vanished, his own cousin Derek Wetherill seemingly murdered, and God alone knew what else.

But it was real and the paralysis sweeping across the nation was neatly symbolized by the Press Conference he'd just witnessed on television. The paralysis was real and the danger to his family and himself was real—as real as the checkpoints and the careening jeeps full of armed troops, as real as the betrayal of Mort Evers, as the truck drivers just short of Kennedy, as real as the legion of other men with red-and-white arm bands who were now spreading like the shadow of a dark winter cloud across the hills of the Northeastern Corridor.

"Letting off steam after a long, hot summer!" exploded the Senator from Illinois. "Christ, either he doesn't know what's going on or Welby's brain was completely destroyed by the stroke."

"It's tragic, but the facts make what we have to do clear indeed." The Senate Majority leader spoke as quietly as ever, his soft Southern voice sounding oddly out of character with what he was saying. He leaned unhappily against the wall a few feet from the television set, his face long and sad, his hands clasped in front of him.

"Does anyone have any really hard information from the doctors on him?"

The senior Senator from Ohio posed his question, slipping into his topcoat as he talked, then standing, waiting for an answer. All he received from Duane Wetherill was a helpless lifting of his shoulders and hands, a gesture to indicate that no one, certainly not he, could provide a meaningful answer.

The Senators were sitting in the living room of Duane's Washington apartment rather than in his home in Virginia because Duane's city place allowed them to get to the emergency Congressional meeting—scheduled to follow the news conference—more quickly. If, as expected, the conference provided no new answers, both houses would open impeachment proceedings. It was something no one in the room relished, but the situation was too critical to allow more time to pass without action. And from what they had just seen on television, little action could be expected from the ailing President. The legal complications of impeaching a President and replacing him with the Speaker of the House were enormous, but the times called for extreme measures, Constitutionally correct or not. Before they left, however, Duane had some additional information he wanted these particular Senators to have, and this was the real reason he had suggested meeting in his apartment.

The Senator from Ohio did not give up easily. "I thought you might have picked up something—about the President's health, I mean—from your brother."

Duane laughed. "Toby? Not a chance. Whatever he picks up at the Court, he keeps to himself."

"Of course. But I thought perhaps in this case, with the Constitutional implications and all . . ."

"The last person Toby would say anything to would be me."

Duane's casual good humor, as was characteristic, stood in direct contrast to what he was feeling. The situation deeply worried him, and he was unable to dismiss from his mind Chase's call earlier that week. He looked around the room and saw that the last of the Senators was on his feet and ready to go. Unknown to the public, the bill of particulars for impeachment had already been drawn up for the House, and probably would pass by voice vote. The Senate would follow suit. Technically, there was supposed to be a Senate trial, but, given the circumstances, an attempt was going to be made to waive it. By midnight if all went as expected, Thomas P. Garvin, the fiery ultraliberal Speaker of the House, would be President.

"Everybody ready?" someone in the room asked. The time for Senator Duane Wetherill to expose the rest of this group to his private information was at hand. "Before we go," he said suddenly, "there are some fragments of evidence you gentlemen should be aware of. I will give you Xeroxes of them, but I would like them all back. If they fell into the wrong hands, the fact that we had them could come back to haunt us all."

The men in the room looked at Duane curiously. Fascinated, they watched him unlock his desk and withdraw neatly slipped sheafs of Xeroxed documents, one copy for each Senator. Quickly, these were handed around in total silence. Some of the Senators read their sheafs of paper standing, others sank back into their chairs. The silence continued broken only by the dry rustle of turning pages and an occasional sharp intake of breath.

Duane had given the Senators the conclusions of the report prepared for Graffa, the substantiating documents, copies of the SYNPAC Telexes and FBI reports, as well as some new documents he'd been able to get his hands on.

In light of the unheard conversation between Tristram Shandy and parties unknown in New York, one of these was of particular interest:

NEW YORK NY 14 NOV XXXXSYNPAC FOR THE EYES ONLYXXXX REPEAT FOR THE EYES ONLY

SEC'Y OF DEFENSEXXXX CONFIRM RECEIPTXXXX
TLX CODE ZR 1212 XXX

REPORTS FROM THIS CITY INDICATE IMPOSSIBLE
TO AVOID CONCLUSION HIGHER ECHELONS OF
CAC ARE IN DIRECT COMMUNICATION AND POS
COLLUSION WITH SAME LEVEL OF PLA XXXX

PENETRATION OF CAC HIERARCHY REVEALS
FUNDING FOR PLA COMES IN SOME PART FROM
CAC XXXX IMPOS TO VERIFY BUT INDICATIONS
OF POWER AND MONEY BEING FED INTO CAC
ITSELF BY VESTED INTERESTS OF BOTH MILITARY
AND INDUSTRYXXXX

REQUEST PERMISSION TO TAKE MOST URGENT
ACTION TO PENETRATE SITUATION FURTHER
IMMEDXXX PRESIDENTS ILLNESS PROVIDES EX-
CELLENT OPPORTUNITY FOR DECISIVE AND POS
IRREVERSIBLE MOVESXXXX PLEASE ADVISE SOON-
ESTXXXX TLX CODE ZR 1212 XXX ENDXXX SIGNED
COLBERT SYNPACXXXXXXXX

Scrawled across the bottom of this Telex was a notation
apparently made in the office of the Secretary of Defense.
The writing was difficult to make out; the import was
clear: "Request for further penetration denied by TLX
sent 1730 14 Nov. Synpac notified Colbert to be termi-
nated with extreme prejudice as of this date."

The rest of the exhibits Duane had prepared for the
other Senators were in the same vein. If there had been
any doubts on the part of any of the Senators as to the absolute necessity of their taking action immediately, these
documents ended them. And terrified them. These were
papers of some other time, some other country, some
other people. Yet, they were being held in their own
hands, in this time, in this country, this people. The reaction was so immediate no one even asked Duane how he
had come by the papers. It was unimportant.

The first words spoken came from the Senate Majority
Leader. "We'd better start going. It's getting late."

"I only hope to Christ it's not too late already," announced the Senator from Ohio. But no one in the room
was listening. One by one, with an even greater sense of
urgency than before, the Senators filed from the apartment
and climbed into their cars for the trip to the Capitol

Building, unaware that it was a trip that would never be completed.

Emlyn came barreling noisily down the stairs of the house in Salisbury, his shirt off, the transistor radio clutched in his hand. "Dad! Mom! You'd better turn the TV set back on. What's happening—well, you won't believe it."

Ever since returning from his walk, Chase had sat in his chair, buried in thought. Occasionally his eyes would rise automatically to the blank television tube. To his mushrooming fears, the press conference had added the burgeoning weight of full realization: it seemed impossible, but the government appeared to be ignoring the rioting, the burnings, even the killings and pretending that they were small, isolated incidents. Either out of wishful thinking or helplessness, Washington was clinging to the belief that the spreading of the uprisings was something that simply couldn't happen, that given time, left alone, the whole thing would go away. He and his family would not be safe here long. Glumly, Chase had tried to measure their chances of survival in Salisbury against any possible options elsewhere still open to them. He had found none.

For an instant he stared blankly at Emlyn, then he strode across the room and turned the television set back on. After a short humming, the tube formed the image of the Capitol Building area.

The streets, empty a little while before, were now teeming with people, streaming out of the avenues that surrounded the Capitol and pouring onto the plaza in front. Above their heads waved a sea of signs and banners, pressed together so tightly that in places the area looked like a moving wall of white. Slowly, this mass of humanity pressed forward and up the steps of the Capitol Building, a relentless chant of "jobsjobsjobs" filling the night air with its angry, threatening chorus. Most startling of all, flying from the Capitol dome, floodlit and flapping in the stiff November wind, was the black-and-white banner of the PLA. Tristram Shandy's order to the man on the other end of the phone to escalate it "to full scale—the works" was being carried out to the letter.

As if released from a long, enforced silence, the networks were no longer playing the situation down. Full descriptions of the rioting and killing in other cities was compared to what their audiences were seeing happening now in Washington. As if aware that the camera was on them, the rioters on the Capitol steps seemed to redouble their efforts. Windows on the building's first floor were broken and men forced their ways into the building. A great roar rose from the crowd as those first inside reached the mammoth main doors from behind and unlocked them, allowing the entire first wave of the mob to surge inside. The announcer's voice rose in pitch, trying to make itself heard above the shouting and chanting. At intervals, the picture would go black, doubtless people were continually tripping over and disconnecting the cables from the remote television trucks parked along the edge of the plaza.

Chase sat mute in front of his set. Emlyn stood behind him with Brannigan, whom Darcie had called back from the kitchen. Hearing the excitement, the twins had come down out of their bedroom and were watching noisily.

The screen went blank permanently at precisely 10:14 p.m. For a few moments, the sound continued sporadically. Chase was staring at the floor, his fingers wandering pensively up and down the sides of his face. The announcer's voice suddenly caused his head to snap upward. "My God," whispered an unbelieving voice into the microphone. "It's on fire. The building's on fire. The Capitol is beginning to burn. You can see flames at the upper window and they're—" Then the voice went dead. The Weimar Torch Option had been called. The announcer on Emlyn's transistor continued, but soon he too was stilled in midsentence.

There had been continual breaks in the transmission throughout the evening, but all further word from the capital ceased as Operation Pull-Plug struck Washington. An unaccustomed darkness crept across the country like the shadow of a great cloud moving across sunlit water. Being without electricity, Chase was not aware of it, but the town of Salisbury went dark early, at 10:22.

As the night advanced, the electricity in every major city in the country went off. Times Square was the last of the major areas to remain a blazing island of light, but eventually, it too was plunged into darkness. Airplanes were grounded as airport lights failed and air communications became sporadic; trains wheezed to a stop as signal systems went out. Radio and television stations went off

the air from lack of electricity to amplify their signals.
Newspaper presses ground to a halt.

Tristram Shandy wanted as few witnesses to what would
happen next as possible.

Dina Wetherill and Alan Peletier had spent November 6
as what could only be called a lazy day. They had gotten
up late, and with the exception of Alan's trip to the small
pile of firewood he kept beside the converted garage, neither of them had been outside. Even at that, Alan had noticed there was something wrong in Darien. People were
racing past on the roads, the cars filled with frightened-
looking occupants who appeared to be fleeing from something. As he watched, Alan saw another of the cars that
had so disturbed Dina the night before, filled with young
people angrily shouting out the car windows. It moved
slowly down the road, apparently looking for something or
somebody. Alan had hidden from them by darting back
behind the garage, until the car and its occupants had
moved on. In the distance, he thought he heard scattered
shooting and screams. The whole thing filled him with
fear. He took his load of wood and quickly slipped upstairs to his apartment again. He would not tell Dina; she
was still too shattered from the day before. This decision
also spared Alan from accepting that he was not only still
shaken by yesterday's events, but had found new reasons
to be frightened today.

The sounds Alan thought he had heard were indeed
real, not imaginary. The crew from the Red Coach Inn
had been pillaging all of Darien, killing, burning, terror-
izing. Some people from this prosperous, upper-middle-
class bastion of suburbia were deliberately allowed to
escape; they would spread the word about the PLA, and
by design that word was to be—terror. All the exits were
then sealed off; anyone still left was to be killed. The only
reason Alan and Dina hadn't yet been discovered was that
the PLA leaders had considered the dilapidated garage
building on the old estate to be abandoned; it hadn't oc-
cured to anyone to check inside.

The weather was chilly, and there was intermittent rain.
Although it had been three weeks since Dina had disappeared into his Volks with him, little had changed in their
playing out of Alan's fantasy. He and Dina spent the day,
then, affecting normalcy, curled up in chairs in front of

the fire, pretending to read books, sipping sherry and listening to Brahms. Toward evening, Dina had slipped back into her gossamer Halston and Alan into his eighteenth-century clothes; Dina knew it would be only a matter of time before their curious nightly ritual took place.

The Brahms on their stereo turned out to be their undoing. For the first time since she had known Alan, Dina had dared to play an even mildly aggressive role. As he stood before her, lost in the music, Dina had unbuttoned the two rows of white pearl buttons on his trousers and let her hand slip inside. There had been no objection from Alan, only a slight trembling as he felt her hand touch him. And as the Brahms soared, Dina grew bolder, feeling Alan's stomach muscles contract as he took a deep breath. He was still taking deep breaths when the front door crashed inward. There, framed in the doorway, finally drawn to the garage by the loudness of the stereo, stood a handful of the PLA, their eyes blinking in the sudden dimness of the candlelight which Alan insisted be the apartment's sole illumination.

"What the hell?" said the leader, a huge black, staring around the room, trying to understand first why it was so dark, and then, back at them, confused by Alan's clothes and the position of Dina's hand.

"Shit, there's got to be a light somewhere," said a second man, running his hand up and down the plaster just inside the door where the light switch would normally be.

A short, red-headed white girl with incredibly pale skin finally found the switch, half concealed behind a needlepoint bell pull. The sudden, harsh glare of the electricity startled all of them. Reddening, Alan was struggling to fasten the buttons on his trousers, but his fingers were shaking and he made little progress. "Well, I'll be damned," the redhead giggled.

Alan's living room suddenly filled with people. His clothes were examined with wonder, they looked even odder now that his hands were tightly tied behind his back, while the Dr. Denton-like flap remained hanging open from his trouser front.

"What the hell is he dressed for?" the group's leader asked the red-headed girl.

She reached out and felt the loose sleeves of his fencing shirt. "Beats me," she answered, in a strangely small, cul-

tured voice. "It's sort of an Errol Flynn get-up." Her arms
whipped the air as she imitated a fencing expert.
"Whoosh! Whoosh! It's Zorro!" She giggled, letting her fingers sink into the flesh of his arm so deeply that Alan
cried out in surprise and pain.

"Don't hurt him," Dina said suddenly.

"Zorro can't be touched by anything but silver blades,
honey." The red-haired girl giggled again, and pushed
Dina back against the wall. Turning she addressed the
man who was leading them. "How do you want to do
these? They like to play dress-up, in old-fashioned clothes
yet. Maybe they should go that way."

The black shrugged. He looked uncomfortable discussing such a subject in front of its intended victims. "You're
in charge of that kind of crap, Esther. You decide."

Esther and two or three of the others huddled in the
center of the room; two men guarded Dina and Alan. On
Dina's face no real expression could be seen; with the exception of her plea not to hurt Alan, she had neither spoken nor allowed any emotion to show. For all intents and
purposes, she was already fully resigned. With Alan, it was
completely different; he was terrified.

For a band of executioners, the redhead and the others
were a jolly group. Neither Alan nor Dina could hear all
of what was being said, but they were trying to find some
form of execution appropriate to Alan's clothes. The word
"guillotine" rose out of the huddle and produced a laugh.
"No basket for the heads to fall into," the redhead said
sadly. Another laugh. A chopping block was mentioned,
but no axe could be found. More giggling.

Finally, the black who was their leader lost patience.
"For Christ's sake, get on with it."

"Well," said the redhead with a sigh, turning toward
Alan, "it's very lower-class, but I guess you'll have to go
like the rest. Sorry, Zorro." She patted her submachine
gun meaningfully.

Two two men guarding Dina and Alan backed away as
the redhead and another girl raised their guns to point
them directly at Alan and Dina, huddled now against the
wall. Alan found his stomach shriveling inside him.

As if delivered by a beneficent God, Operation Pull-
Plug chose that moment to reach southern Connecticut.

The room went black. There was still a dim glow of
light from outside, but after the brilliant glare of the over-

head electric lights, the PLA group could see practically nothing. "What the hell?" demanded the red-headed girl.

One of the group clustered against the wall had already looked out the other window. "The whole town's gone out. Maybe the police—"

A sudden babble of voices, nervous, and a little fearful now, rose from them. Half-blinded, they stumbled around in the dark, shouting to each other, trying to find the door they had entered through. In the confusion, Dina suddenly felt a body push against hers and heard Alan's voice whispering in her ear. "Shhh. Quick. Out the side door and into the car before they can see again. But watch the outside stairs, they're slippery."

They ran. The rain had made the outdoor stairs as slippery as Alan had predicted, although he had the harder time of the two; with his hands still tied behind him, he couldn't help himself with the handrails. Outside they dashed for the Volks bus.

"For Christ's sake, untie my hands," Alan hissed at her.

With a shove, Dina opened the passenger side of the driver's compartment and pushed him in, climbed behind the wheel and jammed the car into gear, and roared down the driveway. "See if you can swing around and open the glove compartment," she yelled at him. "There's a knife in there, isn't there?"

In the rear-view mirror, she could see the other headlights outside the garage spring into life. They had recovered, thumped down the stairway, and were climbing into their own cars.

Roaring down the road, she could make out a roadblock ahead, one that had been set up when the PLA had first decided to cut off Darien. "Hang on, we're just going to have to barrel through."

Alan braced himself awkwardly against the door, his useless hands groping for something to grab. Dina gave the motor full power, closed her eyes as she saw gun flashes from the men beside the roadblock, and drove through the wooden sawhorses blocking the way. The noise of splintering wood and breaking glass, even though she had known it was coming, surprised her. But the car got through. From behind, more sounds of guns firing and the soft splat of bullets into the body of the Volks. Then the roar of the other cars, blowing their horns and tearing down the road in pursuit.

Just past the roadblock, Dina made a sharp right turn, and because there were no street lights and the Volks lights had never been turned on to begin with, the pursuing mob shot past without seeing them.

"Jesus," said Alan Peletier. "Those guys are plain crazy."

Dina had gotten the knife out of the glove compartment and was cutting the ropes that tied Alan's hands together. "But not crazy enough not to guess that we must have turned off somewhere," she added. "We'd better try it overland if we can. There must be help we can find around here somewhere."

Alan was massaging his wrists in the darkness, trying to get the circulation going again. Even in the dim interior of the unlighted car, Dina could see the still-open flap; Alan had forgotten all about it. "You should probably button yourself up, too. It looks funny."

Alan blushed. After a moment's silence, his tone businesslike, he asked, "Do you want me to drive?"

"If your wrists are all right."

"They're fine." Silently, they switched positions. The new sound of firmness in his voice, the new strain of docility in hers, indicated that now the worst of the danger appeared over, they had switched back to their more normal roles.

Shifting carefully and stepping on the gas only tentatively, Alan started the Volks forward up a small slope, trying to make as little noise as possible. Behind him, in the rear-view mirror, he could see headlights racing up and down the road and knew that the hunt was still in full swing. Let them search, he thought; they were safe. With its rugged drive, the Volks made it up the grassy hill easily. Alan looked up and down the road, right and left, and could see nothing. Stepping lightly on the accelerator, he eased the van out onto the upper road and headed in a direction he assumed would bring them to the Connecticut Turnpike.

The blasting glare from perhaps half a dozen cars turning on their headlights simultaneously almost blinded them both. It was a PLA roadblock on the upper road.

"Get down!" roared Alan at Dina as he gunned the car toward what appeared to be a gap between the searing headlights of two cars. The Volks responded with a lurch. But as he plunged through the gap, he saw a large looming shape, on top of which two dark red discs of light blinked ominously on and off. It was a bulldozer, and it inched forward, ponderous, unstoppable, straight toward the Volks. The forward section of the left tread seemed to lift the bulldozer when it first rode up and over the front end of the van, then the shell of the car collapsed and the tread dropped abruptly to the pavement as the dozer ground relentlessly on. Lying on the floor in the back, where the van was collapsed but not completely flattened, Dina watched in numb disbelief as she saw the bulldozer's moving tread pick up Alan's body and crush it between itself and the flattened front end of the car. As the dozer continued forward, each revolution of the tread left a dark, wet imprint of blood and bone as it clanked across the pavement, the way a lawn roller makes several imprints of a squashed spider before finally shaking the flattened insect loose on the driveway.

No one bothered to look into the rear end of the crushed van; there seemed little chance anyone had survived. For a long time, Dina lay where she was. Finally, she heard the banter of men grow more distant and the last of the cars leave. She painfully pulled herself out of the wreckage, and started off on foot, heading for the turnpike, but not at all sure what she would do when she got there.

She could hear a voice and knew that the voice was her own. Unstoppable, the incoherent words kept pouring from her, words sometimes addressed to Alan, sometimes to her mother, sometimes to a Being she had never addressed before and essentially didn't believe in.

She received no answer from any of them.

Sharon is almost a Christmas-card version of what a New England village should look like. Its sidewalks are tree-lined, its homes large but classically simple, its church steeples gleaming white. The only jarring note is a stone library built in the Victorian era, angular, gothic, and ugly; but this sort of architecture is in itself a fixture in most small New England villages, and is no more startling than that Sharon still boasted a working blacksmith. In spite of—or perhaps because of—the wealthy people who had begun moving into the area some years before, the town had remained largely pristine and untouched.

Every time Chase saw Sharon, it reminded him of some

enchanted village that had been frozen in time, an island
of tranquillity. For Chase, that feeling ended at eleven-
thirty a.m., six days after the "Presidential" news conference.

Emlyn saw the man first. He grabbed his father's arm so
suddenly and so hard Chase winced. With his head, Emlyn
indicated something across the street. Chase went white.
This was the first actual man wearing a CAC arm band
they had seen in any of the towns proper, and the sight focused all of Chase's anxieties, doubts, and fears into a
single symbol. The man was doing nothing either note-
worthy or frightening, merely leaning against the store-
front of one of the many bookstores that dotted the area,
absorbing the noon sun full on his face, his hand fingering
the red-and-white arm band a little self-consciously. But
the feeling of an ominous presence persisted. In keeping
with the tradition of any small New England town, no one
had yet asked him who he was or what the arm band
stood for.

Chase and Emlyn darted into the store nearest them,
Englehardt's Pharmacy. Mr. Englehardt, Emlyn told him,
was in the rear of the store fussing with some packages on
the shelf, so Chase allowed himself to look out through the
plate-glass window and study the man further. In the
peaceful, crisp setting of Sharon, the man and his red-
and-white arm band looked out of place and, to Chase,
obscene. And while the people passing by might merely
look at him with curiosity, understanding neither what he
was nor how much of a fixture in their lives he and his fel-
low troopers planned to become, to Chase he represented
pure terror. Automatically, Chase found his hand reaching
toward his face, seeking reassurance in the whiskers
growing there; his beard had come in rapidly and the
chances of anyone recognizing him were now slight.

"He doesn't seem to be doing anything much," Emlyn
said; he was standing beside his father, staring at the man
too.

"Just the fact that he is here is doing enough," answered Chase grimly.

"He's crossing the street." Emlyn hadn't been as disturbed by the sight of the man as his father was, although
the fear was beginning to have a contagious quality to it.

Chase looked. At first, the man appeared to be headed
directly for the drug store, but about halfway across the

street he veered to the right and disappeared from their view.

"Anything I can do for you fellows?" The voice from behind them caused Chase to jump abruptly. He spun around to look into Mr. Englehardt's pale-blue eyes.

With a nervous laugh, Chase tried to recover. He and the druggist had never seen each other, but there was no point of reminding the man of the fact. "Oh, Mr. Englehardt. You were busy in the back and I didn't want to disturb you. We were just enjoying looking at the beautiful weather. I need—I need—three tubes of Crest, some pipe tobacco—Amphora, if you have it—and six bars of Dove."

"Dove's cheaper at the supermarket," noted Mr. Englehardt on his way over to the toiletry counter. "But it's your money, mister."

They waited for Mr. Englehardt to wrap their package, paid him and went out of the store. The man was nowhere in sight. Crossing the street, Emlyn turned to his father. "What about getting the radio?" A short-wave radio was the reason they were in Sharon in the first place; Emlyn felt, if he got the right parts from the local radio store, he could fashion one that would bring in Canada. All U.S. stations were now off the air because of the power blackout.

"I'll try to pick up the stuff in Millerton tomorrow."

Emlyn started to protest, but was cut off by his father. "Look. No more going anyplace off the farm together. It makes recognizing us too easy. When we can get to it, we'll phony up Brannigan's driver's license with your birth date and you can drive yourself. In the meantime, you'll just have to stay at home."

Desperately, Emlyn returned to his original line of attack; he knew his father's knowledge of AM technology was hopelessly inadequate in so complicated an area as buying components. "But the parts for the radio," he began. Chase ignored him. A sense of panic inside him told Chase that he had to get Emlyn and himself out of town quickly. As they drove down the street, they once again passed the drug store. What they saw unsettled Chase even further. The man was leaning against the wall outside of Mr. Englehardt's, and standing beside him, talking, was Mr. Englehardt.

With considerable effort, Chase managed to persuade himself it was a ridiculous thing to let worry him.

Chapter Nine

So long as a man rides his hobby horse
peaceably and quietly along the Kings'
highway, and neither compels you or me to
get up behind him—pray, Sir, what have
either you or I to do with it?

Laurence Sterne,
—The Life and Times of Tristram Shandy

At first, neither Chase nor Brannigan saw them. Chase carried the shotgun under his arm; he had for some days wanted to explore the hill behind the farm, hoping, even though it was late in the season, to find some quail or partridge. Brannigan had pleaded to come along, saying he could use the air, but really because there was something he felt he had to discuss with Mr. Wetherill; a long walk through the wooded hills would provide him with an amply relaxed setting for what he had to say. "You'll scare the game, Brannigan," Chase had complained.

"Yerra, I'll be an extra set of eyes for you, Mr. Wetherill." Brannigan paused a second, then an impish smile broke across his dark face. "Although, if you expect me to get down on all fours and point, I withdraw my offer."

They were almost two-thirds of the way up the first hill when something moved in the underbrush and caught Brannigan's eye; he silently grabbed Chase by the elbow. Chase looked at him, trying to follow his eyes as he indicated a spot almost on top of the hill. "Partridge? Pheasant?" he asked Brannigan in a whisper, his eyes straining to see what the Irishman had sighted.

Then Chase spotted the two. The men's backs were to them. They were lying flat on the ground, and they had a pair of field glasses trained on his farm below. One was wearing a brightly checked plaid wool shirt, while the other appeared to have thrown some sort of white jacket over his own heavy shirt. Inside, Chase could feel the knot of fear and the cold numbness growing again in his stomach. Brannigan tugged his sleeve and suggested that they get close enough to make out the conversation between the two men; at the present distance, all they could hear was a low murmur. "But quiet, real quiet, y'understand?"

With all the modest skill they had as hunters, Chase and Brannigan began creeping up the hill; the dried fallen leaves and dead twigs kept exploding beneath their feet in what seemed ear-splitting bursts of sound.

But it was no particular noise, as Chase remembered, that finally gave them away; rather, it was a series of small coincidences. The man in the plaid jacket, yawning, sat up to stretch himself, and as he did, turned around and stared at them, gasping in surprise. In that instant, Chase recognized him as the man they'd seen outside the bookstore in Sharon. At the same time, the other man, the man in the ill-fitting white jacket, startled by the suddenness of his partner's movement, turned around too. It was Mr. Englehardt.

For a moment, the four men stared at each other, motionless, frozen in place as if by a photographer's flashbulb. The statuelike silence was suddenly shattered by Brannigan. "Look out!" he bellowed. There was a third man, whom neither Chase nor Brannigan had spotted; the man stepped calmly out from behind a tree and raised, with elaborate slowness, a gun to his shoulder. The man on the ground appeared to be fumbling beneath his plaid jacket at his waistband, and Chase could see that a gun was already in his hand and being withdrawn.

The man behind the tree fired.

Chase felt himself thrown to the ground, unaware for a second that he had been knocked over, not by a bullet, but by Brannigan. A second shot rang out, this one from the handgun, and Chase hugged the ground. Brannigan was shouting something at him, and Chase finally realized that it was about the shotgun he still held in his hands. Chase fired only twice; that was all that was required for the two men. Brannigan was already on top of Mr. Englehardt, beating the pharmacist's head with a flat rock.

"Stop it. Hold it. That's *enough*, Brannigan." Brannigan appeared not to hear, but continued his pounding; Chase could never remember seeing an expression like the one on Brannigan's face. He pulled him off.

"My God, Brannigan, dead is dead."

Shaken, Brannigan stared at his hands as if they were objects not completely under his control. "Mother of God," he said and looked away.

Chase was already consumed by a new and growing worry. "Do you think that's all of them?"

"For now. If more was close by, they'd already be here."

Chase studied the squashed Mr. Englehardt, and something barely visible through his white jacket caught his eyes. Trying to keep his eyes off the remains of the druggist's face, Chase pulled his jacket down off one shoulder. It revealed the red-and-white arm band of the CAC. Examination of the other two men produced the same results. Chase sighed heavily.

"I understand the other two. But Englehardt—well, he was just an another ordinary small-town druggist. I ducked in his store the other day, when I saw that guy there. I didn't figure Englehardt somehow. It baffles me."

"Englehardt is one of the reasons I wanted to take this walk with you, Mr. Wetherill. There's more like him in town, you see. I found another black man living in Amenia, and we've been comparing notes. He doesn't dare show his face either these days. Englehardt he knew about. I knew you had to be told, but I wasn't sure how you'd take it, you know, how you'd feel."

"I feel scared about what happens to us next, that's how I feel. God knows how many more Mr. Englehardts there really are in Salisbury. And the first question is how many people knew these three were coming here today. Maybe none, if we're lucky. The second question is what to do with them; we just can't leave them lying there. Emlyn has a dry well outside someplace where he dumps the plastic bags from the chemical toilets. Connected to a leaching field, he says. It's the easiest place to put them, but it's a long haul from here.

"I'm afraid," said Chase after a second thought, "Emlyn's going to have to know. We can use the trailer part of the way, but the rest will be dragging by hand. Emlyn's awfully young for this kind of thing, but I'm beginning to think no one is ever really old enough for it."

The two CAC men and Mr. Englehardt were buried

about two hours later, their bodies dropped down the dry well and covered with quicklime.

Two days after the killings on the hill (or one month less a day following Chase's flight into exile), a remarkable thing happened in Sharon. At first the twins could not believe their eyes, sitting in the early-evening darkness. They had just finished their nightly job of bringing in the wood, and after pausing in the kitchen to pick up Cokes, had collapsed into chairs in the living room, staring at the blank television screen in frustration. The room was lit solely by the flickering deep-yellow light of kerosene lamps, set going a half-hour earlier by Brannigan. Almost without their first being aware of it, the room suddenly became brighter. For a second the brightness wavered, surging between light and dark, then burst into the steady, harsh whiteness of fully working light bulbs.

"Hey," cried Jeremy. "The lights, the lights!"

"The electricity's back!" shouted Raven.

"Dad . . ."

"Mom . . ."

"Emlyn's wiring works!"

"We've got electricity!"

People poured into the living room. Electricity seems such a simple thing—until you don't have it. The scene looked as if Thomas Alva Edison himself might have just perfected the electric light right there in front of the Wetherill family's eyes: the twins were spinning around the room whooping and cheering; Darcie was already in conversation with Brannigan about the possibility of an electric stove; Chase was recording the precise time the power had returned in a notebook, for reasons of which he was not entirely sure; and in the center of it all stood Emlyn, shy and quiet, but enormously proud of himself.

"Actually," he said in a solemn voice, just a tinge of excitement allowed to surface, "all that time with the power off made it easier. I could hook up into the main power lines without having to worry about taking twelve thousand volts D.C." He turned toward Chase, knowing he was letting more of himself show than he really wanted, but unable to do anything to stop. "It's all grounded and everything, so we shouldn't have any trouble as long as the power stays on."

Chase felt a lump rise in his throat. For a long time, he

said nothing, but stared into his son's eyes, sharing his pride, wanting to express his own. "Dammit, Emlyn. I don't know how to—" Abruptly, Chase stopped. Because he had spoken the truth. He didn't know how to tell Emlyn of his pride any more than he knew how to tell Darcie how much he loved her or Brannigan how much he needed him or the twins how much he worshipped them.

"Have we got two-twenty as well, Emlyn?" asked Brannigan, suddenly breaking into the silent dialogue between Chase and his son. "Your mother is wanting to know about an electric stove and all."

"No, but I bet I can do it. There's a step-down transformer on a pole a couple hundred feet farther up the line."

"No." Chase spoke firmly. "No playing around with twelve thousand volts. The clothes washer—well, we don't have water pressure for it anyway."

Emlyn laughed. "Now that we've got the juice, we can get all the water pressure the pipes will take. Brannigan can pick up a shallow-well pump."

"Emlyn!" exclaimed Darcie, laughing with delight. "You mean, real honest to God running water?"

Inside Chase, there was a sudden sadness. Darcie happy over a tap you could turn on. He could remember her so clearly, back in the house on 64th Street, curled up on the library sofa in front of the fire, lost in her private world. She would be reading a book and listening to Mozart on the stereo at the same time, usually dressed in some favorite shade of the yellow she adored; the two corgis would be balanced precariously on the sofa back just to be near her. Motionless as cats, they would lie there for hours, as if inhaling the serenity that surrounded her. Through the French windows, the late-afternoon sun would filter into the room and dance around her blond hair, blinding you a little as you walked in, the room itself steeped in the perfume that followed her everywhere. That Darcie, his Darcie—and this picture of her that he carried in his mind—should be standing in a shabby living room, plonked out in the middle of nowhere, growing excited at the thought she would soon have so simple a basic necessity as running water.

"The screen's blank," complained Jeremy, fiddling with the knob of the television set.

"No picture, no sound," added Raven and turned toward Emlyn.

"Are you sure you didn't do something . . ."

". . . to the aerial when you were fiddling with the wires?"

Chase exploded. "Oh, stop whining, both of you. There's no picture because the stations aren't back on yet. Goddammit, ever since we got here, all you two have done is complain about one thing after another. I don't think you realize the danger we're all in. Emlyn's done a terrific job, in spite of everything. Instead of complaining, you should be thanking him. For God's sake, act your ages. Sometimes . . ."

The twins stood there, silenced. Always their father's favorites in the past, they were not used to being upstaged by Emlyn. Dina had been disapproved of; Emlyn tolerated; but they had been praised, talked about, and exhibited proudly to his friends. Instinctively, they drew closer to each other even as they stood in front of him, suffering what they must have considered a diminution of his love.

None of this was lost on Darcie. With a laugh, she poked the twins with her hand. "You know what we should do, Chase. We should throw a party to celebrate the twins' not having to lug all that wood in every night. What a job they did!"

But her effort was quickly lost in the general excitement. For just short of a month, the entire family had been living under intense pressure: the flight here, the futile effort to get to the airport, the killings of the man in the car, Mort Evers, of the men on the hill, the roadblocks and the realization they were being hunted. None had been immune. And now, after all this strain, the idea of a party suddenly seemed to seize everyone. The danger had not disappeared, the question of their very survival had not diminished, but the return of the electricity provided an excuse, for the first time since their arrival, for them to celebrate something that had gone right.

" 'Tis a good idea, a party, Mrs. Wetherill," agreed Brannigan with enthusiasm. "And maybe we can pick up some wild music from Erin on the short-wave to go with it. I do a mean clog, y'know."

Shouting and stomping his feet on the floor, Brannigan began his clog without waiting for the music from the short-wave receiver. The noise of his feet striking the bare wooden floor of the living room was so great that at first no one noticed the knocking on the door.

The first knocks were soft, but they grew progressively louder. By the time Brannigan suddenly stopped, rooted in the silent stance that ends the clog, the knocking had become a pounding, and everyone in the room turned their heads toward the door.

For a moment, they stood frozen; then everyone began performing the planned routine for any such occasion. "Do we hide that thing?" asked Raven. The twins didn't wait for anyone to respond, but began tucking the television set safely out of sight, stashing it beneath the hanging skirt of a large round table in one corner of the room.

"Just a minute, please," Darcie called cheerfully toward the knocking, waiting until she saw Emlyn dash into the cellar to turn off their illegal electric power supply. Chase moved beside Darcie, his beard looking fierce in the suddenly dim light of only the oil lamps, prepared for the worst. Quickly, the latch was thrown and Darcie pulled the door open.

Outside, hard to see in the frail light coming from the front hall, stood Tracey's lover, Dirk. He had never met Darcie, and, looking at Chase and finding him in an unfamiliar beard, at first wasn't sure he had the right house. Bewildered, he blinked for a minute, his eyes moving from Chase to Darcie and back to Chase.

Chase was the first to recover. But the boy's name escaped him completely. Smudged and dirty, dressed in mud-spattered jeans and heavy walking shoes, he still retained the feline grace Chase remembered from Tracey's apartment. And for reasons he could not explain, it was the gold coin on the chain, barely visible at the open throat of the wrinkled denim shirt, that suddenly brought his name back to Chase, but the boy beat him to saying it.

"Dirk. It's Dirk. We met at your brother's."

"Of course, Dirk. Come in, come in."

Waving him in with his hands, Chase pulled Dirk into the hall. Moving past him, he let the door stand open a crack, peering outside to make sure no one was following the boy. For a moment, he and Dirk stood facing each other in the hall; Darcie studied them briefly and then disappeared. Chase helped Dirk out of his leather jacket and tossed it onto a wall peg. "No one followed you, Dirk?"

"No one. I checked. Hitchhiked. Then by foot from the highway to here. I doubled back twice to make sure. Tracey was very specific about details like that. He doesn't know who may be watching his place, or if they'd try to tail me."

"Would you like something to eat?"

"Maybe later, Mr. Wetherill. I probably ought to get back tonight."

Chase raised his eyebrows; the meeting was making less sense by the minute. "That's a lot of hitchhiking. And even if you do go, you'll certainly need some food first." The offer was not made purely from generosity: at this point, Chase was still not sure how far Dirk could be trusted. Dirk in the house could be kept track of; Dirk gone could not. Pushing him into a small room off the kitchen—the place had once been the "summer kitchen" of the old mansion, but had been outfitted with furniture to make a sort of den for him and Darcie—Chase stuck his head into the living room and asked Darcie to pull something together for Dirk to eat. The sound from Brannigan's impromptu party was deafening; he had all of them—Emlyn, Raven, Jeremy, even Darcie—clapping their hands while he went through the intricate and noisy ritual of the clog. His arms pressed straight against his sides, only his legs moving, Brannigan appeared ready to go on forever. Looking up, Darcie seemed relieved to have an excuse to leave; a little of the clog goes a long way. With a faint smile, Chase went back into the den, closing the door against the din from the other room.

The smile vanished as he sat down to face Dirk. "Is Tracey all right?"

"Fine. Fine." Dirk twisted the gold coin back and forth, fondling it, rubbing it, caressing it, as if he drew his strength from it.

"Well, something has to be up." Chase paused, realizing his statement had a very rude, almost demanding sound about it. "What I mean is, Dirk, Salisbury is a long way to come from the city. Especially with no cars or trains and with all the confusion on the highways." (The trains had been stopped for the lack of electricity to operate the signals; cars could not get gas, because the gas pumps depended on electricity for their machinery to work. Only diesel fuel was available, so only heavy trucks were, for the most part, to be found on the highways.)

Dirk stood up and moved over to the darkened window, staring out into the blackness; Chase could hear the faint click of the coin against its chain. "Tracey says you have to come back, Mr. Wetherill. He has to see you. It's urgent, he says. A family matter, is the way he put it." The words had all tumbled from Dirk in one long phrase, with no pause allowed for breath, as if he were scared that the entire thing must be said in one piece or would never get said at all.

Stunned, Chase stared at him. Tracey's request came unexpectedly and devoid of any accompanying explanation. His first reaction was that something had happened to Tracey, that he was sick or in some sort of trouble and that he should leave with Dirk immediately to help. But, almost as quickly, this reaction was replaced by the picture of the men on the hill and Mr. Englehardt. They were gone, but others would take their place. Darcie, the children: someone had to protect them. Chase floundered. "Is something wrong with Tracey?" He remembered he'd already asked Dirk that question and pulled at his beard to take the edge off his confusion.

"No, Tracey's fine. As I told you. But Tracey gave me the message and told me to give it to you—to say it in those precise words, in fact—and that's all I know."

The one long phrase was now explained; Dirk had been given the message and then dutifully memorized it. Struggling, Chase went over the message in his head once more, searching for some clue, struggling, too, to think of what he should say to Dirk. His answer sounded weak, even to Chase. "I don't know. It's all so sudden," he said, fumbling again.

The door opened and Darcie came in, carrying a small tray of sandwiches and sliced cheese. "This is just to hold you till dinner," she announced. Then she looked at Chase. "Is anything wrong?"

"It's Tracey. He wants me to come to New York right away. Urgent, Dirk says. I'm not sure I can—or should."

Dirk's eyes never left Chase's face. In front of him, his hands automatically reached for the sandwiches, devouring them as if he hadn't eaten for some time. Darcie let her eyes pause on him. "There's more," she said gently, "and dinner will be ready soon."

"It was a long trip," apologized Dirk, suddenly realizing his carefully acquired manners had disappeared. Darcie smiled and let her eyes move away from him to Chase. The smile vanished, replaced by a look of sad resignation. "If Tracey says you have to come, you have to come. He's your brother."

Yes, Tracey was his brother. But regardless of this, regardless of anything else, he had to consider his family here in Salisbury first. Particularly after the ugly incident with Englehardt and the CAC men, the thought of leaving Darcie and Emlyn and the twins with only Brannigan to protect them seemed wrong. On the other hand, Tracey had said he needed him. Of course, Tracey could be overreacting, panicking under the pressure. Who knew? Chase could feel his soul squirming. Like many ordinarily decisive men, he found himself thrown when confronted with a problem steeped in so many private and personal considerations. At the Foundation, if he made a wrong decision, it was an abstract one. People might get hurt, but in an abstract way—and in those situations, even the people themselves were abstracts to Chase. In the kind of decision he faced now, if he made a wrong decision, neither the suffering nor the sufferers would be abstract; they would be either his family or Tracey—or both.

To Chase, it was one of those dilemmas with no possible answer that was either really right or really wrong. It was also one of those dilemmas that he couldn't possibly solve standing on one foot watching Dirk eat cheese and sandwiches.

Seeing Darcie and Dirk staring at him, waiting for an answer, Chase ruffled his beard once more and shifted uncomfortably. "Dammit, I wish the decision was as easy a one as Darcie makes it sound. Of course, I'll do anything in the world to help Tracey. He knows that, you know that. But the situation here—the danger of it— Darcie—the kids . . . Hell, I want to—have to—help Tracey, but there's so many damned practical things to factor in."

Darcie changed the position of a cigarette box on the table with a noisy thump. "We'll all be lined up against a wall one day, while you're sitting someplace 'factoring in' the practical things. God, Chase, you're usually so good with tough decisions. Look, in the end what's practical is that Tracey is your brother and he needs you and this time you'd better damned well do something while you still can."

Dina's name had not been mentioned by Darcie, but by implication, it was the heart of her attack. Chase felt himself growing irritated by Darcie; her way of putting things so that she cut through to the center of any matter—something he usually valued—was backfiring on him. The argument she made might well be right, but . . . The sound of some small animal outside the house startled Chase and brought him back to the core of his own logic, a logic built on the bedrock realities of roadblocks and checkpoints, of the CAC man lounging in the streets of Sharon, and of the killings on the hill. And those realities were just the parts he knew about, the tip of the iceberg. Realities that outweighed the curious, frail-looking boy with the gold coin on a chain and his unexplained message from Tracey.

Basically, Chase's decision was that he had no choice but to stay here, yet the door had to be left open in case the balance shifted and he had to go. Uncomfortably, he looked at Darcie; it was not going to be a decision that sat well with her, and Chase knew it. "The children—you, Darcie—I can't just go breezing off. Not now anyway, not yet. Not until we see what happens here."

"Which means you're not going—-at all. Right?"

Chase flared, his face suddenly furious. "All right, dammit, that's what it means. Right." Chase turned away, then spun back toward her. "And I've heard all the crap about it I'll take. Just drop it. Understand? Drop it." It was as sharp a tone, as crude a set of words, as Chase had ever used to Darcie. But instead of making him feel better, it only made him feel worse.

The door opened and Brannigan came in carrying a tray loaded with everything from whiskey to Coke. To all of them, Brannigan presented a remarkable sight. He had slipped into his white service coat, his shiny black face standing out in startling contrast to the light material. The staring match between Chase and Darcie did not escape him. Holding the tray with one hand, he indicated the jacket with the other. "Wisha, but I thought the occasion called for a mite of the old splendor, you know. The electricity back, the party, and then Lord love us, a guest." Darcie and Chase looked at him dumfounded. Very carefully, Brannigan was putting the tray on a small table beside Dirk's chair. "In the case of the last-named item, however, he appears to have gone into a deep stupor. The truth is, I don't believe anyone has ever looked to be so sound asleep as him. Exhaustion. It's the city life, I expect."

Darcie smiled only faintly as she studied the sleeping Dirk. Then she turned back toward Chase. "Well, he's dead to the world.

"Shouldn't we try to move him—to get him to bed?" Darcie asked Brannigan.

"Try to move him? Never. For all I know the lad may be dead and I'd be disturbing his immortal soul. I'll get a blanket, is what."

"Immortal souls are in short supply around here," Darcie snapped and followed Brannigan out of the room without even glancing at Chase.

For perhaps half an hour, Chase sat and studied the flames burning in the small fireplace. Although not yet winter, the room had a chill to it. Chase drew his chair closer to the fireplace for warmth, watching fascinated as an occasional gust of wind would blow down the chimney and make the flames dance, each time sending small scatterings of ashes whirling onto the hearth. From the living room, the sound of the party occasionally grew loud enough to reach through the door. A subdued moan of exhaustion from the sleeping Dirk caused Chase's head to turn; the boy was fighting some phantom in his restless dreamworld, twisiting beneath the blanket and pulling pulling it tighter around himself, as if for protection. Chase sighed.

The noise from the living room rose in a sudden swell. Some sort of game was being played and someone had won and someone had lost. With a defeated shrug, Chase rose from his chair, opened the door, and walked slowly toward the din in the living room.

He wished his own problems were as simple as someone winning or losing a game.

Chapter Ten

*I characterize the nation's liberal
establishment as exhibiting a failure of
nerve and an immobilized state of mind
that constitute an accommodation to
totalitarianism without precedent in our
history . . . Americans no longer manifest
any interest in freedom, but only with
freedom from involvement.*

> —*Daniel P. Moynihan,*
> *United States Senator*

In the underground retreat built at Usspatpenn, things
were falling into an essentially relaxed pattern. All of the
systems seemed to be in perfect working order. There
had been some small initial difficulty with the water supply, but Dr. Chatteris had quickly diagnosed his inanimate
patient's problem and cured it.

Graffa spent most of the days reading from the extensive collection of books lining the shelves of his underground library, while his wife was content riding up and
down the two-story elevator he had had installed for her.
Occasionally, she would complain about the shortness of
the trip and the small number of passengers, but, between
Miss Dark and Graffa, they finally convinced her that in
the shift to suburbia, two-story department stores were
quite common. This seemed to satisfy her, although to
help her adjust, the doctor, Miss Dark, Granger and
Graffa thought it wise to take as many trips a day in the
tiny elevator as they could bring themselves to.

Standards were being maintained. Dinner was still taken
at eight-thirty. As he always did, Granger would serve the

meal in his chancery coat, and although Dr. Chatteris and Miss Dark both found the process excruciating, black tie and long dress were *de rigueur*. Sometimes Chatteris found himself wondering who was really the crazier: Graffa or his wife.

On November 4—one day before the outside world was to receive full electric power again and be addressed on its television receivers by the White House—a curious event took place at Usspatpenn, rattling the calm. Because the structure was entirely underground, no satisfactory radio reception was possible. Originally, an aerial had been located in one of the exhaust vents, but the wires had apparently been cut during one of the groundkeeper's trimming and pruning sessions. No one had gotten around to try crawling up the long tunnel in what would have probably been a useless effort to repair it. Perhaps they all felt a certain security in their sense of isolation. The tennants thus were unaware that no radio or television programming was being broadcast. Nor did they know of the CAC or the PLA or of the burning of the Capitol. Graffa, his wife, Dr. Chatteris, Granger and Miss Dark lived in an entirely sealed environment, shut off, as carefully buttoned up as astronauts in a space capsule.

At exactly eight o'clock the morning of the twentieth, as the sun slowly climbed over the waters of Delaware Bay, one month less a day after their self-imposed imprisonment, this state of isolation ended abruptly. Chatteris was the first to notice the sound, a scraping of metal against metal, an occasional thud of something heavy being moved into place, the rising and falling of distant voices. A few minutes later, Granger came into the room, his face etched with worry, seeking reassurance that the sounds were not as ominous as he suspected.

Graffa looked from one to the other of them, studying their expressions. "What is it? Is something wrong? You both look terrified."

"Shhhh." Dr. Chatteris listened, one hand held up, struggling to make sense of the noises above their heads. "Go on battery power," he suddenly ordered Granger. "Shut down everything else—the generators, the pumps, that damned elevator, anything that makes noise. Someone is right next to one of the intake or exhaust shafts."

Graffa asked his question again. "Is something wrong?"

Granger, for possibly the first time in his almost thirty

years of service to old Mr. Wetherill, ignored him and, slipping off his shoes, ran for the generator and electrical controls. The elevator whined to a stop, the cage suspended halfway between the two floors. Out of nowhere, Miss Dark materialized; the lighting flickered on and off in the changeover of power systems, finally returning, but at a considerably dimmer level. Bringing over a small stepladder, Miss Dark tried to coax Mrs. Wetherill down out of the elevator, but the old lady sat firmly planted on her camp stool, announcing that her post in an emergency was to stay where she was. Graffa joined Miss Dark in the effort, letting his voice rise in the process, commanding her to leave for the safety of her passengers.

"Shhhh!" repeated Dr. Chatteris; his tone made the command urgent and unarguable. "There's quite a few of them. I can hear voices coming from another shaft too. We have to stay absolutely quiet. I'm going to crawl along one of the deeper shafts, and up to ground level. If there's nobody close, I can lift the outer cover and take a look."

Graffa studied the doctor. "Do you think it could be serious? No one knows about this place."

Dr. Chatteris affected a casual tone, one that conflicted sharply with what he felt. "Probably nothing but snoopers or trespassers. I think I should check, though. And everyone's got to remain completely quiet. If you have to walk somewhere, do as Granger did: take off your shoes. Chance's are it's nothing. Probably nothing to worry about at all."

Granger had removed the interior grillwork covering the air shaft Chatteris had indicated, and helped the doctor pull himself up and into it. Very shortly, Chatteris disappeared inside, and soon even the sound of his clothes brushing the sides of the galvanized metal shaft was gone. Granger stared at the empty opening of the air shaft and hoped the doctor was right.

Aboveground, perhaps a dozen men, all of them wearing red-and-white arm bands, stood around the grounds of Usspatpenn, listening to the orders of a man holding what appeared to be a map. Behind the men were parked two large trucks, each carrying a load of cement blocks; to one side stood a smaller pickup truck, loaded with shovels, wheelbarrows and other equipment. All of these men, including the leader, assumed they were following orders is-

sued by CAC headquarters; in actuality, the orders had
been issued by Mort Evers shortly before he left for the
house in Dennis. When he had issued them to the local
CAC headquarters, he had used a headquarters authoriz-
ing stamp to make them carry more weight.

Between him and Graffa, he felt, there remained a score
to be settled. Years before, when Graffa originally hired
him, he had been assured that his job as head grounds-
keeper was only a temporary arrangement, a stepping-
stone to some higher job in the Wetherill empire.
Somewhere along the line, Graffa soured on the man's potential and the greater visions which Graffa had painted
were quietly put aside. Although Evers had always blamed
this change of heart on Chase, he felt he had an account
to even up with the old man as well. Chase was to be
taken care of at Dennis; the old man in his underground
shelter at Usspatpenn. But the more he thought of it, the
less comfortable Evers felt in his plan to destroy old Mr.
Wetherill; destroying Chase would be enough—as well as
being its own kind of revenge on the old man.

Sucking on his pipe, Evers had written new orders rescinding the ones issued to the men now gathered on Usspatpenn's lawns; these rescinding orders were still in
Evers' pocket when Chase blew his head off in Dennis.

None of this was known to Dr. Chatteris when he finally reached the exit of the air shaft and slowly raised the
camouflaged cover to look around him. For a moment, the
men's actions baffled the doctor; blocks were being off-
loaded from the trucks and placed into metal wheelbarrows, which were being slowly moved. Then the realization
of what the men were up to struck Chatteris like a knee
to the groin. Lowering the cover, he slid himself back
down the air shaft as quickly as he could.

The group waited below. All of their eyes rose as Chatteris slipped out of the air shaft and back into the room.

"Mr. Wetherill," he began. "I don't know how to break
this to you gently, but—"

Graffa's ice-blue eyes fixed him with a disapproving
stare. "Your clothes are all dirty, doctor."

From nowhere, Granger produced a whisk broom and
began brushing the doctor's coat, then his pants. "Those
trousers will need pressing, sir. If you would leave them
on your bed—"

Chatteris looked at them in awe. He was trapped with a

group of the truly mad, a gathering of the politely insane. Giving his head a quick nervous shake to clear it, he forced himself back to reality. "What they're going to do is seal off the air shafts with concrete blocks and cement. Some man with a map is pointing out where the openings are. If his map shows all of them, we're finished. There's a certain amount of air already here inside the bunker, of course; it may last four or five days. Then, there's a little bottled oxygen. But after that, well . . ."

With a nod, as if the doctor's statement came to him as no surprise whatsoever, Graffa indicated the decanter of brandy. "I think we could all use some, Granger."

"Mr. Wetherill," interrupted Chatteris. "I'm not sure whether you understood what I just said. In a short time, there will be no air."

Graffa nodded to show that he understood very well. Looking up, he smiled weakly, as if the doctor's announcement was something that would, in the end, have little effect on them. "No air." He repeated the doctor's words wistfully. "Air. That's the one thing I never got around to patenting."

Dr. Chatteris's estimate of four or five days worth of air became academic almost as soon as he made it. Trying to get Mrs. Wetherill down out of her elevator without hauling her from the car bodily, Graffa had ordered Granger to switch briefly back to normal power. But the battery power was still being fed into the line, so there was an immediate short circuit. To avoid the poisonous sulfuric acid fumes which quickly billowed from the shorted batteries, most of the bunker's rooms and air shafts, with their precious reserves of air, had to be sealed off immediately.

The backup battery system, Dr. Chatteris explained angrily, would still give them a vestige of power, but to keep from being poisoned by the battery fumes, sealing off everything but the immediate area around them was the only possible course of action. This left the group with only the air in the living room, two small bedrooms, and one air shaft to draw on, which would, Chatteris estimated, last them little more than seven or eight hours.

By ten that night, the quickly deteriorating quality of the air was affecting them all; the trapped people wheezed and gasped, doing their best to conserve the small supply that was left by moving as little as possible. Except

for Graffa. He stood in the hallway beneath the elevator
still trying to coax his wife into pushing the button to
bring the elevator all the way down. Graffa had changed
into his black evening tie and velvet smoking jacket, as if
preparing for dinner; the bunker below Usspatpenn might
be rapidly running out of air, but he refused to change the
habits of eighty-three years. He looked up at his wife and
sighed; she was still seated on the small camp stool, firmly
planted in front of the elevator controls, but her head kept
falling farther and farther forward, as if she were sinking
into a sleep. Graffa wondered if this was because of the
diminishing air supply, or because his wife was merely
tired from being in one position so long without the usual
movement of the elevator.

Earlier, he had gathered Miss Dark, Granger, and Dr.
Chatteris and thanked them, telling them they were free to
do with their last hours as they wished; he would require
nothing further. Perhaps, he said, they had letters to write,
or other affairs to put in order. Or, if they wanted, they
could try their luck breaking through one of the newly ce-
mented air vents. Of all of them, Granger had been the
hardest to dissuade from staying with him, but Graffa had
been insistent. In the end, Graffa had had to be quite rude
to Granger and make his leaving an order. Although he
knew how Granger would react, Graffa tried not to see his
look of hurt. He was well aware that Granger could have
thought of no more fitting way to spend his last moments
on earth than in service to the family. But to Graffa, getting rid of all of them was of very special importance. Finally, after a long handshake, Granger had walked slowly
off toward one of the rooms; Miss Dark had simply disappeared, to lie down on a bed and let death come to her as
in sleep; Dr. Chatteris had climbed again into one of the
air vents and was making what he already knew would be
a futile effort to break his way out through the concrete.

Once they were gone, Graffa poured himself more Co-
gnac, then returned to the area directly below the elevator.
Increasingly, it became obvious that his wife would never
operate the buttons herself, and Graffa concentrated on a
way to do it for her. The small ladder was not high
enough. But by standing on it and poking with a broom
handle, he might be able to reach the buttons himself.

Rocking precariously, Graffa leaned far forward and
started jabbing at the buttons, talking to her as he did.

"Come on, you silly old woman, you can't just sit there forever, halfway up and halfway down. We Wetherills always stand for something, never the middle." He poked again with the broom handle, came close but missed, and almost fell off the ladder from the momentum of the lunge. "Easy, now, easy," he cautioned himself, regaining his balance and preparing for another attempt. This time he was successful. With a hesitant whir, the elevator descended slowly to the ground level. "There you are, old girl. We'll have you looking better in a second." From a closet, where he'd hidden it earlier, Graffa withdrew a portable oxygen tank, the kind skin divers use. Quickly, he adjusted the mask over her face and gave her a long shot of the oxygen in it. This tank was the reason he had been so insistent on everyone else's departure. For if the famous Wetherill luck lived up to its reputation just one more time, this oxygen might take him and his wife to safety. Luck. The Wetherills had always been lucky. Sometimes Graffa felt it was their greatest asset. Years before, when the imported Frenchman had built this bunker for him, one exit had never been marked on any map. At the time, this had not been done for any particular reason, but simply because Graffa had forgotten to tell anyone. Luck. This exit was at the end of a long tunnel, and the skin divers' air tanks might provide just enough air for the two of them to make it. If he had told the others, the air would have had to be shared with them as well, and none would have made it. All that remained now was for him to bring his wife back to consciousness so they could try their escape, their last joint effort, the two of them against the world—as they had been back before the strange sickness had robbed her of her reason. A part of Graffa felt remorse at the treachery to Granger this involved, but only a modest part; about Miss Dark and the doctor, he felt only a passing twinge of conscience.

The oxygen hissed through the mask, but nothing much seemed to be happening. He rubbed her wrists, pumped her arms, and talked to her. If they were to have any chance at all, they should already be under way. "Come on, old girl, come on," he urged her. "No time for beauty rest. Later when we're safe, you can have all the rest you want. Outside, there's a world full of passengers wating for your elevator. You wouldn't want to disappoint them, would you?"

For a second, Graffa thought he saw some flicker of life, but leaning closer, he could not see it again. He searched his memory for other things that might penetrate her sleep. With difficulty, he remembered the songs she had liked—old songs—and tried to sing them in his cracked voice, but couldn't seem to remember any of the words, Graffa took a shot of the oxygen himself, then returned the mask to her face. He was surprised at how cold her skin felt, and a knot of fear swept through him. Searching, he groped for her pulse. Finally, after trying several times, he realized that there was none. She was dead.

Graffa sighed. He supposed he'd known it from the moment the elevator reached the ground and he had seen the color of her face. For just an instant, he considered trying the escape on his own. With only one person to support, the tankful of oxygen would be more than enough. But he quickly abandoned the idea. He had lived too long with her, lived too long *for* her, to attempt a life without her. Reaching out, he drew a small chair into the elevator and sat down beside her, cradling her hand in his lap.

He talked to her of things from the past, rocking the hand back and forth in his, conscious of how quiet the elevator was with only his own voice and the hiss of the oxygen mask to fill the silence. Simultaneously, two ideas came to him: a final gesture of his love for her and the words of her favorite song—something they used to sing together more than fifty years earlier.

"Going up!" he called out and pressed the button. When he reached the top, he asked for passengers, pressed the button again, and let the elevator descend. Riding endlessly up and down in her beloved elevator while he sang her favorite song to her didn't seem like much, Graffa conceded, but it would have made her happy. Feeling silly, he searched her face, but it remained blank and unresponsive.

The oxygen ran out about halfway through the song's first verse. The elevator had just left the first floor again and was about to disappear slowly toward the second. "We'll go up in a great big balloon," his voice croaked in song, "and make love to the man in the moon . . . and behind a big cloud, where no one's allowed . . ."

His voice stopped, there was a small cough, and then silence.

* * *

In Salisbury, of course, no one was aware of the sàd course of events at Usspatpenn; Chase and his family had their own problems and concerns.

Dirk left for New York about noon. For what apparently was the first time in some days, he had had a bath, changed into clean clothes (Brannigan found some old things of Emlyn's that were approximately the right size), and ate a breakfast-lunch of gargantuan proportions. When he saw Chase, some instinct steered Dirk away from putting any direct questions about coming to New York to him. For the moment, he left the matter in abeyance and instead provided Chase with a comprehensive set of instructions on how to find Tracey in New York.

"If you should decide to come, Mr. Wetherill, you'll find Tracey's made himself very hard to track down. Actually, he has three places in the Village, not one, and moves to a different pad each day. In no particular order. I'm not sure he knows himself where he'll be on any given day. Anyway, he said to tell you that if you do come, the way to find him is to hang out in one of these three bars and eventually he'll show up. I'll tell him about the beard; with it, I'm not sure he'd recognize you himself." Leaning over the kitchen table, Dirk wrote out the names of the bars and their addresses on a slip of paper and handed it to Chase. Chase studied the list; the names were all unfamiliar to him.

"They're all gay bars, of course. Right now, no one seems to be watching them too closely; they've got their minds on other things, I guess."

More details were discussed, interspersed with Dirk's comments on life as it was today, in the city. After meeting with the CAC, the police had ended their "strike" and returned to duty, Dirk noted; order had been restored, but the price was high: a sunset to sunrise curfew (not very closely observed), identification papers for everyone, frequent spot checking of these cards by policemen, the National Guard, or small groups of CAC troopers who roamed the streets particularly for that purpose. All theaters, motion-picture houses and meeting houses were shuttered. All of this, Dirk said, had been locally explained as a temporary phenomenon, but no one really believed that was the case. Wearily, Dirk told Chase that the stories about people being spirited from their homes in the middle of the night or day were true. Pressed for details,

Dirk had admitted that he had watched, unable to help, as several of his own friends were taken away. They were, he said, suspected of nothing more dangerous than being "potentially subversive." But in spite of its difficulties, the city was somehow managing to survive: schools were slowly reopening, the streets were relatively free of petty crime, garbage collection had been restored, the telephone was sputtering back to life, and mail service was falteringly returning to its usual deliveries, a little more efficient, if anything, than in other days.

Abruptly, in the middle of this recital, Dirk finished putting on a jacket of Emlyn's that was a full size too large for him, turned, and looked Chase squarely in the eye. "What do I tell Tracey?"

"You have no more specific idea of why Tracey wants me to come than what you've told me?"

Dirk shook his head. "If I knew, I'd level. Honestly. All I know is that it's urgent."

"Tell Tracey—tell him that I'm going to make every possible effort I can . . ." Chase knew he sounded totally inadequate. He pressed his lips together and said what he really felt. "No, dammit, tell him I'll break my ass to get there—do absolutely anything I can to show up—if I can swing it without leaving my family in danger."

Solemnly, Dirk nodded. "Travel's tough. Planes all grounded. No gas for cars. No trains, of course. Not yet, anyway. Thumbing your way on a truck is probably the only way. A lot of checkpoints, and an awful lot of people on the road moving from nowhere to nowhere—like refugees, not really sure of where they're going, but convinced that anyplace else must be better."

Chase nodded, and they walked into the living room. In spite of all the pressure he and Darcie could apply, Dirk refused to spend the day and stay for dinner. He would be late getting back as it was, he explained. At the door, he paused and looked at Chase again. "Christ, I hope you can get there. Tracey's counting on it."

"I'll do my damnedest."

At seven-thirty that night, television returned to the screens of the nation. On all channels, the images were the same: an endless succession of shots showing a country at peace. There was no voice, no commentary, only soft music of a borderline patriotic variety played by the full

Washington Philharmonic. When the cameras showed the now orderly streets of different cities, the pictures came in startling contrast to the television the nation had last witnessed: rioting, violence, burning, destruction. The pictures of New York, with lights blazing brightly and even some traffic pouring down its main arteries, would have been hard to distinguish from a picture of the city in completely normal circumstances. Only in Washington was a sour note allowed to inject itself. When the White House was shown, it looked as graceful and softly elegant as ever, the floodlit American flag flapping gently in the wind. This made the sudden, stark pictures of the burned-out Capitol Building, covered with PLA graffiti and the blackened, soot-scarred marks of the fire evident around its windows and doors, seem even more shocking. The ruined structure conjured up the frightening moments when the nation had watched one of its most sacred symbols of freedom attacked and destroyed.

In passing, the rural areas were also shown, looking particularly peaceful in the long shadows of the fast-fading fall light. In combination, the effect of cities and country-side bathed in a sense of peace gave the television viewers of the country a feeling that, at long last, the nation was once again free and safe.

At three minutes to eight, a commentator's voice was heard. Since, he said, the upcoming address from the White House was to be in effect a group one, the American people would be shown pictures of the Cabinet members whom they would shortly be hearing from. Most of them, he noted, were already familiar to the audience. They weren't—some of them were total mysteries, even to Chase. The new leaders of the House and Senate were represented, but, while their names struck a distant responsive chord in Chase, he knew nothing of their pasts, their records or credentials, and Chase couldn't help wondering what had happened to the men who had been the leaders before the news blackout. The Cabinet was largely made up of new faces, too: some of the original Cabinet was still there, but the Secretary of State was a man Chase remembered only as a past Director of the CIA, while the Secretary of the Treasury was Carter Morgan, the "friend" who had tried to keep him on the telephone long enough for his call to be traced. To a man, all of those presented appeared uncomfortable and embarrassed, as if they weren't sure how they happened to be in this room at this time, appearing before these television cameras.

The commentator's voice stopped and the people in the pictures suddenly came to life. The men shown in the stills were seen seated in a shallow semicircle, with one somewhat larger chair, still empty, positioned in its center. For a second, the men on the screen could be observed talking to each other nervously, but too softly to be picked up by the microphones. Then, Senator William Carnass of Alabama—and the man probably most familiar to Americans—indicated that the rest of the group should rise. Simultaneously, Carnass addressed both the men in the room and the television audience. "Ladies and gentlemen, it is my honor to introduce to you, by virtue of Section IV of the Twenty-fifth Amendment to the Constitution of the United States . . ."

All of the men on the screen had turned to the right side of the room, and some were already applauding listlessly. Chase gasped. Carnass continued doggedly. ". . . Associate Justice of the Supreme Court and Acting President of the United States . . . Tobin Wetherill." Into the picture, wearing an expression of gravity, sadness and unwanted responsibility thrust upon him, strode his brother Toby.

Chapter Eleven

"In my thirty years as a businessman," Mr.
*[Henry] Ford said, "I have never felt so
troubled about the future of . . . my country.
It is not too much to say that the very
survival of our free society may depend on
finding good solutions. . . ."*
    —Henry Ford,
        *appearing before the Joint Economic
        Council of Congress, February 19, 1973*

Chase did not hear that anyone was standing outside the
front door, he felt it. At first he dismissed the sensation as
a product of his imagination, a delayed reaction, perhaps
to the killings on the hill. But the feeling of a presence on
the front step was so all-pervasive, Chase was unable to
shake it. The early night of late fall had already wrapped
the house in hostile darkness and the whole family was
gathered in the living room; with his hand, Chase suddenly
signaled everyone to be quiet. Uncomprehending, they
stared at him, but immediately fell silent. Silently, the
lighting of the room was converted from electricity to oil
lamps and candles; the short-wave was switched off and
hidden; the shotgun was brought out of the closet, unwrapped, and placed in Chase's hand.

For perhaps three minutes, Chase stood with his ear
pressed against the door, but could hear nothing. He again
dismissed the thought that the feeling was a product of his
imagination; the last few weeks had so developed his instinct for survival that he no longer rejected any sensation,
however illogical, that warned of imminent peril. With his
eyes, he signaled Brannigan to bring the powerful energy-
pack flashlight and stand beside him; its beam would be so
intense that anyone entering through the door would be

momentarily blinded and Chase would have the advantage. He raised the shotgun.

With a sudden yank, Brannigan jerked the front door inward. The energy pack blasted the doorstep with a blinding incandescence. Darcie's scream shattered the silence of the living room and caused the energy pack in Brannigan's hand to swing its beam up and down erratically.

In the doorway were a man and a boy frozen in place by the brilliant shaft of light. The man's entire head, from his hair to just above his mouth, was clumsily wrapped in makeshift bandages. There were two large, ugly dark stains near the area of the man's eyes, and additional blood had trickled down his face in almost symmetrical patterns, like Indian warpaint. The boy, who appeared to be seven or eight, was holding the man by the hand; Darcie's scream, the suddenness of the blinding light, and the sight of Chase with his shotgun scared him so that he now clutched at the man's other hand as well; yet his movements were slow and dull, as if he were drugged or so familiar with fear he was incapable of further reaction to it.

"Darcie!" commanded Chase, but she was already running from the living room to the front door. Chase gently guided the man inside, while Brannigan steadied him when he tripped over the change in the floor levels. Chase's voice shook as he tried to reassure the stranger. The man tried to speak, but when he opened his mouth all that came out was a bubbling, breathy sound; his face was so badly beaten that there were few teeth left and his mouth and lower face were so swollen that speech was beyond him. Reaching out, the man clutched at Chase, pulling desperately at his sleeve as if to tell him something. The touch stirred something in Chase's memory and he stared at him, trying to figure what it was.

"Sweet Mother of Jesus," yelled Brannigan at the twins. "Get a chair out here fast. The poor soul's about to keel over."

More of the strange bubbling, breathy sounds came from the man, his lips and mouth trying desperately to form words. Darcie patted him on the shoulders and gave a reassuring "Everything's all right," helping him into the chair the twins and Emlyn had dragged into the front hall. Then she turned toward the boy and tried to put her arms around him comfortingly, but the child drew back—eyes wide, but no sound, no tears, nothing but a penetrating stare that was near to hostility. Darcie knelt down in front of him to put her head on the same level at his, her hands still stretched toward him. "What happened, darling? What happened?" The boy only shook his head and reached into his jacket pocket, fumbling for something. She could see that when he had started the day he had been well dressed; a now ripped and torn pair of gray flannels showed beneath what apparently had been a school blazer—part of some emblem could still be seen on his breast pocket—and the remnants of a striped tie were knotted into a messy ball pulled down to his waist. "You can tell me," Darcie said softly. "I'm not going to hurt you, I'm going to help you. Are you all right? Do you want something to eat? What happened to your father?"

The hand emerged from the jacket pocket with some sort of note, which the boy glanced at and then put back in his pocket. When he spoke, the memorized words came out of his mouth in flat, measured tones, as if from some machine designed to speak in a person's voice. "My name is Russell Wainwright. My father and I were in an accident, but we cannot find a doctor. Can you help us, please?"

The moment the boy spoke his name, the bandaged stranger began making desperate sounds, grabbing Chase again by the arm, trying to form words his ruined mouth would not permit. Darcie and Chase looked at each other for a moment, stunned. Unbelieving, Chase turned to the man and asked, "Nicholas? Nicholas? My God, Darcie, it's—" He threw his arms around the man, who half-staggered to his feet and embraced his brother, swaying back and forth. Darcie was no longer looking at Chase; she was forcing her arms around the boy.

Her attempt was brushed aside, as if what was happening was not part of some script he'd been told to follow, and the boy-machine began again, this time with the voice quavering badly. "My name is Russell Wainwright. My father and I were in an accident, but we cannot find—" He stopped in the middle of the sentence and collapsed into Darcie's arms, the tears and sobs finally all coming out of him at once.

Chase's odd feeling of *déjà vu* when the stranger had

pulled on his sleeve explained itself easily enough now. Chase's brother Nicholas—the banking Wetherill—had had one son, Russell Wetherill, by his first wife. When Nicholas divorced her, the boy's mother had taken Russell with her and, to spite her former husband, had changed the boy's name by having her new husband legally adopt him. Chase and Darcie saw little of Russell Wainwright; the hostility between Nicholas and his first wife was such that little Russell was the one Wetherill deliberately kept outside the family. Only when he had spoken his name had the pieces fitted together.

Both Chase and Darcie had felt guilty that they had not recognized Nicholas immediately, although there was no reason they should; very little of his face showed, and the little that did was a swollen, misshapen mess. This, combined with the absence of any voice to orient them, left Chase and Darcie still having trouble believing it really was Nicholas. The more important questions—what had happened, how Nicholas and his son had found them, how Nicholas had been so badly injured—would have to wait until later.

Although most of his face was so hidden, they could see Nicholas was shaken by the sound of Russell's crying; his body began to shake and his hands explored the air in front of him in a sort of frenzy. Suddenly, he stood up, unsteady and uncertain on his feet, then lurched across the room toward the sound to reassure his son. Brannigan reached him quickly and guided him, and the father gathered Russell into his arms, stroking his head and making a sound somewhere between a moan and a breathy sigh.

Shortly afterward, Chase and Brannigan took Nicholas upstairs and put him to bed, undressing him and helping him into a pair of Chase's pajamas. To Darcie fell the job of removing the old bandages and washing the wounds. Chase was gathering up Nicholas' blood-stained clothes when he heard a gasp from Darcie. He started to turn and move toward her, but found her already in his arms, trembling. "My God, Chase," she hissed. "His eyes, his eyes."

Looking, Chase could see as the clotted and matted blood was washed away that the eyeballs themselves had become visible. It required no doctor to realize that Nicholas would never see again. Chase squeezed her arm and stood beside her as she finished the bathing and washing of Nicholas' face.

Once finished, they both thought Nicholas would immediately fall asleep; but he refused the suggestion and made hand signals for a pad and pen. Brannigan brought the writing material. From Russell and from what little Nicholas could write, they were able to learn a small amount more of what had happened. It was difficult, since Nicholas could not see what he wrote, and the letters and words crossed over one another, but they were able to get the gist of the story from him.

Pieced together, what had befallen Nicholas was brutally simple. Originally, in its early days, he had helped the CAC, even advancing it funds through his bank. Business friends, as well as Nicholas himself, had considered its basic philosophy to be honestly in the country's best interests—and perhaps the only possible way to save the country from itself. But as the movement developed, Nicholas became aware that what the CAC really planned was a complete takeover with no pretense of democracy. And so he had begun to withdraw his support. But the CAC wouldn't allow him to, and Nicholas, in spite of their threats, had done the only thing he could: he summarily cut off the funds from his bank. Like Chase, then, Nicholas found himself damned by both sides—the CAC and the PLA—and wasn't even sure which group had cornered him in his house and left him for dead.

Russell had become involved because that particular weekend happened to be one when Nicholas could demand visitation rights from his first wife. As things turned out, the break had been a lucky one for Nicholas.

For Russell, no one could call the incident lucky. On Nicholas' orders, he'd hidden himself in a closet before the savage beating was given his father; he had not seen, then, but had heard the terrible sounds of it. The effect of this on Russell was difficult to imagine; certainly, it was something the boy's memory would never outlive.

Following his father's written instructions, the boy had led him from Greenwich to the turnpike as fast as he could; as did all the brothers, Nicholas knew where Chase's retreat of last resort was—Chase had told it to each on the phone the day he made his try for the airport, except for Toby, whom he had not been able to reach. On the turnpike, Russell had stumbled onto a sympathetic trucker, who had not only given them a lift, but even taken a detour onto the Taconic Parkway to bring them closer to Salisbury.

It was at this point that Nicholas had written out Russell's little speech for him. For while Chase had given him brief directions for finding the farm, he would be relaying these directions to the young boy leading him, and it would be easy to make an error. Nicholas knew that as soon as Chase and Darcie heard Russell's name, they would know who he was; if they got the wrong house, or if Chase's house had already been found and occupied by the CAC, at least they would not have revealed their identity. They had been lucky and reached Chase's actual doorstep.

Gently, Chase went back to trying to gain more information from Nicholas' hard-to-read little notes. But he had gotten all he would of the story; Nicholas' limited supply of energy was now exhausted, and helped by some sleeping pills of Darcie's to deaden the pain, he finally fell asleep.

Back in his own room, Chase found that the events had left him literally shaking with fury. Out of the blue, he had discovered his brother, Toby, was the mastermind behind the CAC. As yet, there was no definite proof of this assumption, but the fact that Carter Morgan was acting as Secretary of the Treasury—and Chase already knew all too well that Carter Morgan was directly implicated—made Toby's own involvement with the CAC hard to escape. Similarly, the name of the new Secretary of State, Randall Davison, had set off a chain of half-forgotten facts in Chase's mind. Davison, he seemed to remember, had turned up in at least one of Colbert's many SYNPAC Telexes as also tied to the CAC in some way. Abruptly, it struck Chase why he had been unable to reach Toby at the Supreme Court Building, the morning of "Situation D"; Toby had deliberately made himself unavailable.

The evidence kept growing in Chase's mind by the minute. He tried to find other explanations and excuses, but they would not come. Worse, Toby's involvement with the CAC made it impossible to exempt him from the whole situation that had enveloped the country, for Nicholas, for Dina's disappearance, for whatever was happening to Tracey, and for his own desperate state of mind.

*   *   *

Chase's stomach turned, thinking of Toby's sanctimonious little speech, designed to lull America into a false sense of peace, assuring people things would return to normal and democracy be restored "shortly." Meanwhile, of course, Toby would be consolidating his own position. Then had come the arrival of Nicholas and his son. Nicholas, too, turned out to be less than above reproach, but when he finally saw what was happening, at least he had had the guts to refuse to cooperate any further. And Nicholas' punishment had certainly been swift and cruel—left blind, speechless, a silent, walking vegetable. Too cruel. Slumping down on the edge of his bed, he turned to Darcie, who was just slipping under the covers of her own bed. "It's hard to believe that people can do things like that. What they did to Nicholas. And it's hard to believe your own brother can do things like Toby is doing. Right now, I feel as if the whole world's gone crazy and that anyone is capable of doing anything."

"Or do nothing." Darcie had raised her head slightly to offer this comment; she now lay back down, turning herself away from him and pulling the covers up close around her. Inside Chase, a lot of bitter words, explanations and arguments came boiling to the surface. Although her comment was presumably about Tracey, behind it lay her bitterness about Dina. Darcie was being unfair, unreasonable, illogical.

To try to shake his sense of frustration, Chase lay in bed, listening to the night sounds and wondering about Toby. Could he really have so badly misjudged his brother for a lifetime? Could they have known each other so well and spent their entire childhoods so closely bound without Chase noticing some sign, some indication, some omen of what he had seen of Toby on television tonight? Chase squirmed, suddenly remembering the prayer Toby had used to finish his speech. Not because there was anything wrong with the prayer itself, but because there was so much wrong with the hypocrisy Toby had displayed in offering it to the country. "Oh, Lord," Toby had prayed, his benign face lowered to precisely the right angle, "We pray for your help in preserving this country from its enemies, both internal and external, and to guide us in our pursuit of justice and freedom."

Across the hall lay his brother Nicholas, who could have told the world all about Toby's pursuit of justice and freedom. Unable to sleep, Chase stole out of bed and took a couple of Darcie's sleeping pills.

Next morning, Chase woke early. The pills had left him with a slightly drugged feeling. He was not sure what had awakened him, but he sensed an uneasiness, some instinct of foreboding. He pulled on his bathrobe and went downstairs. On his way, he noticed the door to the bedroom Nicholas and Russell were using was open and the beds empty. He was surprised, yet he supposed this was a good sign: the boy had probably led his father downstairs and Brannigan was feeding both of them. Chase wasn't sure what to do about Nicholas—his brother should be seen by a doctor, but getting one from Sharon or Salisbury would not be easy; a lot of questions would be asked.

When Chase looked into the kitchen, it was empty. Some second sense brought him to the summer kitchen, and he pushed the door slightly open. As he did, an unseen object sticking out from behind the door brushed against his shoulder, causing Chase to flinch; a hollow thump reached him, and along with it, a repeated sensation of some unknown presence brushing against him; the combination caused Chase to throw the door completely open. Staggered by the sight, he sagged weakly against the door frame.

Nicholas, swinging gently from the movement of the door, hung by his neck. His sightless eyes bulged slightly, as if unable to accept some distant vision which had appeared in front of them. Like all old manor houses, the room had a high ceiling, and his brother had managed to hang himself from a heavy hook just below the molding, kicking over the small chair he had apparently used to stand on. His body, its grotesque head unwrapped from its heavy bandages, was what Chase had felt coming into the room. On Nicholas' pajamas—actually a pair of Chase's—was pinned a short note, written in overlarge, overlapped writing. "I have failed the family, I have failed the country, and I have failed my son. Pls. take care of Russell. I'm sorry.—Nick." For a few moments, Chase stood staring at his brother, shocked at the piece of trivia that flew through his mind: in his entire life, he had never known Nicholas, even as a child, to call himself "Nick".

Chase shook himself free of his shock, spun around, and was about to yell for Brannigan, when he saw him crossing the small hall separating the library from the kitchen; in his hand was a large knife, and from the look on his face, it was obvious that he had already discovered what Chase had just come across. The expression he wore was one of infinite sadness, a weary look of resigned helplessness. Seeing Chase, he merely nodded, then reached up and began sawing through the heavy rope Nicholas hung from. "Something woke me up," Brannigan explained with a small sigh. "Some sound, I don't know what. It must have woke the boy too, because just as I got here I seed him run through the door, poor lad. But when I tried to catch up with him outside, he was nowhere about, and I thought I should get back and cut down this, before Mrs. Wetherill and the children see him. Blind as the dear man was, he must have slipped down here sometime in the night and done it. My heart goes out to the poor soul, but I worry more about the boys." He grabbed the body as the rope was cut, and he and Chase gently lowered Nicholas to the floor. "Soon as we take care of this, everybody can start looking for the child."

But they were never to find Russell. The entire family fanned out through the woods and across the fields and out as close as they dared to the edge of the highway without discovering a trace of him. Weeks later, Chase would still find himself wondering what had become of him, a terrible picture growing in his mind of Russell, his wide eyes blurred by tears of noncomprehension, going from house to house across the foothills, his machine-programmed voice endlessly repeating: "My name is Russell Wainwright. My father and I were in an accident, but we cannot find a doctor. Can you help us, please? My name is Russell Wainwright . . ."

This fantasy of Russell wandering aimlessly, appealing for help, touched Chase strangely, and for a second, the thought of Dina flashed through his mind. But the association of the two ideas was so disquieting that Chase quickly dismissed it; Dina was a resourceful girl and could take care of herself. Shaking his head, Chase set out to join the futile search for Russell Wainwright.

They came and took Eliot Towers away a few minutes after Toby Wetherill's address to the nation began. 8:04 p.m., to be precise. Towers, personal assistant to Chase at the Foundation, was just as floored as Chase had been

when Associate Justice Tobin Wetherill appeared on his
screen, although, since he was not Toby's brother, Towers'
reaction was more clinical than personal. Tobin Wetherill
had just told the country the first order of business would
be new elections to replace the discredited houses of
Congress. After a pause to explain that there would, of
course, be a few necessary delays before this could be accomplished properly, Toby was repeating his desire that
full democracy be restored with all speed—his quiet, dig-
nified manner almost made the statement sound plausi-
ble—when Towers' front door crashed open and four
armed members of the CAC burst into the room. Towers'
wife screamed; his children looked at the armed men with
a mixture of excitement and terror.

"Eliot Towers?" demanded the man in charge, nervously
fingering the red-and-white cloth of his arm band.

"Yes. But what the hell—?"

The leader reached into his breast pocket and withdrew
a document. He waved it in the air but never volunteered
to show the paper to either Towers or his wife. "Acting
under instructions from the Central Office, Citizens Action
Committee," the man said, "I am herewith directed to re-
move you to such place or places as Headquarters may
deem appropriate. You are wanted for interrogation in the
disappearance of one Chase P. Wetherill."

"I had nothing to do with that, I don't know where he
is, or anything about it. The last I saw of him—"

The man with the arm band appeared not to hear him.
"You are hereby notified that you have been placed under
formal arrest and are required to comply with all orders
of the arresting officers forthwith."

"Can I call my lawyer?" asked Towers suddenly.

"If you haven't done anything wrong, you don't need a
lawyer. Let's go."

Towers looked around with a helpless expression. This
room, this house, his children and his wife suddenly
seemed unreal and transitory, as if they might vanish forever the moment he walked out the door. He called the
children to him and kissed them, telling the two boys to
take care of their mother, ignoring a strong hand that
closed around his left arm and was tugging him forward.
His eyes sought out Angela's with a pleading look; then he
shook his head and let himself be pulled toward the door.

"Let's go," repeated the man. Pausing, he pointed to

one of the other men with him. "You, Barker, stay here. No telephone calls out; monitor the incoming. Someone will be along to relieve you about midnight."

Towers tried to shake the hand loose. "Goddammit, that's against—"

The leader of the group pushed him, with one of the other men's help, through the front door. Angela started to scream, beating her fists uselessly against the leader's back to stop him.

The man in charge tried to shake her off; one of his men was more direct. With a swing of his rifle butt, he knocked her down; a total look of amazement and pain twisted itself across her face. The children both screamed, then began sobbing. Numbly, one hand went to her mouth. As she pulled it away, she stared at the blood that had come from her mouth and the tiny, jagged portions of tooth that lay in her palm. Towers tore himself free enough to see what had happened, and when he did, he began to struggle fiercely, but the other men held him firmly, his arms pinioned. Dragged out through the door, Towers began to shout to his neighbors for help.

The same rifle butt that had just knocked out two of his wife's teeth crunched into the back of Towers skull. Limp, he was half-dragged, half-carried into the unmarked car parked at the curb.

The man stationed inside the house winced and gently closed the door; with apparent embarrassment, he offered a grayish handkerchief to the bleeding Angela, who was still sitting on the floor, staring at her hand as if the secret behind the mystery of all that was happening somehow could be found there.

"Anything I can do, lady?" the man asked.

Angela shook her head.

When you are battling the imponderable, there is nothing anyone can do.

Chapter Twelve

A majority can never replace the man . . .
just as a hundred fools do not make a wise
man, an heroic decision is not likely to come
from a hundred cowards.

—Adolph Hitler,
Preface to Mein Kampf

Nicholas Wetherill was buried on a small rise overlooking his brother's farm. After a considerable scouting of the property, Brannigan had suggested this particular site to Chase. It was an ideal spot, not far from two venerable oak trees and silhouetted against the rolling Berkshire foothills.

For a Wetherill, the service was simple, almost stark. Although Brannigan had worked all night to fashion a coffin out of rough-grained barn siding, his efforts produced little more than a crude-looking, rectangular box. The only prayers offered were those intoned by Chase. After reciting the Lord's Prayer, he also read the words of Reinhold Niebuhr: "Oh, Lord, Grant me the serenity to accept that which I cannot change, the strength to change that which I can—and the wisdom to know the difference."

For a few minutes after everyone left, Chase stood staring at the newly filled grave. Reinhold Niebuhr's words, he knew, applied as much—if not more—to himself as to Nicholas.

Back in the house, Chase sat for a long time staring into the fire. Darcie was in the kitchen with the twins, putting them through the intricacies of French without much success (both Jeremy and Raven felt that their stay in Salisbury should be a permanent school holiday, but had been stoutly overruled by both their father and mother). During the month they had been here so far, Chase had handled mathematics and history, while Darcie had tried to keep them going forward in English, French and art. Brannigan, besides appointing himself athletic director, also slipped in a stepped-up course in Gaelic. "You know, Mr. Wetherill, with the way things is going," he had said, "the language may make a comeback yet."

Chase heard the twins yelling to each other as Darcie released them from the agonies of French, and walked into the room where he was sitting. "The twins," she groaned. "Finishing each other's sentences in English is bad enough; in French, it's impossible."

Without looking at her, Chase stood up. "I'm going to New York. In the morning. The last couple of days made up my mind for me. First Toby, for Christ's sake. Then Nicholas. Well, there's nothing I can do about either of them. But Dirk told me how to get hold of Tracey, and suddenly, that seems very important."

Darcie stared at him in surprise. "Don't let what's happened, Chase, push you into something silly. There's nothing you can do about Toby. You said so yourself; Nicholas—well, that's a tragedy, but too late to do anything about now. Tracey . . ." Darcie's voice trailed off. "Chase, what I really am trying to say is, do you think it's safe? They must be looking for you. Especially now that—" She didn't finish the sentence because mentioning Toby at this moment, if painful to her, would be doubly so for Chase.

Chase's answer, when it came, had a barely controlled tone of fury to it. "Dammit, Darcie. You can't have it both ways. You've been complaining that I haven't done anything so far but run away. Well, I'm tired of running. Sure, the New York trip is dangerous. We've been hiding away up here to save our skins, which I'd be the first to agree is damned important. Especially yours and the kids'. But maybe I owe the world more than just staying alive. Maybe there's something I can do. Maybe Tracey has some idea of how I could make a difference down there. Anyway, it's what I have to find out."

Darcie said nothing; there was nothing she could say. With a nod, she began mentally packing what she thought Chase might need. She was about to ask something on this point, when she realized that Chase was already making his way to the stairs, muttering bitterly. With a meaningful

glance at the Brannigan, she signaled him to calm down
the children—already beginning to talk all at the same
time, excited and filled with confusion—and followed
Chase up.

Darcie was unsure how to phrase what she wanted to
say to Chase. There was a certain justice in his complaint
of her "wanting it both ways": she did want him to go do
what the right of the matter called for, yet she was also
desperately afraid that something might happen to him in
the process of doing it. Neither Reinhold Niebuhr nor anyone else had a prayer that covered that paradox.

Dina watched the truck heading up the Taconic Parkway and held up her crudely lettered sign, "Amenia." She
kept the smaller sign with her offering on it out of sight
until she was sure that the trucker could read the figure.
Outside of Danbury, she had met what she first thought
was another girl of about her same age, although, even on
short acquaintance, it became clear that the woman was a
good deal older than she looked. She told Dina she was a
cocktail waitress, and it was she who explained the system
of the signs and cautioned her to watch out for unmarked
cars. At the same time, she explained to Dina that with no
trains or nonofficial cars moving, trucks were essentially
the only means of transportation. People were given rides,
but the price the truckers charged Dina found staggering.
Still, the drivers had plenty of takers. Going through her
pocketbook carefully, Dina discovered that she had, at the
most, a hundred dollars. Close to collapse anyway, Dina
had burst into tears at the situation; the strain of the days
before and the shock of Alan's death had taken their toll.
On top of that, as the other girl pointed out, she looked a
mess: the Halston was in tatters, her hair was uncombed,
the heel had disappeared off one of her shoes.

"You okay, honey?" asked the girl, looking at Dina
strangely.

"They killed him," sobbed Dina. "They squashed him
like a bug and then they laughed and I don't have that
kind of money and why did the world suddenly go crazy
on me anyway?"

With nervous movement of her hand, the cocktail waitress patted Dina's shoulder. She'd met so many people in
the past few days, Dina's state was nothing new to her.
For the appearance of calm and peace which Tobin Weth-

erill had shown the nation on television a few nights before was largely cosmetic; the CAC's control of the
country was far from being a *fait accompli*. In most of
Washington and Manhattan, the CAC had the situation
well nailed down; in the great sprawling rest of the country, no one really knew who was on top.

The police, taking their orders from National Teamsters
headquarters, had delivered as many of the cities to the
CAC as they could, but it had frequently been a half-
hearted effort; their less doctrinaire members were growing
increasingly reluctant the more they witnessed the end
result of their own actions. With the Armed Forces, the
battle lay largely within their own leadership; as a result,
the Army and Navy stayed in their barracks.

The nation, then, was in chaos. News was scanty and,
what there was of it, heavily censored by the CAC. All
there was, was rumor—and feeding on that, fear. To the
cocktail waitress, Dina was one of the products of this fear.

For this whole part of the country seemed to be walking
along the edges of these roads, carrying their belongings
on their backs, pushing them in baby carriages, dragging
them in children's wagons. The story you got from any of
them was roughly the same: they had to go somewhere—where it didn't seem to matter, just go somewhere—but didn't have enough money to pay one of the
truckers, although all of them claimed they had plenty of
money at home, only they hadn't brought it with them,
and what should they do anyway when the government
wasn't lifting a finger to help them, for Christ's sake?

This girl, Dina, struck her as different. She was as
shaken as the rest—on the edge of collapse—but there was
something about her, some inflection in her voice, her accent, something about what was left of the clothes she was
wearing, that set this kid apart. She thought of her own
daughter and hoped she wasn't in the same sort of trouble.

"Look," she said, "there's a gas station up ahead, and
you give the man a dollar, he'll probably let you use the
can. Comb your hair, honey. Wash your face. If you have
any makeup, use it. A trucker is a trucker is a trucker."

Blankly, Dina looked at her. The sense of what she was
saying didn't reach her, but she obeyed automatically. This
waitress was strength; she was order; she was someone to
be trusted and obeyed. Dina came back out, looking a bit
better, but so numbed that she felt no pleasure in it.

"You look like a million bucks. Now let's get hoofing it."

By the time they had reached the first truck stop, Dina was half-asleep on her feet, each leg moving when directed, but only with the greatest of effort. She felt as if she were in some sort of unreal world, jostled by people on either side. Foot traffic along the edges of the highway was moving in both directions at once, disorderly, confused, grumbling, everyone intent on getting somewhere, anywhere. It was a parade of zombies—stumbling, directionless, amorphous. From the slowly moving mass, forming a cloud above it like an early morning mist, rose a constant exhausted murmur, a distilled misery too tired to cry out for help.

Sitting on the edge of a curb, she dimly saw Brenda going in and out of the truckers' cafeteria; Dina had refused food herself, unable to face the thought of eating or drinking anything. Her back was propped up against a sign announcing that the place was open twenty-four hours a day, seven days a week. Dina's eyes closed without her realizing it. A sharp shaking of her shoulder made her eyes fight to open and she stared up at her companion, who was smiling.

"Hey, honey, you're all fixed up. This guy"—she indicated a large, badly shaved man standing slightly behind her—"his name, he says, is Ralph—is going to let you ride with him. Ralph, Dina. Dina, Ralph."

Ralph stopped picking his teeth long enough to nod at Dina; from her curbstone, Dina nodded back wearily.

"Honey, never believe what you hear about eating where the truck drivers go. The food in that place stank."

Although her mind was operating through a thick fog, a thought came back to Dina. "The money, I don't have the money."

Brenda laughed. Then, leaning forward, she whispered urgently to Dina. "Shhh. Don't worry, baby. I've fixed everything."

"Gotta get going. If you're coming, lady—Dina, I mean—let's haul ass."

Pulled to her feet, Dina headed where Ralph pointed, climbing with difficulty into the giant cab of the truck.

Five minutes later, leaning against her door, she could feel herself falling asleep. Ralph didn't seem to mind. Nice Ralph.

When Dina woke up, she wasn't sure where she was. She could tell she wasn't where she had been, leaning against the door of the truck, but it took a second or two for her to orient herself. As with many large trailer trucks, directly behind the driver's seat was a leather couch, a sort of bed, running across the cab; here, on long trips, one man could nap while the other drove, taking turns at the wheel and eliminating the need for stopping to sleep. This area was shielded from the front area of the cab by a makeshift curtain to keep the place dark enough for sleeping no matter what time of day it was. Dimly, through exhausted eyes, Dina could see that she was not alone; Ralph stood, swaying with the movement of the truck, and was pulling off his clothes. Dina must have made some small noise, some unconscious sound of alarm, for Ralph threw himself on her, one sock and one shoe still on his right foot. Dina tried to push him away, but he was too big and she was too tired. Once, she slipped part of herself free, but Ralph slapped her hard. "C'mon, baby. Your friend said you'd do anything for a ride, and baby, you is going to get rode." She wanted to cry out, but his sheer weight made it impossible. Too exhausted to fight further, Dina's mind pulled a merciful curtain across the rest of the trip. She was not aware of the truck jolting to a stop so that the other driver, Zelinski, could change places with Ralph; nor was she conscious of the fact that occasionally the truck would pull off the road completely, so that Zelinski and Ralph could both enjoy her simultaneously. It took approximately five and a half hours for the truck to reach the corner where the borders of Connecticut, New York and Massachusetts meet. The entire trip was erased from her consciousness by a benevolent amnesia. Numbed, she was able to scream only once—when Zelinski and Ralph roughly pushed her out of the truck near a town, and even at that, her mind was so confused that she was not even sure what she was screaming about.

Chase had hoped to make his departure for New York as casual as catching the 8:12 from Rye. Everyone knew this; everyone tried; all of them failed. Up until the last moment, Darcie was superb. While she had helped him pack the small, inexpensive valise of Brannigan's he would be carrying, she kept up a gentle strain of inconsequential chatter designed to conceal her own deep concern, and had not once referred to his going as anything but an absolute necessity. Nor had she shown any trace of the private nervousness she felt at being left here without him. She felt she had to give him every ounce of support she could contrive.

But at the very last moment, all her resolve, all her promises to herself, fluttered away like pieces of paper in the wind. She threw herself into his arms, holding him as tightly as she could. "Oh God, Chase . . ."

He raised her chin and smiled at her. "It's going to be all right, Darcie. Don't worry. Please don't worry."

Branningan had been considerably more direct. Catching Chase alone in the kitchen a few minutes before he was to leave, he sat down in the chair opposite him and made his pitch across the kitchen table. "Yerra, Mr. Weth-'rill," he said in final appeal, his ebony face pleading for a last-minute change of heart, "God knows what you'll run into down there. I should be with you, y'understand. I'm a sight better at handling the working stiff than you—meaning no disrespect, of course—and I know places—a whole lot of places—in the city to hide."

But Chase remained adamant. "Someone's got to stay here, old friend. Even if they never trace those men on the hill to here, more will show up, eventually. So being here is more dangerous than ever; I'm not sure I should be going myself, but I don't have much choice. And while I'm gone, someone's got to stay and take care of the family. Emlyn's competent, but this is a man's job." Chase paused. "Dammit, Brannigan, there's no man in the world I'd trust them with except you. I think you know that."

"Beautiful blarney as all of that is, Mr. Wetherill, my job—"

"Is to do what I tell you." Immediately, Chase regretted putting the statement so crudely. Brannigan's face had dropped, and Chase struggled to put a softer edge on the remark. "The family, Brannigan, the family. Emlyn, the twins, Mrs. Wetherill. Who the hell else could I ask to look after them and know I'd picked the best man for the job? Who?"

With a defeated smile, Brannigan threw up his hands. "You should have been Irish." Resigned, he had helped Chase into the rucksack and stood at the door with the rest.

Awkwardly, Emlyn had shaken his father's hand. All he

said was, "Take care of yourself, Dad." The twins were untypically quiet. With awe they had watched the preparations being made; then, when they saw Chase's eyes settle on them for a second and noticed his slight smile of encouragement, they had raced over to be hugged. With a whoop, they had disappeared to clamber up the hill and watch his receding figure make its way down the road toward the highway.

The big diesel roared as the trailer truck came to the bottom of a slight hill and the driver pushed the accelerator to the floor to try to keep his momentum up. Chase had had little trouble in getting himself a ride, using, as Dirk suggested, virtually the same system of signs the cocktail waitress had explained to Dina a few hours earlier. Because he was in a hurry, Chase had offered double the going rate, and been picked up practically by the first empty truck that went by.

After a few tries, the driver of Chase's rig gave up attempts at conversation. By a sort of unwritten code, these drivers had learned not to ask too many questions of their passengers, but usually were able to strike up some line of chatter that helped while away the hours behind the wheel. With Chase, the driver soon found that even this was impossible. As Brannigan had put it, Chase was no expert at "handling the working stiff."

Earlier that day, traveling in the opposite direction, a truck had traveled that same highway. Inside, its driver whistled softly, forcing himself to keep his eyes on the road. His mind was on the compartment behind the drawn, ragged curtain, and how long it would take Zelinski to get through with his turn so that he himself could go back and diddle some more with this strange kid named Dina.

Ralph and Zelinski were two working stiffs Chase Wetherill would have known how to handle.

In New York, the first thing Chase did was to check his suitcase and the rucksack; they too clearly marked him as a man in transit. Looking around, Chase was amazed at the surface normalcy of the city. Beneath that exterior calm, Chase had heard from Dirk, terrifying things were happening—people dragged from their own homes by the CAC, simply to disappear—yet no sign of it even appeared to ruffle the city's surface. The only evidence was a haunted look on an occasional face, as if only a few knew of the terror that stalked their lives.

Because of this fear, a steady stream of people were leaving the city. One day they would be at home, the next day they would be gone, their apartments left furnished but unguarded, soon to fall prey to the gangs of young, high-living CAC cadremen that were rapidly turning up all over the city.

To look at New York, it was difficult to believe: most of the bars and restaurants were open; the hotels, from the plushest to the seamiest, appeared in full swing; motion-picture houses and theaters were all operating.

Chase walked up the litter-strewn steps of the subway stop nearest the Village. The subway was a new experience for Chase; the Village was not. In his college days, just after World War II, the Village was where one went to stare at the eccentric, the unwashed and the bearded, a place to get drunk and snicker discreetly at the carryings-on of what to him had then seemed another world. Now, he was no longer a tourist; he was bearded and not too well washed himself, and in his pocket was Dirk's list of gay bars where he would find Tracey.

He started with the name at the top: the Purple Moth. In spite of the chill night air, the Purple Moth was almost suffocatingly hot inside. A jukebox blared, its neonized glow casting weird changing patterns across both the walls and the customers' faces.

Turning around, Chase started for the far wall because he thought it would provide him a clear view of the door in case Tracey came in. Almost to the wall, he found his way blocked by a slightly built man, maybe in his middle thirties, wearing a light-colored leather jacket. "My," the man said, "it's cold out tonight, isn't it? I don't think I've seen you before."

Part of Chase panicked. "I'm waiting for someone," he announced. Chase sipped and then studied the contents of his beer glass deeply.

"Do you live around here?" the young man asked, tilting his head.

"No."

"I do. Just around the corner, in fact." A long pause, followed by a subtle change in the position of the young man's head, an unspoken invitation.

Chase repeated almost angrily, "I'm waiting for someone."

"Who isn't?" noted the man, and, with a philosophical
shrug, disappeared. Chase stood bewildered. He looked at
his beer glass and saw it was almost empty. The question
now was whether to stay in this bar, or to move on to the
next on the list. No matter which course he chose, he
stood a good chance of missing Tracey; the system devised
for meeting him was murderously inefficient. Damn
Tracey. A minor point made Chase's mind up for him:
someone had turned the volume on the jukebox even
higher. Wincing, Chase left to try the next bar on Dirk's
list.

Just as leaned forward to put the empty beer glass on a
nearby table, he felt a squeeze on his elbow. For a moment, he thought the man with the leather jacket was
back. But, turning, he saw Dirk standing at his side.

Dirk said nothing. He merely nodded, indicating with
his head that Chase should follow him. As they walked
toward the door, Chase could feel a roomful of eyes
watching, keeping score. Dirk, a familiar sight to most of
them, had picked up the stranger with the beard.

A curious combination, the regulars of the Purple Moth
decided.

Chapter Thirteen

*If I may cite the French Revolution, we're
coming to the Thermidor. The accusations
hurled about in the Terror, so to speak, will
be forgotten. I think people will discount the
charges that were leveled but never proven
in the last two or three years. . . .*
                                    —*Kevin Phillips,*
                                    Conservatist Strategist,
                                    April 19, 1975

Tracey's apartment, one of four new "safe houses" he
now had (instead of the three he'd operated from the
week before), was not far from the Purple Moth. Dirk
was almost entirely uncommunicative, indicating by mono-
syllables when Chase should turn, when he should walk
straight, and, finally, which door to enter. Chase followed
him up three flights of carpeted stairs. The building, he
learned later, was a converted brownstone, with the lower
floors rented to tenants of whom Tracey felt sure. Dirk arrived at a small wooden door, painted the same color as
the walls, so insignificant the casual visitor might have
thought it led to a closet rather than to another apartment.

Feeling along the door frame, Dirk found a concealed
panel. Behind this was the door bell, which he rang in a
series of three short and two long buzzes.

Almost immediately, the door opened, and Tracey
pulled Chase inside. Dirk appeared to hesitate, but Tracey
dismissed him with a gentle but forceful "Thanks, Dirk.
I'll see you later." With a shrug, Dirk disappeared.

"Thank God you got here," boomed Tracey, once the
door was closed and the locks slid back into place. "Was
the trip awful?"

"Not bad. The roads were a mess, though. All those

people." Chase caught himself, realizing how unimportant what he was saying was; he had not traveled this distance, taken these chances, to exchange light banter with his brother. "Is something wrong, Tracey? Your message—"

"No, something's right. I have a surprise for you."

As he led Chase into the small but elegant living room, a sound behind Chase made him begin to turn around. The roar of someone bellowing his name almost deafened him. "Chase!"

It was Duane Wetherill. "Jesus," groaned Chase, shaking his head in a series of rapid movements and leaning against his brother weakly, half-laughing. "You could scare a man to death like that."

"You could stand a little scaring." Duane's finger explored his stomach. "Getting heavier every time I see you."

"Thanks."

Tracey watched them, enjoying seeing the two of them together again. "Sit down, sit down, both of you. Coffee, a drink, anybody want anything?"

As soon as they were seated, Duane turned abruptly solemn. "I asked Tracey to get you, Chase. We need you. I'm sorry about the cloak-and-dagger routine, but you can't trust anybody any more. Particularly when you're on their list. I've seen a copy of the CAC list, and I'm on it—high up on it. You're there too."

Chase was unsure whether Duane knew about Nicholas, but knew the subject had to be brought up eventually. "Hell," he began. "I understand your precautions damned well. Too damned well. You ought to know—"

"Chase, I know it's going to be hard for you to accept all that I'm going to say about Toby. We have informants inside the CAC, and what we've learned is shocking. To me, it's difficult to believe it's the same brother we grew up with. But the facts are unshakable. I don't mean just what you saw of him on television, but the things he has had his people do."

"I know."

"Sometimes, of course, I'm sure it's not Toby himself. His people are issuing orders right and left, and nobody seems to know who's doing what to whom. For instance, the CAC has Moira locked up in their Interrogation Center."

"Moira?" Chase was shocked.

"I'm sure Toby doesn't know about that—too strong a
sense of the family to let it happen. But some of his lieu-
tenants are out-and-out bastards," Duane noted bitterly.
"I've sent an anonymous message to him telling him where
she is so he can spring her. Christ, I'm working full time
against the CAC, which means against Toby, and I can see
how anybody'd regard me as a threat. But Moira! Hell,
Moira doesn't represent a threat to anybody—except possibly Dudley."

Remembering Nicholas, Duane's statement about "too
strong a sense of the family to let it happen" was hard to
take. He was on the point of finally bringing up Nicholas,
when another thought struck him. "What about Graffa?"

"No sign of him. Someone checked Usspatpenn and
said everything was quiet. I'm sure Toby wouldn't harm
him either. Graffa would give Toby hell himself, but he's
too smart to say anything in public. Myself, I guess I'm
dumb. I talk to everyone I can. And besides having been a
Senator, I'm also Toby's brother, which makes what I say
sound even more damaging. I guess that's why Toby wants
to shut me up."

From the other side of the room, they heard Tracey
give a small laugh. "I suppose he thinks of me in the same
league as Moira. Not dangerous to anybody. And maybe
he's right."

Duane spoke with a touch of anger. "Stop feeling sorry
for yourself, Tracey. You're doing a lot. Hiding me is a
risk you don't have to take. Sending that boy to get Chase
was another. You're helping plenty."

Watching, Chase could see a feigned diffidence cross
Tracey's face; inside, he knew, Tracey was proud.
"Duane's right, Tracey. You're taking just as big a chance
as any of us."

"Chase, I said a moment ago that we needed you. To
repeat myself, I realize it is hard to accept the incredible
things Toby is doing. When a man's your brother . . .
well, it's not easy to believe."

"Duane, I do believe it. I know it. And I know it because of something that was probably done on Toby's
direct orders. They killed Nicholas."

For a moment, the three of them sat in a stunned, painful silence. Quietly, Chase talked about Nicholas' arrival,
his suicide, the note about failing the country and the
family, and Russell's panicked flight.

· The effect of this on Duane and Tracey was completely different. Tracey sat quietly, shaking his head as if unable to accept the fact. Duane was on his feet, pacing back and forth in a sort of nervous frenzy. "Damn it, it's probably my fault. I talked with Nicholas a couple of times. You know, bankers are a surprisingly naïve lot. He'd been financing some of those people at the beginning, but it never dawned on him what they were up to. I told him. At the time, I didn't think he believed me, but I guess I underestimated him. I suppose he tried to bail out and they . . . Jesus." Duane walked over to the window and kicked the wooden cabinet concealing the radiator so hard its wicker front caved in. Suddenly: "Maybe Toby didn't know."

At first, Chase said nothing. He realized Duane was grabbing at excuses, trying not to let Toby be responsible for Nicholas' death. And even though this was probably unrealistic, he also knew Duane had to think it through for himself. Finally, Chase decided this process was too agonizing a one. "Somehow, Duane, I doubt if Toby was as much in the dark about killing Nicholas as you'd like to think. I also wonder if he's as ignorant about Moira. I know that for you to hold yourself responsible for either of those things plain doesn't make sense."

Turning from the window, Duane shrugged. "The world's gone crazy is all I really know." He slumped into a chair and nodded in appreciation as Tracey handed him a drink.

Studying him for a moment, Chase decided it was time to get Duane out of his self-destructive mood. "Why did you send for me, Duane?"

"Because we need you. We need everybody, but particularly people like you. People who are respected, people who have nothing to gain and everything to lose by opposing Toby. Particularly, someone of your standing, who's as much of a Wetherill as Toby is. Look. Toby's setup is built on the myth that he and the CAC stepped in to correct a situation he had nothing to do with creating. You know better than that; you saw the report Graffa had made up. Right now, it looks as if Toby's scheme worked, but that's only here and in Washington—what Spiro Agnew used to call the 'Eastern Establishment.' And that's because all the communication centers are here—Toby has control of the newspaper, radio and television. And with limited telephone and mail service and with travel restricted, he believes the rest of the country will accept his voice, as one not just of authority, but of justice. Well, there's a hell of a lot of country outside this narrow Eastern strip he doesn't have control over, and out there he's vulnerable. And the irony is that his isolation in the capital prevents him from realizing this himself. A lot of the people who were with him at first are now against him. From his own press people, he gets the impression the thing is all locked up. Just like a lot of people do. Well, it isn't. People only think it is. It's a horse race. And that's what we need you for."

Chase looked at Duane with genuine bafflement. "I'll do anything I can, Duane. But I don't even know where to start."

"Start with people. You know a lot of very influential men. People who are just as confused as the rest of the country. Start by telling them—in person. Then, we want to start an underground radio station of our own, something to offset Toby's controlled newspapers and his doctored television news programs. I'm stunned to discover how many intelligent people believe what they read in his captive press and what Toby tells them on TV. Someone like yourself—respected, highly placed, politicially non-aligned—is the perfect person to offset Toby's propaganda of success. And at the same time, we need as many Whetherills as possible visibly working against him, just to overcome the fact that Toby is a Wetherill. And to take some sort of luster off his position on the Supreme Court."

A wave of uncertainty swept across Chase. He didn't know anything about running a radio station. More important, contacting people and heading a station would keep him in New York indefinitely. "God, Duane, I'm no writer. Or radio impresario. And more important, there's Darcie and the kids to consider. I can't disappear and leave them up there to fend for themselves. I can't just leave my family."

"I did."

Glancing at his watch, Duane saved Chase from having to answer. "There's a meeting I can't miss. I know I've thrown an awful lot at you all at once, so, stay here, think about it, and give me an answer when I get back. Tracey can fill you in on more of what's really going on."

And before Chase could say anything, Duane was gone.

Helplessly, he looked at Tracey. "Goddam. What am I supposed to do? Duane doesn't leave a guy much room."

"One thing you can't do, Chase, is run from yourself. I've spent a lifetime doing that, and it just doesn't work. Rod wasn't really killed by that stranger in Grand Central. In a way, I—oh hell, it's too complicated to explain, but I do know that running from the truth is impossible; it runs faster than you can."

He didn't understand what Tracey was saying about Rodney. But as he started to ask, the door, double dead-bolt locks and all, came crashing in. The room was suddenly filled with police and men in the familiar red-and-white arm bands. Shouting back and forth between the rooms, they at first paid very little attention to Chase and Tracey. Outside in the hall, Chase could see and hear one of the CAC men berating Dirk. "Goddammit, you said he was here."

"He was. He must have just left."

"Bullshit. What the hell do you think the money was for? It was to tell us when he was here, not when he's 'just left,' for Christ's sake."

A list was gone through, and Chase's name found on it. But not on the same kind of list that Duane's apparently was. A telephone call was made and Chase found himself handcuffed. Tracey was ignored, although he was told a man was being put in his apartment to wait in case Duane returned. When Tracey objected, he was knocked to the floor.

"We ought to take you in too," the CAC man told Dirk. "For phony information. For crap. You took the money and gave us crap. You'll be hearing from us, count on it." The man turned and nodded to the others, who then took Chase forcefully in tow. As Chase left, he twisted his head slightly and saw a stricken Tracey staring at Dirk—Judas Iscariot with limp wrists.

Moira Cantrell sat on the edge of a plain steel cot and stared at her legs. She decided they were not unattractive, considering her fifty-three years, but was disturbed by her feet. Sometime during the flight from Bermuda, one of her shoes had been lost; probably, she decided, when she was placed aboard the plane. The missing shoe broke the symmetrical design the shadows of her legs and feet cast on

the floor. Studying the light in the ceiling, she could think
of no way to change her position.

The cell contained nothing but Moira and the cot. The
fact that there wasn't even a pillow in her cell reminded
Moira of her beach bag full of jewelry. She wondered if
the beach bag had also been lost during the plane ride, or
whether it was lying in a wire-mesh locker, neatly tagged
with her name, awaiting disposition. Someone had used
those words when she first arrived, and Moira pondered
whether the phrase referred to her belongings or to herself.

Outside in the corridor, she heard hard footsteps fall
upon the cement. The small steel shutter covering the
viewing slit in the door slid back. Standing up, she
watched the action of the bolts; the small lugs that penetrated the door turned when the outer locks were thrown.
So far, no one had even touched her, but at two different
times, she had heard women screaming in their cells.

Flattened against the wall, Moira stared at the dapper,
middle-aged man who entered. Unlike the rest of the offi-
cials she had seen up to now, he was dressed in a business
suit, not work clothes. His hair and his clothes were different, and when he spoke, it was with an accent of the right
schools.

"Mrs. Cantrell," said the man, looking at Moira huddled
against the wall, "there has been some mistake. I don't
know how to account for it. Your brother Toby learned
about the error only a few minutes ago, and was horrified.
I can only extend our apologies, which I realize are insuffi-
cient." The man paused in embarrassment. "Sometimes, as
in any bureaucracy, people with the best intentions get
tangled up by orders that are intended to apply to others.
Frankly, I don't know what else to say."

Moira felt as if a tremendous weight had been lifted
from her. There was to be no screaming trip down the
hall, no return in mental tatters. A mistake had been
made. Toby had heard of it somehow, and now she was to
be treated as she always had been treated—as a regal, per-
ishable commodity. With her self-confidence suddenly
back, she could find no reason to make things any easier
for this man, pleasant as he was trying to be. "You're
quite correct about one thing," she announced coldly.
"Apologies are not sufficient."

The man found himself beginning to sweat. Being Tobin
Wetherill's personal aide was not easy; Moira's reply, un-

derstated but icy and chilling, indicated Toby's sister was an equally difficult person. Moira watched with feigned lack of interest as he leaned back out into the corridor and began issuing a stream of orders. Personal effects—on the double. A pair of shoes—and quickly please; Mrs. Cantrell could not be expected to go anywhere wearing one shoe.

The matron looked bewildered, staring at Moira's one unshod foot. "Your size, ma'am . . ." she began halfheartedly.

Moira looked down at the matron's flat-heeled shoes.

"If you'll just lend me some carpet slippers, I have plenty of shoes at home," Moira noted icily.

A moment later, the head matron came into the cell breathlessly, carrying the beach bag; it was neatly tagged with her name.

"Are you sure you want to stay here in New York?" asked the man. "We'd be delighted to fly you to your place in Florida—or anywhere."

"No. For the time being, I shall stay in New York." Moira was not being considerate; she simply could not face returning so soon to Florida. She hated New York and used the apartment there rarely, but any place would be better than Florida, haunted by its ghosts of Dudley, Captain Struthers and Sail Island.

"We'll have a car brought around to the front immediately." He nodded to the head matron, who had reappeared with a pair of fluffy carpet slippers.

"Thank you," Moira said and left.

Chapter Fourteen

The ruling ideas of each age have ever been the ideas of its ruling class.

—*Manifesto of the Communist Party (1848)*

Chase's treatment was entirely different. He was not taken to the Interrogation Center, but to the Tombs. Even there, he was not put into a cell, but told to sit in a waiting room, given coffee, and treated with courtesy. Two CAC men guarded him, but in such a deferential manner that a stranger would have had a difficult time believing Chase was even a prisoner.

At a small desk in one corner of the room, Chase could hear part of a conversation that, from the snatches he could make out, obviously concerned him. But he was unable to hear enough to make any sense of it.

After three hours, the two men led him across the interconnecting bridge, out onto the street, and into the Federal Courthouse Building at 120 Center Street. There he was once again shown into a small room with barred windows and told to make himself comfortable. This time, the guards left him by himself.

Ten minutes later, the door sprang open and Toby strode in. He advanced, one hand outstretched. Chase automatically began to take Toby's hand but then brought his hand down to his side. Toby ignored the slight, and studied Chase's face, allowing himself a gentle smile.

"My God, Chase. That beard. You look like Sigmund Freud."

"I didn't grow it from choice," Chase noted bitterly. "It was a necessity. Some of your supporters are less than gentlemen."

Sitting down, Toby sighed. "I know, I know. But in a situation like this, you can't expect people to follow orders strictly. Too much is going on."

Chase stared out through the wire-mesh screen that covered the window. His hands were shoved in his pockets, and his back turned toward Toby. "What is going on is your responsibility."

"Look, Chase," began Toby. "Let's get some things straight. I did what I thought was necessary. Given the circumstances, I would do those same things again."

Turning abruptly away from the window, Chase faced Toby. "Killing Nicholas was necessary? Locking up Moira? Tracking down Duane to do God knows what to him? You can look me in the eye and tell me those things were necessary?"

Still sitting in the small straight-backed chair, Toby shook his head sadly. "None of those things were supposed to happen, Chase—not the way they did, anyway. You'll just have to take my word for it. Moira has been released; there was no plan to put her in prison to begin with. Nicholas—well, obviously there's nothing I can do to set that straight now. But I didn't know anything about what was happening until too late. With Duane, it's a different matter. He's actively working against what I'm trying to do. And yes, we are 'tracking him down,' as you put it, but when we catch Duane, nothing much will happen to him. For a while, he'll be put out of circulation, for his own good, that's all. His own good and that of the country. No decision like that—none of the decisions about any of the things you've mentioned—is easy. But someone has to make them, and that someone is me. Because the decisions are necessary."

"Shit, Toby. If you really believe it's for the good of the country, you need a psychiatrist, not an army. 'For the good of the country,' you've imprisoned thousands of people, killed others and terrorized the rest. You've suspended freedom of the press, junked normal judicial processes, and aborted the Constitution. Now you try to cloak the whole mess in a shroud of doing it 'for the good of the country.' Hell, it was mostly for the good of Toby Wetherill. And if you expect me to buy anything else, you're crazy. You say it wasn't easy to do; you say it was necessary. The only thing necessary right now is to get rid of you and your whole bunch of two-bit bully-boys with arm bands. Quite frankly, if I had a gun, I'd shoot you myself, and do the world a favor."

For a second, Toby stared at Chase. "You really think

it's that easy, don't you, Chase? Destroy the evil head and the whole thing will go away. All right." Turning, Toby strode to the door, knocked on its inside, and waited for the guard to open it. "Give me your gun, please."

The guard looked first at Toby, then at Chase, hesitating.

"The gun," repeated Toby impatiently. "First, fire a round. I want my brother to know they're real bullets, not blanks."

Still visibly uncomfortable, the guard drew the revolver and fired into the cement edge of the barred window, chipping off a large piece. The noise was deafening. Toby took the revolver from the guard. "That will be all. Continue to wait outside." Baffled, the guard backed out of the room, closing the door behind him.

Chase studied Toby's face, trying to make some sense out of what was happening. "Are you planning to kill me with that, Toby, or just scare me to death?"

"No. You said if you had a gun, you'd do the world a favor and shoot me. All right. You now have a gun." He handed the revolver, butt first, to Chase. "Here's your chance."

For some moments, Chase stood staring at the revolver. He was surprised to discover that both hand and gun were shaking. Tentatively, he raised the revolver in the direction of Toby, but was unable to make any real effort to actually aim it.

"Come on, Chase. Where are all the brave words now? I'm evil, you said. Getting rid of me is necessary, you said. The whole problem would go away if someone shot me, you said. Well, here I am, less than ten feet from you. There you are, a loaded gun in your hand. The decision would be easy, you said. Prove it."

"Goddammit, Toby," Chase yelled. "This is a fucking trick of yours—"

Toby remained infuriatingly clam. "Perhaps you didn't really mean what you said. Perhaps a part of you knows that what I am doing is right. Or perhaps it's because this way you have to look me in the face. Very well." Toby turned, presenting his back to Chase. "Now, you don't even h ve to look me in the eye, Chase. I'm not your brother, I could be anyone. An anonymous back that you could pierce with a bullet and rid the world of a major problem."

Setting his jaw, Chase let the revolver slowly rise until it was pointing directly at Toby. Although he steadied it with both hands, the barrel moved up and down from the shaking of his arms. He tried to picture again the sight of Nicholas in his doorway, swathed in his mummy bandages, Russell roaming in the hills with his pathetic, prepared little speech, the CAC men shooting at him on the hill, Mort Evers' unctuously smiling face just before Chase blew his brains out through the window. But forceful as the images were, they became all mixed up with Toby as Chase's brother. Chase pulled the trigger hard. The gun fired and the bullet slammed into the ceiling, showering both of them with pieces of plaster and a chalky rain of plaster dust.

Toby turned around. On his face, the smile remained, knowing, confident. The sound of the shot had made him flinch, and his eyes were still blinking. Otherwise, he appeared unaffected. "You see, Chase, the exercise of power is not as easy as it sounds. Making a decision is one thing. Carrying it out—well, I shudder at a lot of things I have to do. But if I didn't do them, nobody would—certainly not any electorate. When you're a trial judge, the maxim is that if you get a jury too dumb to bring in the verdict you know is right, declare a mistrial and get yourself a new jury. Well, I got one."

Then Toby turned abruptly and strode out the door. One of the guards quickly came in and recovered the revolver from the floor where Chase had dropped it.

Five minutes later, Chase was ushered out of the building and turned loose on the street.

The Dragonfly, the third bar on Dirk's list, was where Chase again found Tracey. From there, they went to the largest of Tracey's safe houses.

"This would be an ideal place for you to work out of, Chase. It's safe enough, certainly. Of all four of the setups I have down here, this is the one I like most. Frankly, I would enjoy the company. Now that Dirk has . . ." the sentence trailed off.

"Are you sure I wouldn't be in the way?" asked Chase. The question was a senseless one, since there was more than ample room. But Chase had felt he had to say something to rescue the moment.

"Of course not. On the other hand, if you'd rather be by yourself . . ."

"No, no. It would be just great, Tracey."

"Good. I thought maybe we could talk Duane into moving from the small one into here too."

"That would be tremendous." Chase's comment was not an empty one. In a way, having himself, Duane and Tracey under one roof would be like a return to the days when the world still made sense and the Wetherills made the most sense of all. The idea filled Chase with sudden enthusiasm. As he packed away his meager belongings in the closet Tracey had pointed out as his, Chase discovered he was actually whistling.

In Salisbury, Brannigan was out in the kitchen humming. doing the last of the dishes and wondering how Chase was faring in the city. In the library, Emlyn was trying to make sense of the complicated set of instructions he'd been able to dig up for hydroponic gardening. Upstairs, the twins were noisily enjoying a shower from the new system of hot running water Emlyn and Brannigan had rigged, and Darcie was sitting in the living room trying to read a book. She was annoyed to hear the twins were still running the water and had asked the Brannigan to go upstairs and remind them—again—that there was just so much hot water and no more. For all of them, the sense of relative well-being was to be short-lived.

Just as Brannigan began clomping up the bare staircase, Darcie heard someone knocking at the front door. Although there had been no signs of CAC activity since Chase's confrontation with them on the hilltop, the family lived in constant fear of their return. Emlyn tore into the room and headed for the cellar to shut off their illegal electricity; Brannigan came back down and quickly lit the kerosene lamps; Darcie set the candles going.

The knocking continued. Brannigan held the shotgun in one hand, and with the other indicated that Darcie should open the door, then stand back. Softly, Darcie pulled open the heavy oak door. Outside, even in the dim light, it was easy to recognize who was there.

"Dina!" Darcie shrieked, and threw her arms around her, pulling her back inside the house.

"Dina, where have you been?" asked Darcie gently, then bit her lip and stopped. Dina's eyes were like those of a stuffed animal: glassy, unmoving. Darcie explored her daughter further; the dried blood that had soaked through the front of Dina's dress, the scratches on her face and the blackened right eye, told Darcie more than anything Dina could ever have said. Darcie reached out her arms and folded her daughter into them, rocking her back and forth.

For the first time Dina spoke. "Mummy? is everything all right, Mummy? Dina's so tired."

"Yes, sweetheart, everything's all right," Darcie reassured her, and furiously motioning Emlyn and Brannigan out of the way, led her upstairs. There, she carefully undressed and washed her, shocked at the evidence that covered Dina's body. Darcie tried to talk to her reassuringly, but the moment Dina lay down, she fell sound asleep, her right hand clutching her mother's.

Outside of his longstanding position as Associate Justice of the Supreme Court, Tobin Wetherill still had no legal title. He was not President of the United States, nor even Acting President. In his own words, the Constitutional crisis into which President Welby's repeated strokes had plunged the nation had forced him to act as a surrogate head of state, an arbiter, a temporary chief executive, until the glaring loophole in the Twenty-fifth Amendment could somehow be altered. Under ordinary circumstances, Toby would carefully point out, his assumption of power might not have been so urgent, but the state of virtual chaos produced by the PLA was a national challenge that had to be met. With that in mind, he would add, he had had little choice but to accept the job when it was thrust upon him.

Actually, Toby found the very vagueness of his position gave him far more power than any President had ever had (at least, he had power along the Eastern Seaboard and in Washington; the rest of the country was still uncertain). And it was the kind of nonaccountable power which allowed Toby room to experiment as he wished. On December 8—four and a half weeks after he had assumed control—he decided to revive an old American custom: the public execution. For years, Toby had held a private theory that the death penalty had lost its deterrent effectiveness only as executions were transformed from public to private events.

In an earlier day, executions would have been by hanging and the public able to attend would have been no larger than could fit inside, say, a stockaded area. The new public executions would be different: death by firing squad in front of an audience of millions watching on television. To Toby, it seemed the ultimate deterrent.

The PLA, the enemies of the state, those areas of the country still not secured, needed examples to learn from; there was no shortage of people who deserved to become object lessons. With the awesome feeling of power any man in his kind of position feels at such moments, Toby picked up his pen and signed the papers which formally doomed the first group. He sighed, stood up and stretched. It was done.

Sweeping out of the Oval Office, his right arm brushed the early Christmas tree set up near the door, sending a bright-red Christmas ball crashing to the floor, where it lay in a thousand glittering pieces.

Chapter Fifteen

The familiar story, that, on seeing the evil-doers taken to the place of execution, [John Bradford] was wont to exclaim: "But for the Grace of God, there goes John Bradford. . . ."
— *The writings of John Bradford, 1853*

At another of Tracey's safe houses, Chase and Duane were considering their options. For almost a week, Chase had the suspicion that they were taking on the impossible. "Duane, you know, I keep wrestling with something. I wonder if we're really going to make progress against the CAC or just think we are. The damned thing's so big, and people are so easy to intimidate."

"Wait until your station hits the air. Wait until they begin to hear the whole story." Duane was a good judge of Chase's moods and knew what his brother needed most now was a sense of forward movement. "When's your first broadcast? Tomorrow?"

"Barring incident."

"How far can you reach? I haven't had too much chance to keep filled in."

"Not clear across the country yet. Except by word of mouth. The studio's all set and we got tapes of anti-government statements from some pretty prominent people. Then, the program goes by a private phoneline to the transmitter, which is in a trailer truck—it's got Coca-Cola painted all over it—so that no one can get a fix on it. They pull off the road and pick up part of the broadcast at one place, then drive on and pick up some more, twenty miles farther down the road. If mobile tracking units begin zeroing in, all they find is another truck barreling down the highway. We're going to repaint the truck every couple of days."

"That's ingenious, Chase. Great. And believe me, enough of those broadcasts won't leave Toby anyplace to hide. A lot of people really believe the crap he's been spoon-feeding them."

"Okay, so a lot of people discover Toby is a son of a bitch. A lot of people knew that about Nixon, and it still took the threat of impeachment to shake him out of office. Now there isn't even a Congress to do that. And CAC men crawling all over everybody."

"These things have to move slowly. General Akroyd—I told you I got his support last week—had been nosing around among the likeliest of the Air Force brass, and says it's going very well. He's even gone outside of the Air Force and talked to some of his buddies at Army and Navy Staff. Thinks they're beginning to see the cracks in the CAC, too. Damned brass. They're never ready to jump until they're sure who looks like the winner."

Duane wasn't getting to the heart of what was bothering Chase. "The Air Force, the Army, Navy, fine. But what bugs me is what can they actually do? Drop a bomb on the White House? Shell it? Lob a missile into the Rose Garden?"

Duane shrugged off Chase's grim humor. "Well, certainly all the Senators—the ones still alive and functioning—are lined up. I talked to Beedle of California this morning—he's in hiding too—and he's not only with us, but said there's a growing sense of revulsion on the Coast against what they've heard of Toby's maneuvering. And when the radio station starts putting the people behind men like Beedle . . ."

A sudden look of confusion came across Chase's face. "Talked to? On the phone?"

"Not from here. But we do have a system to handle that kind of thing. At a prearranged time, I called a phone booth near L.A. from a phone booth here." Duane gave Chase his easy smile. "Had to carry so many quarters I looked like a conductor on an old-fashioned trolley. That's how we make all our calls now. The CAC can monitor home phones until they go blue in the face without picking up anything. And monitoring phone booths—we change the ones we use each week—is impossible."

Chase nodded. One of Duane's men would probably be

able to make the same arrangements so that he could talk to Darcie. He kicked himself for not having thought of this idea himself; Duane had had messages delivered to her, reassuring her that Chase was all right, and his messengers had brought back the same reassurances from her. But Chase had been in New York a week now and wanted to talk to her, to reassure her with his own voice, to tell her he loved her. Two people married as long as Darcie and himself, used to sharing conversations and intimacies daily, feel as if half of them is missing when suddenly reduced to communicating only by letter.

"Hey, Chase! You're drifting off. Listen, please." Duane's own relationship with his wife, Virginia, was such a loose, informal arrangement—what Washington circles refer to as a political marriage—that while he was concerned about Virginia's safety, he was not lost at not being able to see her, or at least talk to her, every day.

"Sorry."

"Anyway, besides the word I got from Beedle, the poop from around D.C. is getting better every day, too. Fedders of the CIA, I hear, is quietly moving in our direction. Likewise Green and Whiteford of the Bureau. We're making progress."

"Yes, but what kind of progress? I mean, is there really any hope at all?"

Duane looked at Chase, annoyed at the question, yet recognizing its truth. An Army general here, a CIA chief there, a cabal of disenfranchised Congressmen and Senators, could hardly be viewed as a sure success against the entire organized weight of the CAC. "I realize it all sounds pretty jury-rigged. But our objective is to begin the resistance. To fight back now, no matter how impossible the odds against success may seem."

"O.K., but Toby has police, CAC troopers, elements of the Armed Forces, parts of the FBI and CIA, and a whole countryful of people scared to death of more disorder. That fear of disorder is how Toby got where he is. Now, I'll be damned if I know how we can get over all those hurdles."

"The answer has to be the weight of public opinion. And that's why your radio broadcasts are so important. The public is not as stupid as politicians sometimes like to think. And, somewhere along the line, if it requires more disorder to set things right, I have enough faith in the

American people's common sense to believe they'll accept it."

Chase's opinion of this response was to tell himself that Duane had spent so much of his political career making speeches, he'd come to believe his own pat statements about the responsibility of the legislative branch and the native wisdom of the general public. Quickly he changed the subject.

"Duane, what *is* our responsibility? None of us would be where we are if it weren't for the Wetherill money."

For a long time, Duane studied the carpet, not quite sure of what the answer was, or even if there was an answer. Then he looked up. "I don't know. I do know that regardless of how we got where we are—you, Nicholas, I, Toby—the family's personal responsibility now is to get Toby out. Nothing else is even thinkable."

The magic words had been spoken—"the family." In spite of everything, Chase could feel the power of the words. The family. A ritual invocation drummed into his and his brothers' heads since they were old enough to understand what the word meant. The family. Chase stared at Duane. "I guess that there isn't any choice." Inside him, the nagging question of how Toby, raised to respond to the same invocations, brought up in the same tradition of devotion to the country and public service, could sincerely believe in what he was doing, was brushed aside. The family. It had its duty to perform.

How brilliantly the family would satisfy its obligations, how thoroughly it would fulfull its mission, was a matter locked, for the moment, inside somebody else's head.

Chapter Sixteen

*Even so my bloody thoughts, with violent
  pace,
Shall ne'er look back, ne'er ebb to humble
  love,
Till that capable and wide revenge
Swallow them up.*

—*William Shakespeare,*
Othello

In Washington, inside a curious-looking building apparently constructed without any windows, a different view of what the Wetherill family's duty was churned angrily in the mind of a man most of them had never even met. Sturgis Lockridge, Toby's top aide, sat at his desk staring fascinatedly at the transcript of a tape he held in his hand. His head remained motionless, the usual frequent tic for once still. (Back before the advent of Tobin Wetherill, when Lockridge had been a leading municipal-bond salesman, the tic had been a source of polite amusement in the financial world; now the tic was an object of fear, not only to the financial world, but to everyone in the government who had the misfortune to run into him.) Carefully, the tape transcript was reread, phrase by phrase. Then, Sturgis tossed the transcript a few inches into the air and caught it in his hands, an expression of delight crossing his somber face. The CAC had been almost as effective in penetrating Duane's organization as Duane had been in infiltrating Toby's CAC. But this time, what Sturgis' man in Duane's operation had provided him was a lever to break the logjam of worries that had been building up: a tape duplicate of what Duane and Chase would be inaugurating their station with tomorrow. It was this duplicate tape from which the transcript had been made. Most important of all, the

taped program identified Chase Wetherill as the station's
volunteer manager, and the lead item—a particularly bitter
attack on Toby—was read by Senator Duane Wetherill.
Sturgis Lockridge wanted to laugh.

Because with this transcript, Lockridge could finally
prove to Tobin Wetherill what Lockridge himself had suspected all along: that the rest of the Wetherill family was
of actual danger to the state. With this transcript, he could
stop operating behind Toby's back in his constant tracking
down of the remaining Wetherills; with this transcript, the
awkward questions about Nicholas Wetherill would cease;
Lockridge could get Toby to denounce the validity of the
transcript before its broadcast as well as forcing Toby to
let him mount a nationwide manhunt for Chase and
Duane. Lockridge planned this maneuver to be so highly
publicized and so intensive it would be guaranteed to
deliver.

For some time now, Lockridge had been aware of a
nagging fear, something that had caused him night after
night to wake soaked in a clammy sweat. The failure to
expand CAC control very far in from the East Coast, the
irrefutable evidence of rising resistance to both Tobin
Wetherill and his CAC-dominated government, was, to
Lockridge, a symptom of impending possible disaster. This
curious-looking transcript, its pages typed like a play, with
the speakers' names in all-capital letters at the top of each
block of reading, could help him slow, if not halt, the dangerous erosion of power.

Picking up the phone, Lockridge set a conference to
plan the mounting of a manhunt for Chase and Duane:
their pictures on every television program, on the front
page of every publication, on every wall of every building.
This exposure would be coupled with a sizable reward for
information leading to their arrest. Not a complete plan,
to be sure, but enough to go with for the moment. Then he
dialed the White House and asked for an urgent meeting
with Tobin Wetherill, a conference at which both the
transcript and the plans for the manhunt would be revealed. He must, Lockridge reminded himself, be extremely careful to avoid anything that could be interpreted
by Toby as an "I told you so."

Well, almost anything.

Down the hall from Sturgis Lockridge, a man named

Michael Traynor was struggling with his own set of worries. (Chase would have recognized him from their encounter on the abortive trip to Kennedy, as the truck
driver with the habit of saying "person" with an accent
that made it sound like the French *peu.*) Being more devoted to the thoughts of his own personal future than to
any political ideology, Traynor's concerns were different
from Lockridge's—but equally powerful. And while he
shared many of the same doubts about Tobin Wetherill's
recent actions as Lockridge did, Traynor was currently less
absorbed by the need for tracking down Chase and Duane
Wetherill than he was consumed by a passion to settle
scores with Lockridge. For the trim efficiency with which
Lockridge had shifted the blame for Moira's arrest from
himself to Traynor was something Traynor could not for-
give. Like Lockridge, he had looked ahead and glimpsed
the apocalypse, but first, he wanted to be sure that his
treatment at Lockridge's hands was avenged.

To accomplish this, Traynor had struck on a curious,
perhaps diabolical idea. Since the day he had taken Moira
Cantrell home after her release from the Interrogation
Center, he had been to see her twice. Tobin Wetherill's sister, he had figured, was not a bad person to get to know.

From the beginning, she had appeared receptive, partly,
he assumed, because she had recently lost her husband and
seemed genuinely distressed and lonely. Traynor also knew
he was an attractive man, with the kind of right schools
and background that would appeal to her; although much
younger, he felt he could build some sort of relationship
with her that might help him in the future.

Then had come the double-cross by Lockridge, and suddenly, the future was staring him in the face. Traynor
made a third visit. In their earlier meetings, Moira had remained neutral on the subject of both her brother Toby
and the CAC. Knowing, however, the famous closeness of
the Wetherill family, Traynor had assumed that Moira was
a supporter of Toby's; her release, when Toby learned
where she was, Traynor considered one proof of this.

Sitting in Moira's elegant living room, Traynor proceeded to build, as offhandedly as he could, a damning
indictment against Lockridge. Traynor told her that
Lockridge was systematically destroying any chance Toby
had for permanent success. Possibly, Traynor suggested,
this was because Lockridge had his own plans for displac-

ing her brother. To give his case the ring of authenticity when she reported the story to Toby, Traynor revealed an astonishing amount about the CAC's inner workings. The fallout shelter in Delaware, the collusion with the PLA movement, and even that most secret of secrets, Toby's private code name of Tristram Shandy—all of it was revealed to Moira. These details, Traynor knew, would force Toby to think Moira's information about Lockridge's plan to overthrow him could only come from a highly placed source—Lockridge himself. And he knew that any man who has seized great power spends a good deal of his time worrying about who covets that power and who may be plotting to steal it from him. Once the suggestion was offered that Lockridge could be deliberately allowing CAC missions to fail, Traynor knew he could count on Toby to do his revenge-taking for him.

To Tobin Wetherill, the idea of such treachery on Lockridge's part would at first be greeted with some doubt, but then there would be all those details Traynor had provided Moira with. They could not be ignored.

From the beginning of this long recital, Moira had appeared intensely interested. If she had been the type, he suspected she would have taken notes. By the time Traynor left, he felt he had triumphed; Moira would shortly be calling her brother.

Moira, indeed, had been interested, and, as Traynor had hoped, soon called Toby. But her reasons were quite different from what Traynor had imagined. Moira blamed Traynor for the kidnapping in Bermuda and her stay at the Interrogation Center. Lockridge, from what Traynor had said, could be blamed for something bigger: the need to flee the country and the subsequent massacre of Dudley on Sailfish Island. And Toby could be blamed because he was in charge of the entire process that had resulted in all of these events. She could not punish him directly, but Moira could guess her brother would be, at this point, an easy man to rattle.

Moira's method had been simple. When she called Toby, she had been put through immediately. Toby had listened, at first with little apparent interest. What Moira related initially seemed impossible to believe, yet her story gained weight with every detail she added. Two men, she said, had been to visit her—one's name was Michael Traynor, the other had been a municipal-bond expert, now

very high in his councils, with a name that sounded like
Lockheed.

"Lockridge? Sturgis Lockridge?"

"That's it. Red-faced man, very nervous, has a tic."

"Impossible. Lockridge's one of my right hands."

"And referred to you as Tristram Shandy in the Delaware fallout shelter."

The long silence from her brother told Moira her shot
had hit home. And as Moira told Toby more and more of
what Traynor had told her—although changing his basic
message entirely—it rapidly became apparent to Toby that
someone indeed had talked to Moira. Someone very high
up. Moira had learned too much for the person to be anybody less highly placed than someone—well, someone like
Lockridge. The code name Tristram Shandy was the
clincher, as Moira had suspected it would be.

After thanking Moira, and asking if there was anything
he could do for her, Toby hung up, thought for a few moments, and reached his decision.

Three days earlier, after he had had his meeting with
Moira, the most Michael Traynor had hoped for was that
she would call her brother Toby and repeat what he had
said. Now, seventy-two hours later, Michael Traynor could
have wished Moira had never made the call at all. At four
a.m., the door to his apartment in Georgetown was torn
off its hinges as a heavily armed squad of police and CAC
men burst inside. In spite of Traynor's identification of
himself and his own position in the CAC, Traynor found
himself in the back of a police car being rushed to some
unknown point outside Washington, where he was thrown
into a heavily guarded cell.

He was in his cell for about half an hour. Then, Army
guards appeared and he was led to a small room, window-
less, whose only architectural feature of interest was a set
of steel double doors leading somewhere. Traynor studied
them and questioned the guards, but received no answer
except a grim shaking of heads. Since he had left his
apartment, he had been unable to get a single word from
any of the men holding him. After about fifteen minutes
of waiting, the inner door through which he had come
opened again and Sturgis Lockridge was shoved into the
room. He was as bewildered as Traynor, but when the two
of them attempted conversation, a newly arrived Army of-

ficer curtly told them to "Shut the fuck up." MPs were
stationed behind Traynor and Lockridge.

Ten minutes later, at precisely ten o'clock, the double
steel doors opened and the Army guards hauled them out,
the prisoners blinking in the sudden harshness of artificial
lighting.

At five minutes before ten p.m., sharp, January the first,
the pictures from Blakeslee Army Barracks began appearing on the country's television screens. Blakeslee's courtyard was harshly lit by high-intensity floodlights, the
shadows cast by any object appearing in stark relief against
the concrete surface of the compound. Surrounding the
area, the enclosing walls were also of concrete, topped by
electrified barbed wire and punctuated by cupola-like guard
towers. Against the far wall and rising from the concrete
ground cover stood two heavy wooden posts, each perhaps
eight feet in height. It was, as Duane whispered to Chase,
the almost classic setting for a military execution.

Leaning against the wall of the Golden Cockatoo,
around the corner from one of Tracey's new safe houses,
Duane and Chase stared at the scene with fascination
mixed with loathing. There was a certain element of danger in their being together in a bar like this, but Tracey,
after Dirk's defection, had moved from his old quarters
into three new safe houses. As yet, none of these had television antennas hooked up, so Chase and Duane had had
to take the risk of going to a public place to watch the
event. It was not mere curiosity; Chase's new assignment
running the underground radio station made him want to
get a first-hand feeling of the public's reaction to tonight's
bizarre happening.

The Golden Cockatoo was jammed, everyone's eyes
glued to the set suspended high in one corner of the room.
The announcer's voice was hushed as he explained the details of what would shortly take place; once again he reminded parents in the audience that their children should
not be allowed to watch the proceedings (and thus guaranteed that any who were still awake, would). One camera
showed the crack Army rifle team put together for the occasion giving their weapons a final check; then, another
camera again cut to a picture of two small steel double
doors. The riflemen were called to attention and you
could clearly hear the slap of their hands on their rifle butts

as they snapped them into place. Simultaneously, a team of unseen drummers began a slow, muffled drum roll. Abruptly, the two small steel doors were flung open and Traynor and Lockridge, flanked by additional riflemen and a chaplain, walked slowly out of the main building into the courtyard. In the harsh incandescence of the flood-lighting, the group's shadows were grotesquely elongated. In what seemed to take an agonizing length of time, Lockridge and Traynor were slowly bound securely to the posts. No hoods were placed over their faces; in a firm voice, clearly audible to the television audience, Lockridge declined for both of them, saying they wished to look their murderers in the eye. Then the drums began their eerie tattoo; an Army colonel, visibly nervous, unfolded a large sheet of paper and first read the charges against the two and then Tobin Wetherill's orders for their executions. Although a great deal of what the colonel said was swallowed by the sound of the muffled drums, it was obvious the colonel was having considerable difficulty with the legalistic language of the charges, most of which appeared to concern a conspiracy by Lockridge and Traynor to overthrow the government.

Finished, the colonel folded the document neatly and leaned forward to ask the men if either had anything to say before the orders were carried out. Once again, Lockridge elected to speak for both of them; after a brief pause, he leaned forward slightly and spat in the officer's face.

The crowd at the Golden Cockatoo had been completely silent until the spitting incident. But the gesture was so unexpected that now there was some nervous laughter, even some light applause. Chase thought perhaps the crowd was reacting to Lockridge's response at being asked if he had anything to say, when it was obvious nothing he might say could possibly alter the deadly circumstances in which he found himself. Looking around the room, Chase could also sense a feeling of pity for Traynor and Lockridge, probably the last thing Toby expected. Lockridge and Traynor were doubtless loathesome people, but to the crowd they were, for the moment, victims of a terrible situation. With the public executions of another time, the crowd could easily grow angry at the criminals; they were horse thieves, they had robbed the bank, they had shot the sheriff. But these two men were unknown people, abstracts, guilty of some complicated crime the crowd could not understand; the pair's situation was not too different from that of anyone there, and instead of anger, the people in the bar were feeling pity. On the other hand, Chase noticed, not one of them could tear their eyes away from the scene.

The colonel saluted, and as he walked farther from the two posts and closer to the camera, everyone could see a large, dark stain on the front of his army jacket's lapel. On signal, the guns were raised; the drums increased the speed of their tattoo, and, on the falling of the officer's arm, the oddly insignificant sound of eighteen rifles being fired simultaneously brought the drums to an abrupt halt.

Traynor and Lockridge appeared to jerk backward, then hang suspended for a moment. The holes torn in each of their faces and foreheads were visible, but as yet, bloodless. One after the other, they slumped forward. An Army doctor stepped forward and after briefly applying a stethoscope to the collapsed forms, pronounced them officially dead. From the announcer came the superfluous information that this fact would be confirmed, as the law required, by immediate autopsy.

The conversation in the bar took on a curious quality, as if the men there were unsure how to react. It was like the crowd at the Indianapolis 500 which comes half hoping to see a mammoth pile-up; yet when it happens, what the crowd expresses is horror, or at the very least, shock. To some, seeing two men executed on television was a genuinely obscene sight, and they felt sick inside. To others, it was the ultimate high.

But to Chase and Duane, watching the execution at Blakeslee only served to remind them that it was the slenderest of threads that separated them all from the same fate.

Slumped in a chair, Tracey Wetherill sat by himself and sipped at his drink as if his life depended on finishing it as quickly as possible. Although he had refused to go along with Chase and Duane to the Golden Cockatoo—the idea of a public execution sickened him—he had also found himself inexorably drawn to seeing it. At the last moment, he had called a friend, Henry Platt, who lived in one of the apartments below his, and asked if he could watch it there.

The effect of the execution on Tracey left Platt open-mouthed. As the drums began to roll, Tracey had suddenly raced across the room and started screaming at the television set; then Tracey had picked up a heavy ceramic garden seat and hurled it through the screen. Staring straight ahead, he had raced out of Platt's apartment, with tears streaming down his face.

Now, half an hour later, calmed and partially anesthetized by liquor, Tracey was embarrassed. He must, be told himself, either call Platt or write him a letter, promising him a new set to replace the one he had destroyed. He shifted uncomfortably and mixed himself another drink; as with so many things in today's world, the blame for his outburst belonged to his brother Toby. But almost as soon as that crossed his mind, Tracey realized the blame behind his explosion in Platt's apartment could not be fixed on Toby; it belonged to him, and him alone.

For, in Tracey's mind, sudden death was inextricably intertwined with his twin, Rodney. It was a death Tracey had no choice but to accept responsibility for. Once again, for what must have been the thousandth time, he let the details of that night with Rod float through his brain, in all their ugly detail. How could something still be so clear, twenty-seven years later? He had been eighteen then. He was forty-five now, yet every minute of that night was still a vivid, violent, terrifying picture to him.

"C'mon, Rod, lay off," he had said. "Those places stink."

"Okay, what do you do tonight, then—play with yourself?"

"I'm not going to do the bars, dammit, and that's that."

"Shit, Tracey—you're crazy."

They had had one of their fights—or, to phrase it precisely, one of the continuing battles in their same fight—about going out to cruise the bars. Originally, Tracey and Rodney had cruised together, although Rod, as the more homosexually active, had always been the leader. But as they had grown older, Tracey had had increasing doubts about himself in the role Rodney kept casting for him; more and more, he felt twinges and stirrings toward girls he knew, feelings that Rod continually belittled and made fun of. Increasingly, he struggled to free himself from the homosexual world Rod had immersed him in; the subject became the first genuine point of difference between the twins either could remember.

"You're chicken," taunted Rod. "You're afraid someone'll see you there."

"No, I just don't want to go."

"Sure, Tracey, sure."

The whole ugly subject came to a boil inside Tracey— and along with it a way to get Rod off his back, at least for the evening. "If you're such a damned hero, why don't you try Grand Central like you keep talking about all the fucking time?"

For a second, there was silence. Then, from Rod, the faintest note of pleading in his tone: "You won't come with me?"

"Now who's chicken?" jeered Tracey.

"Shit," snarled Rod, throwing a book at Tracey and storming out of the house, caught, challenged, and now forced to prove himself. The men's room in Grand Central had been a constant preoccupation with Rod for months; he himself could never have explained why. Most probably it had something to do with the risk involved in picking up a stranger there. At a queer bar, you were relatively safe, surrounded by others looking for the same thing; at a public washroom, you were inviting danger, taking high risks to seek the ultimate thrill of gambling on who would and who wouldn't play along. The stakes were high; if you guessed wrong, you could get beaten up or worse.

And as Graffa had told Chase two years earlier, on that particular night, Rod had guessed wrong, very wrong. Although his death had technically been an accident, to Tracey, it had been a murder—a murder of which he was guilty. If, in his own anger, he hadn't provoked Rod, if he hadn't deliberately taunted him into going to Grand Central, Rodney wouldn't have been killed.

For a long time after Rod's death, Tracey had gone into what can almost be described as a state of hysterical paralysis, wrestling with himself, struggling with his conscience, blaming himself for everything that had happened. On top of his sense of guilt, Tracey could now add the realization that his entire family knew about him. That part of what had killed Rod was his own emerging feelings about women would count for nothing; they must consider him the family fag, the queer, a disgrace to the Wetherill name, someone to be whispered about when absent and treated with hidden mockery when present. To them, he was now an object of contempt, a sudden stranger who had to be tolerated, but not understood, for the gay sub-culture was a world as far removed from them as poverty.

The result of all this—even to this day—was that Tracey had started running. And had been running ever since. The time had come to stop. With a slight, half-drunken sigh, Tracey picked up his den phone and made several calls. The comfort and safety of the chair in his living room was abandoned for the unknown; he packed his bags and took the next Metroliner to Washington.

Chapter Seventeen

*It is the most complicated matters which
we find have the simplest answers.*

—Albert Einstein

"Brannigan," whispered a soft voice, quiet urgency in its tone.

Brannigan, stamping his feet in the cold, was trying to fix the door to the root cellar so that it would come open without needing a fierce yank. He spun in surprise.

Behind him, he discovered his friend from Amenia, whom he had described to Chase as the only other black in the entire area. Brannigan had been so startled that he forgot his carefully affected Harlem accent and lapsed into brogue. "Mother of God, Sully. You're enough to scare the wits out of a saint."

Sully blinked at him, the unaccustomed Irish accent throwing him off his stride. Recovering, he filed the information away. "Sorry to sneak up on you, Brannigan, but I weren't sure who was around, y'know?"

The Harlem patois was hastily summoned forth. "Man, you hit it on the chops. I got a cold feeling the whole town's playing cozy-baby with my life." For a moment, Brannigan considered the sentence; it was overdone, he decided. "Like a beer?"

"Ain' got much time, y'know?" Sully pursed his lips and reconsidered. "On the other hand, you got less. Sure."

His eyes troubled by the ominous sound of Sully's statement, Brannigan gave a great heave and finally succeeded in pulling open the root-cellar door, coming back out with two cans of Bud. With a solemn nod, Sully accepted his, yanked off the snap-tab, and took a long pull. "What I mean is, Brannigan, you is in trouble."

"What kind of trouble?" Sully had not offered any explanation yet, but Brannigan had sensed his statement demanded one.

"Well, there's another brother, y'know, over in Limé Rock, y'know, only I didn't mention him before on account he passes for white. Skin like a cream puff. Anyhow, he works at the Iron Plough, behind the bar, see, a lot of them CAC dudes drink there, y'know? So he picks up a lot of talk, 'cause they don't pay him no attention, thinking he's white." Sully seated himself on a fallen tree and pulled at the Bud, caressing the cold can with his fingers. Brannigan sat down on the trunk himself and waited for Sully to drop the other shoe, but Sully seemed content to lounge there, drawing on the Bud, thinking. Maybe, thought Brannigan, he was half-enjoying being the bearer of ċad news and didn't want to end it too quickly.

"Like you was saying, Sully . . ."

"Anyhow, my friend at the Iron Plough heard the CAC guys say the man you work for is one of the Rockefellers or the Wetherills. Is that true, Brannigan?"

"Shit, Sully. Can you picture someone like that living in a fallen-down heap like ˈthis?" Brannigan let his arm's sweep take in the whole complex of dilapidated farm buildings. "Or having *me* working for them? Them CAC dudes got˙ their heads on crooked. Either that or your friend swallows as much as he serves."

"Swears that's what he heard. Not only that, Brannigan, they is planning a raid out here. You seed on TV how they is trying to catch any Wetherill they can get their hands on now. Well, they is going to round up the whole bunch of you living here and see if they is right about one of the Wetherills hiding on the farm. That's why I came out. To warn you, y'know? Us brothers got to stand together."

Brannigan was staggered and fought back the obvious question. He trusted Sully, but the magic name of Wetherill could be dangerous. "They won't find nothing. No Wetherills here." He paused to come at his question tangentially. "When is they staging this raid? On account old Brannigan better hide his ass when they come. Them CAC bimbos ain' partial to us brothers."

"Tomorrow night."

"You sure?"

"That's what the man said. Tomorrow night. Two-three a.m., my friend says, when everybody's asleep, y'know?"

Brannigan knew. "Well, they won't find nothing, but Brannigan figures he'll curl up in the chicken coop for the night anyway. Them cats scare me."

Sully finished the Bud and seemed to hesitate, as if wondering whether more Bud might be forthcoming. Brannigan's face remained blank and he made no move to go back into the root cellar. Finally, Sully stood up, dusted off his pants and stared into space. "Anyways, I just thought I should tell you."

"Thank you, brother. I'll be scarce."

After more hesitating and some nervous shuffling, Sully left, slipping along the edge of the field until he could reach the forest and get back to the road without anyone seeing where he had come from.

With a low whistle, Brannigan sat back down on the log. He could picture a force being assembled in Lime Rock tomorrow night, the shotguns silhouetted against the headlights of half a dozen automobiles. The family had to go. But where? And when? Sully had said tomorrow night, but there might already be somebody back in the woods or up on the hill keeping track of their comings and goings. His instinct was to tell Mrs. Wetherill the story now, to pack the whole family into the car and go quickly. But some deeper instinct told him that that approach would be risky. Leaving wouldn't be safe until it was dark; then they could drive away from the farm without headlights and try to reach the open road before an alarm was sent to the roadblocks and checkpoints. He even debated telling Mrs. Wetherill, at least, so she could prepare, but decided that she and Emlyn and the twins should not know until the very last second.

"Hey, isn't that something?" Chase switched off the tape playback and turned, beaming, toward Duane. Today, January 16, marked the end of their second week of broadcasting. The programs had been so successful they were expanding the programming to a full three hours a day. To mark the occasion, today's program—the one he had just played for Duane—would include two former Presidents of the United States, three former Governors, statements by leading actors, writers, artists, and even two major-league baseball players.

Duane stood up, looking at Chase warmly. "It really lays things out. Those baseball players are a great touch;

they sound so damned down to earth after all the intellec-
tual types."

"Aren't they great?" To Chase, putting together a radio
broadcast was a new experience and one he had approached with some misgivings. But now that he'd grown
used to the director's and engineer's private language and
watched each program progress agonizingly slowly from a
set of notes with estimated times to a finished tape with
each second accounted for, punctuated by musical cues,
effects and segues, he was growing increasingly overcome
with parental pride.

Infected by his brother's enthusiasm, Duane watched as
the engineer fed the tape through the playback head,
started the powerful generator (so that the underground
station could not be traced through its power drain during
broadcast, the station had its own diesel-driven generator
in another building). Throwing a cue with his left hand,
the director started the tape rolling. Simultaneously, an
improvised "On the Air" light flashed on. "Christ, Chase.
I'm impressed. You're doing one hell of a job. If things
ever come to the worst, you can probably pick up a job at
some network."

"If things come to the worst, there won't be any networks."

Fascinated, they watched as the technicians began monitoring their dials, listening to the words going out to the
mobile transmitters for rebroadcast. Recently, as the station had grown in influence and effect, they had added
additional rebroadcast points, and were now able to
penetrate some distance across the country. From an editing panel on the opposite wall of the dingy little studio
came the strident sound of tape being run backward at
high speed. The room was small, dusty and hot, but to
Chase, it was CBS, the Voice of America, the BBC, all
wrapped into one. He felt exuberant and oddly safe; the
studio was a hole in the wall, one flight down, below 34th
and 35th streets, on the West Side and a stone's throw
from Orbach's. Except for the men actually in the room,
the writing, editing and recording was done elsewhere, a
precaution Chase felt necessary. Everyone connected with
the project had been carefully screened and thoroughly in-
vestigated, but, with the exception of himself, none of the
hierarchy was ever allowed to come here to the studio.

Tonight, though, was to be different. The programming's expansion in length, the recent ability of the station to reach more people at greater distance, Chase felt, called for a celebration; some of the stringent rules had been relaxed. The top writing and editorial staffers had been called in, and, with Duane, Chase was holding an impromptu champagne bust as the tapes rolled endlessly on their broadcast decks. For an affair staged by the Wetherills, it was modest; California champagne served in paper cups. But to Chase, no vintage year ever tasted so good.

The engineers continued to adjust their dials, pausing only to take an occasional sip from one of the paper cups. Duane had just left the table and crossed the room to refill the engineers' glasses again, when a buzzer in the room began ringing stridently. The faces of the men in the room stared at one another in disbelief; the buzzer was the emergency alarm from upstairs indicating trouble. Chase listened as the tape whirred down in a decelerating whine. The buzzer rang again, this time more urgently, and the room broke into confusion. Reels of tape, scripts, and champagne were swept off the long tables onto the floor; most of the men headed for one of the two stairways that led out of the studio. Chase dashed across the floor and pulled Duane to one side.

From upstairs, they could already hear the shouts and scufflings. "Quick," whispered Chase. "There's another door over here—nobody knows about it." They slipped out of the room, pulled the door closed behind them, and slipped down a long cement corridor.

The passage seemed to wind endlessly, the only sounds being that of their footfalls on the cement. Several times, Chase reached out and slapped the concrete sidewall in frustration. Abruptly, he stopped, turning to face Duane, who had been walking behind him. "They infiltrated us, somehow. They've got the studio, and they came damned close to getting us."

"Everybody had been tripled-checked. My men did some of the checking personally."

"Triple-checked, hell. No amount of security checks could have been enough. Toby had no intenion of letting that station stay on the air; he couldn't afford to."

"Well, it was working—that's what counts. We can get another studio. Maybe outside the city somewhere this

time. There are tape dupes for the old programs. We just
have to shrug it off and start over."

"The whole damned editorial staff was there. I should
have figured that probably one of the engineers was CAC.
Toby may have known about the whole thing all along. For
all I know, he may have even known precisely where the
studio was for days and just bided his time. I should have
seen it coming."

"No, I should have," sighed Duane. "That was my department."

"We'd better use the phone relay system and let them
know in the mobile transmitter, so the same thing doesn't
happen to them." Duane looked depressed, squatting on
his haunches, leaning against the sidewall for support.
"It'll work out, Duane, so let's get moving and make
sure it does."

"You're right, of course. But where the hell are we, anyway?"

In spite of everything, Chase managed a small smile.
"It's an old interconnecting tunnel. Wait'll you see what's
at the other end." He began trotting down the passageway,
Duane panting along behind him, until they came to a
dusty steel door. Just before turning the knob, Chase gave
Duane a long, sly look. "Just act natural, Duane. This
place may come as a bit of a shock."

They went through the door and came into the "Paris
Copies" fitting rooms of Orbach's. Several women, in various stages of discount déshabille, half dressed, looked at
them with alarm. "Pardon, *mesdames*, pardon." Chase
spoke in his best St. Mark's French, bowing from the waist
to the undressed ladies, mincing elegantly, the stock
comedy version of a French dress designer. Duane, less in-
hibited, fluttered his hands wildly, constantly nodding to
the store's customers.

Pierre Cardin and Yves St. Laurent walked calmly out
of the dressing rooms toward the elevator, out of the store,
and into the street.

Earlier that day in Lime Rock, the CAC, purely as a
matter of routine, notified their Great Barrington headquarters that they were planning a raid on a farmhouse
near Salisbury, occupied by "persons unknown." In passing, Lime Rock had mentioned that some suspicion existed
that one or more members of the Wetherill family might

be hiding there. As their source, they mentioned a local pharmacist named Englehardt, although making it clear they could not vouch for his reliability since the man had disappeared almost immediately after giving them his information.

The Lime Rock group was not prepared for the reaction the name Wetherill produced in Great Barrington. Tobin Wetherill had been infuriated to learn from Lockridge about the radio station and the part his two brothers were playing in the movement to dislodge him. But even though Chase and Duane had escaped the raid in New York, Toby had thought that with the seizing of the studio near Orbach's, his troubles with counter-propaganda were over. Instead, almost immediately, the programs began appearing again from coast to coast. As a result, Toby, so long tolerant of his brothers' activities, had stepped up the campaign to capture them.

Thus, when the name of Wetherill surfaced in Lime Rock's report, Great Barrington contacted Lime Rock and told them to surround the farmhouse immediately, and let no one escape.

The order was greeted in Lime Rock with consternation. Notifying and gathering men would be a near impossible operation in itself, because just surrounding the house would require every man they could get hold of. Reluctantly, Area Overseer Griswold decided he would have to move with only as many troopers as there were in the village. Now, in the early dark of a winter night, the men stood around outside the Lime Rock Lodge, stamping their feet and blowing on their hands against the sudden cold, their shotguns and automatic weapons slung over their shoulders. On the road in front of the lodge stood the ten cars these thirty-six men would use, their exhausts making great clouds of warm vapor in the chill air.

Grisworld, a burp gun hung over one shoulder, marched out of the building and ordered the men into the cars. He himself climbed into the lead vehicle, the town police car, and with an ascending growl from the siren, the party roared westward toward Salisbury.

In a straight line, Lime Rock is roughly five miles from Salisbury. But the roads Griswold had chosen formed anything but a straight line, and were something less than smooth-paved, as well. The cars bounced along at great speed, following the flashing blue light on top of the police car, its siren stilled once they were outside the town proper. In the car immediately behind the lead vehicle, four men clutched their weapons as the uneven road jounced them up and down. One of the men in back swore as the wheels of the car hit an unusually bad bump and made his shotgun stock crash into his ankle. Up front, the squad leader, Peter Filger, sitting beside the driver, told the man to keep it quiet—and then, in what appeared deliberate contradiction of his own order, turned on the car radio.

Avoiding the center of Salisbury itself, the procession of cars cut across the state highway north of the town, heading directly toward Chase's farm in the back country. At the road junction, perhaps half a mile from Chase's, the police car halted and Griswold stepped out, striding over to Filger's car with instructions.

"Turn that damned thing off," he growled at Filger, indicating the blaring radio with a nod of his head. "Now, then. I'll take five of the cars and we'll circle around the old road behind the farmhouse. You, Filger, fan your men out through the trees up the hill. Keep 'em quiet. In exactly fifteen minutes"—Griswold checked his watch against the squad leader's—"that'll be eight-oh-twelve—eight-oh-twelve—break into the farmhouse. I'll send about half of the men in through the back door, and keep the rest spread out in the woods to catch them if anybody tries to make a run for it. And I know it's tough when there's kids involved, but if you have to, shoot to kill. Got it? Eight oh twelve. You, Filger, stay in your car in case I have to get hold of you on the police band. Let's go."

Filger nodded and watched as Griswold climbed back into the police car and drove off, followed by six of the other cars filled with men. Quickly, he sent his own men into the woods and settled back into the front seat. Almost immediately, the men were devoured by the darkness as they climbed up the hill. Filger suddenly felt very alone, listening to the small animal noises coming from the woods and the eerie hooting of some distant owl. Twice, up through the trees, he thought he saw light from the farmhouse. Stupid, he thought; if these people were really wanted for something by the CAC, they shouldn't have lights burning at night.

The squad leader, Filger, leaned back in his seat and checked his watch. Five and a half minutes to go. Leaning forward, he scaned the woods to see if he could make out any of his men outside the farmhouse, but they appeared invisible. From the woods, the owl gave its lonely cry again, and Filger turned his car radio back on, letting the raucous blare of the folk rock roll out the open window.

Five—no, four minutes. The squad leader yawned and checked his gun, patting it in rhythm to the heavy beat of the rock group. Then he slowly eased his great hulk out of the car, crooked the shotgun under his arm, and steeled himself to do what he knew would have to be done.

Tracey was nervous as a cat. The house he had bought in Washington was finally decorated to suit his taste; the painting and replastering work was newly completed, and the place, he had to admit, was both elegant and handsome. Just off Embassy Row, the mansion rather looked like an embassy itself, with huge, ironwork gates hanging from the brick and stone posts that graced both exits and entrances to the semicircular driveway. The mansion was of the same brickwork inlaid with a limestone pattern, a combination of Federal period with late French chateau architecture (complete to mansard roof). Inside, the receiving rooms were done in pale shades of blue, with darker blue silk damask wall coverings. Louis XVI antiques predominated, as well as portraits of noble gentlemen and their ladies from the last days of the Bourbons. Hanging inconspicuously among them was an oil copy of the Hendryk Wilhelm Vederyll portrait, keg of nails and all, to make sure no one lost sight of the symbolism.

Toby initially had not been overcome with enthusiasm at the idea of Tracey's moving to Washington. "My fag brother, for Christ's sake, setting up shop practically in the shadow of the White House?" he had exploded to his press secretary when told of Tracey's new quarters. But as the days passed, the idea grew on him. Certainly, Tracey had never been a favorite of his, but a Wetherill, any Wetherill, living in town, attending functions, throwing the right sort of parties, added an extra veneer of legitimacy to Toby's status. This was particularly desirable in view of the defection that Chase and Duane's association with the violently anti-CAC underground radio station signaled to the world. Tracey so far was the only Wetherill to come out openly for his brother, and that in itself would make a

difference with some people. As for unfavorable comments
about Tracey's private life, well, Toby controlled the
media, so no gossip about Tracey could appear anywhere.
Besides, Toby reassured himself, while the Washington in-
siders might know about Tracey, to the general public, his
brother appeared as normal as anyone else in Washington's precious society. As a result, Toby found himself
appearing as the guest of honor at Tracey's first party—
nothing lavish, just himself and perhaps one hundred others
—to be held that night. The Wetherill name would make
its influence felt.

Toby's attendance at the night's gala was what was
making Tracey so nervous. It was going to be difficult
enough putting the last touches to the décor and steeling
himself to hold forth in straight circles without all the confusion that now attended having his brother to any func-
tion. Secret Service men, CAC Security men, and members
of the CIA had been crawling over this house all day, examining every corner, poking into closets, scanning the
guest list. A food taster had been installed in the kitchen,
almost causing Tracey's new chef to quit in a very French
huff. The first arrival, Wanda Berrylson—Tracey's hostess
for the evening—had been astonished to find herself
searched by a CAC matron. Because her name was unknown to the security forces, she had been considered suspect and given the most rigorous scrutiny.

"Tracey," Wanda told him wearily, "if I could hide a
machine gun in some of the places they looked for one,
I'd be in a side show."

Signaling one of the waiters for drinks, Tracey laughed
nervously. Wanda was striking, tall and slender, with
shoulder-length blond hair. She was also one of the more
notorious dykes in New York, but few straight people
knew of it; as with Tracey, she could "pass."

Before long, the house was filled with guests. After the
ritual playing of "Hail to the Chief," Toby arrived with a
cluster of Secret Service men and CAC Security agents
grouped around him in wedgelike formation. If one had
not known that President Welby was still alive, slowly
recovering from the ravages of his stroke in his bedroom
at the White House—and there were many who did not
believe that this was the case at all—one could almost believe that Toby really was the President. As Toby came to
the center of the room, the crowd—as carefully selected as

the blue damask wall coverings—broke into loud applause. As far as the gathering was concerned, Toby *was* the President.

Following the dinner, which was long and sumptuous, served at small round tables of eight (with the exception of the one with Toby and Tracey at it, which held sixteen), it was time for the toasts to begin. Tracey, suddenly composed, rose to his feet and tapped his champagne glass. From the other tables came the usual scraping and shuffling as chairs and bodies were turned to face the head table. Then, silence fell.

"Mr. Justice Wetherill, distinguished guests, ladies and gentlemen," began Tracey. All glimmerings of nervousness disappeared; Tracey appeared as poised and urbane as a professional speaker. "Before proposing an actual toast, I would like to say a few words about our family. As you know, this country has been good to the Wetherill family. Too good, some people seem to think, particularly in the range from Walter Cronkite to John Kenneth Galbraith. (*Gentle laughter.*) But we're a family like any other, with any family's weaknesses and strengths, successes and failures, members we're proud of and"—Tracey took just the right beat of silence to make the remark effective—"well, some we're not so proud of." (*More laughter, this time relaxed and easy; Tracey was winning their confidence.*) "Thinking of my own five brothers, I guess the same thing goes. Some I was very close to, some I was not. For one thing, at least two of them regularly tried to beat me up." (*Laughter, and a sprinkling of applause.*) Toby was smiling now, proud of Tracey. He had never realized his youngest brother would be so relaxed and charming on his feet. Tracey went on, growing more confident with each sentence: "But I suppose, being the youngest, my twin and I were probably pretty hard to put up with sometimes— particularly since we were also the brightest." (*Laughter.*) Suddenly bowing in Toby's direction, Tracey added with a small smile: "Excuse me, Mr. Justice, that's a family secret I probably shouldn't have let out of the bag." (*Laughter.*) "But about my own brothers. As with any family, we have our share of skeletons in the closet—members of the family we do our best to pretend never existed." Now that Tracey had his audience with him, he suddenly allowed his expression to grow serious, as if he were releasing a great burden he would rather have done in private.

"To get personal for a minute, my own twin, Rodney, had he lived, could only have brought shame and disgrace on the family. With any of you who are familiar with how close twins are, you will appreciate how such a statement must pain me. But while in general we could not be proud of Rod and could not escape from the sense of shame that surrounded him, it didn't mean we loved him any the less."

There was a nervous rustling among the people at the tables; Tracey was becoming too personal for a speech given at so formal an occasion (and being broadcast, via radio, to the country; Toby was making the most of his opportunity to show the nation that the Wetherills were standing behind him). But Toby remained smiling. He doubted if anyone in the room knew what Tracey was really saying about Rodney, and certainly the great masses of listeners would only be baffled.

"In contrast to my twin Rodney, we are honoring tonight an Associate Justice of the Supreme Court and a man who is acting—if he is not actually—President of the United States. He has given us—the nation, the family—everything he has to give." Tracey had paused to make sure that everyone's glass had been filled, and then raised his own. "So I ask you all now to rise and drink in honor of my brother, Tobin Wetherill, who, for the first time in years, has made the whole family realize how stupid we were to feel ashamed only of Rodney."

Toby's hand was already wrapped around his glass, preparing the beneficent nods with which he would accept Tracey's salute; the smile appeared frozen on his face, fading only slowly. The crowd, on its feet, had its glasses half raised while the full impact of Tracey's insult sank in. One could almost see their minds running through Tracey's remark to make sure they understood it correctly. There was no escaping it; the insult was direct, brutal, and calculated. The guests looked at each other, trying to find some glimmer of how the rest of the people were going to handle the situation, so that they could behave accordingly.

They did not have much time to find out. Tracey slumped into his chair, his left hand fumbling for something under the table; for a second the room seemed to rise, then ripple like a ribbon in the wind. An instant later, the mass of plastic explosive buried beneath the new plaster in the redecorated rooms and thus immune from all the searches of the Secret Service and the CAC Security men reached maximum force. The dining room, the adjoining reception rooms, then the house itself burst apart, scattering broken stonework, pieces of antique furniture and fragments of guests from one end of Embassy Row to the other.

At the edge of the woods, Squad Leader Filger stopped and turned around. The music coming from his car radio, still playing distantly behind him, had stopped abruptly. Checking his watch again, he turned and ran back toward the car; someone had turned the radio off, and while his own presence at the farmhouse was important, finding out who was creeping around the edge of the woods was equally so. As he drew closer to the car, he went into a crouch to make himself less visible; it was then he realized the car radio was still playing and that the music had stopped because an urgent voice had cut into the broadcast and was telling the world that Acting President Wetherill had just been killed.

Filger straightened up and raced toward the car. The announcer was repeating himself, but the early news appeared fragmentary. At one point, the man said Tobin Wetherill had been killed by a bomb; at another he said by an explosion at his brother's house that killed everyone in it. The announcer paused, apparently absorbing something just handed to him. All CAC units were to report to their headquarters immediately, the announcer said; the Executive Committee of the CAC had declared a national emergency. Then the announcer went back to his repetition of the news about the President.

Filger did not wait to hear it. His radio was not equipped with a device so that he could signal Griswold, so he began running up the hill toward the farmhouse Griswold and his squad were surrounding. His flashlight was unreliable running through this kind of tangled underbrush, and Filger kept tripping over fallen branches and unseen outcroppings of rock. He was unaware what effect the announcement he had just heard would have on Griswold's planned assault on the farmhouse, and didn't really much care; all he was certain of was that Griswold must ? told of what had happened, and of the CAC Executive Committee's order for all units to return to their bases. Panting, Filger struggled up the hill.

When Chase and Duane heard the news of Tobin's death they were first dumfounded, then ecstatic. The long period of cajoling, persuading and waiting was over; people, important people, who up until now had lain back, suddenly sprang into action. Duane's operation came out into the open, with Chase's rapidly expanding radio network demanding an end to all of the CAC's repressive tactics. Quickly, Duane organized an impressive list of former Congressmen, Senators, and statesmen to give speeches everywhere and anywhere they could attract a crowd. Newspapers—the small ones at first—returned to their old freewheeling ways, printing the truth as they saw it, and were quickly joined by independent radio and television stations. Without Toby, the old administration, constructed without benefit of law or precedent, was already doomed. Because of the jury-rigged nature of the whole structure, uprisings sprang into being everywhere, and this time they were legitimate, not contrived rebellions.

The networks and newspapers followed the lead of the local stations and went back to factual reporting of the situation, not the carefully controlled government handouts fed to them by the CAC's PR men. It was from one of these that Chase first heard the death of Tobin Wetherill and most of his official cabal had been by Tracey's hand, and that Tracey himself had been killed. He shook his head in wonder. Tracey, of all people, to be the Wetherill who would finally bring down the seemingly invulnerable head of state, his brother Toby.

The remnants of the old government tried to react swiftly, but were hampered both from within and without. Many of the top CAC leaders had died with Toby at Tracey's gala, and Duane's opposition forces seemed to be everywhere; Army generals still loyal to the CAC would order units out, only to find half of their troops were already aligned against them, commanded by anti-CAC officers. Tanks from one armored regiment would roll, only to be met by two regiments led by opposition commanders. The Air Force, which throughout the Tobin Wetherill period had kept itself judiciously sitting on the fence, followed Lieutenant General Alwyn's orders and came out against the CAC; while they didn't obviously resort to the use of planes, they had considerable ground forces and helicopter regiments to throw into what appeared to be the beginnings of a civil war. These troops, along with a regiment of Marines, retook the White House and there discovered President Welby. He was still alive, but almost completely paralyzed. Propped up, and with two men to guide his hand so that he could write at all, he signed an order to defederalize the National Guard, which then reverted to control by the various state Governors. Most of these were, by now, thoroughly disgusted with the CAC and promptly turned the guard units to mopping up the CAC units in their states.

When President Welby was told what was going on—he had been kept completely in the dark by the aides around him—he was stunned. Welby waited only long enough for a quorum of Senators and Representatives to meet and approve his nomination of Thomas P. Garvin as Vice President. Then, he resigned, making Garvin the country's legal President.

Chase relaxed in the back of the Mercedes 600. The limousine, with its six doors, was one so ostentatious that Chase rarely if ever used it. ("Yerra," said Brannigan the first time he saw it, "but you need a second driver to steer the back end, like on a hook and ladder, don't y'know.") But with so many of the family to bring down from Salisbury at once, and with all of them, he knew, wanting to ride in the same car with him, he'd been forced to resort to it.

The car hummed along the highway, smoothly, noiselessly, the silence broken only by the occasional sound of the driver clearing his throat or blowing his horn. The ride had given Chase a lot of time to think. Ahead of them all lay an uncertain future. While it had been one Wetherill, Tracey, who had actually brought an end to the conspiracy, it had been another Wetherill, Toby, who had provided the leadership to start it. Where this left him and the rest of the Wetherill family was, as yet, unknown. Where the whole conspiracy left the country was another question.

A week before the death of Toby, Chase had managed a telephone call to Darcie—he from a telephone booth in New York, she from one in Salisbury—and had told her he thought they were making real progress. Soon, he had said, he suspected it would be all over. She had bubbled with happiness, chattering about the town house on 64th Street, imagining a life suddenly normal again and a family not constantly living in the shadow of fear. "You mean you think it's really going to be all right again, Chase? Everything the way it was?"

"I think everything will be all right. As to whether everything will be the way it was, well, nobody can even guess that yet."

Shifting in his seat, Chase shook a feeling of unexplained uneasiness that swept over him. A little later, the car bounced up the bumpy road to the farmhouse in Salisbury. As the car stopped, he saw Brannigan's back disappearing around a corner and called to him. The man turned and stared. It was not Brannigan, but another black, probably the man Brannigan described as the "only other colored in the area." Chase began walking toward him, but the man looked startled and fled, disappearing somewhere behind the house. A few seconds later, Chase could hear him fighting his way through the underbrush.

Pulling his overcoat tighter around him against the cold January wind, Chase walked quickly toward the front door and threw it open. "Hello!" he shouted. "I'm back! Hello! Anybody home?"

In the silence he could hear his own voice echoing through the house, and from somewhere the sound of mice racing for their hiding places. "Hello!" he called again. Perhaps they had seen the car coming and were hiding from him. Chase found himself almost angry at the thought.

When he walked into the living room, Chase slumped weakly against the doorframe. The long, bare plaster wall of the living room was riddled with bullet holes—bullet holes and blood. On the floor near the wall, the wide uneven boards were soaked with large, dark, irregularly shaped pools of dried blood. His family had been executed. Quickly, before he could lose control of himself, Chase spun and walked out of the house back to the car.

The driver had the trunk open, and began opening three of the doors to receive the six people Chase had told him to expect. As he saw Chase walking toward him by himself, he raised his eyebrows in a silent question.

"No one else will be coming."

In the days and weeks that followed, the country appeared to return to its old ways, but you could feel an undercurrent of something different surging just below the surface. In a way, it was symbolized by a subtle change in the vast lobby of the Wetherill Foundation Building. Hendryk Wilhelm Vederyll hung, as always, in his position of honor on the main wall, his hand resting confidently on the keg of nails. But he was flanked now by two smaller portraits. Graffa hung to his right, his bright eyes twinkling to greet the people milling below him in the lobby. On the other side hung a portrait which, a year earlier, might have surprised some people. The oil was of Tracey Wetherill. He had no keg of nails, and his past was open to many questions. But he had lived up to the finest meaning of the family.

He had served.